# The Adventures of Mortimer deRose

# Prologue

She watched as they all prayed before her, most of them with no idea she even stood before the statue they had erected in her honor. One set of eyes kept wandering up to her, not towards the statue, but directly at her. Slowly she walked to the other side of the statue and watched as the one pair of eyes followed her, finally she waited for the eyes to meet her own and she nodded her head slightly. "This one is different from the rest," she thought to herself as she stepped down from the dias and walked through those who worshiped her until she stood before the young woman.

The woman's eyes once more rose from the floor in front of her, and she blinked when she saw the midnight robe directly in front of her.

"Come with me child," she said to the girl, "I would speak with you."

The young lady bowed her head and stood in front of her, there were gasps all around, none had ever stood during worship.

A nearby priestess turned to admonish her and froze for a second, "Goddess, it is your right to take her." She looked at the young woman, "you are blessed to be chosen by our goddess, do not fear her child."

She reached out one pale hand and placed it on the young woman's shoulder, "why do you weep my child," she asked as she guided the young woman out of the room. As she passed through a doorway, she sealed it behind them; with a wave of her hand human bones materialized and formed a solid wall, while more clattered together to form chairs and a table. Upon the table sat a cordial and two small glasses.

"I weep for your beauty, goddess," the young woman answered.

"You have been taught well, but need not lie to me. I can see what burdens your soul," she replied.
The young woman bowed her head and fell into the chair the goddess guided her to. "I am sorry my goddess, I know I should not let my troubles become your own," she replied.

The goddess laughed gently, it had been a long time since anyone had ever considered her feelings. "Please, tell me of your troubles my child," she said, determined now to help the young woman.

The young woman didn't say anything for a minute, "It is not my place to second guess my goddess," she finally replied.

She was tired of this woman not looking at her, and reached out to cup her chin gently, "my child it is easier to speak when you look at each other," she said gently.

The young woman blushed and wiped away her tears, "I'm sorry goddess."

With a sigh the goddess said, "you are a battle priestess, correct?"

"Yes, goddess," she answered.

"Your duty is to save lives on the battlefield, and to offer a quick death to those who are too far gone to heal," the goddess continued, "do you wish to be reassigned my child?"

5

"No," the young woman fairly screamed as she leapt from her chair and prostrated herself to the goddess, "oh goddess no," she sobbed.

"Then please sit and talk to me, tell me what it is that has you so distraught," the goddess replied. She was used to battle priestesses asking for reassignment after a short time, but never saw one so adamant that she stay one.

"Goddess," the woman began, before she started to cry again.

"Have a drink," the goddess offered and poured her a glass from the cordial. The liquid that came out was a vibrant red in color and smelled of copper. The goddess was taken by surprise as the young woman took the offered drink without hesitation and drank it in a single gulp. She poured herself a glass and sat back to listen to the young woman speak.

"As you know, I have been with a mercenary group for a couple years now," she started. "I have been healing wounds whenever possible, and being a faithful servant. However recently I have found myself putting one man's injuries before everyone else's, and it has occured to me that I wish to be with this man." She took another drink before she continued, "he has turned me down several times and yet continues to always be there when I need someone to talk to."

The goddess smiled to herself, and poured another glass for the young woman. At the rate she was drinking she would soon be either dead or a very faithful servant.

"Anyways," the young woman continued, "I wanted to know if I could be out on the battlefield, in order to protect him from harm."

The goddess smiled at her and handed her another drink, "my child I have never heard of one of the healers wanting to enter the field of death for a soldier's sake." She gently reached out and caressed the young woman's face, "you have scars of your own from those battles, not everyone is happy to be healed on the battlefield. Drink some more, and I will offer you a deal, sound fair?"

The woman did not hesitate, but drank everything in her cup and filled it again, she continued this until the cordial was empty. "You do not have to offer me a deal goddess, you have simply to order and I will obey as I always have."

"My child, death is inevitable, I am inevitable, but it does not mean that I force my will upon others," the goddess replied. "Here is my deal, you have drank from my own cordial, as such your life as it stands is over. You have two choices, the first is to forget everything about the battlefield and become a healer in a nearby town, the other is to become my handmaiden, assigned to this young man you care so deeply about." She looked at the young woman, curious to see which path she would take.

"I will become your handmaiden," the woman said without hesitation.

"You understand your duties to him will be multiple?" she asked in surprise.

"Yes, oh great goddess and I will not fail in my duties," the woman replied, "please tell me what they are."

Death smiled, she had never seen such an eager worshiper before, "The first, is you will need to do your best to protect him, should he die you will die. The second is that

6

when he dies you will need to guide him to me, making him as happy in death as he could have been in life."

"It will be my honor goddess," the woman replied.

"That is good child," the goddess said as she handed her a small black vial. "Give this drought to him the next time you tend his wounds, if he won't drink it then pour it in his wounds." She frowned slightly, "the sooner the better, you drank enough of my blood it will kill you within a week if this is not mixed with his blood. Remember whoever you use this on you are bound to protect and guide."

"Yes, goddess," the woman said with a smile, "I will go to him at once and get him to drink it."

The goddess smiled as she faded from view, a quick wave of her hand and the young woman had a new body and now wore leather armor, on the inside of the breastplate was the image of a skull.

The high priestess saw her armor as she walked out of the room and bowed deeply, "handmaiden, do you require anything to aid you in your journey?" she asked.

The young woman laughed as she replied, "the goddess has provided me with everything I need." She ran from the hall, mounted a horse and flew down the road to where the mercenaries were camped after today's battle.

As she entered the tent she found him still asleep in a cot, the wound on his side had re-opened in her absence. Gently she woke him up and waited for him to see her face, "What if I told you I have something to speed up your healing and allow you to return to battle sooner?"

He smiled at her and asked, "Why are you wearing armor?"

She returned his smile and answered, "I will join you on the battlefield from now on, now will you drink this or not?"

Mortimer laughed slightly and coughed up some blood, "if it will make you happy I will drink the blood of death herself," he answered.

Rose smiled as she poured the vial into his mouth, and watched as the wound started to visibly heal, "I pledge to watch over you on the battlefield, to protect you from harm, and upon your death I shall guide you gently to my goddess," she said softly under her breath.

The goddess watched and wondered why she felt a tear on her cheek, she would have to keep an eye on these two. She checked her schedule and frowned, a closer eye than she had realized. "Make the most of your brief time together my children," she whispered as she moved on to the next dying soldier.

# Scarlet

He darted through the shadowy street, avoiding the few people who traveled in the dusk. Across the street he saw a young man stretching up and lighting the lantern which hung above a doorway. Soon the streets would be empty of people, it wasn't safe to be out after dark, at least not for most people. He noticed a slight sound coming from the other side of the stone wall on his left side and frowned, very few people would venture into the cemetery at night, but the occasional grave robber would venture inside in the hopes of finding riches buried with the dead.

With a low sigh, he ran forward a few feet and vaulted to the top of the wall; crouching he moved swiftly along the top of the wall, stepping gently on the old stones. There, he saw a slight movement next to a headstone. He watched in silence, counting on the shadows to hide him from casual observation as he surveyed the area. There was definitely someone there, but why? Graverobbers had already picked these graves clean decades ago, as it got darker he closed his eyes and concentrated on his sense of hearing and smell. There was no scent of freshly dug earth, but there was a strange floral scent he didn't recognize. He heard a faint rustling sound coming from the headstone, and off in the distance the sound of footfalls.

With a shake of his head he dropped silently to the soft earth inside the cemetery, and crept closer to the grave. As he approached the grave, he noticed the flowery scent was stronger, and wondered if someone had simply been late in placing flowers on the grave, but then again nobody visited this part of the cemetery anymore. "Well," he thought, "whatever is here is just the other side of this statue." He looked up at the back of the statue and frowned, he knew this grave and knew what he would find.

For the past couple of years people had been leaving sacrifices at this grave in order to ward off bad luck, it was believed that the woman who was buried here had been a witch and that she hungered for the blood of the living, as such it was not that odd to find dead livestock left at the foot of the statue. "Oh well," he thought, "nothing to do but clean it up again."

He stepped around the statue, mentally prepared to find an eviscerated sheep or cow, but let out a gasp, the body of a young woman lay there. "Crap," he swore under his breath, "the sergeant is going to be livid when I report this one." He closed his eyes and slowly counted to 10 to steady his nerves, as he counted he caught the smell of fresh blood and heard a slow ragged breath. His eyes snapped open and he crouched down next to the body. Placing his hand on her neck, he noticed it was still warm, and there was a very faint thump under his fingertips as her heart continued to beat.

"Oh god," he whispered to himself, "she's still alive." He slid one arm under her knees and the other behind her shoulders in order to pick her up, only to discover her wrists were tied to the statue.

Cursing under his breath, he lowered her back to the ground and drew his dagger, "Forgive me," he whispered to the blade as he sliced through the cords at her wrists, "I know you hunger for blood, but she has lost too much already." He felt a stirring in the short blade and knew it was not happy, "Very well," he told it, "drink of my blood." A quick slice along his arm, and a line of red appeared, the blade glowed as his blood touched it and he felt its anger subside. Quickly he sheathed his dagger, and lifted the girl from the ground. He knew he wouldn't make it far carrying her like this, so he set her in the lap of the statue and pulled her arms across his shoulders to carry her as if he was bringing home a trophy buck.

The question now was where to take her, he could take her to the barracks, the doctor there could tend her wounds and he could get started with writing his report, but at the same time he wasn't sure if he could carry her that far. "Just my luck," he said, "been home for a day and I stumble on an attempted murder." He frowned as he thought about what people would say seeing a mercenary carrying a bloody girl through town, "I'm going to have to find a place to patch you up myself," he said to the unconscious girl, "then I can go get help."

It only took him a second, and he remembered the old caretakers cottage along the west wall. He had played there as a child, and the old man who lived there had always been nice. He started off towards the west, relying on his memory to guide him, his ears constantly listening for any signs of other people in the cemetery.

Based on the stars he had only carried the girl for half an hour, but it felt like it had been all day when he reached the cottage. He had been correct, after the old man had died, it had been abandoned, the door protested slightly when he pulled on it, but eventually swung outwards. In the pale moonlight, which came through a good sized hole in the thatched ceiling, he could make out the table and chairs the old man would always serve food on. As gently as he could, he laid the young lady on the table and smiled, "If it could hold a fully dressed out hog 10 years ago, it should be able to hold you," he chuckled at the memory of the feasts the old caretaker had every holiday.

Looking around the room, he found a couple of old lamps, and used his flint and steel to light them. With the light shining in the room, he smiled, "it hasn't changed a bit since I was last here." He hurried back to the table to check the girl's injuries and frowned, it was obvious in the light she was of noble birth, and the entire front of her gown was covered in blood and cut in several places. "Please forgive me," he said to her, as he ripped open the front of her gown in order to check her injuries. He stood in shock for a moment, as he saw what she wore under her gown, boiled leather armor, "oh, well," he said, "at least since you're a warrior you'll understand what I have to do."

He unbuckled her armor and removed it, now he could see how bad her injuries were. The armor had kept her from receiving a lethal blow, but she could still bleed out if he didn't tend to the multitude of cuts. He checked her entire body, wishing he had some clean water to flush her wounds with. He turned her gown into bandages and bound her wounds, as they proved superficial. A quick check of her head, and he found a slight lump near the base of the skull indicating she had been knocked out, and based on the lack of any clear defensive wounds, probably before someone tried to cut her up.

He buckled her armor loosely back in place and sat down to think. Who was this lady, why had somebody tried to kill her, and why was it he couldn't bring himself to report this to the barracks. He looked down at the red line across his arm and winced, feeding his dagger his own blood always came at a price, the question was, what was that price going to be? He pulled out the cursed blade and concentrated on it.

"What do you want?" the beautiful voice came into his mind, as if an angel were speaking to him.

"I wish to know what the price is for your aid," he replied, "Who do I have to kill for you this time?"

The blade gave a musical laugh, and he realized that it wasn't just in his mind this time. A quick glance around, and he spotted the ghostly shape of a gorgeous young woman, so beautiful that it hurt to look upon her directly.

"I grant you my help freely this time." she said

"I am confused,: he answered, "I was told that if I ever called upon you, I would be required to perform an act of vengeance for you."

The ghostly figure smiled, "Normally that would be true sweet child, but I am making an exception as I see now you truly want to help this woman. You would be amazed how many men have used me and carried ulterior motives in their hearts, and with the taste of your blood I see you are pure, so I help you freely, until such time as your desires and mine no longer coincide." With this the ghostly woman dissolved back into his dagger, and he could feel a new kind of strength coming from it.

He jolted awake, not sure when he had fallen asleep, but the injured young lady had groaned, and the sound had awoken him. His dagger sat in his lap, its crimson blade glowing slightly in the lantern light, he sheathed it and went to the young lady's side, "It's all right, I've bandaged your wounds," he said gently.

The young lady rolled off the table away from him, landed on her feet and went into a fighter's crouch.

"Easy," he said gently, "if I had meant you harm you wouldn't have been able to move, trust me."

Her head whipped around to look at him, and she staggered for a moment, "Ooh," she replied, "that wasn't a good idea."

"You took a nasty blow to the head, before I found you," he replied, "When you're a little more stable maybe you can tell me what you remember of your attackers."

She gave him a half smile, "Not much to tell, I felt a blow to my head and then woke up here. Now, can you tell me where my gown is? I can't exactly blend in at a masquerade in just my armor."

"You're wearing it," he answered, "as it was the only cloth I had to bind your wounds. You wouldn't have blended in very well anyways, covered in blood as it was."

She chuckled softly, and winced. "You obviously aren't a town guard," she said, "and mercenaries are forbidden from walking around town after sunset, so who are you?"

"You are only partially correct," he replied, "Mercenaries are forbidden in the town after dark, unless they are native to the town, I grew up here."

The lady scrutinized his features as best she could in the dim lighting, and shook her head slowly, "You can't be, there is only one man who left this town to become a mercenary, and last we had heard he killed his commander."

"Please, let me explain, before you jump to conclusions." he replied, "There is a lot that happened in that battle and I had no choice but to kill him."

She shook her head slowly, "You were cleared of all charges, you know."

He nodded his head slowly, "I know, but I don't want anyone to know where I am, I do not want to bring enemies to my hometown. I just came here to say my farewells to my family before I go into battle with those who are seeking me."

"You know the garrison would stand with you," she replied.

He shook his head, "No, I can't ask them to do that, the people looking for me will kill everyone here to get to me. I must fight them alone."

A dull pain along his thigh made him look down at his dagger, "Okay, maybe not exactly alone, but I can't ask the town to sacrifice itself for me." He told the blade.

The young lady across from him smiled and said, "This is the first time I've ever seen someone talk to their weapon before."

He smiled at her, "This is the first time she has ever made her presence known when around others. There must be something special about you." Slowly he drew the dagger from its sheath, "This is the crimson dagger, also known as the bloody bitch," he said. The crimson blade flashed bright red, and he felt the presence of the spirit behind him again.

"How dare you call me that?" the spirit growled at him.

"I don't," he smiled, "everyone else who meets you does." He couldn't resist smiling at the young lady, "I have taken it upon myself when I acquired this lovely blade to keep it from falling into the wrong hands. Truth be told, she is the reason I killed my commander. I couldn't let him take an innocent life to satiate the thirst of the crimson blade. It wasn't until after I killed him that I found out about the thirst of the blade."

The spirit cut him off by stepping between them, "It has been a long time since I have seen a witch guard, sister," She said.

The young lady instantly dropped to one knee, "Mistress, does this mean the legends are true?" She asked.

"Dear child, there is some truth in every legend," answered the spirit, "there is no need to bow to me. Come, let me get a closer look at you."

Meekly the young lady stood up and came around the table to stand in front of the spirit.

The spirit reached out and laid a hand on the young woman's shoulder, "she will assist you," she said bluntly as she looked over at him.

He frowned at the spirit, "Are you sure?" he asked, "I don't wish anyone else to get hurt."

The spirit smiled coldly at him, "It is only fitting that one of my heirs protect you while you right the wrong which was done to me."

"So that was why you were so angry back at the headstone," he said.

"The fact that someone bound one of my heirs to my grave angered me, but I would have been angered no matter who they had left there," the ghost replied. "Sadly though we do not have time to hunt them down right now, we will return when you have collected all of the pieces of my spirit."

He sighed deeply, "As you wish, it is the least I can do to repay your kindness."

The spirit smiled more gently at him, "You make your ancestors proud, now I must rest."

He sheathed the dagger, as the spirit faded away, and chuckled gently, "It appears we are to be traveling companions."

The young lady bowed to him, "If that is your wish, bearer of the crimson blade."

He shook his head, "Call me Mortimer," he replied. "We should get you checked by a doctor before we continue on." He paused for a moment and asked, "What should I call you?"

"You can call me Red," she answered, "it is the name I was given when I joined the guard."

Mortimer looked closely at her, "You appear to have recovered from your wounds quite rapidly, perhaps we should see my family and then leave town."

"That would probably be best," Red replied, "I will need to stop at the armory and inform them I have a new mission assigned from our lady."

He smiled, and offered her his arm. "At this time of night it would be best if we appeared to be together, as opposed to looking like a pair of brawlers."

She laughed gently, "As covered in blood as we both are, I just hope we don't get arrested."

"Normally I would have to agree with that statement," a deep voice said from the doorway, "but in this case I'll make an exception." The two of them looked at the door, and saw a town guard standing in it. "Your father sent me to find you when you didn't show up at his house, he even suggested I look for you here." The guard frowned, "Something about paying your respects to the dead, and not being able to keep your nose out of trouble."

Mortimer snorted, "Good to see you again too, Captain. Mind telling me what you were doing at dads?"

"He invited me over for dinner," the guard frowned, "He also told me it was time we buried the hatchet and learned to get along."

"So you never told him the truth?" Mortimer asked.

"No," the guard answered, "I can't bring myself to tell him it's my fault you left, and now that you're back it doesn't matter. Seeing you have a woman now, I don't feel as worried about you seeing my wife."

Red frowned, "Oh, we're not together, well not romantically. We are simply traveling companions."

The guard frowned slightly, "I find that hard to believe, any single man would be throwing himself at the feet of such a lovely woman."

Mortimer burst out laughing, "I am sure most of them do," with a wry smile he added, "after she kicks the crud out of them." A sudden throbbing sensation in his thigh made him fall to the floor all of a sudden, dragging Red down with him.

"Are you all right?" Red asked, a look of concern on her face.

Mortimer smiled back at her and chuckled, "Yes, apparently she doesn't like my sense of humor."

Red glanced over towards the guard who had now stepped closer to them, and leaned closer, "Or, she wants us to play a part and is putting a stop to both our protesting."

"Why do you say that?" He asked her.

She nodded towards his arm where he had cut himself earlier, and clearly written in blood was the word "Couple". They both watched as it drew back into the cut after they read it.

Together they slowly got back to their feet, "We had best get to my dad's place, before anything else happens," Mortimer said.

The guard chuckled, "Come, I brought an escort, just in case." As they stepped outside he noticed the blood and frowned, "Apparently I was correct in assuming you had found trouble, how many bodies are there?"

Red laughed, "Oh, this is all my blood, it's not nearly as bad as it looks."

Mortimer chuckled, "Don't worry Robert, I'll give you all the details over dinner. Honestly, I'm glad you found us, because now I won't have to report all this at the barracks."

Robert grinned darkly, "Oh, you'll still have to come by, review and sign the report, otherwise it will only be classified as hearsay."

Mortimer frowned, "Just so long as nobody sees me, there are many people who would rather I never returned to this town."

Red frowned at him, "Oh really? Am I going to have to protect you from a bunch of jilted lovers?"

Robert laughed and said, "No, more like you're going to have to protect him from all the fathers throwing their daughters at him."

Red looked thoroughly confused and Mortimer just said, "You'll find out when we get to the house.

Robert led them through the cemetery and to a carriage which stood just outside the gate, "Your ride awaits you my lord," he said with a slight grin.

Mortimer frowned, it was his fathers carriage, and beyond it sat two house guards on their horses waiting for them. "Well, I guess we can forget about keeping my return quiet." he said, as Robert laughed.

"Did you honestly think your father was going to keep your homecoming a secret?" Robert asked.

Mortimer sighed, "I suppose not." He turned and helped Red climb into the carriage as both guards bowed to him from their horses. In the light of the carriage, he could see clearly the tattered bandages and blood that covered her body, a quick glance down confirmed his dark clothing masked the sticky fluid fairly well. His shoulders gleamed slightly in the light, showing clearly where her blood had soaked into his doublet while he carried her.

Robert climbed in with them and frowned, "It would be best if we used the back entrance, so you two can have a chance to get cleaned up before seeing your father."

Red laughed musically, which caused Mortimer to jump slightly, "Good luck with that," she replied, "your lordship here destroyed my only gown."

Robert raised an eyebrow, "That is alright, you can borrow one of his sisters dresses, I'll have the maids bring one to your room once we arrive." He looked over at Mortimer, "You do remember how to get from the stables to your chambers unseen?" he asked.

Mortimer laughed slightly, "The only ones to see me shall be the servants, and that is only if I allow them to."

"Good," Robert replied, "it wouldn't be appropriate for the guests to see you in this state."

"How many did he invite?" Mortimer asked.

"Everyone with a single daughter," Robert replied, "I'm just glad I listened to you and married my wife when you told me to."

Mortimer chuckled, "That was to protect you, we were like brothers, and I knew if I didn't order you to marry her you would have let her slip away. At least this way you won't have to go to war, and she won't have to worry about her husband getting killed."

"Why did you choose the mercenary life anyways?" Robert asked.

"Because of what my father said, 'War is just a waste of life, best leave it to the professionals.' so I figured I would become a professional and be able to choose which side I would fight on." he answered. "I have learned a lot in a short time, and I will continue to fight, so that the people I care about don't have to. It's good to see father gave you the Captains position, but then again I figured you would inherit your fathers post."

"Assistant Captain actually, "Robert replied, "my father refuses to retire."

Mortimer smiled slightly, "You know all that stuff we were taught about honorable combat? Well, in war you can forget all that, there is no waiting for your enemy to be ready for your next attack, there is simply striking and moving on to the next foe all while hoping you kill the first one."

# Home

They rode on in silence until they got to the house, Mortimer glad that the carriage prevented Red from seeing exactly how big the estate was. As the carriage came to a halt, he jumped out, and offered his hand to Red as was protocol when with a young lady.

Red took one look at his posture and after what she had heard on the ride, gracefully accepted his hand as she stepped down from the carriage. "You are such a gentleman," she said.

Mortimer grimaced as if the comment pained him, and slipped his arm around her waist, "Please come with me," he whispered, guiding her through a nearby doorway and into a dark tunnel. He led her down a flight of stone stairs, then around a couple of turns and up another set of stone stairs, after which the floor continued sloping upwards as he led her through multiple twists and turns. They reached the end of the tunnel and stood facing a solid slab of stone, with the ease of experience, he ran his hand down the right side of the slab and pushed. Soundlessly the slab pivoted outward and they found themselves in a small empty room.

Mortimer smiled to himself, and crossed the room to the doorway, opening it slightly he peered out, the hallway was clear, "Come," he whispered "if we move quickly we can avoid being seen."

Red followed him as he moved down the hallway, past two other doors and then turned into one on the left hand side. Once inside, he closed the door and locked it. A fire roared to life in the fireplace, and several torches burst into life on the walls, the blue flames of fairy fire lighting up the entire room. "Wow," she gasped as she stepped back in surprise.

"It's nothing," he said, "just a gift from one of my fathers friends."

"You never did think much of extravagance." a deep voice said from across the room.

Mortimer frowned, "I am surprised you are still here, I was told you were released from service when I moved out."

"You may have released me from being your servant, but you cannot release me from a life debt old friend." came the response.

Red kept looking around, trying to find the speaker, but having a hard time pinpointing where the voice was coming from.

Mortimer sighed, "You owe me nothing, if it hadn't been for your training I would have died many times on the battlefield, as such I feel your debt has long since been paid in full."

A shadow moved along the wall, before detaching itself and standing in front of him, "Very well, then as friends I welcome you home." the voice said as the shadow solidified into the form of a tall young man. "I have missed you, but as you know I cannot abide the touch of iron, or I would have gone with you."

Mortimer gave the young man a hug and said, "I know, it is good to see you again, how is your family?"

The man smiled, "My son is growing rapidly, and my daughters are all begging to see you again. I don't know what you told the woodsmen, but they now only cut down trees a good distance from our home."

Mortimer smiled, "I simply explained to them who and what you were, and that having you there would bring them prosperity and well being. It took them a bit to understand that the shadows were children, simply playing and not meaning any harm."

"Yes well, thanks to you, we are able to prove that fairies can live alongside humans peacefully," he answered, "and the council is even now talking about asking some of the smaller towns if we might move a family into their parks to better maintain the trees."

Red was surprised, she had never seen one of the fairies before, even the witches guard believed them to be a myth.

The young man smiled at her and said, "Well, I shall be off it appears you and your young lady need to get cleaned up, my eldest will be so disappointed that you have been spoken for." With that he blended back into a shadow and slipped out under the door.

Red looked at Mortimer and giggled, "Sorry, but apparently there are quite a few young ladies that are interested in you."

Mortimer frowned, "Very few of them truly know me and most only seek me for my fathers money. The curse of coming from a rich family is that you can't trust if someone loves you or your money," he growled a dark glint in his eyes.

She could tell it was a sore subject with him, and was about to apologize when there was a light tapping at the door.

Mortimer's frown deepened, as he turned and unlocked the door, "What?" he growled as he opened it.

A young girl stood there holding a box, "I'm sorry my lord," she whispered, "but I was informed you would be needing a dress for your lady right away." Her eyes never left the floor, as she offered up a red bundle of cloth.

His expression softened, "No, I am sorry, I was just reliving a bad memory. Tell your mother thank you for us, and please come in and put it on the bed. I am afraid if I touch it I might get blood stains on it."

The young girl came into the room, and glanced around, as her eyes came across Red, they widened a bit and she whispered "she is so beautiful." Quickly she spotted the bed, set the bundle upon it and ran back out the door.

Mortimer laughed for a moment, all signs of anger left his face, "In case you were wondering, that is my niece. It would appear the family has decided we are treated as a couple." He smiled at her, "Through that door there is a washroom, when you are done, let me know and I will clean up."

Red shook her head, "Sorry my dark eyed friend, but if we are a couple then we should act as a couple." She glanced around the room, "Who knows if anybody else is watching. Besides," she said as she headed towards the washroom, "you've already seen me unclothed, it's only fair you return the favor."

He shrugged, he had bathed with female mercenaries in the past, he had only been trying to be considerate of her honor. He burst out laughing, "I'm sorry my bloody lady, but all this time I have been treating you as if you were one of the noble girls I had grown up around, even though based on your armor you are a warrior, forgive me?"

She laughed in response, "I was beginning to wonder what you were playing at, and now it makes sense. I suppose you had best use my given name when you introduce me to your father." She took a deep breath, "My father named me Scarlet after my hair, but people have always simply called me Red. You could say my work name is Red, but my real name is Scarlet."

He shrugged, "Thank you, for trusting me with that information, I know the witches guard takes true names very seriously."

Together they entered the bathing chamber, and her eyes lit up as the tub started to fill with steaming water, "another gift?" she asked.

"Yes," he answered, "my family has done a lot of favors for many people. The water is controlled by a water sprite, she can be a bit playful sometimes, but she is harmless."

Red watched as he unbuckled his belt and set it along with his dagger next to the tub, a water hand reached up and gently touched the dagger before receding back into the tub. "She senses its power," she said, as she stiffly removed her armor.

Mortimer watched her as he removed his clothing and threw it in the corner, "would you like some assistance?" he asked, "I left the buckles a little loose, but it may be too much to expect you to remove your armor without some help."

She shrugged, as he started to unbuckle the thick leather straps, and she smiled at him, "You know this is the first time I've been able to get a good look at you."

He shrugged, "I was thinking the same thing, the question is are you now upset with your task of assisting me on my mission?"

She laughed and then winced, as the bandages and armor were removed, her cuts burned when exposed to the open air, "No," she answered, "the scars on your body show you have been through many battles, and as such you know how to handle yourself."

After he removed all of the bandages he helped her step into the tub, and watched her wince as the hot water touched the first cut. He had to admit, having had only cold baths for the last couple years, the water did seem to be a bit on the overheated side.

As they stood knee deep in the water, he watched it turn pink and then fade back into its natural blue color, "I am sorry sprite," he said, "I should have warned you she had wounds."

Suddenly there was a watery female form standing in the tub with them, looking over Scarlet slowly, almost as if trying to determine how bad the wounds were. Slowly it turned to him and he said, "this is her blood on me, I am uninjured." With a quick nod, the water girl disappeared back into the tub.

"You had best sit down," he said, "she didn't look too happy."

Scarlet sat down, and he sat across from her to soak in the tub, she felt hands on her and resisted the urge to jump out. The hands ran over all of her injuries, new and old, they scrubbed her body and massaged her muscles, she was very surprised when they grabbed her hair and began scrubbing and brushing it out.

Mortimer chuckled as the sprite washed and brushed his hair and massaged his body. He jumped slightly and said, "Yes I know, I should have visited sooner, and I know you would have prevented most of the scars."

Scarlet looked puzzled for a second and then noticed the cuts on her arms were healing visibly in the water, "Thank you," she said "you are a most amazing sprite." The water around her turned a bit pink as the sprite blushed with pleasure.

Scarlet smiled and said, "I could get used to this."

Mortimer laughed, "You would soon become bored," he replied as he stood up. "We should get dressed for the party."

She stood up to join him, and thought to herself, this guy is actually a decent man, I wonder why no woman has snatched him up yet. Seeing the dagger casually carried in his left hand, she realized that he refused to let anyone get close to him. "So, out of curiosity, did you have someone in your life before you acquired the crimson dagger?"

He laughed, "No, I never found a woman I could trust," he answered as he glanced over his shoulder. "I trust you on the other hand, because of this dagger. What about you? Any jilted lovers I need to be worried about?"

Her pale skin turned the same dark red as her hair as she replied, "No, men avoid me because my red hair and green eyes are considered a bad omen. If my eyes had been brown or blue like my mothers, it might have been a different story."

He smiled at her, "Then I am thankful for the bad omen, and will add it to the rest of them I carry."

She noticed his eyes had changed color and were now a deep dark blue, but his hair was still nearly jet black in stark contrast to his pale skin.

He noticed her staring and said, "It's called being a child of death, if I didn't use coal to darken my hair it would be pure white. You could say it is my own bad omen. For a while I kept it white when on the battlefield, as it terrified my enemies, but at the same time it also meant I drew a lot of the archers attention. As they say, those who get too close to us soon perish, just like my mother died shortly after my birth."

She saw a cloudiness come into his face, and without thinking stepped closer to him and gave him a hug, "It appears our two omens are perfect for each other."

He smiled and a scarlet blush ran up his face, "We should probably get dressed," he gasped.

She blushed as well, "Oh my, I didn't even think about how this might look if someone walked in."

"If you can do without your armor tonight, I am certain the guard captain will have it cleaned by morning," he said. "Tomorrow I will need to stop by the barracks to pick up my gear anyways."

"I can manage one night without armor," she replied as she picked up the clothing his niece had left on the bed for her.

The outfit his niece had dropped off turned out to be a beautiful burgundy dress with pink rose petal lace trim, Scarlet was surprised to find that it fit her perfectly after Mortimer tightened the laces in the back. Once in the dress, she went back into the wash room so she could fix her hair, only to find the sprite sitting on the edge of the tub with a brush and ribbons in her hands. "Well hello," she said to the sprite, "are you offering to do my hair for me?"

The sprite smiled and nodded her head happily, so Scarlet sat down in front of her while she brushed and braided and did who knows what with her hair. When the sprite was done, she handed scarlet a mirror.

Scarlet gasped, "Oh wow, my hair has never looked this good before."

The sprite blushed furiously and slipped away down the drain of the wash basin, clearly pleased with the praise.

When Scarlet came out of the wash room, Mortimer was dressed in a navy blue tunic with crimson trim, along with matching pants and knee high dress boots. His hair was tied back into a single ponytail with a crimson ribbon. The crimson dagger hung on his hip, its blade bare with only the last 3 inches in a sheath strapped to his thigh. "She wasn't too happy at first, but when I explained to her the importance of the display, she agreed on one condition," he frowned, "we must remain at each other's side no matter what."

Scarlet smiled, "I can do that, does she require a blood oath?"

He laughed, "No, I don't think so, but you never know when she will require your blood."

A musical voice answered, "When you two get married, I will do everything I can to make that happen."

"Why?" asked Scarlet.

"Sister, when you have been dead as long as I have, you learn to read souls," answered the voice. "I am running out of energy, so must rest, it wouldn't do to have either of you bleeding when you present yourself to his father."

Scarlet looked at Mortimer, and he answered her unspoken question, "She gets her energy from the blood she draws, if she kills someone she becomes very powerful for a few days. Granted," he added, "the weaker she gets, the less aware of her surroundings she becomes."

"I'm not so sure how comfortable I am having my future decided by the dead," Scarlet replied.

Mortimer chuckled dryly, "You get used to it, in a couple more hours I will be the only one able to hear her voice, and in a day or two she will be completely oblivious to what is going on around us.  Come, we should head to the banquet hall," he said as he looped her arm with his.

# Family

As they left the room, Scarlet found herself to be nervous, she hadn't been out in public without her armor on for quite a while, and as late as it already was, she was certain what type of people would still be waiting to greet them.

A servant spotted them in the hall, and bowed slightly, "Ah good, right on schedule my lord and lady. If you would please follow me I will be honored to be your escort for the evening."

Mortimer returned the servants bow and said, "It is good to see you again, I take it his lordship has decided to have a formal reception for us?"

The servant straightened up and answered, "Naturally, my young lord, you know how he loves to show off." He bowed to Scarlet and said, "I do not believe we have had the pleasure of being introduced."

She curtsied back to the servant and answered, "Allow me to introduce myself, I am Scarlet of the witches guard."

His eyes widened as he straightened back up, "It is a high honor to meet you Lady Scarlet, I do believe this is the first time I have ever heard of the guard not wearing any armor."

Scarlet blushed slightly, "It was in need of repair, so I left it in my lord's room," she replied with a sideways look at Mortimer.

The servant chuckled to himself and said, "Oh, this is going to be a most interesting night I must say. Is there by chance another woman present with us tonight my lord?" he asked with a glance at the crimson dagger.

Mortimer smiled, "She is observing at present, it would not do to fully wake her."

"Very well, my lord," he led them to a pair of huge ornate doors decorated with copper and brass roses. "I shall announce your arrival, and then you may mingle as you see fit." the servant said as he reached for the doors. With ease, the doors swung open. The servant stood tall and called out, "It is with the greatest of pleasure I announce the arrival of his lordship Sir Mortimer of the order of the rose, and his Lady Madame Scarlet of the order of the witches guard." As he finished, he stepped to the side and performed a flourishing bow to the two of them.

Mortimer kept a smile on his face, as he escorted Scarlet into the huge room, hoping it wasn't going to overwhelm her. He glanced over at her, and noticed she had a similar smile on her face. "We can get through this," he whispered to her.

Scarlet brought her left hand up to her face as if to hide a laugh, and whispered back, "This reminds me of a few training sessions I had back with the guard. Why didn't you tell me you were of the order of the rose?"

"Why didn't you tell me the witches guard are supposed to always wear some form of armor?" he asked back.

"Because I was unconscious when you removed it the first time," she answered. "Besides, it's not exactly a taboo, we just don't run around without our armor because people are always trying to kill us."

As they walked casually through the crowd of people, towards the head table, he whispered, "I wasn't sure how you would feel about me if you knew I was part of an order which seeks out witches. We don't exactly have a good reputation with the witch's guard after all."

Scarlet smiled at him, "Darling, you don't exactly have a good reputation with anyone, except perhaps me."

He glanced at his fathers table and grimaced, "good point. Maybe you should have worn your armor, most of the people in this room are not happy to see me returned."

She chuckled, "I think those dark looks are meant for me not you."

"Well, if any of them have a problem with you, they are welcome to cross blades with me," he said, his voice had a sudden hard edge to it and his eyes had gained a reddish tinge to them.

A broad shouldered old man stood up from the head table and approached them with a smile on his face and a twinkle in his eye. "My son, you have stopped by for a visit I see," he said with his arms open as if to give them both a hug. "And you have brought along quite a beauty as well." He smiled and asked her, "So how did you manage to catch this dark cloud?"

Scarlet was slightly taken aback by this greeting, but she let it roll off her shoulders and answered, "He rescued me from a certain fate, and as such he is now stuck with me."

The old man wrapped them both in a huge hug and whispered to them both, "Keep your cool, no harm may come to any under my roof. I am proud of you my son, always have been, but to peel the armor from one of the witch guard, that takes a certain amount of courage few men can muster." He released them and spoke a little louder, "So how many curses and bad omens do you bear on your shoulders now son?"

Mortimer chuckled dryly and his eyes returned to a dark blue color, "Not enough to kill me father," he replied. "Although, I am still curious about the rest of that prophecy from when I was born, how does it go again?"

The old man paled, "You deliberately challenged it didn't you?" He then looked at Scarlet, and grew paler still, "Please tell me he did not pull you from the grave and summon the dead for you."

She looked him directly in the eye and answered, "He woke the spirit of the crimson dagger with his own blood in order to unbind me from the grave to which I had been tied, why?"

He waved a hand and a group of guards came over to them, "We must go to my office, make certain nobody follows us." he said to them. "You two come with me," he said to them as he turned and moved with ease through the crowd and out a side door.

In this new room hung several ornate daggers and a matching sword, all of them had a reddish hue to the blade. "My grandfather collected these blades in order to free the witch who was trapped in them," he said, "Now you have gone and started a new collection." He took a deep breath and slowly spoke, "The prophecy dates back long before you,"

'A child born of death, shall possess the witch and through her soul shall retrieve his wife from the grave, together they shall release her'

He leaned against his desk, "My grandfather fulfilled that prophecy, and when you were born I knew you too would try to fulfill it, it is by no means a guarantee of success, after all many people have failed in regards to this particular prophecy, but I believe you can do it if you truly are going to try."

He looked at Scarlet, "His mothers last words were, he shall be reborn with fire by his side. I believe she may have foreseen this coming. I am curious though if I could meet the witch within the blade?"

Mortimer nodded his head, "In the morning if you desire, I will ask her if she will meet with you."

Scarlet shook her head, "Are you sure it is safe to continue feeding her your blood?"

"Oh, he won't need to bleed in order for me to meet her," the old man answered. "The order of the rose has a special ceremony that will permit me to meet her on the spiritual plane, provided she is willing." He smiled at the two of them, "Come let us get back to dinner, after the ceremony tomorrow you two will be wanting to get started on your journey."

They returned to the banquet hall, and Mortimer led Scarlet over to a table laden with food and drink, "Our banquets are a bit different than most, as everyone is expected to serve themselves, once the head table has eaten then musicians will play and there will be dancing."

Scarlet smiled at him, "I am torn in two, part of me hates the fact that my path has been chosen for me, and part of me is excited and happy that it is with you my lord."

He looked at her as he loaded some roast pig onto his plate, "My dear I would have preferred to have you wishing to be with me, than being ordered to be, for you are a far more beautiful woman than I could ever deserve. Now please join me in this meal and every one after it."

She blushed deeply, "You do not realize how lucky I am that I was chosen for you, and you were chosen for me. You are perhaps much nicer than one such as myself deserves." She then focused on selecting her own food, as he watched her with a puzzled expression.

As the two of them finished filling their plates and took their seats at the head table, she noticed the other guests moving quickly along the table of food and heading to their seats. They waited patiently for everyone to take their seats, and then a young woman in a pink and red dress stood up and addressed the crowd, "Please take a moment and thank the animals who have so freely given their lives in order to provide us with this meal, and thank the earth and sky for supplying us with the vegetables to go with it and the fruit for our drinks." She smiled at Scarlet and Mortimer, "I would also like to thank the powers that be for allowing my brother to come home to us, if only for a visit and ask they continue to watch over him in his travels. Finally I would like to say welcome to our family to our new sister." She looked directly at Scarlet and nodded her head with a faint smile.

Scarlet looked at Mortimer who grinned back at her, "Congratulations, my eldest sister has just formally declared you a part of the family." he said.

"What exactly does that mean?" she asked, as she picked at her food.

Swallowing a mouthful of roast pig, he answered, "By morning everyone in the town will know you are a part of the family, and anything you purchase will be invoiced back to my father. I am quite certain that by morning you will have a new piece of jewelry to wear when you go out."

"You realize I don't wear metal," she said.

His father chuckled, "Do you see my daughters wearing any metal jewelry? You aren't the first witch in our family, and I certainly hope you will not be the last."

"How do you know so much about the guard?" she asked as she tried some of the steamed vegetables.

He smiled as he replied, "My wife was a member of the guard, as was my mother. It's funny how the witch guard knows so little about us, when so many of them have married into the order. For that matter, several decades ago the guard would have been wiped out had it not been for the order of the rose intervening. They weren't too happy at the price we asked for our aid though."

"Oh, what was that?" she asked.

"They would provide a wife for the head of the order for as long as the order existed," Mortimer answered for his father. "When they heard of mothers death, a dozen of the highest witches showed up and offered themselves to him."

His father laughed, "You should have seen the look on their faces when I told them they had already met the requirements for my generation, and the conditions of the contract were met until it was my son's turn to find a wife."

Scarlet laughed softly, "I can just imagine the relief they felt, not knowing the truth about your family." She continued to eat for a few minutes, before she said, "I am beginning to understand why I was assigned to come to this party to begin with, I was to be a sacrificial lamb, wasn't I?"

Mortimers father smiled, "No, you were to be here with the rest of them," he nodded towards a nearby table, "in order to give us the opportunity to find out if there was one within the guard my son would be willing to marry. Since he first took interest in girls, I have thrown these parties and invited the guard in the hopes of one of them wanting to get to know him." He let out a deep sigh, "Sadly, every year he has managed to avoid or upset every member of the witch guard that has been willing to attend." He smiled at Scarlet, "If I had known he was going to bring you tonight, I wouldn't have bothered to invite them."

"Honestly, I was ordered to attend before I even met Mortimer," she replied. "I was on my way here when I was ambushed and left chained to a grave, I am still not sure how they failed to kill me, as my armor didn't cover my entire body."

Mortimer winced as a sudden burst of heat exploded along his thigh.

Scarlett noticed and asked, "Are you alright?"

"I think she just bit me," he answered as he looked down at his leg. His dagger glowed a vibrant red and was vibrating rapidly, "If you have something to say, you can just say it, no need to bite me," he said to the blade.

"I'm sorry," the musical voice said, "but the reminder of how they tied her to my grave upset me. Her blood spilling on my resting place combined by your proximity to my grave gave me the strength to protect her. The anger you felt in me at the grave was not directed at you, it was directed at them."

"Thank you, for protecting me until he could get there," Scarlet replied to the voice, "I'm sorry we woke you again."
"Do not ever be sorry for waking me child," the ghost replied, "now put the darkness aside, for now is a time for you to enjoy yourselves there will be plenty of time for us to get to know each other better later."

Mortimer could feel the spirit return to a restful state, and then realized everyone at the table was staring at him as if he had grown a second head, "What?" he asked.

His father smiled at him and said, "It is only appropriate that you would hunt for those particular blades. That was your great, great grandmother's voice."

Mortimer went a little paler than usual, before he said, "I swear I will avenge her death."

Scarlet laughed softly, "There is no point in swearing an oath of vengeance, especially a blood oath, since you already have sworn to free her spirit. I admire your loyalty, but honestly I feel you gave her your loyalty before you even knew who she was."

Mortimers father chuckled, "You are very observant for such a young witch, you will go far if you survive the task before you."

She blushed in response, "You are such a flatterer, I see where your son gets his silver tongue from."

Mortimer snorted, "We just speak our minds, it does no good to speak a falsehood. Come, we should start dancing so our guests don't get bored."

"You realize, witches are not trained in dance," she said to him.

"That's alright," he replied, "neither am I, but a friend of mine once gave me great advice. Think of it as a form of combat, you move to compliment your partner's moves."

Cautiously she accepted his offered hand, and he led her out into the center of the floor. The room became silent and they felt all eyes upon them. Mortimer turned and bowed to her, before pulling her into his arms and sweeping her sideways. She lost track of the movements as a drum started to beat, followed quickly by the whistling scream of the pipes and the thrum of a lute. His eyes had transitioned to a steel blue, bright and beautiful, one strong hand always held one of hers, while the other wrapped gently around her waist. The room itself melted away, as she spun around it with him holding her in his arms. She wondered why there was a red glow around them, there was no heat coming from it, but the glow seemed to be getting stronger the longer they danced.

As they danced, he noticed the fire building around them, he felt the heat along his back, but he didn't care, for the first time in his life he felt pleasure. He saw the shadows dancing with the flames, and he knew this was no trick of the mind, this was the combination of both of their powers manifesting themselves. He didn't care if he died, he was drawn ever more into her emerald green eyes, and watched as her flame red hair wrapped itself around her neck. It would be a most pleasant way to die, he thought. Finally I have found someone who understands me, someone who compliments me and knows when to contradict me.

Suddenly there was stillness in the air, they both could feel the mixture of light and darkness, the music had stopped and the crowd was silent, and they were locked deep within each other's eyes as the flames and shadows wrapped tightly around them. Slowly, they became aware of their surroundings, and even more aware of each other.

Scarlet started to say something, but Mortimer pulled her in close to him and kissed her passionately. The wall of flames and shadows collapsed as if washed away by a great waterfall, as the kiss ended.

"I'm sorry," Mortimer said, "but I just couldn't hold back."

Scarlet let out a musical laugh, "You have nothing to apologize for, that much power had to be released somehow, and I really enjoyed it." She smiled happily as she looked him in the eyes, "The happiness I saw in your eyes while we danced, I hope I will continue to be the source of your happiness in the future."

Mortimer smiled back at her, "I could say the same to you, I was lost in the passion of your eyes, and thinking of how much I hoped I was bringing out that passion in you. The fire in your eyes, the wonder and amazement, all I could think of was that I wish it was for me."

She couldn't help it, a tear ran down her cheek, as she wrapped her arms around his neck and pulled him in, "It is all for you, now and for as long as you'll have me." she said as she kissed him.

Applause suddenly exploded around them, and they both started laughing with embarrassment. "I do believe a contract has been renewed," an older woman said as she approached the two of them.

Mortimers father snorted, "I told you before, the witches will always have the support of the order of the rose. That stupid contract was only written because your ancestors tried to stop the marriage of a single witch to the man she loved."

The old woman glared at him, "I know," she grumped, "but a magical contract is a magical contract." She looked at the two of them closely, "I have never before witnessed such growth in power." She looked directly at Scarlet, "this morning you could barely light a candle, even though you have the gift of fire magic, and now you not only summoned a great wall of fire, but you controlled it to the point that it didn't burn anything." She looked at Mortimer, "You on the other hand, have never shown any aptitude for magic in your life, but upon meeting her you broke through antimagic bonds, and just now you summoned a wall of shadows and you controlled them as if they were an extension of your body." She shook her head and looked at Mortimers father, "You may be correct in your belief that when the right people get together, their skills grow exponentially."

Mortimer stepped in front of Scarlet, "What do you know of the attack on her?" he demanded, "Did you have something to do with it?" All of the shadows in the room moved towards him, twisting and pulling, breaking free of their bonds and stalking across the dance floor.

Scarlet put a hand on his shoulder, "Easy love, she would never allow harm to befall one of the guard, let her explain." She looked at the old lady, "high priestess, would you please explain how you know what type of bonds were used."

The high priestess frowned, "Love truly is one of the most powerful forces of magic. I investigated immediately after I received word you hadn't shown up here at the appointed time. When one of the guards told me what had happened, and that you were being tended to at their headquarters, I decided to go to the graveyard and see what I could find out." She shook her head, "I was completely puzzled at how the bonds had been cut when I saw the spell that was inscribed on them, even a crimson blade wouldn't have the power to cut those bonds. No magic can affect such bonds, so it would have had to be a non-magical item that cut them, but at the same time no ordinary item could have cut that cleanly. Shadow magic though, is the opposite of almost every type of magic out there, and when used properly can cancel out almost any spell, and after this display it makes sense, he subconsciously used his shadow magic to counter the spell on the chords and then the crimson blade easily cut through them."

Mortimer relaxed a bit as she explained this, and the shadows faded away once again, "The only thing is, I didn't summon the power of the dagger to cut the bonds, I gave it my blood as an apology for using it for such a utilitarian purpose."

"You gave her your own blood as an apology?" The priestess asked, "Even knowing the price you would have to pay for summoning her even if you didn't use her magic?"

"Yes," he answered, "and I would do it again if I had to."

"The elders are still clueless about the crimson blades it would appear," a musical voice suddenly spoke. "I must say, you two are much stronger than anyone could have dreamed when your love is exposed. It probably helps that the family never removed my old prayer circles, they only covered them up." The spirit of the sword appeared before them, this time she looked almost solid. "It is sad that since my time at the guard you still have not bothered to research the crimson blades. You do know part of the contract allows for the exchange of information between the two different groups in order to better protect witches, but I bet you still don't even know what becomes of the witches the order of the rose discovers." She looked at Mortimer and Scarlet, "I will tell you a secret, that neither group knows, we draw our power from blood, that is true, but we also can draw energy from our wielders directly if they have the talent. It is a convenience, I have not bothered to use, as it tends to leave my user tired afterwards." She looked at the high priestess, "You have a lot to teach when you get back to the guard, oh and one more thing, you're standing on the very spot where I died, and there are hundreds of witches buried under this hall, that is why any witch trapped in a crimson blade can manifest in this room without draining their handler." With that she vanished in a crimson cloud.

The high priestess looked around the room in shock and asked, "What does she mean by there are hundreds of witches buried under this hall?"

Mortimers father snorted, "You ever wonder what happened to all the witches we found over the generations? We accepted them into our family and when they passed away they were entombed in our own private catacombs, unless they had a specific request for where they wished to be buried. It was the easiest way to prevent the creation of more crimson blades."

"I have a lot to think about," the high priestess said as she turned and left the hall. The other witches in the room curtsied to them, and followed her out, many of them had a look of amazement on their face as they left.

Mortimer laughed, "Our family has never kept it a secret as to what we do, or why, I'm quite surprised she didn't know."

A nearby merchant laughed, "Considering the entire town knows what your family does, I'm a bit surprised as well. It was definitely the most entertaining night any of us have ever had, and it will be the talk of the town for many years I believe."

Mortimers sister laughed, "I guess that priestess is a little upset, she thought they had all the witches, and now come to find out more witches turn to us than them, that must really sting."

Mortimers father snorted, "It was never about controlling the witches, it was about protecting them. The stupid thing is the contract was their idea, not ours. We went to their aid against the witch hunters, after the battle they asked what the price was, and my great grandfather said he would like my grandmother to be his wife. Their elders then decided to draw up a magical contract that promised, our family, could take any of their members as a wife provided we continued to provide protection." He smiled at them, "Honestly, they did us a favor, as ever since then the men in our family have always found love in the witches guard. You could say their marriage back then married the two groups to each other. Stupid thing is if they remembered their own history, they would know the order of the rose was founded by the witches guard."

He shook his head at the stupidity of it all and started to walk away, "Well, I'm off to get some rest, I'll see you in the morning."

"Father speaks the truth," Mortimers sister said, "I have been studying the history of our family, and we only left the witches' guard because they would not allow the witches to marry people who they thought didn't have any magical power. It was quite the embarrassment when Great great Grandpa marched in and saved them from being annihilated."

Scarlet smiled at this pretty young woman and said, "I should thank you for loaning me this dress, before you head to bed."

"Oh, I didn't loan it to you," she replied, "It's yours to keep. I simply can't wait until I get to see you in your wedding dress, I have already begun designing it."

Scarlet blushed, "Thank you, doesn't this complicate our sleeping arrangements though?"

Mortimers sister laughed, "Are you kidding? The wedding is just a ceremony, as far as our family is concerned you two are already married. Nobody in this family would even think of trying to untangle the magic binding you together."

Scarlet shook her head, "I have to admit, your family is a lot different than I had expected."

Mortimer laughed, "You don't know the half of it, come we should head to bed ourselves, we have a long day ahead of us tomorrow." He led her back through the myriad of passages to his chambers and opened the door for her.

Scarlet smiled as she entered the room, "Do we have any more unexpected visitors tonight?"

"No," he laughed, "we are alone, why?"

She untied her hair and let it fall down her back, "Because I'm not sure if I want everyone in town to know what I look like underneath this dress."

Mortimer pulled her into him, "Trust me if anyone saw you without it, they would keep their mouth shut for their own safety." He untied and loosened the ties on the back of the dress, then tentatively kissed her, only to have her kiss him back with a fiery passion.

# Mercenaries

He woke in the morning, and froze it took him a moment to remember why there was someone else in his bed. He looked over to see a pair of emerald green eyes watching him, and said, "I am sorry, I shouldn't have taken advantage of you last night."

She laughed, "I am not sorry, and neither should you be." she replied. "Unless of course you didn't mean it," she said coyly.

"I meant it," he answered, "but are you sure this is what you really want?" He asked.

"Lay back down with me and find out," she whispered.

Gently he lay back down with her, he would stay there all day if she asked him to.

It was almost noon when they got out of bed, and dressed. Their clothing and armor from the day before had been cleaned and repaired.

Scarlet was happy to be back in her leather armor, while Mortimer wore a simple traveling outfit of black pants, and tunic, with a matching black cloak and boots. "Is that all you wear when you travel?" she asked him.

"No," he answered, "the rest of my gear is at the barracks. I will change when we get there, I'm sure you have items to retrieve from the guard as well."

She laughed, "Just my sword and bow, we don't keep a lot of personal belongings."

"Let's eat lunch, then we must get on the road," he said, "it wouldn't do for me to stay in town too long."

They headed out of the room arms looped together, and he showed her the way to the family dining room. As they entered, his niece looked up and said, "Leaving already uncle?"

"Right after we eat," he answered, "there is something I must do in the next couple of weeks."

His father entered from another doorway and said, "I insist your lady wear your mothers amulet when you go." He held out a beautiful silver chain from which hung a single copper rose, "It will protect you in your travels," he said as he slipped it over her head.

Scarlet could feel an icy cold power coming from within the rose, "Are you sure? This is quite a valuable piece of jewelry."

Mortimers father smiled, "I am quite certain, and don't worry, it won't be affected by your magic."

Mortimer bowed to his father, "Thank you, I know how much it means to you."

"Just be sure she makes it back alive," he replied.

"I will father," he answered.

They all sat at the table and ate lunch, Mortimer told them all about the various battles he had been in and the lands he had seen, before long though lunch was over and it was time to leave.  Scarlet was surprised at how silently everyone left, there were no hugs, or words of farewell, just a simple nod as if everything had already been said.

As they left the house, Scarlet wondered if she would see any of them again, and at the same time she knew it didn't really matter as long as he was by her side.  They drew a lot of attention as they walked through the town, a quick stop at the witch guard building and she received her sword, a bow, and a quiver of arrows from the guards at the door in silence.  She knew she would never be welcome back into that building again, she was now an outsider.

"I'm sorry," Mortimer said to her as they walked away.

Scarlet shrugged, "I knew last night this would be the case," she replied.  "I will miss my sisters, but I have gained so much more," she said as she hugged him.

The barracks was another matter altogether, as some of the people staying there had fought both alongside and against him on the battlefield.  Many of the men and a few of the women watched him with open jealousy in their eyes, one even asked "How did the grim reaper get such a pretty thing at his side?"

Another answered, "Careful, hair like that is a bad omen, he must have summoned her from the halls of the damned."

One of the women walked up to him and frowned, "You never once showed any interest in the women here, were we not good enough for you?"

Mortimer chuckled dryly, "I told you before, I would not sleep with a woman I might have to kill the next day."

The woman swung a fist at him, but before it could come close to connecting, Scarlet stepped forward and drove her fist into the woman's stomach, doubling her over, a quick knee to the face and the woman dropped to the floor unconscious.

"Anyone else have a problem with me being with him?" she asked the room.

Mortimer calmly stepped over the prone woman and approached the bar, "I have come to collect my things," he said to the bartender.

Without a word, the bartender went into the back room and returned with a large duffel bag, "Rumor has it you're going into war by yourself," he said as he set it on the bar.

Scarlet frowned, "What am I? Chopped liver?"

Mortimer laughed, "Red," he nodded towards her, "will be joining me.  I do not recommend anyone signing up for the other side."  He opened the duffel bag, turned to Scarlet and said, "I will be right back, please try not to hurt too many people."

"Define too many," she said with a mischievous smile, it was a well known fact you couldn't show any weakness when dealing with the mercenaries guild.  She leaned against the bar and winked at the bartender, "Would you be a dear and bring me something sweet to drink?"

The bartender noticed her amulet and bowed his head, "yes Mistress," he said and slipped into the room behind the bar.  When he returned, he carried a small wine bottle and a crystal goblet. "I hope it is to your liking, my lady," he said as he poured the fluid into the goblet.

Scarlet smiled sweetly as she watched the crimson fluid fill the glass, "It looks perfect," she said as she lifted the glass. A quick sip, and her smile broadened, "Thank you barkeep."

"Anything your ladyship desires, just ask," the barkeep replied with a bow.

Everyone in the room stared at this strange behavior from the bartender, they had never seen him behave like this before. "What was that about?" someone asked softly.

A dry laugh answered, as an old mercenary at the end pointed to a broken sword up on a shelf, "The last time someone offended a lady of the order, it cost over ten thousand lives, that sword is one of many broken over the bare arm of the man defending his ladies honor. It has been a long time since anyone from the order has ventured into a mercenary barracks."

"Not as long as you might think," Mortimer said, as he walked back into the room, he was wearing black studded leather armor with the imprint of a large rose on the chest, the studs were shaped like thorns with vines twining between them. Across his back was a black recurve bow, and on his left hip hung a black short sword, and on his right thigh was strapped the crimson dagger. Under his arm he carried a bundle of what looked to be chainmail, from which protruded a pair of sword hilts. "Would someone please wake her up?" He asked with a nod towards the unconscious woman on the floor.

Everyone in the room stared, as the bartender went over and dumped a glass of cold water on the unconscious woman.

As she sputtered and picked herself up off the floor, Mortimer strode over and threw the chainmail bundle down in front of her, "I told you, you could have this when I no longer had a use for it."

The bartender smirked at the look of shock on everyone's faces as he went back behind the bar and poured a drink for Mortimer, "It's good to see you in your house armor your lordship, I take it you are on a quest."

Mortimer took the drink, and smiled, "yes, my lady and I will be leaving after this drink to free the souls of the crimson blades." He looked around and chuckled, "You all look a bit surprised."

The old mercenary laughed, "I knew I recognized your fighting style, I just couldn't place it."

Mortimer bowed to the old mercenary, "I am thankful you didn't recognize it, it would have made it hard to blend in if you had."

The woman on the floor shook her head, "Red, you have one hell of a punch. You're the first to knock the wind out of me in a long time." She looked at Mortimer and laughed, "Well Grim, I guess I missed my chance at you."

Mortimer laughed, "fate showed me my soul mate before you took that chance."

She laughed painfully, "the story of my life, at least invite me to the ceremony would you?"

Red laughed, "Only if you promise not to hold a grudge."

The woman smiled, "I learned a long time ago not to hold grudges, I also learned not to date my coworkers as quite often I ended up across from them on the battlefield."

The bartender shook his head, "Red and the Grim Reaper, this is a bad omen, the Red Death, there is going to be a massacre in the near future."

Mortimer raised an eyebrow questioningly.

"An old witch stopped in here once, and told me that when the Grim Reaper mates with Red, it will create the Red Death. She said that the team would slaughter all in their path in the name of revenge." He shook his head slowly, "She also told me to warn all mercenaries when they left my bar, to avoid those two at all costs."

Red frowned, "There are stories of the Red Death in the guard," she said, "it is said they were the most powerful fighting duo ever seen. A pairing of a fire witch and a shadow warlock, the like none had seen before. They slaughtered thousands of soldiers before they disappeared, rumor has it they retired after they accomplished their goal. It is indeed a lofty name, but I do not believe us to be them, as they would be very old now."

A mercenary laughed, "No offense madame, but he earned the name Grim Reaper, and you are obviously Red, so on the battlefield, people will revere you as Red Death."

Mortimer chuckled, "I should have hung out around the fire more often instead of being a loner all the time, maybe I would have learned about all of this. Oh well, it's a moot point, let us be going, we have a few people to hunt down."

# First Contact

As they left the barracks, Scarlet looked at him and said, "You don't seem too concerned about being associated with such a bloodthirsty team, why is that?"

He laughed, "Probably because I already have a reputation on the battlefield," he answered. "They call me Grim Reaper, because none of them have ever seen me happy after a battle, and because I have survived mortal wounds while at the same time killing my enemy. If you look closely at my scars, you'll see that some of them are from weapons that went through my body. The first time that happened I killed the man who stabbed me, and with his sword still stuck in my body turned and killed the man next to him. I spent a month in bed after that battle, but had been given the nickname of the Grim Reaper. What's wrong with a reputation that will keep most people from even thinking about attacking us?"

She didn't have a response to this line of thought, but she did have one more question, "Are you truly a shadow warlock?"

He smiled at her, "Yes, does that make you regret being with me?"

"No," she answered, "I was just wondering, since there hasn't been a shadow warlock in many generations."

He sighed, "I'll tell you a family secret, the original Red Death, are my ancestors, from back before the order or the guard even existed. They were not bad people, they only did what they had to do in order to bring peace to the area."

Before long, Mortimer started to chuckle, "We shall have a guest tonight, he will not stay for long though."

"Oh?" she asked, "What makes you say that?"

He pointed off to the side of the road, "Fresh corpse, and only a human would take their time killing another human."

Sure enough, soon they heard the noise of several people ahead of them on the road. As they reached the top of a small hill, they could see a family kneeling with their backs together in the center of the road. "Stop," sobbed an old man in the family, "it's a trap."

Mortimer laughed as he drew his sword, "it is the nature of traps to be sprung."

Scarlet grabbed her bow and stayed close to his side, an arrow nocked. "While it is true a trap is a trap until sprung, are you sure we should trigger this one?"

A voice called out from the trees, "Give me the witch and I will release the family, otherwise we shall have to kill you both."

Mortimer frowned, "I do not revel in the idea of meaningless death, but in your case I shall gladly make an exception."

The air filled with arrows coming at them from the trees, Scarlet acted and fired her own arrow towards the treeline. Fire spread from her arrow and created a flaming shield above the road, protecting all of them from the arrows.

A flick of Mortimers sword, and a shadowy spear leapt up from the ground cutting the bonds of the people in the road, "Go, get out of here," he told them as he ran towards the enemy coming from the trees.

Her fire shield in place, Scarlet drew her sword and smiled as flames licked its blade, yes she thought we are the combination of red and death.

Mortimer encountered the enemy a half a minute before she could reach his side, and yet, the ground was already littered with corpses. "I find it funny that your leader is a coward who keeps sending his underlings to fight me," he yelled as he fought.

Scarlet noticed the corpses on the ground had all been killed in a single slice, and yet he had not drawn the crimson dagger. Shadows danced amongst the dead, and slowly rose in a protective circle, that's when she saw it, a Crimson blade coming straight towards her. She brought her sword up to defend herself, but knew she was in trouble, this attacker was on horseback, he had the advantage of speed and weight.

Suddenly Mortimer was there, his sword billowing a black cloud as he stepped out of the shadows. His first swing cleaved the horse's head from its body so smoothly, the rider was barely able to deflect the blow that would have cut him in two had it connected. As it was, the rider was thrown backwards off his horse to land hard on the ground.

"He's as magnificent in battle as my husband was," a musical voice said from beside Scarlet. "Don't worry dear, I am absorbing quite a bit of energy from the battlefield, the fool thinks to use me against my own heirs?" The spirit laughed, "Don't worry about Mortimer, he gains energy from death, and he has a lot of that energy lying around right now."

"Don't you have to give your power to the one who holds your blade?" Scarlet asked.

"Oh no dear," the spirit shuddered at the thought, "that is the myth of the crimson blades, we are constantly at war with our handlers and seeking revenge against our creators. That is why we set a high price for them to borrow our powers, we created the war within their own ranks trying to convince them to bring all our pieces back together accidentally." She smiled at Scarlet, "Your husband, my great great grandson is quite a powerful warlock, I am impressed he has learned all this control without any instruction."

A slight disturbance in the air caused Scarlet to whirl around and raise her sword into a guard position, as an arrow glanced off the blade. "Really?" she asked, "very well then," she raised her sword above her head and brought it slicing downward. The shield above their heads, suddenly dropped down to the ground, and they heard the screams of soldiers being burned alive by the smokeless flames. More shadows stepped out of the flames, these ones had red and orange eyes, soon they joined the ranks of shadows around them.

As the flames died down, the shadows all pulled up shadowy bows, and the air was filled with black, red and orange arrows. Humans and animals alike screamed in fear and pain as the arrows found their mark amongst the trees on either side of the road. Scarlet turned to the largest of the shadows and said, "Eliminate the rest of them, but bring me their leaders alive."

With that the shadows charged, they dropped to the ground and flowed like a black wave between the trees.

She turned back to watch as Mortimer removed his opponent's arm at the shoulder, and the crimson blade fell to the earth.

He picked up the man's fallen sword, and chuckled dryly, "there is a special hell that awaits you," he said as he plunged the crimson blade deep into his chest.

The spirit hummed with power, as she raised her hand and with a flick of her wrist the man's limbs were rent from his body. "Begone from this world, never to return," she said icily, and his body turned to dust and vanished.

Mortimer retrieved the crimson sword and its scabbard, belted them to his side and frowned, "There is another piece nearby."

Scarlet shrugged, "Can the crimson blade affect the shadows?"

"Only if I want it to," the spirit answered, "and I really don't want it to. She is trying to flee," the spirit was definitely upset by this development.

""Which way?" Scarlet asked, as she drew her bow.

Mortimer grabbed her shoulder, "follow the line, two of my shadows are near her."

She nodded in understanding, and whispered a spell as she released the arrow. "That will not stop her for long, we need to catch up to her."

With a snap of his fingers, a shadowy horse appeared before them, "Then let us ride like the wind," he said as he leapt astride the dark horse.

Scarlet had never ridden on a shadow before, it was a strange sensation, the animal moved from shadow to shadow faster than any horse could gallop. The air about it was cold as ice, but the very shadow itself seemed full of life and warm to the touch.

In no time at all they had caught up to a group of riders fleeing the battle, shadows pulling them down one by one. In the lead was a dark haired woman, two shadows clung to her horse's legs but still she forced the animal to try and flee.

As they passed, Mortimer leapt from the shadow horse's back and drew his dark blade. A single slice and her horse faltered and fell to the ground.

Scarlet drew her bow as her shadowy stead changed direction and circled the two combatants, she had a clean shot, but didn't take it, something wasn't right here. From out of the trees came another rider, covered in blood and heading straight for the woman, a spear aimed at her heart. On instinct Scarlet released the arrow and watched it plunge deep into the man's throat, the force of the arrow strike was such that it ripped half of his neck out as it continued out the back of his neck.

The spear dropped, and he fell from his horse, as a crimson mist rose from the ground, "I told you I would kill you eventually" the spirit said as she manifested in the mist. She turned to the woman and smiled, "I thank you for removing me from his hands, but if you do not wish to share his fate I suggest you give that little piece of me you're carrying to the man in front of you."

Mortimer sheathed his sword, "I am not a witch hunter, I am with the order of the Rose," he said calmly. "We will protect you if you allow us to."

Scarlet directed the shadow horse to his side and smiled at the woman, "Sorry for shooting your horse earlier, but I was aiming for that piece of crimson steel you carry. I am a witch and can vouch for this man's word that no harm will come to you if you give us that piece of steel."

The woman looked at the three of them and collapsed on the ground, "You can have it, if you swear you will put it to rest."

The spirit started to laugh musically, "sweety, that is the entire reason they are hunting for the pieces of my soul."

The woman handed them a small dagger.

"Now to get you someplace safe," Scarlet said.

"That's an easy task," Mortimer replied, "provided she trusts me. We are close enough to town, I can create a portal with the extra energy from this battle, it will place her at the gates of our home." He looked the poor woman in the eyes, "When you appear, the guards will be a bit surprised, just ask to speak to the captain and tell him and only him that Red sent you there for your protection."

The woman nodded her head in understanding, and Mortimer made a few gestures with his hands. All of the shadows gathered beneath the woman, and she dropped out of sight.

"Why Red?" Scarlet asked after the lady had vanished.

He smiled at her, "It gives him two messages, the first is that she needs our protection, and the second lets him know we are in a battlefield situation and to double the guard. The witch hunter leaders are not going to be happy losing two members of their leadership."

Scarlet looked around at the corpses lying around, "This is going to be quite a task to clean up."

"No," he replied, "we will leave the bodies, the scavengers will eventually clean it up."

"Shouldn't we at least give them a proper burial, to prevent them returning as vengeful spirits?"

He shook his head and frowned, "There is no returning for them, that is the power of this sword," Mortimer replied. "The yielder of the blade determines the fate of the souls it takes, and in this case only the spirits of the animals have been released."

"What happens to the others?" she asked nervously.

"They remain trapped within the blade until their power is used up, and then they are destroyed. It is not ideal, but it is necessary to prevent them from causing problems in the future," he smiled at her, "when we are done with our task, I will cleanse the blade and they will be sent to the afterlife, at least those who are still bound in the sword."

"How did you get such a blade?"

"Through shear dumb luck," he answered, "The first battle I was involved in, was very chaotic and I didn't know that I had any power. We were outnumbered, and although we all thought we would die, we continued to fight. An enemy soldier thrust his blade at me, and I felt it go through my heart, but I had to protect my fellow soldiers, so I swung my sword hoping to take his life with mine. It was a clean cut, his blade was lodged solidly in my chest and he was unable to defend himself. As his head left his body, I felt strength flow into my limbs, and I turned and struck down another foe. Soon, I stood alone surrounded by corpses, this sword through my chest. One of my comrades ran to my side with a shield on her arm as a hail of arrows came at me. She was struck by several arrows, but held her ground to protect me with her shield."

He took a deep breath and continued, "I couldn't let her die trying to protect me, after all I knew I would die when the blade was removed. I tripped her, and kicked a couple of corpses over top of her body to protect her from the next wave of arrows. At least a dozen of them pierced my body, but that didn't matter, she had risked her life to protect mine. So, coughing up a lung full of blood, I charged the enemy archers. A pair of spearmen caught me with their spears, but my swords chopped cleanly through the wooden shafts and soon removed their heads. I wreaked havoc amongst the enemy archers, and soon they broke and fled. That is when I realized I was still alive, and the spirits of the slain were coming to me and filling the sword. I went back and helped my comrade to her feet, she had been lucky, none of the arrows which struck her had hit a vital spot. Together we limped back to our tents, where the healers looked at me and began to question if I would survive."

He laughed dryly, "I did, they were a bit shocked when I grabbed the sword sticking out of my chest and pulled it out. I told them I wanted to keep it, right before I passed out. A week later I awoke to find out the enemy had surrendered, afraid of the berzerker we had in our ranks."

Scarlet looked at him, and said, "In the heat of battle you created your own athame without even realizing it, impressive. What happened to the woman who tried to protect you?"

He laughed, "She later died."

"So you've been using your magic in battles all this time and nobody knew it," she said, "that's pretty impressive."

"You could say that," he replied, "it took me quite a while to get used to the feeling of the spirits and to control the power of the blade. Now it is more like an instinct when using it, but I still have no formal training in the art."

Scarlet thought about this, "It makes sense, the witches guard does not allow men in, and I have never heard of a warlock group, so in reality warlocks have to learn their powers by trial and error."

Mortimer shrugged, "considering that the witches guard at one point hunted down and killed all warlocks, you can understand why they don't go around showing off their magic. You know the witch hunters, they were originally founded by the witches in order to hunt down warlocks, and when they ran out of warlocks they turned on the witches."

Scarlet suddenly took a step back from him, it felt as if she'd just been kicked by a horse, this was a part of her orders history she had never heard about. As she collapsed, the wind taken from her lungs, she felt Mortimers strong arms catch her and she knew she would be safe.

She was moving through a world of shadows and spirits, but she didn't have the power to enter the spirit realm. A familiar crimson spirit approached her and gently brushed her hair back from her face. "Poor child," the spirit said gently, "you couldn't take the truth, at least not with all that spiritual energy about. He needs formal education if he is going to continue down this path."

She looked at the spirit and returned her smile, "So much anger and hatred coming from him all of a sudden, where did it come from?"

"From those he killed on the battlefield," she answered, "when he takes in their souls, he gets their memories and emotions. The emotions will fade quickly, as the blade absorbs their energy and makes them a part of it, but the memories will always be there for him to access."

"But, he has been fighting on the battlefield for a while, why now?"

"Those are different emotions," the spirit answered, "on the battlefield he was getting feelings of protection and devotion, that is much different than this type of battle where the enemy hates you simply because you exist. You are going to have to help him learn to use the power he can, and to release the power he doesn't want around him." The spirit pulled her close and said, "It is time to return to your body, please remember what I have told you."

# Druids

Scarlet gasped and opened her eyes, there was a crimson haze around her, and Mortimer lay barely breathing, a dagger deep within his chest. She rolled over, grasped the hilt of the deadly blade, and pulled it from his body, "Please tell me you didn't accept his offer," she said as she dropped the blade next to him.

"Of course not child," the musical voice came, "that was the sweetest act any in the spirit realm had ever seen. He will be fine in the morning," the spirit giggled, "but I do believe he will be much better educated than any warlock in history."

She looked around and asked, "Where are we?"

"The site of a great massacre," the spirit answered, "it was here that hundreds of warlocks were slaughtered, along with many druids and fairy creatures. There is only one way in or out of the grove, and that is through magical portals only a magical creature can open."

Scarlet looked around and noticed a small pile of dry wood nearby and asked, "Would it be alright if I light a fire?"

The spirit laughed, "Oh certainly child, the trees gave you that wood so you might stay warm. If you keep your fire small they will not take offense to its presence." She looked around, "Oh how I longed to someday visit this place, and yet as a witch they would never allow me entry."

"Wait, if witches are forbidden here, then how did I get here?" Scarlet asked.

A single shadow stepped into the circle and solidified, "You are here because a warlock gave his life for yours, or at least tried to." It turned to the crimson spirit and bowed, "Mistress it has been a long time since our paths have crossed. It is not quite your time to be here, but once your soul is whole, please know I will be most honored to welcome you to our land."

The crimson spirit blushed and bowed to the shadow, "Then I will rest until I am needed again and I would be most honored to have you guide me in the future," she said and vanished.

Scarlet looked at the shadow closely, "You look familiar for some reason."

The shadow laughed merrily, "Few can tell us apart, but yes I was on the battlefield today. I have watched over him since I was awoken. I also am the one who summoned help when he tried that stupid stunt of trying to exchange his life for yours."

"But what exactly happened," she asked.

"You basically got your soul knocked out of you, he didn't shed the energy fast enough and when the wrong thing was said, boom it basically knocked your soul out of your body. He instantly regretted it, but not knowing how to catch your soul and return it to your body, he turned to the crimson witch. If the fool had been thinking he would have turned to me instead, after all I knew exactly where you were and how to reach you." The shadow shook its head, and its eye sockets momentarily turned red in frustration.

"Exactly who are you?" Scarlet asked the shadow.

The shadow laughed, a long hard laugh, before it regained its composure and answered, "I am the first to carry the name Death on the battlefield, my wife and I were the Red Death." The shadow gave a short bow, and slipped back into the trees with one last comment, "Tell my wife I still love her."

She thought that was a strange thing to say, but then noticed the crimson dagger on the grass, "it couldn't be," she said under her breath as she tucked the dagger away in her pack, and proceeded to build a small campfire.

As she thought about it, she stripped all of the crimson blades from Mortimers body, and strapped them to her own, "If you are to be death, then I shall truly play the part of Red," she said to his motionless body.

"Your fate will be the same as hers," a voice hissed from the darkness. "Little girls should not meddle in affairs they know nothing about."

Scarlet's anger flared, and flames suddenly leapt up along her body, she could feel the power of the crimson witch flowing freely through her, "I know only that the love of my life sacrificed himself to save me, and I cannot allow that to continue. I will no longer allow him to get injured in order to protect me," as she spoke the flames grew hotter and brighter. The trees around the clearing leaned away from her and their branches rustled nervously.

"Enough serpent, leave this young couple alone," a deep earthy voice said from behind her. "My dear child," the voice continued softly, "please turn down the heat a bit, the trees don't deserve to burn because you are angry with a trickster."

She turned to see an old man shielding his eyes from the radiant flames covering her, and smiled, "I'm sorry I didn't mean to offend the spirits here, and by no means do I intend to threaten such beautiful trees."

She could hear the trees whispering to each other all around her as the light from the flames died down.

"Thank you," the old man said, as he looked at Mortimer and chuckled, "the sprites did a good job at healing his wound. You have quite the temper on you, reminds me of the Crimson Witch in her day." Looking closely at her, he shook his head sadly, "The serpent is correct though, if you allow yourself to follow the path of the Crimson Witch you will end up sharing her fate. It would be best if you let him finish this on his own."

"I can't do that," she said to him, "I can't let him go to his death if there is any way I can use my power to save him."

"Then I suppose I had best teach you how to protect yourself from his magic," the old man replied. "The first thing you have to realize is that his is the power of death, everyone thinks it is antimagic, but in reality it is the second strongest magic of all. Do you know what the strongest magic is?"

She thought about it and asked, "Is it life?"

"Oh, I see why he loves you," the old man answered, "you are much smarter than the average witch. Everyone believes it to be love, but in reality it is life, the act of creating life is extremely powerful, much more powerful than creating death. When his magic is in full swing the most important thing to do is remember your love for him, and your desire for him to live, it is this that will protect you from the backlash of his magic."

Scarlet nodded her head in understanding, "Love is life, it is through love that we create life," with a frown she continued, "my own power is destructive, but also through its destruction it can bring new life."

His smile broadened, "I see you understand, all magic is a circle, as is all of life. Your flames can destroy, but the ash they leave behind can be used to nurture plants and in some cases heal wounds. It can be used to cook food for people to eat, or it can be used to destroy entire villages, it is all up to the person who uses it." The old man smiled, "this is a timeless place, and I have lived here for centuries, but you are the first witch to ever be invited here since the witch wars."

She frowned, "I was taught that was when the jealous warlocks attacked the witches and nearly destroyed them, but now I have heard it was they who started the war in order to destroy the warlocks and maintain power."

The old man frowned, "It is a convoluted mess, back in the days before the war, there was a balance of power, the fairy creatures and druids had the power of bringing new life to the world, while the warlocks had power over the shadows and death, and the witches power spanned all that was in between with control over the elements. When the three different powers came together they could accomplish great things, but when they fought against each other there was often great tragedy. The witches decided they would band together and destroy the warlocks, thus eliminating the power of death, but in order to do that they had to destroy the druids to maintain a sort of balance. So they created the witch hunters, a group of normal humans who were given weapons that could kill warlocks, druids, and the fairy people."

The old man paused for a moment, then continued, "After the battle that took place on this very spot, the witch hunters turned on the witches and demanded they be given more magical weapons as so many of their number had died in the battle. Naturally the witches refused and the witch hunters turned on them, and slaughtered many of them, before the order of the rose came to the rescue. They were an order of knights who had sworn to protect the innocent, and their leader was in love with one of the witches, a powerful fire witch. Unbeknownst to everyone he was an unawakened warlock, and during the battle a blade pierced his heart and woke his power. The crimson Witch saw the blow and sent a wave of fire to surround him as she opened a portal to his side, and held him close. He drew the sword from his chest and told her it was an honor to die for her. Needless to say he didn't die, a witch hunter leapt through the fire about to remove her head while she was distracted, and the knight of the rose suddenly shoved her aside and with a great heave and cut the man in two. The sight of her tears, streaming down her face, thinking he had just sacrificed himself for her, drove the young knight into a frenzy. He carved a path through the witch hunters, killing with every strike of his sword, it sliced through steel flesh and bone, nothing could stop him, until the Crimson Witch called his name and told him she loved him." The old man chuckled, "After that the two of them were known as the red death, the witches gave them permission to marry and the rest is history. I do believe I did a pretty good job of writing the magical contract the witches were required to agree to, it bound their powers and forbid them from ever using them against a warlock or druid ever again. They can't even use third parties to do so or they will lose their powers."

Scarlet was in shock, "But then how did she become the crimson blades?"

The old man frowned, "She is the second to take that title, and it was because she sacrificed herself to save his life in the end. You see, many years later, they were attacked by the witch hunters, and he was taken prisoner. In order to save him she offered to give them weapons powerful enough to destroy any magic user. Naturally they agreed, so she had the leaders meet with her on the grave of many witches, there she instructed them to kill her with the blades they wished to have enchanted. They did so, and her spirit entered into those blades, being the treacherous fools they were, they then gave the command and killed her husband. With his death, his sword exploded killing quite a few witch hunters, for you see he had not willingly given his life to become a weapon, instead he channeled his death through his sword seeking to avenge her death. At the same time, the Crimson Witch, having now been betrayed, refused to give them the power they sought unless they paid the price she demanded, and as you can imagine she has been quite vengeful and taken the lives of everyone they loved."

Scarlet shook her head in wonder, "I can't say as I blame her, I would do the same thing."

"Not if I can prevent it," the old man muttered, "I have had enough of the witch hunters, it is time to put an end to them."

"How do you plan to do that?" she asked.

The old man laughed, "I will get them to break the magical contract they had with the witches originally, especially since none of them know the details of that contract these days."

"What clause are you talking about?" she asked.

"Oh, it's quite simple," the old man smiled, "the witches were concerned about the witch hunters betraying them on the battlefield, so there was a clause put in there that if any witch hunter were to allow the blood of a witch and warlock to mix on the same blade, they would simply cease to exist. Basically," he produced a small red vial, "all you have to do is recover the crimson blades and then get any witch hunter to break this vial with their weapon. It contains a small amount of your blood and mortimers blood. There is another way, and that would be for the witch hunters to kill a child, of their own accord, but I personally find that idea to be distasteful."

"As do I," she replied, "I'm sure even the crimson witch would find that to be a bit too much."

"Agreed," the old man said, "I leave it in your hands then to destroy the witch hunters forever." He bowed as he backed into the trees, leaving the vial of blood next to Mortimers body.

"Strange," Scarlet thought to herself, "I'm surprised the contract wasn't broken when the hunters turned on the witches, but then again, maybe hunters were smart and cleaned their weapons before they fought the witches. It would have been even smarter if they would have simply put a betrayal clause in place, but then again I'm pretty sure the witches were planning on using them to hunt down each other eventually."

She practiced using her magic for a little bit, then studied a bit, before finally digging a travel blanket from her pack, and lying down next to Mortimer.

# An Honorable Foe

The two of them woke at the same time, it was as if they had been asleep for quite some time. They didn't talk much, Mortimer kept his distance from her, and after saying good morning simply apologized. Scarlet on the other hand waited for him to say anything that would give her an excuse to hold him.

After an hour of awkward silence, he said, "we should get going, you'll need to hold my hand as we go through the portal."

Silently she stretched out her hand to him, and as soon as he grabbed it, she jerked hard on his arm. As he was unbalanced for a moment, she pulled him into her arms and kissed, "If you ever try something like that again, I will find a way to bring you back and kill you again, understood?"

"How can you care for someone who literally just killed you?" he asked.

"You didn't kill me silly, you merely disconnected my soul from my body." she replied, "besides your sword knew where I was at and was more than happy to guide me back if need be."

He gave her a confused look, "what are you talking about? How could you talk to my sword, or it talk to you?"

She laughed, "Oh the stories I could tell, let's just say I had a very long talk with the Crimson Witch and the original Death, and they have been keeping a very close eye on you. That sword you carry, is the sword of the original Death, the leader of the Order of the Rose during the witch wars. He also happens to be an ancestor of yours, as is the Crimson Witch, so instead of demanding help from them, in the future just ask alright?"

"Does this mean you forgive me?" he asked.

"You don't need to ask my forgiveness," she replied, "I love you, and I know you would never deliberately hurt me."

He shook his head, "This love thing is new to me, so I'm not exactly sure how to respond. You appear to be comfortable with the crimson blades, and since she talks to you, you should carry them for now." He frowned, "If they become a burden, please give them back to me."

"Oh, she'll never be a burden for me," Scarlet said, as a small flame ran from her fingertips to her shoulder and back, "if anything she is teaching me new things."

Hand in hand, they entered the trees surrounding the clearing, and soon they were back on the road, what road Scarlet wasn't sure, but it was the road. "Where are we now?" she asked.

He looked around and laughed, "about a month long march from home, and unless I miss my guess, about three weeks closer to our goal."

"If your goal is death, you're a lot closer than three weeks," a guttural voice said from behind them.

"Oh, why do you say that?" Mortimer asked as he casually rested his right hand on the hilt of his sword.

"Because the only people out here are witch hunters," the voice answered.

"Does that mean you're a witch hunter?" Scarlet asked cheerfully, "and, can you provide us directions to your leaders?"

"Yes I am," the voice said pridefully, "and the only place you're going witch is to hell."

Mortimer spun around drawing his sword, just in time to see the ground beneath the man open up and flames shoot out engulfing the man.

"Too bad he couldn't be more helpful," Scarlet said coldly, "I guess I'll have to ask someone else." She looked directly at the flames and simply said, "Hunt." and the flames shot along the ground weaving between the trees and under bushes.

"You might as well come out," she yelled, "far better to play with me than with my pet."

Mortimer looked over at her and recognized the glow in her eyes, there was a rage burning deep within the emerald green eyes and it showed itself as a single slice of red. He shook his head slowly, and said, "Better a quick clean death in combat than to be slowly roasted in your own fat. I wonder how long it takes for someone to roast to death anyways, I bet it takes several hours."

Suddenly the air was filled with screams as people came charging from the trees with weapons raised, "oh good, they want to play," Scarlet said as she drew the crimson daggers.

Upon sight of the red blades, everyone froze and stared, Mortimer laughed and said, "Which way to your leaders?" As one they all turned and pointed a look of absolute fear on their faces, "Thank you," he said to them. "Red honey, are they innocent or guilty?"

Scarlet laughed, "they are witch hunters, what does that tell you?"

"Guilty it is," he replied and drew his sword, "sorry folks, but you chose the wrong side in this war."

After the slaughter, Mortimer turned to Scarlet and asked, "How much of that was you, and how much of that was the Crimson Witch?"

She frowned, "It was all me, now that I know their history, and their intentions, I can't let a single one live. I don't want our children to be hunted down by them some day, it is time we brought an end to the witch hunters."

Still covered in blood, they headed in the direction the witch hunters had indicated, "You know, so far we have only been dealing with underlings, they are only going to get tougher from here on out," Mortimer said.

Scarlet let out a low laugh, "That is fine by me, I only feel one crimson blade nearby, so I am sure he will know where to find the rest."

He shook his head and laughed, "You have definitely been spending too much time with the crimson witch, careful you don't become her."

She smiled, "No, I am not becoming her, but I am learning a lot from her. You realize that when this is done we both will be without weapons other than our magic."

"That is when they are most likely to seek revenge, unless we completely annihilate them," he replied.

They followed the road for a ways, before they came to a clearing, a single man stood in the center of the clearing. "I get the feeling this is some sort of trap," Mortimer said.

The man laughed, "No, no trap, I prefer to face my fate head on, so I sent the rest of my troops to report to my commander." He lifted up a large bastard sword and picked up a shield which had been leaning against his side. "No sense in using a crimson blade against you, I already know that she will not serve me in this battle."

"You seem to be much smarter than your comrades were," Scarlet said as she drew Two of the crimson daggers.

"That is because I listened to the stories my father told me as a child," he answered, "he told me how he had sought revenge for the witch wars, and how afterwards he realized it was wrong to take innocent lives no matter what their ancestors may have done." The man frowned, "He also told me that I was cursed to the same fate as him, when he gave me the crimson sword. I have never used it, nor have I called upon its power, but at the same time I know that bearing it means I must die."

"Myths often get twisted in the retelling," Mortimer replied, "have you not sought to ask the one trapped in the blade itself?"

The man laughed, "I would gladly do so, if it didn't mean having to use the blade. The thing is cursed, it brings death to all who yield it, unless they are of the order or a witch. The witches gave us hunters a lot of power in order to kill the warlocks, but what they didn't tell us was that it would cost us everything in the end."

Scarlet smiled at the man, "The crimson witch says she holds no animosity for you, as you simply inherited the crimson sword. She is even willing to let you walk away if you simply surrender the sword to us."

"I wish I could, but if I were to do that, then I would in turn be hunted down and killed, along with those I love." He frowned, "even if you bring all of the pieces together and froo tho witch, thoco who curvivo will hunt mo down ovontually."

Mortimer smiled to himself and said, "Then I suggest you sleep on your decision, we can take this up in the morning when you are rested and well fed." As he spoke, he made a few subtle gestures to the shadows, and willed them to knock the man out. With the speed of a striking serpent, a shadow detached itself from the trees and slammed into the back of the man's head.

They watched him crumple to the ground, a look of disbelief on his face before his consciousness faded. "Now what do we do with him?" Scarlet asked.

Mortimer smiled at her, "I believe we will need to imprison him somewhere, then we can talk to him again when this is over. Retrieve the crimson sword from his belongings, while I create a place to hold him.

Scarlet did as he asked, and watched as he pulled his sword and drew a strange symbol on the ground around the man, when he was done the man simply slipped into the earth and vanished. "Where is he?" she asked.

He shrugged, "he is in the realm of dreams, and his body is being guarded by the fairies. Should we fail, he will awaken and they will determine his fate, should we succeed, he will be brought to wherever we are and awakened."

"You've been learning from your sword," she said, "there is no way you knew that spell earlier today."

"Correct," he replied, "since you told me who it is that inhabits my sword, I have been listening to it and learning from it. I have also learned that the only reason the blades are crimson, is because she was a fire witch, like you are. If she had been a water witch, the blades would have been icy blue in color, and an earth witch they would be an emerald green. A wind witch would have created clear blades, almost impossible to see, and yet deadly and almost indestructible."

"It is good you are learning, but don't let your learning distract you from the task at hand." she said, "the final blade won't be just handed over to us, and even then we still have to bring an end to the witch hunters."

"Very true," he replied, "but how are we to find the last blade? I know the blades you have are drawn to it, but if you can't sense it's direction how do we know we're going the correct way?"

Scarlet laughed, "Easy, we just ask the ones who have been watching us this entire time." The puzzled look on her face made her laugh even more, "We need to ask the animals around us, and any local fairy folk."
He shook his head, "I really should have thought of that, you do realize though the fairy are not easily found if they don't want to be."

"That's why you're here," she replied, "for some reason they are attracted to you."

"Not entirely true," a deep voice came from the tree line, "it's just the fact that we are all curious as to what type of human would go out of their way to help one of our kind. As for the witch hunters, yes we do know where they are at, but are you sure it is a good idea to give you that information?"

"Why wouldn't it be?" Scarlet asked, "after all we are intending to put an end to the witch hunters, and that would make life easier for the fairies."

"You say that now," the voice replied, "but who is to say what your intentions will be when you find them? Many have tried, and all have failed, of those at least half have ended up being captured and used by the witch hunters. No matter how powerful you may be, given enough time they would eventually find out from you where we live."

Mortimer laughed, "You know the more information we have, the less likely it is we are going to fail. Besides, the red death defeated them in the past, so we should be able to do so now?"

The voice laughed, "The Red Death, you would compare yourselves to them? First of all, they only succeeded in freeing the soul of the witch they held captive back then. Second of all, it was when he went back to finish the job that death was captured. I am just thankful that very few witches know how to bind their souls to weapons, and even more thankful the witch hunters have not learned the secret."

They heard movement among the trees and then the voice continued, "Know this, you cannot defeat the witch hunters unless you have the crimson blades and the soul sword. If you retreat from the battlefield after releasing both of their souls, you will fail to defeat the witch hunters."

"Does this mean you will help us?" Scarlet asked the voice.

"Yes," the voice replied, "but I pray for your unborn child that you succeed. Follow the road until you reach the beach, from there you will need to head towards the setting sun. As you approach you will come across the remains of many armies, it is amongst those corpses you will find your enemy."

The crimson witch suddenly appeared, "You know some secrets are not meant to be shared, but now that everyone knows, I suggest we finish this quickly."

"Do you know where we are going?" Mortimer asked her, "ignoring for the moment that he was going to be a father."

"Yes, it is the same battlefield where my husband and I defeated the witch hunters back in our time." she didn't seem to be too happy.

Scarlet laughed, "So I am with child," she said, "this could be an interesting battle."

The witch looked at her and frowned, "Remember deer you carry a precious life inside you, and even though it will augment your powers, it will also wear you out." She faded out in her usual crimson mist, as Mortimer tried to hide a laugh.

"What's so funny?" Scarlet asked.

He couldn't resist laughing anymore, "Nothing, it's just that when she disappears, it is almost like when you remove someone's head on the battlefield."

She shook her head at him and frowned, "You know this will complicate things, magic becomes very unreliable when a witch is pregnant."

Mortimer laughed, "Then we will have to rely on my magic," he said, "I swear you will make it home alive no matter what."

There was something in his eyes that told her this was not a time to question his resolve.

# Clarice

It took them a week to reach the coast, they hadn't run into any signs of the witch hunters the entire time, but they knew they were out there somewhere. They set up camp just inside the trees, where their small fire would not be noticed and they could easily watch for anyone coming along the path from either direction.

Shortly after dark, a female voice asked softly, "May I join you for a bite to eat?"

Scarlet and Mortimer both leapt to their feet and spun towards the voice, "Step into the light of the fire and we shall discuss it," Scarlet said, a hint of worry in her voice.

They heard a slight scraping sound, and the top half of a naked young woman appeared near the ground, it looked as if she were arching her back to maintain her position, and she used her hands to pull herself towards them. "I mean you no harm," she said as she pulled herself closer, "it is just so rare to see a witch in the area I just had to come over to say hello."

Mortimer watched her for a second longer and then stepped towards her, "Here, let me help you."

The young woman's face flashed with fear for a second, before she said "I suppose if you're traveling with a witch you might be alright."

As he approached her, he realized the dragging sound was a great big fish tail, which appeared to come out from her waist. Carefully he squatted down next to her and spread his arms as if to give her a hug, "Can you swing your tail around so I can get an arm under it?" he asked her gently.

The young woman laughed, "Oh my, aren't you the gentleman type," she said as she rolled over so she was sitting up.

Mortimer carefully scooped her up in his arms and carried her towards the fire, the sweet salty scent of the ocean filled his nose, and a strange desire started to overwhelm him.

"Oh, I am so sorry," the young lady said, "I do that when I get nervous."

"Do what?" Scarlet asked.

"It's a defense mechanism, when I get scared I automatically release an odor which drives men crazy, and usually makes them follow me wherever I go." She stroked Mortimers cheek, "there there my young hero, the effect will go away in a few minutes."

Scarlet raised an eyebrow and said, "Mortimer set her down over here by the fire, she can lean back against the log there to get comfortable." She eyed the young woman closely and then laughed, "I should have known, you're a mermaid. Will you please release my husband, he will not hurt you."

The mermaid laughed gently, "He couldn't if he wanted to, but you most certainly could. I have already turned off my lure, mother did warn me it could cause quite a bit of trouble if I used it on land."

It took Mortimer several minutes to shake off the effects of the lure, but when he did he laughed about it. "I am going to have to find a way to become immune to that, for

58

my own safety," he said, then a quick glance at Scarlet he added, "and the safety of mermaids."

Scarlet smiled sweetly at him and asked, "What am I too much of a woman for you?"

He started laughing at that and replied, "No, you're perfect, the perfect woman for me."

The mermaid laughed softly, "You two must have been together for quite some time the way you banter with each other. I wish it was that easy for us mermaids."

Scarlet moved closer to the mermaid and asked, "Do you mind if I get a closer look at you? You are the first mermaid I have ever seen."

"Sure," she answered, "but I am not a true mermaid, only half of one."

"That sounds like an interesting story," Mortimer said.

"Not really," the mermaid answered, "it's how my mother discovered that our scent could be a hindrance when on land. She was laying on the beach one day sunning herself, when a young man happened to startle her, her instincts kicked in and he was overcome by her scent. As she said humans are faster on land than us, and it didn't take long for him to capture her. It was a bad cycle, he had his way with her, but she was so afraid her scent glands were in overdrive. It took weeks for her to get them under control, and when the young man realized what he had done, he tried to kill himself."

Mortimer raised an eyebrow, but didn't interrupt.

The mermaid smiled, "my mother rescued him from drowning, and took him to a deserted island to talk. You see she discovered he wasn't a bad man, he just couldn't control himself when she spooked. Needless to say, they ended up staying together, she would catch fish in the sea and he would grow plants on the island." She smiled briefly, "There are advantages to being half human, once I fully dry out I will look human for one, and for another my scent glands are not nearly as strong as my mothers and as such have much less of an effect."

"So if you can look like a human, why didn't you wait until you were fully dry before coming to meet us?" Scarlet asked.

The mermaid blushed faintly, "I'm not very comfortable on my feet," she answered. "If I had to fight back, my tail is much more powerful than my legs."

Mortimer chuckled as he picked up a blanket and handed it to her, "You should cover up when in mixed company, and considering your mother was caught on land because she didn't have legs, it makes me wonder if your tail would be better for defense than running away on human legs."

The mermaid looked at Scarlet and then Mortimer and started to blush a deep red, "I am so sorry, I just realized. My kind usually doesn't come on land near human settlements, and I have often wondered if my mother didn't deliberately get caught by my father."

Scarlet laughed, "it sounds more like your mother caught your father, not the other way around."

The mermaid frowned, "That is possible, it is our nature to seek out a mate when we hit adulthood, and when the need to breed hits us, we are almost unstoppable, entire ships have been sunk when a sailor catches wind of our scent."

"How do you know when that time has come?" Mortimer asked.

"In the city under the sea, they keep track of it, and the females are locked up as they near adulthood, but for those of us in the open ocean we have no way of knowing," she answered. "My mother told me it usually starts with a desire for company, and then we find ourselves doing things we normally wouldn't do, usually dangerous stuff, almost as if trying to impress somebody." Suddenly she put her hand to her mouth, "Oh no, it must be getting close to that time."

Scarlet frowned, "Well, that would explain a few things."

Mortimer chuckled, "On the positive side, according to my sword, when she is fully human her scent glands shouldn't work. Granted if a man didn't have self control and caught wind of her as a mermaid, it would end in the same way."

"What are you saying?" Scarlet asked.

"Basically if she had waited until fully dry before coming to visit us, her natural defenses would not have kicked in." he answered, "At the same time though, if she is between forms, or a full mermaid, her scent glands would override even my self control given enough time."

The mermaid frowned, now that her legs had fully formed, "So you are saying if I stay human I do not have to breed in the near future, but if I return to the sea I will have to breed soon."

"Not necessarily," he answered, "after all you're not fully a mermaid. Due to your unique lineage you may be able to ignore the need to mate, as if you were a full human. It would be best if you asked your mother if she ever heard about any other half-breeds and what happened to them."

"I will do that right away," she replied as she stood up and dropped the blanket. "Thank you so much for talking with me, I hope we meet up again some day soon."

As Mortimer watched her walk back towards the ocean, Scarlet said, "I hope not too soon."

She almost screamed as Mortimer launched himself from his seat and wrapped his arms around her, "You don't have to use any sort of magic to get my attention love."

"I was beginning to wonder if you still desired me," she whispered.

"All the time," he whispered back as they cuddled together on the dropped blanket.

They woke up later than usual the next morning, but neither one of them complained, they had learned quite a bit from the mermaid the night before and about each other after she left. They now knew of one more danger on this beach, and that was the merfolk. It was rare to encounter them anywhere, but it was also true they were deadly in the defense of their territory.

They broke camp quickly, Scarlet made certain the fire was completely out with a simple flick of her wrist, while Mortimer made a quick gesture of his own and the shadows packed their blankets into their packs.

They made their way towards the west, the sun bright overhead, but for some reason there seemed to be a cloud of doom far off in the distance.

"That does not bode well," Scarlet said as she watched the cloud.

"I guess that depends on who you're asking," Mortimer replied. "There is a lot of power to be drawn upon in that cloud."

# Witchhunter General

It took them nearly three weeks to reach the end of the beach, where a narrow trail turned and went between two cliffs, the setting sun appeared to be going down at the end of that trail.

"I don't like the feeling I'm getting," Scarlet said.

Mortimer chuckled, "You're just now feeling it? Beyond those cliffs I can feel the weight of the dead, and they do not like it when the living visit."

Together they stepped into the narrow passage, "It would be a good place for an ambush," Scarlet said as they entered.

"It was used as a choke point," Mortimer replied as he pointed to a pile of rocks lying atop a skeleton. "I'm pretty sure someone tried to create a landslide in order to kill as many of the enemy soldiers as possible."

Suddenly pulling his bow from behind him, he notched an arrow and let fly, off in the distance there was a piercing scream, "I guess they know we're here," he said with a sigh, "I was really hoping to be able to sneak up on them."

A voice ahead of them laughed, "That was a pretty good shot, or were you firing at random?"

Mortimer laughed, "Nothing is random, I just thought about where I would put my sentries, and aimed for one of those spots, thanks for letting me know where you are though, I appreciate it." He laughed as he let fly another arrow and heard a grunt of pain. "Guess he wasn't fast enough," he said to Scarlet as his eyes surveyed the area.

"Would you like some more light?" she asked him, it was nearly noon, but with the clouds overhead, it was nearly pitch black in the area.

"Not yet," he replied, "it should open up in a minute here, at least if great great grandfather's maps are accurate." Sure enough, in about thirty feet the area opened up into a big flat field of dust, bone and smoke.

"Welcome to hell," a voice said off in the distance. "I can hear your breathing, but not quite see you yet. How about you come down to the camp and give yourselves up? I promise none of my men will attack you if you are heading into the camp, only if you try to go around or away from it."

Scarlet winced, "I can't believe this, I am unable to step back, it hurts if I try to turn away from his voice."

Mortimer frowned, "You know, using magic to force us to visit with you is really bad form for a witch hunter, but that's alright, I was expecting something like this." He took a deep breath and exhaled slowly, "ah the taste of death is truly strong here." Under his breath he whispered, "One last chance to fulfill your quest brothers, protect my wife and child."

As the smoke swirled around them, he launched himself towards the center of the camp, leaping over skeletons and ducking under fallen trees. Every step he took skeletons rose from the ground, humans and animals alike slowly regained their feet and started to battle once more. He leapt into the witch hunters camp as the sound of dozens of war horns was heard throughout the area. Ancient arrows rained down upon the camp as the witch hunters paused in shock at seeing the army of dead rising around them.

Mortimer fired three arrows in rapid succession, and then broke his bow over the head of a man who stepped in front of him. His desire to protect his wife, his witch, and his family drove him into a battle frenzy. He swung the broken bow sideways and wrapped the string around another witch hunter's neck, the force of him pulling it tight cut through the arteries in his neck and the man fell. He left his bow there and drew his sword, it hummed with the power of the dead, as men and women fell back from him in fear, more skeletons clawed their way up from the earth, for centuries war had been fought on this land, and now all of the dead soldiers were being called back to service.

The enemy broke and fled before him, and with them the skeletons on their side crumbled, the order of the rose had the field and now it was time to face the enemy's general. He looked around the battlefield, but could not find him, then a scream told him where he was. His head whipped towards his wife, and there stood the general with sword raised, "Make one move and I will kill her Warlock," he called to Mortimer.

"I doubt that," Mortimer replied, "you can't kill her with that blade."

The man looked up and frowned, the crimson glow of the blade in his hand was almost completely gone, "What?" the man looked at the blade, "But how?"

Mortimer started to laugh, "Oh what a silly man, he doesn't even know the rules of using a crimson blade, you should realize they cannot be used against the family of the witch whom they contain? Should you draw her blood with it then your contract with the blade is broken and the witch contained within will be set free."

With a scream of rage, the general threw down the crimson sword and picked up a nearby fallen sword, "I will kill her with this then," he yelled as he turned toward Scarlet, who at this time had picked up the discarded weapon.

"I doubt that," Mortimer shouted, and slammed his hand down hard on the ground. "Now my shadows, return her to the realm of dreams and let no man harm her."

There was a thunderous boom, as the shadows around Scarlet twisted and turned, as they closed into a solid bubble which imprisoned her. She screamed in fury as the battleground disappeared and she once again stood on a beautiful green clearing surrounded by trees. The druid sat there tending the man whom Mortimer had knocked out over a month ago, he looked up and smiled at her.

"I didn't think he had it in him," the druid said to her, "come child I must make certain your baby is alright."

Scarlet looked at him in shock and said, "How did you know?"

The druid laughed, "Oh, the spirits have been so excited ever since the child was conceived, never before has a child been conceived in both life and death magic. You two don't even realize what you did by having that much magic flowing around you at the time of conception, then again you probably don't even realize when you conceived." He grabbed her arm and guided her to a small stump, "Now sit down my child and relax, it was the fairy who brought you here, not the shadows, but boy was it a close one, that young man has no idea how much power he has gathered inside himself."

At this point Scarlet was in too much shock to react to anything the old man said, she just sat down and let him check her over for injuries. As he checked her over, she found herself crying, she had lost him, the one person who had ever loved her, and whom she had loved in return, and she had left his side on the battlefield. With that thought, she collapsed into the old man's arms and cried herself to sleep.

Once she was fully asleep, a deep voice said from amongst the trees, "Thank goodness, I thought she'd never sleep. Mortimer would go on a killing spree if we hadn't gotten to her in time."

The druid laughed, "Oh, I am quite certain it would have been the massacre of the ages."

"You do understand," the voice continued, "it was a calculated risk, his shadows don't actually create passageways, they just obscur the person from sight, if we hadn't pulled her out when we did, that general could have killed her."

The crimson witch suddenly appeared in the clearing, "Be quiet you two," she ordered, "I am trying to listen to the battle, it's so far away it's hard to hear. And," she continued, "for your information I would have stopped the general from killing her." The look in the eyes of the crimson witch told them both, she was not to be trifled with.

Back on the battlefield, the general cursed and swore as he turned his rage towards Mortimer, "That was a neat little trick, but don't think any tricks like that will save you."

Mortimer shrugged, "I don't need any tricks to defeat you, haven't you realized that this area is a warlock's dream come true? All of this death just lying here waiting for someone to claim its power and a stupid witch hunter sitting in the middle just begging to die."

The witch hunter general charged at Mortimer, who simply deflected the attack and spun away from him.

"I must say, thank you," Mortimer said as he dodged another attack, "if it hadn't been for you I never would have met Red. If your men hadn't tried to kill her, I never would have been there to rescue her. Too bad you still have not figured out how to make more crimson blades, you could use a few dozen of them right about now."

The general kept swinging wildly at him, and Mortimer continued to dodge, "Stand still and fight," the general roared at him.

"Very well," Mortimer replied, as he stepped forward into the generals slash, his blade angled just right so the generals sword deflected up over his head, and Mortimer punched him squarely in the jaw. "You realize, I have already won," Mortimer said with a smile. "We have taken your precious crimson sword, and even now the blades are being reunited. It is only a matter of time before the Crimson Witch is standing before you and getting her revenge."

Enraged, the general charged Mortimer and battered at him with a rapid series of vicious swings, each one deflected by the black blade in Mortimers right hand.

"I suppose it really isn't fair of me to use this blade against you," he said to the general, "I believe it would be better if I used a blade of the order to defeat you." With a smile, he charged at the general and pushed him backwards onto the ground. He looked over at a blade one of the witch hunters had dropped and smiled, "ah, that one will do nicely." he said as he picked it up. "Would you look at that, it was once used by a knight of the rose," he said as he spotted the vine engraved in the blade and the rose bud pommel.

Mortimer stepped back, thrust his black blade into its scabbard, and with a flourish spun the rose sword in his hand. "Oh, I can most certainly kill you with this blade, after all it would only be appropriate." He performed a slight bow and said, "General of the Witch Hunters, I challenge you to a duel to the death."

The General froze for a moment then as he was standing back up replied, "I accept your duel, let no living creature interfere, on pain of death."

Mortimer laughed and unbuckled his black blade and dropped it to the ground, this was the fight he had been waiting for, and he could feel the pressure of death lifting as souls were finally able to rest.

The two of them came together with a crash, sparks flew from the impact point of their swords and the sound of steel ringing on steel echoed through the air. Blow after blow, block after block, neither opponent seemed to gain ground, but neither lost ground either. Soon they were both covered in sweat and dust, and panted heavily.

"I must say, you are a pretty good swordsman," Mortimer said to the general as they both paused for a second, "it'll be a shame to kill you."

"I would say the same about you," the general panted back as he charged once more at Mortimer. "I have never met a warlock who could handle a blade as well as you do, where did you learn to fight?"

Mortimer laughed as he deflected a strike and counter struck, a slight cut to the generals arm, not much, but first blood. "If you really must know, I've been a mercenary for the last couple of years, before that I was raised by the order of the rose. My father is their leader after all."

At this the general faltered, it was only for a second, but it was long enough for Mortimer to get in a strike to his thigh, as the blood started to flow, the general knew he would bleed out if he didn't bandage it soon. "Damn," he swore and threw something at Mortimer.

Mortimer deflected the dagger the general had thrown and then thrust forward with the pummel of his sword, the rose bud pommel connected hard with the general's nose, and blood gushed from his face. He wasn't quite fast enough to avoid the general's next swing though as it came in low under his sword arm and cut deep into his side. "I should have seen that coming," he said as he grunted and kneed the general in the gut.

The two backed away from each other and the general laughed, "If I didn't know any better I would say that is a fatal wound."

Mortimer laughed, "I guess it's a good thing you don't know any better." The wound burned slightly, but wasn't bleeding too much. "A little higher and you would have killed me for sure, as it is I have survived similar wounds in the past."

The general stared at him in shock, "How could you possibly survive such a wound?"

Mortimer laughed, "It is time to cleanse all your ilk from this world." With that he pulled a broken vial from under his breast plate, "I was honestly worried you would break this before I could get it on your sword."

"And what pray tell is that?" Ask the general feeling dizzy.

"Witch's blood," Mortimer answered, "as per the magical contract granting your powers, should you ever get a mixture of witch's blood and warlock's blood on your blade at the same time you forfeit all of the witch hunter's powers."

The general laughed, "You are only slightly correct, it takes druids blood too, and you can't get that anymore."

Mortimer chuckled dryly, "Are you sure about that, I wasn't certain if you knew the contract or not, so I had my druid friend give me some of his blood too." He pulled out a second vial and frowned, "Oh look you broke that one too, so I guess you just threw away all of your protections against magic, not to mention your ability to lock it up. I wonder what your dungeon guards are thinking right now?"

"No," the general cried, "you tricked me, I will kill you." as he lunged at Mortimer one last time.

Strangely the lunge seemed half hearted and weak, and Mortimer knew why, the general no longer had his magically enhanced strength. One quick sidestep, and a swipe with the rose sword saw the general's head flying through the air. "May the dead find peace now," Mortimer said, as he knelt to retrieve the black blade.

As he stood, he felt slightly light headed, "Damn, I guess he cut deeper than I expected," he said as he looked at his wound. He slowly started to walk back towards the entrance to the vale, it was easy to see now that the dark clouds of death broke up and the sun started to fill the area.

He had just about reached the entrance, when he collapsed. "This is not good," he said with labored breath. Bloodloss had weakened him now to the point he couldn't even unbuckle his breast plate to tend to the wound. As he lay there on the ground unable to continue, the rose sword twinkled in the sunlight. "I guess this will be the last thing I see before I die," he thought as his eyes closed.

Mortimer found himself standing next to his own body, he looked down and shook his head sadly, "That was pretty stupid letting that sword strike get through," he said to himself.

"I have to agree with you," a voice said from behind him. "Sacrificing yourself for another is very honorable, but as we all learned on the battlefield, honorable acts are usually stupid acts."

He turned to look at the speaker and laughed, "Look who's talking grandfather, come to lead me to the afterlife?"

"That's great great grandfather to you," the man replied, "and no I am not going to lead you to the afterlife. I am simply keeping you company until your wife gets here." He looked at him closely, "Your great great grandmother will want to have a few words with you, I am quite certain they will be about how much like me you are. She will show Scarlet a way to save you, but you must understand you will forever be bound together afterwards."

Mortimer frowned, "I do not want her sacrificing herself for me, she has more important things to worry about."

"There is nothing more important than love in this world," he replied, "without love you will find your existence to be quite miserable. Now watch for their arrival and let her take you back to your body."

# Healing

They watched as a portal from the fairy world opened up, inside were Scarlet and the Druid. As Scarlet stepped out of the portal, they could see the crimson witch was at her side. They couldn't hear what was being said, but they could watch as a ring of fire sprung up around Mortimers body. The fire rapidly turned from red to blue and then to white as Mortimer felt a strong pull, suddenly he gasped and screamed as pain erupted from his side.

His very blood felt as if it were on fire, it was absolute agony, and then he felt a pair of hands holding him, and the pain subsided.

"Easy," Scarlet said to him, "let the fire do its work. Once the wound has closed then you can sit up." She held him down with both hands on his chest, the white fire danced along her body as it worked to cauterize the wound so that his body could heal naturally.

He smiled up at her, "You were supposed to stay away from the battlefield."

She smiled down at him, "The battle is over, your armor is ruined, but your body will be whole."

As the pain subsided, he grasped her hands with his own and laughed, "War is never over, it just simply fades away for a while."

Scarlet laughed at him, "Then I suggest you get yourself some new armor." She pulled him upright, and waved away the remaining fire, "Come, we had best see if our mermaid friend is still along the beach, rumor has it they have amazing healing skills."

The druid laughed gently, "He is now truly been reborn in fire with fire at his side." He looked at Mortimer, "have you tasted enough of the realm of the dead?"

Mortimer laughed, and winced, "You could say that, but we still need to free the spirits of my ancestors."

"When you get back home, your father will explain the process to you," the druid said with a smile, "besides I believe the two of them would be happy to see your wedding. Rumor has it your sister has already started organizing it. I may even make an appearance, it's been so long since I last saw someone from the order get married." With that he turned and went back into the portal closing it behind him.

"What happened to our sleeping friend?" He asked Scarlet.

"Oh, when the contract was broken, he woke," she answered, "he asked if there was a way to atone for his sins, and the druid laughed and told him he would teach him." She winked at Mortimer, "apparently he didn't realize his family had druid blood, and that is why he was always at odds with being a witch hunter."

Mortimer chuckled, and winced again, the wound was closed, but it was obvious his injuries were much more severe than he had realized. "We had best start looking for that mermaid," he said as he struggled to stand up.

Scarlet shook her head and laughed, "Always in a rush."

"No," he replied, "I just can't stand sitting still when there are things to do. Besides, if we don't get back soon my sister will make certain we have the most outrageous wedding possible."

She laughed, "I think we can handle one crazy day, especially after today, and what were you thinking spiriting me away like that?"

"There is no way I was going to let you be hurt on that battlefield," he replied, "until I broke the witch hunters spell, any injury would have resulted in death." He picked up the rose sword once more, looked at it, and with a smile he said, "Thank you my friend for your service, may your services never be needed again." Slowly he tucked it into his belt, "I'll need to get a scabbard for this blade at some point."

Scarlet laughed, "Ever the mercenary."

"Not quite, this blade needs to be returned to the hall, it's one of a very few blades made from fairy steel. All of them were given to the heads of the Knights of the Rose. I'm pretty sure my father will be glad to have it returned." He replied.

She looped her arm around his back to help support him as they started walking, she could tell he was in a lot of pain, she could feel it herself. The crimson witch had warned her it would be this way, she wouldn't feel all of his pain, but she would take as much of it as she could handle.

It took them the remainder of the day to get back out to the beach, and then they still had several weeks of travel before they reached the mermaids' territory.

Scarlet led him to the edge of the water and sat him down. She wasn't sure if it would work, but if she could find the right shell, she should be able to call the merpeople. It took her about an hour, before she found a beautiful conch shell. With a silent prayer, she picked it up and rinsed it in the ocean, before she lifted it to her lips and blew a clear strong note. As she listened to the sound, it brought back memories of being a child and learning to make music with the shells on the beach.

Gradually the sound faded, and she took another deep breath and blew three quick sharp notes, followed by a single long one. Now it was a waiting game, she had never tried to call on the merpeople, but her father had taught her the signals for a friend in distress, and the one to signal a trap or warning.

They sat there for a couple of minutes, before a man's head emerged from the water, in his right hand was a trident, and on his back was strapped a pair of spears. "Who calls, and what is your purpose?" he called from the water.

Scarlet knew he was ready in case they attacked, "A pair of travelers in need of aid," she called back. "We met a young half-breed several weeks ago, and we were hoping she would be willing to help us."

The tritan appeared to think about this for a moment before he answered, "Stay here and I will check with her mother, if she agrees then maybe she will come help you."

They watched as he slipped back under the water and disappeared, "Well," Scarlet said, "all we can do is wait and see."

Soon a woman's voice called out to them, "Scarlet, Mortimer, I'm so glad you are both alive."

They looked down the beach and saw the young mermaid heading towards them, but slowing down as she drew nearer. She smiled at them both when she was only a dozen feet away from them, "I'm not sure if it's safe for me to approach, mother had to run interference while I am in my breeding time. My kind does not appreciate half breeds, but the scent overpowers their will."

Scarlet laughed, "If you can heal my husband, I will deal with any problems that should arise, besides if you are in your human form your scent is almost non-existent."

Mortimer frowned, "If she is fully human, she shouldn't have a scent." As she got nearer to him, he suddenly noticed the smell of the ocean, faint though it was.

The mermaid looked at his blood soaked armor and frowned, "This is a pretty nasty injury judging by the amount of blood." She turned to Scarlet, "I hate to ask this of you lady, but can you help me strip him from the waist up?"

Scarlet smiled, "Of course dear, no need to be nervous, neither of us will hurt you."

The mermaid blushed, "Sorry, but while I trust you won't, I'm not sure if I trust he won't. Since our last meeting, I learned a bit more about our breeding scent, and my human form no longer stops it completely."

"That's alright," she said with a smile, "if need be I can block it with magic, after all nobody can smell much of anything when their face is covered in fire."

"That sounds a bit harsh," the mermaid replied, as she knelt closer to Mortimers injured side. "I see you used fire to stop the bleeding, but it doesn't really stop the wound from getting worse." She sighed and continued, "I am going to have to reopen the wound in order to properly heal it."

"I understand," Scarlet replied tensely, she now understood what Mortimer had tried to tell her about the mermaid's scent, even she was being drawn to her. "The scent of the sea is a powerful thing," she whispered under her breath. She noticed her husband was lying very still, and breathing in a slow steady rhythm.

Scarlet suddenly heard the crimson witch in her head, "I'm impressed, he is meditating in order to avoid being drawn into her spell. She can handle this Scarlet. I suggest you meditate as well, this mermaid is a dangerous creature."

"If you don't mind, I am going to meditate for a bit, you'll get my attention if you need me?" Scarlet asked.

The mermaid laughed musically, "I will come get you if I need your help, I'm sorry if I am distressing you."

Scarlet found meditating was not as easy as she had thought it would be, every time she would slip deeper into her meditation, a sudden twinge or jab of pain would come, and her mind would leap to Mortimers injury. "This is useless," she said finally and walked back over to where the mermaid had her hands shoved inside Mortimers body.

"He's pretty resilient for a human," the mermaid said as she approached.

"I'm surprised he is able to meditate with you working on him like that," Scarlet replied. "Especially considering how much of an effect you're having on me."

The mermaid looked at her curiously, "What do you mean?"

"I can smell the scent of the sea on you," she answered, "it's faint but still there, along with the desire it compels."

The mermaid smiled, "You are the first female to ever be drawn by the scent of a mermaid, it could be a glitch in my magic because I am a half breed, or it could be something to do with your connection to your husband. If it's the latter, then I must say you two have a pretty powerful bond."

Scarlet chuckled, "You could say we have a very special bond, and by the way that kind of tickles."

"What does?" the mermaid asked.

"Whatever you're doing inside his wound, it kind of tickles." she answered.

"You can feel what I am doing to him?" the mermaid asked, "that could be useful. So far I have only been cleaning the wound and closing all of the internal wounds."

"How are you closing the wounds?" Scarlet asked.

"Oh, it's pretty simple," she answered, "since blood is so similar to water, and our power is over water, I am simply having the blood create a thin layer over every cut so the skin itself can heal naturally."

"That sounds pretty complicated," she replied.

"Well, you are a pyromancer," the mermaid said in response, "it would be kind of like when you reach inside the fire and manipulate it so as to create the amount of heat you desire."

"Pyromancer?" Scarlet asked.

"I see much knowledge has been lost to human kind," the mermaid said, "let me see if I can give you a lesson in magic while I work."

"Sounds great," Scarlet replied enthusiastically, "all they ever taught me was how to control my natural ability with fire."

"Well, first of all you need to know the different types of magic, earth, fire, water, and air." She smiled at Scarlet, "the techniques for each of these often called, geomancy, pyromancy, hydromacy, and aeromancy. There is also life magic, but that is the purview of the Druids, and revolves around the circle of life. Spirit or Shadow magic is the domain of warlocks, and revolves around the shadows or spirits that no longer inhabit their mortal body."

The mermaid looked up at her for a moment and then continued, "The fairy has only one type of magic, and depending on their species will determine what their magic is. While a witch can learn all four schools of magic, very few have, as I recall the last time a witch learned more than one type of magic it was the Crimson Witch, she still favored fire over all the others, but it was her command of all the elements which gave her such great power." She smiled at Scarlet, "I would have loved to meet her, it was said she was a great friend to the magical creatures."
Scarlet returned her smile, "That may still be possible, if you traveled with us back to our home."

"You mean she's still alive?" the mermaid asked.

"Not quite, she is dead, but her soul is trapped in the weapons I carry, and when we get home we plan on freeing her," she explained, "When we do so, there might be a chance for you to actually meet her briefly."

"I would really like that," the mermaid replied. "Anyways, back to the different types of magic, if you can find a witch that practices each of the different arts, they should be able to teach you. I would, but since magic is inherent in my species you wouldn't quite be able to learn to do it the way we do it. Although you might be able to feel the way water magic works, if you don't mind putting your hands inside your husband."

Scarlet shrugged, "Okay, what do I have to do?" she asked as she knelt down next to the mermaid. This close to her, the mermaid's scent was overpowering, and she wondered how Mortimer was able to ignore it.

The mermaid pulled one hand out of the wound, and grasped Scarlet's hand gently, and then slid it back inside the wound, "Can you feel the pulse of his blood?"

Scarlet nodded, "Yes, there is something else there too, a kind of vibration."

"That is my magic, it is the water inside his blood, humming to my will." The mermaid replied, "I would let you try to manipulate it, but that would be a bit risky, just focus on that hum, and see if you can pick out the patterns in it."

She started to feel variations in the hum, and noticed every time a certain pattern arose, a small patch of red skin would appear along the inside of the cut.

After several hours, the mermaid pulled both of their hands out and said, "That is as much as I can do today, provided he is careful, he should be able to travel now. I will be able to do some more work on him tomorrow, but right now I am exhausted."

"Please, don't push yourself too hard," Scarlet replied, "we didn't really expect too much help anyways."

The mermaid laughed, "Are you kidding, the druid told us you released the grotto, if you hadn't specifically asked for me they would have sent several healers to tend to your wounds." She frowned, "Sadly it is your association with me that means others won't come to help."

"I wish your people were more accepting," Scarlet said to her.

From atop a rock in the ocean a female voice replied, "So do we, I dare not come closer or I would, I must return to my husband before the guards patrol this area. Will you please keep an eye on her for me?"

"Do you see why I trust them now, mother?" the mermaid asked the voice.

"Yes, I do see now, I will be able to come closer tomorrow." the voice answered, "Please be sure to guard my daughter closely."

"I will," Scarlet replied, although she herself was not sure how good of a guard she would be.

"You two rest," a musical voice suddenly said, "I will keep watch, there is enough blood on the ground to keep me fully energized for several days anyways."

Scarlet looked up and saw the crimson witch, "Oh thank you, I didn't think you had the power to manifest right now."

The crimson witch laughed, "My dear sweet child, I was saving my energy for the battlefield, and then to suddenly be removed from it was quite a surprise. Guarding is a simple task, and if need be I can even blast a few enemies."

"Who is that?" the mermaid asked.

Scarlet smiled, "This is the manifestation of the crimson witch. I guess you will get to meet her now instead of having to wait."

"That's good," the mermaid replied, and collapsed next to Mortimer.

Instantly Scarlet moved to check on her, but the crimson witch laughed, "Don't worry, she is just sleeping, she expended a lot of energy to save his life. Now you should sleep too child."

In the morning, Scarlet was awakened by Mortimer laughing, "What's so funny?" she asked sleepily.

"I was just thinking of how many mercenaries I know would kill to be where I am right now," he answered. "Waking up between two extraordinarily beautiful women, the only problem is that only one is naked."

Scarlet sat bolt upright, and looked down to see him smiling mischievously at her. The mermaid was still sound asleep, her right hand resting gently on his wound, her left arm curled under her head, and a smile on her face. "She looks so innocent like that," she whispered.

He smiled at her and answered, "I know, I'd rather not wake her, but I really need to relieve myself." Carefully he lifted the mermaid's hand from his side, and rolled away from her.

Scarlet stopped him when he got to his side, "Don't you dare let that wound touch the ground, or we'll have to start all over again."

"That doesn't sound like such a bad idea, but can I make a request that you be the naked one and she be clothed?" he winked at her as he very carefully got to his knees. "Damn, you can't imagine how much it hurts just to get this far."

She put a hand on his shoulder, "Yes, I can, give me your hand and let me help you." She knew he was only joking around in an effort to hide the pain.

It was not easy getting him to his feet while trying not to disturb his wound too much. Together they managed to get over to a clump of brush, and Scarlet held him steady as he relieved himself. "I guess it's better than being in the medic tent and trying to piss in a pot," he said as they hobbled back to the sleeping mermaid.

As they approached, the mermaid opened her eyes and sat straight upright, "What? Where did you two go?"

Mortimer smiled at her, "I had to relieve myself."

Scarlet squeezed his arm slightly to warn him to behave, "Just be glad you didn't have to hear his bad jokes this morning."

She laughed at this, "Oh? It couldn't be any worse than the jokes one hears on ships." She shook her head, "sailors have a dirty mind, but as my mother says, most of them would flee if confronted by an actual mermaid."

He chuckled, "I am no sailor, but I can attest mercenaries are just as sick minded. At the same time though we would not flee from a mermaid, or her guards."

Scarlet shook her head, "Well, there goes the illusion of innocence you had," she said to the mermaid.

"Either way, we should start moving, we can't stay here forever," he replied. "Thank you for all of your help," he said to the mermaid.

She looked at him and frowned, "Oh no, you are not leaving me here. Until you are fully healed I am coming with you."

Mortimer looked at Scarlet to see what she thought, and she just smiled and replied, "I agree, she is coming with us, after she talks to her mother. We can wait until then, I am curious though why her scent isn't as compelling this morning."

The mermaid smiled, "Oh, a nice elderly gentleman stopped by last night and watched over you two for a bit. He gave me some instructions on how to help control my pheromones, as he called it. He also explained to me that due to my dual nature, my pheromones were different from other mermaids in that they affected both men and women. He really was a nice old man, it was strange that he could disappear so easily and never left any footprints."

Mortimer shrugged his shoulders and winced, "Suppose then we should start by packing up my armor, obviously I won't be wearing it right away."

Scarlet laughed at him, "always the mercenary, when are you going to relax and enjoy life?"

He grinned at her, "I do enjoy life, but at the same time there are things which need to be done." He looked at the mermaid and smiled, "If we are going to be traveling together, what should we call you?"

She smiled back at him and answered, "Clarice, that's the name my father gave me."

"Well then Clarice, if we are to be traveling together we shall have to find some clothes for you to wear." He said, "we didn't exactly expect to run into you, so we don't exactly have anything on us right now, but I am sure we can figure out something."

Scarlet helped him sit down, and went to her back, "It's not much, but I did bring along a spare chemise, we could use a small section of rope as a belt." she continued, as she pulled the clothing from her bag.

Clarice looked at the simple garment, and pulled it on, "Thank you, while we wait, I should take another look at your wound Mortimer." She rolled up the sleeves and started to gently poke and prod the wound, "Not bad, you'll be sore for a while, I can easily repair the flesh and stop the blood flow, but the bones will take longer to heal. Would you mind leaning a bit more to your left? I need to look inside and see how the internal injuries are healing."

He followed her instructions, wincing slightly in pain, but found her touch to be rather cool and soothing, "Don't wear yourself out," he said, a little gruffer than he intended.

She grimaced, "I won't, but you really need to let me tend to your wound. As I said, in a couple of days it will be mostly healed, at which time if you want you'll be able to wear your armor again. With the bones though I wouldn't recommend going into combat any time soon."

Scarlet smiled to herself, "Don't mind his tone, he's just grumpy because he's in pain. There," she said as she finished packing all of their stuff up. "I guess I'll have to carry both packs, as there is almost no way you're going to carry one with that wound."

Clarice looked at her and said, "Oh don't worry about his pack, I'll carry it for him Lady Scarlet."

Scarlet winced at this honorific, "Please, just call me Scarlet, anyone will tell you I am no Lady."

Clarice looked at her strangely and replied, "As you wish, but you are the most beautiful lady I have ever met."

"Clarice," came a voice from the water.

"Oh hello mother," she replied, "come to say goodbye?"

The older mermaid laughed, "I figured you would want to travel with them. You look strange in human clothing, but then again clothing is something new to our kind."

Scarlet moved to the water's edge to better converse with the mermaid, "I am sorry for disrupting your family, but do you mind if she joins us for a while?"

She looked at Scarlet and smiled, "No interruption really, she is at the age that all merfolk leave their families, you have simply provided her with companionship she would have lacked otherwise my lady."

Scarlet blushed a bright crimson, "You are the one who best deserves to be called a Lady," she replied, "I can only hope to age as well and wisely as you have."

The mermaid turned bright red momentarily, "Oh my, I haven't blushed like that since I was Clarice's age. You will take care of my daughter won't you?"

"As if she were my own," she replied.

The mermaid looked over at Mortimer, still shirtless, and said, "He would make one fine husband, I can see why my daughter wishes to travel with you."

Scarlet frowned, "I'm sorry but he already has a wife."

"Oh, don't get me wrong child, you would make an excellent wife, but as we know humans are not the best at staying with one partner." the mermaid said with a smile. "If you ever grow tired of him, I'll be willing to take either one of you in."

"Mother!" Clarice exclaimed as she stood up, "they are not like us. These two will be together for the rest of their lives, I am sure of that. You should go see father, and let him show you how deep a human's love can run compared to our own. Quit trying to run from him when you know you only truly want to be with him." She glared at her mother, "Sometimes you are so stubborn, you know he would gladly sacrifice everything for you, he already has, and now it's time you sacrificed something for him."

"I gave up my people for him, what more do you want me to sacrifice?"

Clarice laughed, "You never wanted to be around the other merfolk, so that wasn't a sacrifice. I bet if you were to actually make the effort and go into his home, you might find that happiness you are constantly seeking."

"I thought your parents raised you together," Scarlet said.

"Oh, they did, but they always kept their distance from each other," she answered. "It's sad when you see how much they love each other, and yet they both refuse to acknowledge that love."

Mortimer laughed, "Sounds like this might be a good time for you both to discover who you are and what you desire." He looked at the older mermaid and smiled, "You have a beautiful and intelligent daughter, I promise we will take good care of her, but I cannot tell you how long she will be gone for. I can say that when she returns to the water, you will be surprised at how much she will have changed."

The mermaid started to laugh, and then looked more closely at him, "You are not a man to mess with, even with your injury. Do you believe my daughter is telling the truth and that I can be happy with her father?"

He smiled, "If you wish to be happy with him then you shall be, but if you continue to keep your distance you will never know."

"Very well," the mermaid replied, "then I shall go to him, and try to live his way for a while, although being on land for too long can be painful for our species." With that she turned gracefully in the water and swam away.

Clarice laughed softly, "She's in for a big surprise, father built his house with her in mind."

"Oh?" Scarlet said.

"Yes, every room has a pool of water in it, and there are interconnecting passages between them." She smiled, "he even went so far as to build himself a bed that floats in a pool of water so if she ever decided to spend the night she could be comfortable."

Mortimer chuckled, "She is going to be in for a rude awakening making him wait for her for that long."

Scarlet turned and slapped him on the chest, "She's too young to hear about that sort of thing."

Clarice laughed, "You kidding, that was part of our education as kids, our people believe you should know about all the adult stuff before you become an adult and experience it. It's you humans who are concerned about innocence and age, not the merfolk, or any other magical creature I have met."

She had to think about that for a moment, "Be that as it may, we do need to help you learn how to blend in with humans, and the best way to do that is to treat you as a human." She smiled, "By the time we get to the nearest town, we'll have you walking, talking and somewhat thinking like a human."

Mortimer snorted, "This could be very interesting, hopefully I'll be healed up enough to protect her honor before we have to test her ability to blend in." He retrieved both of his swords and buckled them to his waist, slightly below his wound. Taking a few steps he laughed, "All right, I'm ready to get moving."

It was Scarlet's turn to snort, "You have no idea how barbaric you look with those swords on and your chest bare, but you're correct it is time we get going."

The three of them walked along the beach towards where they knew the road would lead them back home, bantering about inconsequential items and the day to day lives of humans. In the end they decided it would be best if they told everyone that Clarice was a water witch, at least with that explanation most people would steer clear of her and would overlook any peculiarities she might exhibit.

The going was slow, and the two women kept insisting that he take a break every couple of hours so Clarice could check his wound, but they at least made it a good distance before nightfall.

# Entanglement

Mortimer sat on a large piece of driftwood and watched Scarlet instruct Clarice in the proper way to set up camp, upset that every time he tried to help the two of them would snap at him to sit down and rest. "Least they could do is let me help in some way," he grumbled under his breath.

"Listen to them," a deep grating voice said from behind him, "Any man would kill for a chance at those two."

Mortimer didn't move, but simply replied, "Any man would be stupid to try and take that chance."

"With an injury like that, you're unable to protect them," the voice replied.

He heard the movement and knew exactly what the person behind him was planning. With a painful, deep breath he leapt up and spun around, his left hand drew the rose sword from it's temporary scabbard. His grip on the hilt was backwards, but it worked as the attacker's short sword clanged against the rose sword. Mortimer took a step back from the man and drew the black blade with his right hand, a flick of the wrist and he held both swords in front of him ready for a fight. "I warned you it would be stupid to take that chance," he said.

The sound had alerted Scarlet, who drew the Crimson sword, with her right hand, as her left hand flung outwards shooting streamers of fire off into the night. "Damn," she said, "it looks like we have company."

Clarice looked over at Mortimer, saw the attack and then saw fresh blood start to drip from his wound. "Who dares to interrupt my healing?" she said in a low hissing voice.

Scarlet looked over at her, and saw her eyes had turned an ice blue, the very air around Clarice had suddenly become very cold.

Clarice was now speaking in some strange tongue, as she marched towards Mortimer, a man with a dagger lunged at her, she slapped his arm and he screamed in pain as ice formed around it.

Scarlet swung the crimson sword with both hands, while she chanted and suddenly a circle of fire surrounded them. A dozen dirty men had gotten inside the ring before it closed, the rest screamed and fled as the flames moved outwards.

Mortimer chuckled dryly, even as he felt the moisture on his side, "All within those flames will perish, and we shall dance on their bones tonight." His opponent hesitated for a split second, and the rose sword leapt forward through his chest and out his back. Mortimer simply let go of the blade and turned to the other men, "Who will feed my thirsty blade next?" he asked.

Screams arose from the circle of fire as men were consumed by the flames, Scarlet was mad and so was the crimson witch, the flames moved faster than any man could run and burned hotter than any fire should.

Clarice in her rage turned the water in the ground into ice which clung to the feet of her enemies, and any enemy that got within a few feet of her suddenly found their blood frozen.

Soon Mortimer found himself getting dizzy, and he knew he had lost too much blood to continue the fight. It was at that point he felt an icy cold hand touch his side, he looked down to see a patch of ice forming over the wound and a pair of ice cold blue eyes looked into his for a moment before Clarice released her rage in a wave of frozen bloody shards. He found himself standing still and watching as red shards of ice ripped themselves from his enemies and flew into those who still looked able to fight.

When he next opened his eyes, he found himself encased in ice and unable to move. "What?" He asked.

Clarice and Scarlet looked at him and said together, "We have decided we will stay here until your wound has healed more."

He looked at Clarice and said, "You're not as innocent as we had thought." He then looked at Scarlet and continued, "You are enjoying this way too much, but you are correct, it's obvious I can't fight in this condition. Just remember, I will get my revenge someday."

Scarlet smiled at him, "I am looking forward to it."

Clarice laughed, "Can I watch?"

This made Scarlet frown momentarily, "My deer, be careful of what you say, he may take you up on it."

"Why would that be a bad thing?" she asked.

Mortimer laughed, "Because, entire wars have been fought over something like that."

Soon enough he got bored watching the women, and fell back to sleep. He didn't have the heart to tell them they didn't need to lock him down, he didn't have the energy to move a muscle.

After a week of being stuck in one place, Mortimer was getting more and more aggravated. He constantly struggled against the block of ice Clarice had trapped him in, and even tried to bite Scarlet when she tried to give him a kiss. Both of them were now worried that if he kept struggling he would make things worse for himself, so they decided to release him from the ice in the morning. Neither of them knew what state of mind he was in at this point, but Scarlet was pretty sure she could handle anything he threw their way.

Clarice was more worried than Scarlet, keeping the spell going was wearing her out, and every time he struggled against it she worried he would break free. Summoning ice was easy, but keeping it frozen while not freezing the person encased in it was difficult. It didn't help that he was still able to manipulate nearby shadows while trapped in the ice. She saw the look in his eyes, he wasn't completely rational anymore, in his sleep he summoned nightmarish creatures, twice the Crimson Witch had manifested to back them off from killing Scarlet and Clarice.

When morning came, they had a real surprise, Mortimer had vanished. Scarlet looked around and found the rose sword where she had put it, but his black blade was nowhere to be found. She concentrated, and could feel a slight throb from her side, which meant the connection was still there, but something was definitely wrong about it. "This can't be good," she said to Clarice.

Clarice frowned and pointed to the ice, "He broke the ice, and as you can see he injured himself again while getting out." She looked closely at the ice and gasped, "There is a shadow stuck in the ice."

Scarlet shook her head in amazement, that meant he had drawn power from the spirits somehow. She drew one of the crimson blades and said, "Okay, can you explain this to me?"

The crimson witch laughed, "I went through this once with my husband, whatever he does, remember your love for him, if you forget that then he will be lost to you forever."

"You're not being very helpful," Scarlet said to the blade.

"This is a battle only you can fight," the blade replied back to her, "every member of his family has had to fight this battle, if you love him you'll forgive him no matter what he does."

Scarlet turned to Clarice, "Okay, I want you to stay here, if he shows up, give a shout, and whatever you do don't fight him."

Clarice nodded her head, "alright, do you think he'll come after me?"

"No," was her brief reply as she took off following the feeling in her stomach. It didn't take long for her to find his footprints in the sandy soil, she could tell he had used his magic to hide them closer to camp, but away from it he didn't appear to be hiding.

Scarlet followed his tracks until they came to a large outcropping of rock, she found him sitting calmly sharpening his sword in the shade of the rock.

"So, you decided to follow me," he said in a strange hollow voice. "You shouldn't have done that, you know."

She didn't like the tone in his voice, or the blackness of his eyes, "You knew I would follow you," she replied. "I couldn't let you just leave me like that, after all you promised we would be together for the rest of our lives."

He frowned at her, "Yes, I did, but you fail to realize something"

"Oh, what is that?" she asked.

"This is the end of my life," he answered as he stood up and stepped out of the shadows.

Scarlet gasped, his entire right side was covered in black dried blood. She stepped towards him, only thinking of holding him and trying to save him. That's when it happened, the dried blood on his body suddenly moved, and she found herself bound tightly by ropes of blood.

He smiled at her, "I told you I would get revenge." he said as he walked over to her. "Oh, don't worry magic won't work against my bonds, they are made up of my own blood so only I can control them."

She didn't struggle, she simply waited, she could see the madness in his eyes, and she had a feeling she knew what had caused it. "You left the battlefield, but it never

83

left you," she said softly, "I'm sorry my love. I give you my life, but I ask that you spare that of our child."

Mortimer staggered for a moment, and the bonds loosened a bit, not much, but enough that she could breath and possibly get loose if she tried. "You have to leave me," he whispered, "please while I can still control it."

"If you really want me to, then I will," she answered, "but first I want to taste your lips on mine one more time."

"Why?" he asked as he staggered a step closer to her, the bonds tightened momentarily, they pulsed as if in time with his heartbeat.

He was close enough now for her to touch him every time the bonds loosened, she knew she had to time it just right or she would pay the price. Suddenly she gasped, "I'm ready to pay any price to be with you my love." she said, as she tried to throw herself at him.

Amazingly it worked, he caught her in his arms and held her close to him, as she kissed him passionately. Her arms were still bound to her sides, but she could feel a resurgence of strength, both in herself and within him. The darkness fell back from his eyes, and she could feel the wounds on his body beginning to knit themselves together.

He smiled at her and pushed her back from him a little bit, "I think I will keep you like this for a little while. I did warn you I would get revenge."

She smiled back at him, "I don't care as long as we are together," she answered. She was surprised to see tendrils of shadow moving over his body and knitting it together as if it were a shirt, "How are you doing that?" she asked.

He frowned, "With the release of the dark spirits, I find myself with something to live for, so those spirits that sacrificed their lives for the ones they loved are doing what they can to keep me with the ones I love."

"So you could have done this the entire time," she replied with a glint of anger in her cyes.

"No," he answered, "not until I was able to purge the darkness from myself. When you receive energy from the dead, you also receive it's emotions, so until I resolved the battle going on within me from all the emotions I collected from the dead on the battlefield, I couldn't use any of my powers. It's why I said I would be useless in a fight, do you really think I have to rely on a sword to defend myself?"

Scarlet couldn't help it, she started to cry, "All those battles, and I never knew how much you were suffering, I'm sorry." In her mind she heard a soft chuckle and the words, "I told you this was a battle I could not help with."

"We should go back, I still have to take my revenge on Clarice, after all I did promise," he said as he raised his hand and the black sword flew from where it rested against the rock into his hand.

Scarlet gasped, "You've never done that before."

Mortimer chuckled, "You have never seen me filled with so much love of life before either," he replied as he swooped her up onto his shoulder and started to trot towards camp.

She could tell, he was more powerful than ever before, and yet he was still holding back, she wondered why. The words came to her mind, "Silly girl, he's afraid he'll hurt you."

As they approached their campsite, Scarlet realized she was happy, she had never seen him so playful. She remembered their first night together and realized he had been quite reserved compared to the energy that was coming from him now.

With an off handed wave of his hand, shadows rose up around them, and he let go of Scarlet as they slipped into them. The shadows hid them as they approached the camp, even with the evening sun at their backs.

Clarice was getting worried about Scarlet, she had been gone most of the day, she was quite surprised when a shadow grabbed her arms and pinned them to her side. She didn't even get a chance to summon her magic, before she found herself completely encased in a shadowy cocoon. It was strange in the shadows, everything appeared fuzzy, and strange figures moved around her vision. Suddenly she felt a strong arm wrap around her waist and pull her to the side. When she was able to see clearly, Clarice found herself lying down next to a laughing Scarlet. "What happened?" she asked.

"Let's just say, he is following through with his word to get revenge for tying him down," She answered. "I must say though, your pheromones kicked in pretty good. I don't think they work on him anymore though."

"Why do you say that?" Clarice asked.

Scarlet smiled at her, "Because, I have a very strong desire to be with you, and he simply set you down and went to make dinner." She chuckled slightly, "At least you're only bound by shadows," she wiggled a little bit, "he bound me with blood, which is a much stronger magic."

Clarice tried to summon her magic, but a pressure against her ribs made her stop. "The only magic I can use right now is my pheromones, anytime I try to use any water magic, the shadows get tighter."

"Oh," Scarlet replied, "that doesn't surprise me, just relax, he won't hurt either of us. He is merely proving a point of what we did to him, he can do to us." She smiled, "Just be glad he isn't the truly vengeful type, or we would be in some serious trouble." She thought about the madness she had glimpsed within him earlier, and realized how horribly wrong things could have gone if someone else had come across him.

Clarice shrugged, the shadows weren't uncomfortable, if anything it was like a thick blanket. Slowly she began to fall asleep, only to be woken by Mortimer approaching.

"Dinner is ready, if you two are ready to eat," he said.

With a gesture of his hand, the shadows fell away from Clarice and she was able to move. She raised her hand as if to strike him, and the shadows suddenly gripped it. "You are different somehow," she said as she lowered her arm.

He laughed softly, as he reached down and offered his hand to Scarlet, "Coming my deer?"

Scarlet found her arms and legs were free, but the blood rope was still wrapped around her limbs, "You're not going to completely let me loose are you?"

"Never," he answered, as he reached down and offered Clarice a hand.

She took his hand and let him help her to his feet, "Well, at least you're going to let us feed ourselves," she frowned.

"It was never my intention of harming you," he replied, "simply to teach you a lesson, as I would my own child. You see when you challenge someone's ability to follow through with what they say, you are in fact inviting them to make the effort." He lifted a finger, and the blood chords wrapped around Scarlet's limbs suddenly pulled her to his side. "Not knowing your enemies strengths and weaknesses makes it even worse," he continued as he hugged Scarlet close to him and kissed her.

Clarice thought about it before she asked, "Why didn't you use the same bonds on me as you did on Scarlet?"

"Would you like a demonstration as to why, or are you just asking for an explanation?" He asked with a frown.

Immediately Scarlet made a quick move and wrapped her arms tightly about him, "If she requires a demonstration, then use me it would be safer that way."

Instantly the look on his face softened and he kissed Scarlet again, "You are somewhat protected from the bonds, I am kind of surprised you haven't tried to break them." He smiled softly at her and then looked at Clarice, "Basically the blood bonds spell is a particularly nasty one, as it first traps the victim in chains of blood, and then it will seek a way into the victims bloodstream. Once it has entered the victim's blood stream it creates an unbreakable bond between the two and the victim becomes subservient to the caster, until such a point as the caster releases them from servitude." He paused and looked at Scarlet closely as he continued, "Usually the victim struggles against such a bond, but you have not, and once the spell has been cast it is impossible to revoke it."

"Can it be countered?" Clarice asked.

"The only way to counter it is to block it from reaching your body," he answered, as he looked into Scarlet's eyes, "You could have easily burned away the blood before it reached you, but you didn't even try, why? Is this what you wanted?"

Scarlet laughed, "That's been bugging you, has it?" she replied, "to answer your own question, why did you try to sacrifice your life to save mine? Why did you offer up your free will in order to tend my wounds?"

"Yes, it has been bugging me," he answered her first question. "As for the other two, the answer is the same, because I felt that I had to save you no matter what."

She smiled back at him, "Then to answer your question, I realized the only way to save you from the madness was to get close to you. The only way to do that was if the darkness no longer saw me as a threat, so I took the same chance you took for me on the day we met." She chuckled softly, "Besides, we are already bound permanently together. When we danced our magic merged, our blood merged the day we met, and on the battlefield when I tended your wound I used a fire magic that bound us together so I could take some of the pain away. So this," she looked at the blood bond and smiled, "it is just another way that we are bound together forever."

"That is so romantic," Clarice said with a smile, "are you sure you two aren't related to the merfolk?"

Mortimer smiled as he swept Scarlet into his arms, "You could never be my servant, but the bonds will need to stay in place until the spell is finished."

Scarlet smiled as she curled into his shoulder, "I wear them proudly for you my love, but if you don't get me some food soon I might take a bite out of you."

He carried her over to the fire and set her down next to it, "I hope you like fish stew," he said, "that's about all we have right now."

Scarlet frowned slightly and Clarice laughed and said, "Smells just like mom used to make."

Mortimer laughed and softly said to Scarlet, "Thanks to you, she," he nodded towards the young mermaid, "isn't on the menu."

"I'm not sure if I want to know what else you thought in your madness," Scarlet replied softly. She looked again at the blood bonds and frowned, "Then again I can't stop you from sharing now either." A sudden look of realization came across her face, "Oh god, I just realized what is going to happen next."

Mortimer laughed, "You just realized what was coming? After explaining everything about feeling each other's pain and strong emotions, it just dawned on you that we are now going to share a lot more?"

"No, I already figured that part out," she answered, "I was talking about the bond, you're holding it back. I know I will lose my free will when it's complete, but you can give that back to me any time you want."

He frowned, "Not completely I can't, that is the truly horrible part of the bond. I can grant you your freedom, but I could also rescind it at any time using the bond. Until I am sure it is safe to finish the bond, I will have to hold it back."

"You know I can't allow that," she said to him, "I will find a way to break your concentration on it. You need your strength and holding back this spell is only going to weaken you." She wrapped her arms around his neck and kissed him deeply.

"Thanks," he said after the kiss, "you are helping strengthen my resolve."

Clarice, having listened in, frowned and said, "Lady Scarlet, if I can be of assistance, all you have to do is say the word. There is one thing that I know of which will break any man's concentration."

"You do know," Mortimer replied, "if you do that you will be putting yourself at risk."

Clarice laughed, "I know, but I will do whatever it takes to make your wife happy."

Scarlet looked at her and said, "If you think you can safely break his concentration, then go ahead and try, but do not put yourself in harm's way for my sake. I am only frustrated that he is hurting himself to protect me from my own choice." As she spoke, she watched as Clarice turned back into her mermaid form, and then she caught the scent of the ocean coming from her.

Mortimer caught a whiff of the pheromones Clarice was sending his way, and the bonds on Scarlet's limbs tightened, she felt them dig into her flesh seeking a vein, and winced in pain, then she felt them stop digging, "damn it the pheromones are not enough," she thought.

Clarice noticed, and pulled herself out of the clothing, which was now tangled somewhat with her tail, and dragged herself over until she was right next to Mortimer, "Now what are you going to do?" she asked him as she wrapped his arms around his neck and pulled his face down to hers. She kissed him very briefly before everything went dark, "Well, how rude to dump a girl like that," she said. She could still feel his skin where it had contacted her body, and suddenly she realized what had happened. Somehow she had fallen in love with him, her mother had mentioned this possibility if she ever used her powers on a person with a pure heart. With this realization, she burst into tears as she sat alone in the ball of shadows he had created.

Scarlet couldn't help but to scream as the blood bond plunged into her veins and flowed through her body, as Mortimers concentration was broken. She watched with tears in her eyes as his arms wrapped around Clarice and he kissed her briefly before his head snapped in Scarlet's direction and shadows erupted from the ground to encase the mermaid.

There were tears in his eyes, as he looked at her and said, "I'm sorry, I failed you."

Scarlet grinned through the pain, "No, you didn't fail me," she gasped. "This is what I wanted, as an added bonus, you proved your love to me by defeating Clarice's pheromones. I can feel how much you desired her, and I desire her too, but you were strong enough to hold your desire in check long enough to contain her pheromones."

Crying softly, he put his arms around Scarlet, "I never want you to feel subservient to someone else, please remember that."

The pain stopped once the bond reached her heart, and Scarlet started to laugh, "You know I don't feel any different, I mean I feel your emotions strongly now, but I don't feel any more compelled to do your bidding than I did before the bond." She stroked the side of his face gently, "You do realize you weren't going to win, once Clarice stepped in, it isn't fair for you to keep her locked up in there," she nodded towards the shadowy ball.

"I know," he replied, "but I am not sure if I am strong enough to handle her right now."

"Together we can handle anything," she said as she pulled him in for a kiss.

It was that kiss which disrupted the shadow ball and caused it to fall apart, suddenly Clarice was sitting just a few inches from them, tears running down her face. It was too much for her to handle, being that close to them at that moment, she tried to drag herself away, but she had no strength left in her arms and she collapsed on the ground crying. Suddenly she felt strong arms pick her up and brush her hair out of her face. "Please, don't," she cried through closed eyes.

"It's alright," Mortimer said softly in one ear.

"We understand," Scarlet said from the other side, her hand gently wiping away the tears.

Clarice slowly opened her eyes and realized she was pressed against Mortimers chest, she tried to jerk her head away, and found that put her against Scarlet's chest. A moment later she realized they both were hugging her, "Wait, what?" she said, completely confused.
They both smiled at her, and suddenly it dawned on her, that hungry look in their eyes, she had seen it before in a man's eyes, but this time there was no escape and she wasn't even sure if she wanted to escape. "It could be worse," she said with a smile.

They both laughed, and Mortimer said, "True, I could throw you in the fire and serve you for dinner."

Scarlet chuckled, "That's not fair hun, I really have a strong desire for her and you want to filet her?"

Clarice looked down at her tail and blushed furiously, "Oh, I thought that hungry look was for something else."

Scarlet's face turned serious, "Darling, if you don't get control of yourself, and put some clothing on you will most definitely find out what the hungry look in both our eyes is for."

As if to emphasize her point, Mortimer tightened his grip on her and gave her a malicious grin. "Trust me, we both feel the desire your pheromones create, and I'll be honest after they're gone, that desire does not go away until satisfied." He glanced at Scarlet and continued, "That's why you are going to get dressed and finish making dinner while we go deal with our desire."

Clarice started to cry softly, as her tail slowly changed back into legs, "I'm sorry, I didn't realize it had a lasting effect." She looked at the two of them and asked, "Will my desire ever go away?"

"What do you mean?" Scarlet asked, suddenly aware of the naked body she was holding so close to her."

"I desire both of you," she answered, she looked at Mortimer, "I can still feel your skin against mine from earlier, and I wish to continue being pressed up against you." She looked over at Scarlet and smiled, "I am enjoying being pressed against your body right now, and desire to feel your skin against my own as well, I desire to please you both, even if I know I will be hurt in the process."

Mortimer frowned, "I think it is best you get dressed, and we can consult some more experienced people, we will deal with this together."

They couldn't help but watch as Clarice slipped her gown back on, frustration building in all of them. It didn't help that both the crimson blades and the black sword were both shaking with spiritual laughter.

Clarice herself kept glancing at them, and wondering why they suddenly were treating her like a servant, it was when she caught them both staring at her she understood, they were fighting to control themselves and she was pretty sure it was a close battle.

She wiggled her hips a little bit, and smiled to herself as they both started to step towards her. "No," she suddenly said to herself, "I shouldn't be teasing them."

"We need to deal with this soon," Scarlet said to Mortimer, "she's going to get herself hurt without meaning to."

Mortimer smiled, "While I quite agree with you, a part of me really wants to see where this goes." He looked over at the black blade and said, "I know you have enough energy to manifest, so please do so."

A shadow drew itself from the blade and coalesced in front of him, "You have definitely gotten yourself into a sticky mess this time," it said.

Scarlet drew the crimson dagger, "You too, we need your advice as well."

A crimson mist drew itself from the dagger and formed into the crimson witch, who was laughing so hard she jiggled. "Oh my, this reminds me of a story," she started.

"We swore not to tell anyone about that," the shadow cut her off.

She smiled at him, "good to see you again babe, it's been a long time."

The shadow smiled adoringly at her, "Good to see you too," it replied, "How about we show these three how to solve this problem they have?" he asked with a malicious grin.

"Oh my," the crimson witch replied, "I would love to, but we would need solid bodies for that."

"Brings back memories of our wedding night," the shadow said.

Scarlet suddenly burst into laughter, "Now I see why you two avoided manifesting at the same time, were you two always this way?"

The crimson witch smiled, "oh yes deer, ever since that accident with the mermaid a month before we got married. I wonder what happened to her anyways?"

The shadow laughed, "She returned to the sea after the knight she married died, took their daughter and returned to the ocean. He looked around, "The rose sword would know, he kept a better track of his family than we ever did."

The crimson witch laughed, "Morti, be a deer and summon the knight of the rose sword would you?"

Mortimer shrugged and picked up the rose sword, "Not sure if you'll talk with us, but will you please try to manifest here?" He shook his head, "it doesn't appear to want to talk, and I'm not about to force it."

Clarice looked at the two spirits and said, "You said the knight died during the witch wars? What was his name by chance? He might have been married to one of my relatives." She looked a little embarrassed as she spoke.

The shadow laughed heartily, "I take it your family is outcast because of their tendency to find mates among humans?"

Clarice turned bright red, "Yes," she muttered.

"Give her the rose sword," the crimson witch said, "then tell it to awaken before it's heir is hurt. No knight can resist the temptation to rescue a damsel in distress," she said to Scarlet with a wink.

It was Scarlet's turn to blush, "You arranged my meeting Mortimer didn't you?" she accused.

"Only slightly," she answered, "I only drew his attention to your situation, you can thank me later."

Clarice gingerly took a grip on the handle of the rose sword, and drew it from its scabbard. She felt a strange energy travel through her arms, and brought it up over her head prepared to defend or attack as needed, "What?" she asked.

Mortimer smiled, "Only one of the knight's bloodline can awaken the spirit that resides within the sword," he said. "Anyone can use the sword in battle, but only a descendant of the man it was forged for can unlock it's knightley powers." He reached towards the sword with one hand and said a strange series of words.

Clarice felt the sword in her arms relax a bit, once the sword tip touched the earth a grey mist came out of it and formed the shape of a young man. He looked at the other two spirits and bowed, "My lord and lady, what do you command of me?"

The crimson witch laughed, "We were wondering what happened to your wife, and heirs. We kind of have a situation similar to the one we had with your wife."

The knight smiled, "It would be a great honor to have one of my heirs join your family, but I get the feeling he is already bound to another."

"Correct," the shadow said, "and of course they both have desires for her and vice versa. Apparently our heir accidentally mirrored her power back onto her."

The knight laughed, "I really shouldn't laugh at this situation, but it is funny in a way." He gave out a ghostly sigh and continued, "She brought it upon herself, she will have to suffer the consequences. You know she will of course forever desire him, but at least after they have their fling it will be easier for all of them to manage."

"Of course we know that," the crimson witch declared, "we were just curious as to what happened to your wife after you passed."

The knight laughed, "She returned to the sea, my daughter married a merman, and their son married a water witch. Their son had a fling with a mermaid, and now lives in isolation hoping she will return to him. I lost track of their daughter, but apparently you found her, why do you ask?"

"That would explain her icy abilities," The shadow exclaimed, "I never heard of a mermaid able to create water or ice when none was around."

Clarice interrupted them, "So you're saying I am part witch?"

"Yes deer," the crimson witch answered, "which also explains why Scarlet could feel your magic so readily. You are untrained, but you are definitely a witch and a mermaid, oh how wonderful."

Mortimer interrupted them, "So you two," he looked at the shadow and the crimson witch, "had an affair with a mermaid, and nobody knew about it?"

"Oh no," the crimson witch exclaimed, "everyone knew about it. After all, you couldn't help but notice a guest visiting a knight's bedroom almost every night a week after the wedding, but nobody talked about it. It was when she found a man worth loving, that the desire lessened for her, and until then we were more than happy to give in to her desire."

The shadow laughed, "at one point there was talk of having a second wedding and declaring her our wife."

The knight laughed, "I have to admit I was completely shocked when I asked her to join me for dinner and she accepted. It was amazing how well she got around for having a tail and not legs. It was even more amazing when she told me she wanted to marry me, but that she knew no man would marry someone who had slept with another woman's husband."

The crimson witch laughed, "Yes, she was so happy when you told her you didn't care, that you just wanted to see her happy."

The shadow smiled, "It was a very exciting wedding I must say, how many people did I have to beat up for trying to disrupt the ceremony?"

"Too many," the knight laughed. He looked over at Clarice and smiled, "Don't worry my child if he's anything like his ancestors, he'll be gentle. Do me a favor though, return my sword to the hall of roses so I might finally know peace."

Clarice smiled at him, "I will be happy to, but are you sure things will turn out alright between the three of us?"

All three spirits looked at each other and laughed, "We know it will," they said in unison as they all faded back to their own weapons.

Scarlet looked like she had received the best gift ever, as she sheathed the crimson dagger, "This is going to be a rather interesting night," she said with a purr.

The fish stew went from being a stew to being a burnt block, as the three of them explored their individual desires and wore themselves out completely. They were very thankful they had several spirits to watch over them, as they slept through the night.

# An old relative

When Mortimer woke in the morning he thought it had all been a pheromone induced dream until he realized he was sandwiched between two naked women. He lay there with his arms wrapped around the two women and smiled to himself, "This will be difficult to explain," he said to himself softly.

Scarlet heard him and whispered in his ear, "Do you think she'd be up for a little more fun?"

Clarice started to cry softly and whispered back, "Yes, hearing you say that makes me so happy."

It was another hour before they were ready to make something for breakfast, but none of them cared, it wasn't like they were on a schedule or anything. It took them forever to get dressed as they all kept stopping to admire each other's bodies.

Finally dressed, they decided on dried meat and fruit for breakfast, so they could eat as they walked. "We really need to get Clarice some proper clothing," Mortimer said as they walked.

"I wish I had a map of the area," Scarlet replied, "at least then we would know what villages are nearby."

Clarice laughed, "I don't have a map, but I do know that if we walk along the coast for a couple more weeks, we will come to a fishing village. There is a very nice old lady there that gave me sweats one day when mother and I came across her fishing all by herself."

Scarlet laughed great, "Now if only we had some horses, I am getting tired of walking everywhere and I doubt the fairies are going to be nice enough to allow us passage through their lands again."
"No horses," Clarice replied, "but I could tow a small raft or boat much faster than I can walk."

"No," Mortimer replied, "we are not going to use you like an animal. We'll walk to the fishing village and then see if we can't purchase some steeds."

Scarlet smiled, "agreed, besides we will want to make certain you," she looked at Clarice, "are not in heat when we get to the village."

Clarice smiled at her, "Sorry, but I am in perpetual heat when it comes to you two, and really feel no desire for anyone else."

Scarlet and Mortimer blushed, even though they knew she wouldn't feel this way if he hadn't reflected her magic.

It took them a month to get to the little fishing village, they still couldn't seem to get enough of each other no matter what, and it didn't help that the spirits in their weapons were enjoying every minute of it.

As they walked into the little village people moved out of their way, even though Clarice had cleaned all the blood from their clothing, neither of them quite figured out what magic she used to do this, the sight of several armed people made everyone in the little village nervous.

Clarice asked about the old woman she remembered, and they were directed to a small dilapidated hut at the edge of town. When they knocked on the door, they were greeted by a very old woman with thin white hair and Mortimer swore more wrinkles than anyone should ever have.

"Hello," the old woman said as she answered the door, "How can I help such noble young guests?"

Mortimer stepped forward and bowed deeply to the old woman, "My companion here told us of your kindness to her when she was a child, and we thought we would stop by and pay our respects."

"Oh my," the old woman said with a smile, "you truly are a noble warrior, please come in." She stepped back into the hut and let them all enter. "I would offer you lunch, but it would not be of sufficient quality for ones as noble as you."

Scarlet laughed, "It is us who would like to offer you lunch, noble woman, come let us take you to the tavern where you may eat your fill."

The old woman smiled, "You truly are generous, but I must decline, they don't much like me in the town and only stay away due to fear."

Mortimer frowned, "Excuse me ma'am," he said as he stepped outside and yelled to the nearest villager, "You there, come here."

The villager approached him nervously and said, "Yes sir?"

He handed the village a couple of coins and said, "Go and get as much food as that will buy and fill this ladies pantry. If you are done before I am gone, I will give you a gold coin."

"Yes m'lord," the villager exclaimed as he ran off into the village.

The old lady laughed, "You are way too generous, m'lord."

"Nonsense," Scarlet replied, "a village like this should be taking proper care of their elders."

The old lady looked closer at Clarice, "My deer child, you need better clothing than that if you are going to be traveling with these two. Come with me child," she said as she led Clarice into another room.

Mortimer looked over at Scarlet who nodded, she could tell what he was thinking at this moment, "How much," she asked.

He handed her a pouch, "whatever it takes to fix this place up properly."

She smiled as she took the pouch, "I'll go find the carpenter."

It took her less time to find the carpenter and return than it did for Clarice to pick out an outfit, "Word must have spread," she said to his unanswered question, "people were lining up outside her door to see the prestigious guests who are visiting the 'old witch' as they call her."

"That's an apt description," the old lady replied as she came back into the room followed by Clarice. She looked at Mortimer, "Yes the order knows I live here, but they haven't been in the area in a long time."

Mortimer didn't answer right away, he was too busy staring past her at Clarice. She was stunning in an ice blue gown with white trim, the rose sword was buckled to a dark blue split belt, the top strap ran above her hip and the lower strap below her hip.

Behind him Scarlet whispered, "I think we're all in heat now."

"Uh huh," he grunted in response, then smiling at Clarice he said, "You look simply delicious, my deer."

"Yes," Scarlet said, "I can't wait to get my hands on you."

The old lady frowned for a second until Clarice replied, "I was hoping you two would still feel that way, but was afraid the extra layers might upset you."

"Oh my," the old lady said, "then you three," she laughed, "well I guess it happens more often than I thought. She smiled, "This sort of thing happens quite often when witches and warlocks travel together through the lands of magical creatures. Magic attracts magic after all."

Clarice smiled at her, "Since we are going to be here for a little bit would you mind teaching me some of the ways of witchcraft?"

The old woman smiled, "I would be happy to, but I am quite certain that the witch you are traveling with can show you more than I could."

Scarlet laughed, "I can instruct her in the ways of pyromancy, but she needs someone who can instruct her in the ways of hydromancy."

The witch smiled even more, "It's glad to hear the old terms are not forgotten, I can indeed instruct her in the ways of water, but being a creature of water she will know most of it instinctively." She proceeded to get a bowl of water from the kitchen, "Now, why don't we sit down over here and we can see what you already know."

Clarice sat down across the bowl from the witch, Scarlet shrugged and sat down next to her and said, "I should learn this too."

Mortimer watched from the side, as they started talking about the different types of magic and how it was traditionally used. He learned that earth magic was predominantly defensive, while fire magic was offensive. Water magic was utilitarian and could be used for healing while air magic was primarily travel magic used for moving things around. The old woman turned out to be a 'wild' witch, or someone who learned her arts without formal instruction; she could do a little of each type of magic, but was not strong in any particular art form.

When there was a knock at the door, he answered it and let the villagers in to restock the kitchen and pantry, when they were done he gave each of them a silver coin, and the one he'd talked to earlier he gave the promised gold coin to. Along with a strong suggestion that properly taking care of the elderly could be very rewarding. He also made a note to send a small contingent from the order this way to help protect the village from possible bandits.

Soon there was another knock on the door and a carpenter waved for him to join them outside, "You have questions?" he asked the carpenter.

"We would not wish to intrude on the old witch who lives here," he said, "but, we have drawn up some plans to replace her home so we can be certain it is comfortable and secure." He paused before he continued, "We have tried to convince her to move several times since her husband died, but she refuses for sentimental reasons. I was wondering if you would look at the plans and give us any advice you may have."

Mortimer laughed, "What is your first idea?" he asked.

The carpenter looked nervous as he pulled out a parchment and answered, "It's something I have been working on, but have not found anyone to let me try it with their home. Basically instead of moving her out and rebuilding the house, I thought maybe we could just build a new house around it." He showed the scroll to Mortimer, "I have pre-assembled walls that with enough people we can put up around the sides and back of the house, then we attach them together and put a roof on over the entire thing. The last part would be to make doorways into the new rooms and repair the front wall and door of her existing house."

"I kind of like the idea," Mortimer replied, "How long will it take?"

"We could be done by tomorrow night, if we get a team of horses from the merchants guild even faster," he answered. "As I said before I already have the walls built, I just need to build the frame for the roof and then assemble it all."

"Then let's do it," Mortimer replied, "tell the merchants guild a knight of the rose requires the use of two teams of horses, if they give you any trouble tell them to come talk to me here."

"Yes my lord," the carpenter said as he bowed and ran off.

Mortimer barely made it to the door of the hut before a richly dressed gentleman called out to him, "Yes" he replied as the man came huffing up to him.

"You can't just demand teams of horses from the merchants," he complained, "we'll lose too much money if they aren't out hauling fish to market."

Mortimer laughed, "You look like you can afford to lose a few coins every now and then, especially compared to the rags the rest of the village is wearing."

The man started to puff up as if to tell him how important he was and Mortimer simply raised his hand palm out and said, "You will lose a lot more money if the order starts transporting all of its own merchandise and buys directly from the farmers and fisherman, the last time I checked we could easily pay them a lot more for their goods than you are willing to pay."

The man deflated almost immediately, "I will have my two best teams at the carpenters within the hour," he whined.

"How much does a team of horses make for you in a day?" he asked.

"One to two silver, depending on the day," the man answered, looking a bit embarrassed.

Mortimer smiled and dug out a gold coin, "Then this should cover their cost and we can forget we had to have this conversation."

The merchant's eyes grew huge, "You are most gracious my lord," he said as he bowed deeply. If you need anything more from me, just send someone and I'll be here immediately.

Mortimer gave him a nod of his head, "Thank you, you have a prosperous day good merchant."

He knew he had overpaid, but he didn't really care, he still had a lot of money left if need be and he knew this village was going to begin to prosper once a proper outpost was built for the order.

Mortimer laughed as the women practiced their magic, Clarice was already quite talented for being untrained, and Scarlet was a fast study, water wasn't easy for her, but she was getting the hang of the simpler spells.

Soon they could hear the noise of people working outside, and stopped their lessons for the day to go out and watch the work being done. Even the old witch smiled as the first walls were put in place and bolted together, "I never imagined anyone would build a house around my own," she said in awe of the idea.

The carpenter smiled at her, "Ma'am when we are done, you will have the nicest house in the village. I even found a way to keep your old house in place so you wouldn't feel out of place."

The old witch gave the carpenter a hug, "Thank you, here I thought you all were just trying to get rid of me."

One older gentleman laughed, "No beautiful, ever since Tim died we've all been trying to help you, we know you miss him, but we sure as heck didn't like seeing you suffer because he wasn't around to take care of the place."

She couldn't help it but to cry, "Oh and here I have been a cranky old witch all this time." She smiled to the carpenter, "You go ahead and do whatever you need to do, I'm going to go visit with Tim and then I believe we'll have dinner at the tavern tonight,"

At this all of the workers cheered, it was the first time in ten years they had seen her smile.

Mortimer watched as she headed down the path towards what he presumed was a cemetery, "I think I'll just help out around here," he said, "I've had my fill of the dead for a little while."

Scarlet and Clarice laughed, "We'll stay and help too."

The carpenter smiled, "Don't worry, even the bandits in these parts don't mess with that old witch. You three see much battle? I only ask because you all carry your weapons like professionals." He eyed Scarlet and continued, "As pretty as you are I would not want to run into you in a dark alley."

"You could say that," Scarlet answered, she leaned in closer to the head carpenter and whispered, "My husband has killed more enemies than you have villagers, and who knows how many I have killed in the past couple of months. Our mistress, though, is a real hero, she has healed some pretty terrible wounds for us and keeps us always at our best."

The carpenter looked at her and realized she was telling the truth, "My lady, you terrify me."

She laughed, "What can we do to help with the construction?" she asked.

"Well, I could use an extra set of eyes around the back to make sure the joints are flush," he answered, "Other than that, help with the ropes would always be appreciated."

"Great," she replied, "Clarice, can you go around back and make certain the joints are all flush with each other? Mortimer, you're on rope duty, myself I'll be assisting with removal of the old wood around the front door and ceiling." She said as blue mage flames crackled along her hands.

As the sun began to set, the villagers stopped and admired their work. "We got a lot farther than I expected today," the carpenter said with a smile. "Tomorrow we can put on the finishing touches and she'll be able to move her furniture into the new spaces whenever she likes."

The entire work crew quickly cleaned up the debris around the house, and headed towards the tavern for a drink before they headed home to their families.

# Tara

Mortimer, Scarlet and Clarice all headed to the tavern as well, after all the witch had said she planned to eat dinner there tonight. They were surprised at how crowded it was, "Good luck finding a seat," Clarice said with a slight chuckle.

"Over there," Mortimer said as he scanned the room.

Sure enough the witch had staked a claim on a table in one corner of the common room and waved them over. "I thought it best if I got here early and saved all of you some seats," she said as they approached.

"Is it always this crowded?" Mortimer asked.

"Not really," she answered, "but when there is a big project going on it tends to get very crowded for a few hours after the work is done."
A barmaid came over to the table and asked, "Are you just having a drink or would you like dinner too?"

Scarlet and Clarice eyed the barmaid wearily, they both felt she was showing a bit too much bosom for their liking.

The witch smirked, "We will be having four bowls of clam chowder, provided the cook still knows how to make it, and bring us a bottle of the chardonnay you keep in the cellar deer, the one with the thickest layer of dust if you don't mind."

The barmaid looked at Mortimer as if to confirm, and he ignored her.

Scarlet caught the slight nod from the witch and said, "If you wish to spend the night with my husband just say so otherwise I expect you to get a move on."

Clarice laughed as the barmaid blushed, and said, "She doesn't know how much fun such a night can be."

The witch burst out laughing, which in turn caused several nearby people to turn and stare at them for a moment. "Oh, you three are so much fun," she exclaimed.

Scarlet laughed and said, "I wasn't joking."

"Neither was I," Clarice replied, "I really enjoy my nights with you two, I'm not looking forward to it coming to an end."

Mortimer laughed, "I would have thought after traveling with us this long you would be ready to leave and head home."

The witch laughed, "Oh to be young again, I would run off and adventure with you three if I was but a bit younger. It has been a long time since this village has seen good honest travelers."

"That will change when I get home," he replied, "I am thinking it would be good if the order were to send a unit of young knights out this way to keep the bandits at bay."

"That won't make you very many friends amongst the men in this town," the witch said, "we have always had a shortage of young women. Apparently the pirates feel we are easy prey, they steal young girls, and I am not strong enough to hold them at bay anymore."

Scarlet smiled, "When do you expect the pirates to return?"

"Any day now," a nearby villager answered, "they didn't arrive last month, so I am pretty sure they'll be here soon."

Mortimer thought for a moment before he turned to the witch and asked, "Do pirates usually explode in shards of frozen blood?"

Clarice burst into laughter, "you don't think those men we killed were them do you?"

Scarlet chuckled, "If so it may be a while before another pirate ship comes here, I made sure none of them escaped."

Mortimer laughed, "Well the man I killed had mentioned how you two were easy prey with my injuries and all."

Clarice's eyes suddenly turned ice blue, "I am still upset with both you and them for re-opening your wounds."

Scarlet put a hand on Clarice's wrist, "calm down deer, we punished the men, and Mortimer survived, that is the important thing."

The nearby villagers all looked impressed at hearing their conversation, one of them approached and said, "If you did indeed defeat one ship of pirates that would slow them down, but they will still return."

The witch looked at Clarice and said, "If they return while she's here I would feel very sorry for them."

The barmaid soon returned with their wine and bowls of chowder.

Scarlet flipped her a copper coin and watched as it landed perfectly on her chest, "If you stay put your tip may get larger," she said with a grin.

Mortimer shrugged, he wasn't sure what game she was getting at, but he knew what she wanted.  With a flick of the hand he tossed a copper at the barmaid and watched it land right next to the first, "Your turn door," ho said with a smile.

The barmaid froze, not sure what was going on, Scarlet smiled and pulled a copper coin, "The rules are simple, you get to keep whatever lands on your bosom, but when a coin misses or lands on the floor the game is over."

The barmaid glanced around before she said, "Yes ma'am."

After Scarlet's coin landed next to the other two, Mortimer pulled a coin out and as he tossed it said, "Remember you can walk away at any time."

Soon enough they ran out of copper and started on silver coins, at which point the barmaid went to her knees and said, "My lord and lady you have already given me enough to buy me from my master, I must beg you please do not humiliate me any more than necessary."

Scarlet dropped the coin in her hand, "Buy you?" she asked.

Clarice grabbed a nearby chair and pointed to it, "Please sit down," she said softly.

As the barmaid sat down, Mortimer scooped the coins from her breasts and put them in a pouch. He was a bit surprised she didn't even flinch at his touch, as he took her hand and put the pouch in it.

"Please explain," he said to the barmaid, he noticed everyone at the table had a dark look in their eyes.

The barmaid shrugged, and her breasts moved rather impressively, "I have been a slave ever since childhood," she explained. "The pirates come and take the young girls from the village, and then after they train them for a while they sell them to another village. The local merchant purchased me and assigned me to work at the bar until I made enough to pay him back. He informed me that because we didn't have slavery laws, there was no way I could ever get my freedom except to work it off." She looked at the pouch of coins and frowned, "This is enough to pay off my master, but now how am I going to pay off you folks." She began to cry softly, and handed back the pouch, "I can't take this as there is no way I can ever repay you."

This time it was Mortimer who had to be calmed down, his eyes had turned coal black and the shadows throughout the bar were starting to move rapidly around the room. A quick glance around told Clarice the villagers had cleared out of the tavern already. She leaned across the table and kissed him deeply, at the same time she grabbed Scarlet's face and pulled her in for a kiss.

The shadows subsided, and the barmaid sat there in complete silence, while the three of them stared at each other, "If you don't calm down Mortimer, there won't be a living soul in this village," Clarice whispered, she turned to Scarlet and pulled her in for a kiss and afterwards said, "That goes for you too." She looked at the barmaid and said, "You will take that pouch and pay off your master, if you believe you need to repay us, we will come up with something for you to do."

The barmaid nodded her understanding, a slight look of fear in her eyes as she scooped up the pouch and stood to leave.

"I really do want her," Scarlet started as she watched her walk away.

"I know," Mortimer answered, "but she is correct the only slavery laws we have is regarding debt, and she has to pay off that debt or technically she will always be a slave."
The witch frowned, "You are referring to the servitude law which states if a person is unable to pay their debt then they must work as a servant for the one they owe until said debt is paid in full."

Mortimer nodded his head, "Yes."

She laughed gently, "Better you than her current master, at least you won't use her body and cast her aside when you get bored with her, as he has done with so many other girls." She spat on the floor, "all of the villagers wives were his slaves at one point, and when he got bored of them he sold them to the villagers. They're good people, don't get me wrong, but it is the only way for them to get a wife. It's actually funny to watch because they will all flirt with the girl until she shows an interest in one of them, and if she ever says she wants to marry one of the men, they will all pool their money to buy her for that man. So even though they technically are property of their husbands, they were able to choose who bought them."

"So they gave the husband the money to buy his wife," Mortimer asked.

"Correct," she answered, "now finish your dinner before it gets cold, your new servant will be back soon."

Sure enough, just as they finished eating, the merchant appeared with the barmaid, "She's all yours," he said as he threw a piece of paper on the table. "A bit of warning though, don't try to bed her, or she'll try to rip you to pieces."

The barmaid chuckled, "Not them, I only did that because it was you," she said and spit in his face.

The merchant raised a hand as if to slap her and Mortimer said, "If you damage my property I will have to file a grievance with the council, and you really can't afford to pay me the price I would charge."

The merchant scowled and stalked off, he knew when he was beaten.

The barmaid looked at them and bowed, "What do my masters wish me to do?"

"Certainly not bow like that," Scarlet said, "we weren't joking earlier when we mentioned we wanted you to join us at night, but we also did not mean it like that."

Mortimer laughed, "She is correct, I was thinking we needed someone who could keep an eye out while we slept." He looked at the contract the merchant had thrown on the table and winced, "This will take a lifetime to pay off, it appears every month your debt was growing," he shook his head slowly, "well, I guess we now have a nanny."

Scarlet laughed, "The baby will come along soon enough." she looked at the barmaid and asked, "What should we call you?"

The barmaid looked thoughtful for a minute, "It's been so long since someone has asked me my name I all but forgot it, my parents named me Tara."

Clarice smiled at her, "What's up with the fancy shackles on your legs?"

"They are to prevent me from running away," she answered, still bowing to Mortimer.

Mortimer frowned, "Sit down and let me take a look at them," he said. "I am not at all worried about you running away."

Tara sat down in a nearby chair and lifted her skirt so he could get a look at the shackle.

"That looks painful," Clarice said.

Tara shrugged, "It can be, if I try to run."

Mortimer pulled her leg up into his lap and frowned, "You have very powerful legs, but these aren't just normal shackles. Do all of the slaves the pirates sell come with these type of shackles?"

"Yes master," Tara answered, "but it varies as to where the shackle is worn." She was blushing slightly and trying not to let him notice his touch had left her entire leg tingling.

Scarlet knelt down next to Tara's leg and gently lay a hand on her thigh as she too looked at this strange shackle, which ran from the ankle, around the calf, over the knee to the thigh. "You are correct love, she does have powerful legs, and really nice skin," she said as she slid her hand from Tara's leg. "I don't like the feel of those shackles, can you remove them?"

Tare laughed, "They are impossible to remove, unless you have the key."

Mortimer frowned, "the bastard didn't give us the key, but there is a way to remove them without a key."

"Are you sure, love?" Scarlet asked, "We don't want to frighten the poor girl to death."

"Yes," he answered, "but it is best if we do it in someplace that isn't so public." He looked at the tavern keep and said, "Tara and I require the use of your cellar," the look in his eyes was enough for the tavern keep to simply bow and lead them behind the bar.

Once behind the closed door Mortimer smiled, "This is perfect, very little light and lots of shadows." He placed one hand on her shoulder and said calmly, "You will either need to hike up your skirt all the way, or remove it all together. I need to be able to focus on both shackles at the same time."

Nervously she hiked up her skirts, unsure if he was going to be a better master than her last one or not. At the same time she wondered what kind of woman would let her husband wander off alone with a strange woman.

Mortimer chuckled to himself, he hadn't tried this spell with metal before, but he knew it worked well on cloth. He inspected the shackles closely and realized they were linked together up around her waist, "interesting design," he said to himself. "It's a good thing the merchant doesn't have any skill with magic." He looked up at Tara's frightened eyes and said, "I'm sorry you'll have to disrobe in order to remove the chains."

"Please master," she started to say.

"I promise I won't do anything to abuse you," he cut her off, "If I wanted to do so, these chains would have made it easy." He spread his fingers as he stared at the chains, and she felt her feet slide apart on the floor. He clapped his hands together and suddenly she found her legs locked together and the chains hooked into each other. "Now please," he said gently, "remove your skirts and any other clothing that covers the chains. I have to find the first and last link in order for this to work."

Tara did as he requested, completely ashamed of herself, "Please master, do not punish me for not obeying faster."

Mortimer ignored her, he was completely wrapped up in tracing the chains, it was quite an intricate little spell, but it was still breakable. He gathered the shadows around him, and traced the chains slowly sending little tendrils between each link testing the strength of each one until he found the one he was looking for. "Naturally," he grumbled under his breath, "they would have to put it in a place you couldn't get to easily. Well, nothing to do now, but break the chain." He looked her in the eyes, "This will be painful, so please forgive me." With that said he wrenched the chains apart, and she screamed as little silver hooks ripped out of her flesh.

It took a good ten minutes to untangle the chain from her flesh, and she was bleeding heavily in lines along her legs, waist, parts of her breasts and arms. She lay on the floor sobbing, as he bound the chain in a shadow ball, wishing Scarlet was in the room to melt it down.

Soon the door opened and Scarlet poked her head in, "You alright?" she asked.

"I need you, to destroy this chain," he said, "and I need Clarice to tend to her wounds," he finished as he lit a nearby lantern.

"Yes deer," she replied as she and Clarice came into the room. "Oh and deer, the witch suggested we should get a room here tonight, a strange crowd has suddenly arrived and she called them the night fishers."

Mortimer sighed deeply, "Very well, I shall have a talk with the tavern keeper." He headed out the doorway of the cellar, and got the man's attention, "Do you by chance have any spare rooms we might rent for the night?"

The tavern keep smiled at him, "The old witch suggested I have a room readied for you and your traveling companions, I suggested two rooms and she said one room with two beds would be fine."

"That will be perfect," Mortimer replied, and put his hand out for the key.

The tavern keep was a little surprised that he didn't ask the price, but shrugged and gave him the key to the room, "Up the stairs last room on the left, it has a window overlooking the harbor," he dropped his voice so others wouldn't hear, "If need be you can slip out the window and lower yourselves to the ground should trouble arise." He glanced at the new patrons entering the tavern and back at Mortimer.

"I appreciate your kindness," he said as he slipped a gold coin into the tavern keep's hand. "My wife and our entourage will head up there shortly."

When he returned to the cellar, Scarlet and Clarice had assisted Tara in getting dressed, "Did you have to be so rough with her?" Scarlet asked.

"I've stopped the bleeding," Clarice said, "but she could really do with a good night's sleep. Those cuts are definitely going to leave scars."

Mortimer frowned, "I wish I could have been more gentle in removing the bonds, but whoever crafted that chain intended that anyone bound in it be bound for life." He picked Tara up in his arms, "Come let's take her to our room and get her in bed, Clarice you can further tend to her injuries if need be. I am going to do a little snooping before I go to sleep myself."

He carried Tara up to the room and set her on one of the beds, he turned to Scarlet and Clarice, "I have a feeling the night fishers are not a group to be trusted, I will return shortly with some food and drink."

As he left he heard Scarlet tell Clarice, "I think that's the closest he has come to actually giving me an order."

# An unsavory lot

Sure enough, once he returned to the common room, he noticed a difference in the way the guests were behaving, they barely touched their drinks and they kept their voices low.  It was obvious these folk were up to no good, he approached the bar and in a loud voice said, "Barkeep a couple more bottles of wine if you please."

Sure enough he could feel everyone in the room listening to him now, "be sure it's the good stuff, as it wouldn't due to present my daughters without a decent bottle to offer the host."

"What are you presenting them for, may I ask?" a nearby man asked.

"You mean you haven't heard? A young noble is seeking a beautiful bride, and is offering a handsome reward to the father of the bride he picks," he said enthusiastically.  "Now, my girls have turned the heads of many low ranking nobles, but this is a high rank one, and so his reward will also include titles and land.  Every eligible woman in the country will be there."

"I take it then you are leaving in the morning, good sir," the man asked.

"Oh no, we'll be leaving just after noon," he answered, "after the other girls arrive. With the bandits on the road between here and the capital we thought it would be best if we all met here tomorrow morning and after a good lunch we would all travel together."  He winked at the man slyly, "it'll give my daughters a chance to scope out the competition if you know what I mean."

The man offered him a drink and said, "Well, good luck to you sir, what time did you say they would be arriving here again?  I would love to see that many beauties in one place at one time."

"Two hours after dawn," Mortimer slurred slightly, and took the two bottles of wine from the bartender.  "I'll see you in the morning good fellow," he said to the man as he staggered up the stairs.

He walked in the room and found a crimson dagger pointed at him, "How dare you use us as bait?" Scarlet asked, "Especially without asking me first," she finished as she put away the dagger.

Mortimer rolled his eyes, "I already knew you would be up for it, but I should have asked Clarice first."

Clarice laughed musically, "I am used to being used as bait, it's kind of our nature after all."

He hugged and kissed both of them, "Thank you for understanding."

Tara pushed herself upright slightly and said, "For the first time in my life I feel like chopped liver."

Scarlet looked over at Clarice and grinned as she lifted one of Tara's arms and licked her wound, "Good news you don't taste like it," she said with an evil grin.

Clarice grabbed her other arm and licked a wound as well, "Nope, not chopped liver, but very earthy tasting wouldn't you agree Scarlet?"

"Most definitely," she licked her lips, "very tasty blood too if I might add." She looked at Mortimer, "Come on you know you're craving it, the fact you didn't take any of her blood earlier surprised me, but you need to replenish your strength you know."

"She did not give me permission to partake of her flesh, so it would be rude of me to do so," he replied, "It's not nice to tease me like this either, besides if I was worried about my energy I would simply kill someone."

Tara's eyes grew huge at this, "Master you should not weaken yourself on my behalf, if you need my flesh to regain your strength then please take all that you need of it."

He noticed the women had left him only one place to sit and be eye level with her, so he knelt down on the end of the bed and put one hand on either side of her so he could easily look her in the eyes. "First don't call me master, just call me Mortimer." He paused as the girls pulled down the sheet exposing more of her wounds, "Second I don't wish to force you to do anything you don't want to do."

He was silenced when she ripped her arms out of the two women's hands, wrapped them around his head and pressed it between her breasts, "This heart is still beating freely because of you, take from it whatever you need to make yourself strong enough for tomorrow's battle." she said.

Mortimer had no choice, his mouth was next to a wound along the bottom of her breast, and the blood called to him. The girls were correct, there was a strange earthly taste to her blood, almost as if he had licked it directly from his blade. "Damn the needs of blood magic," he said as he sucked at the wound. He knew it was intoxicating, and could be very corrupting, especially when taken without permission.

In the morning the room had been rearranged and somehow both beds moved together and their feet encased in stone. Tara's wounds were healed, and her muscles were even more well defined than the day before.

Mortimer smiled at her and said, "Welcome to the family, but I think we discovered why they used magical bonds on you." He stretched his arms and arched his back, as he got out of bed, "well, I suppose it's time to get ready for a little fun, I have never felt this energized before."

Clarice laughed, "I would think not, hers isn't the only blood you drank last night," she rubbed gingerly at her chest as she got out of bed as well.

Scarlet grinned from ear to ear, "But it was so much fun and felt so good," she too had a few deep scratches on her shoulders and torso. "Remind me to never let you deplete yourself that much again deer, you easily could have bled us all dry last night."

Mortimer frowned, he had memories of losing control the night before, but he had been hoping it was only a bad dream. "Sorry," he replied, "I should never have lost control like that. Ever since the battlefield I am finding myself losing control more and more easily, and when you offered her to me and she agreed to the offering well, you know I feel the emotions of the blood and spirits I interact with."

Scarlet laughed, "that's why I stepped in to stop you last night, she was eager to give her life for you," she looked over at Tara.

Clarice smiled, "and when I saw Scarlet having so much fun I wanted to join in and did so, which triggered an even more intense reaction due to our current magical entanglement."

Tara laughed, "I realized I had started something and should finish it, it took all my strength to pull you off of them, and when you sank your teeth into me again, I focused on how much I wanted to please you and your ladies." She smiled at him, "It was strange how you settled down, it was the best night of my life honestly."

They all got dressed, and headed downstairs for breakfast, the old witch was there waiting for them and her jaw dropped immediately upon seeing them, "You just can't resist, can you young man," she said. She looked at Tara and smiled, "I see he freed you in more than one sense of the word. I brought you some traveling clothes more appropriate to your new status in life."

Tara looked at her, "You knew?" she asked.

"I had my suspicions when I saw the chains," she answered, "Now hurry up and get dressed, sails have already been sighted heading this way."

Mortimer chuckled, "I guess my suspicions panned out and they took the bait."

"As you may have noticed," the witch said, "the menfolk in this town are not warriors, and when the waters told me of the pirates approaching, I had to do something. I am prepared to sacrifice my life for the villagers, but when I saw you, I couldn't help but try and find a way to keep you here until their arrival." She looked at Mortimer and continued, "I don't know what you said to them last night, but they are arriving a day early now."

He laughed, "A drunken old man talking about dozens of beautiful young women all leaving town at noon today, must have really hit home with them."

"You're not old," she said, as he waved a hand in front of his face and his eyes developed deep shadows and wrinkles appeared on his face. "How did you do that?" she asked.

He moved his hand to the side, and his great great grandfather stepped away from his body, "Meet my great great grandfather," he said with a smirk, "better known as the dark half of the red death."

The witch bowed slightly, before the spirit put his hand on her shoulder, "No, you do not need to bow to me, granddaughter."

She turned to Mortimer once more, "then you are my sister's grandson?"

"Not quite, he's your brothers grandson," the spirit replied.

"But, he died before he got married," she said.

Mortimer laughed, "Well, not before he got the witch who was tending his wounds pregnant," he said. "Your sister took my father in as her own, as is only appropriate, she even married the witch so as to protect her honor."

The witch laughed, "I always wondered how my sister got her wife pregnant." She looked at Scarlet, does this mean you carry the spirit of my grandmother with you?"

111

Scarlet nodded her head, "Yes, I do."

"Oh my, I feel sorry for those pirates," the witch said, "How many pieces of her soul have you gathered?"

"All of them," Scarlet answered, "now how about you get all the villagers to vacate the area between the docks and us, this could get messy."

The witch laughed, "I already sent them up to my house, and told them about the secret room beneath my root cellar. They will be safe there."

Tara came down the stairs at this point and said, "Then I guess we had best eat while we can, I can't let my mas.., I mean Mortimer go into combat on an empty stomach without me can I?"

The spirit faded away with a smile as it said, "She does look tasty doesn't she?"

Tara shook her head, "why does everyone see me as a piece of meat?"

"We don't," Mortimer replied, "but as you found out last night, warlocks get their powers from death, and the two things most closely tied to death are blood and spirits. The more magical energy is consumed from a warlock, the hungrier they become for either type. As for Scarlet, well she is bound to me by a blood bond spell, among many other spells, and as such she feels my desires almost as strongly as her own. Clarice on the other hand is caught in a magical entanglement caused by her magic and my magic clashing while emotionally charged with mine and Scarlet's feelings, as such she herself desires to please us both in whatever manner she can."

"So who's magic did I feel in the room last night?" Tara asked, "It drew me into your relationship, and when it was over this morning all I could think was how much I wanted to do it again."

Clarice giggled slightly, "Sorry that was me, when we got going my pheromones were released and you got caught in them."

Mortimer smiled at her, "And considering tho amount of carth magic cast last niyhl," he stroked her cheek and her knees started to buckle, "I would say you got caught in the entanglement."

Tara grabbed onto him to steady herself, and suddenly pulled her against him. She kissed him deeply and said, "Knowing what I know now, I would gladly do it again."

The old witch laughed, "Oh to be young again, come let's eat before breakfast gets cold."

The five of them sat at a table and waited while the tavern keep brought them all plates of eggs, sea bass and toast for breakfast. He smiled at Tara and said, "I am so happy for you, it is a great pleasure to be serving you for once."

She smiled at the man, "It was never hard working for you, you were always honorable and kind to me."

As he set a plate in front of Mortimer he whispered, "You take good care of her, she's a good woman."

Mortimer smiled back at the man, "I intend to, she owes me nothing and is free to go any time she pleases," he said loud enough for the entire table to hear.

Tara blushed, "I will not leave you Mortimer, I wish to be there to assist you in the raising of your child."

The witch looked around the table, it was almost a complete circle, death magic sat next to fire, which sat next to earth, while water sat across from fire, all that was missing was air. As she looked around the table a second time she saw the Crimson Witch watching her, a strange sad smile on her face as if she knew something the others did not. She nodded to the fire witch in respect, and was surprised when she bowed back to her before disappearing.

They ate breakfast and chatted as if they knew nothing about what was going to happen in the next couple of hours. Shortly before noon, word came that the pirates had entered the harbor and were heading into the village, "Well, I guess we had best meet with our guests down near the docs," Mortimer said cheerfully.

# Pirates

He led the group out of the tavern and down the street towards the docks, sure enough several large sailing vessels were tying off at the ends of the two longest docks. "Tara, would you be so kind as to limit our guests to only one dock please?" Mortimer asked as they got near.

She shrugged nonchalantly, and watched as the beach shrugged with her, "Oops," she said as the sand and rocks were thrown up onto the nearest dock, blocking any passage until it could be dug out.

Scarlet looked at Clarice, "Please assist Tara in preventing any ship from tying up at the other docks."

Clarice smiled a very chilly smile and answered, "It would be my pleasure." With a wave of one hand over the other, a sheet of ice formed on the surface of the water between all of the docks, leaving only the longest one available for mooring.

Mortimer smiled at his wife and said, "You will prevent anyone but me from coming back across this dock," he gave her a quick kiss and whispered, "I love you and I promise I will return."

Scarlet kissed him back, "I love you too, but don't have too much fun."

He laughed to himself, "There's no such thing as too much fun." Half way down the dock, he unbuckled his black sword and set it down on the dock, "You'll come when I call," he whispered to it with a smile.

The pirates weren't entirely stupid, they knew something was up, but figured it was probably the old water witch who lived in the village. They also figured this was the extent of the magic available to her, so they lashed their vessels together and used their own boats to extend the dock.

Mortimer made it about three quarters of the length of the dock, before he came across the first pirate, "I see you didn't get the message," he said cordially to the group of men charging towards him. When they didn't acknowledge his greeting, he simply swept his left arm across his chest and watched as they slammed into a shadowy wall. "Much better," he said as he continued to walk towards them. "As I was saying, it would appear you did not get the message. I will give you one opportunity to turn your ships around and never return, failure to do so will end in the forfeiture of your lives."

The pirates were a bit confused as to why they couldn't get through the shadow, and Mortimer watched them press against it over and over again trying to break through. "I guess they're deaf," he said to himself as he took a deep breath.

"We heard you perfectly clear," one pirate replied, "there is no way that one man can stand against us all."

"Very well," Mortimer answered, as he raised his right arm and said, "You were correct grandfather, we shall have to kill them."

The pirates all burst out laughing as if he had told a bad joke, the laughter died when a smoking black sword severed six heads from their respective bodies as if it was a hot knife through butter.

Mortimer heard footsteps behind him and laughed, "I didn't think any of you would be willing to wait out all the fun my lovelies." He let the shadow wall drop, as a wave of flaming arrows arched overhead. Hundreds of small stones flew past him at the same time that giant shards of ice sprouted up from the sea to impale people.

There was no more laughter from the pirates, as their ships' sails had caught fire and those on the dock lay impaled by a combination of ice shards and rocks. The ship's captains gave the order to cut the mooring lines, only to find the ropes were entombed in thick ice.

"I gave you a chance to flee at the beginning and you laughed," Mortimer called out to the pirates, "now your blood will be an offering to those who have suffered at your hands. As per the edict of the order, your lives are now forfeit as payment for those lives you have taken illegally." He knew his speech would incite the remaining pirates to fight to the last man, but he didn't care, he knew he could get the answers he wanted from them whether they were dead or alive.

The nearest pirates charged at him, and he quickly dispatched them. "Hmph," he grunted, "not a single decent fighter among them." He marched towards the nearest ship and watched as flames spread rapidly on the furthest ship, "Thank you love for driving them towards me," he said with a smile.

Scarlet laughed, "I was only making sure none of their ships got away, be sure to leave some alive for me, my blades are very thirsty."

One of the pirates looked towards Scarlet and saw the crimson blades in her hands, and without a word drove his own sword into his chest, soon other pirates followed his example. It took a couple of hours to clear the pirates completely from the docks, but that was mostly due to having to chase down some of the pirates as they attempted to flee.

Eventually they cleared all of the ships of pirates, and managed to salvage a good portion of the cargo from the ships, before burning them to the waterline and letting them sink.

As they watched the last ship sinking, Mortimer chuckled, "I believe this shall serve as a pretty good warning to any future pirates to stay away." He glanced over at Scarlet and smiled mischievously, "Do you desire what I desire?" he asked with a laugh.

Scarlet returned his grin, "The fires burn long and hot, are you sure you want to play?" she asked in return.

Clarice saw the look in their eyes and laughed, "There is no love but of the sea, and none love deeper than I love thee," she said with an icy cold smile.

Tara stomped her foot on the dock and caused all of them to turn towards her, "lean on me in your time of need, for I shall be the stone which holds you and the earth that protects your back," as she spoke her voice echoed back as if it came from a deep cavern.

As the shadows spun and twisted around them, they glowed for a moment, three different colors danced with the shadows. The blood and dirt and grime from the battle was pulled together and washed into the sea, as the shadows collapsed and Mortimer laughed, "I so want to pillage a village right now," he said with a grin.

Clarice, back to her usual cheerful self laughed, "Come we had best get you something more positive to feed on," she wiggled her hips suggestively, "Maybe a little sea food?"

"I'm pretty sure he's tired of fish," Tara shot at her with a grin, "I bet he could go for some good old fashion flank steak," and she slapped herself on the butt.

Scarlet laughed, "I am quite sure he worked up enough of an appetite for both, but I also know neither of you is spicy enough to satisfy him." She winked at both women, as a tiny wisp of smoke curled up from her hair.

Mortimer laughed and chased all three of them down the dock and through town, until they reached the witch's house, where they all stopped in wonder at what the villagers had done in a day and a half. It used to be a small little hut, but now it was a huge manor house.

"Oh good, you've returned," the old witch said when she saw them. "Come in and join the festivities," she invited, "there will be plenty of time for a proper cleansing after the guests leave."

They quickly calmed themselves down, and followed the old witch into the house, and mingled with the other villagers, all while listening to people who had watched them battle against the pirates tell the story to everyone.

When the sun started to set, the villagers began heading for their homes, "You know," the old witch said, "the pirates will return after you leave."

"They won't be the same ones," Mortimer replied, "and it will take them a while to return."

Scarlet chuckled softly, "especially since we now know who in the village has been contacting them."

"Oh?" the witch asked, "how do you know that?"

Tara chuckled, "That's easy, who keeps getting a new slave every time his current one gets her freedom? It's actually quite obvious when you think about it," she answered.

"But, you can't do anything about it without proof," the old witch replied, "trust me I've tried."

Clarice laughed, "I wouldn't say that, we left a few surprises for the noble merchant, I'm quite certain he'll be willing to confess by morning."

"How can you be so certain?" the witch asked.

Mortimer laughed, "Have you ever spent an entire night without sleep because the dead keep lecturing you about how you caused their death? By morning he will be willing to confess everything in order to get me to send them off to the other side."

The witch laughed, "That is just plain cruel, but I like the idea. How long will they torment him for?"

Scarlet laughed, "Mortimer only opened the door to his victims, and suggested they continue to haunt him until they feel justice has been served."

Tara laughed, "That could be a very long time."

The witch chuckled dryly to herself at the idea of the merchant being haunted by those whom he had wronged, "You should get some rest deers, you have a long day ahead of you tomorrow."

Mortimer grimaced, "It may be longer than you might think, I have a nagging suspicion that tomorrow will find us heading away from home, not towards it."

"The missing girls?" Clarice asked.

Scarlet nodded her head, "I feel the same, I don't like leaving without trying to retrieve them."

Tara smiled, "then I guess we are all in agreement?"

Mortimer nodded, "Yes, tomorrow we will go after the missing girls, after we have a friendly little chat with the local merchant."

The four of them retired for the night in a guest room, and in moments the girls were sound asleep. "You should sleep as well child," the crimson witch said as she manifested before him.

"It's not that easy," he replied, "you know how energized a warlock is after battle, how can I just go to sleep with all that energy built up inside me."

She laughed, genuinely amused, "Why child, why don't you tell me what is truly bothering you? You know I can keep a secret better than anyone."

He smiled at her, "Thank you for letting her sleep, I know you're the one who is absorbing my excess energy so it doesn't keep her awake."

"The men of your family have always cared more about others than themselves," she said with a smile, "it's the reason why I fell in love with your great great grandfather. I often lay awake after a battle, filled with energy which overflowed from him, and too many times he kept his distance when he should have been close to me." She smiled ruefully, "But that is not your problem, your problem is the desire to protect her from what you feel is coming. So what is it you fear is coming?"

"A repeat of history," he answered.

"Then you must be sure it does not repeat itself," she replied, "You must collect the wind and you must properly complete the ritual, and for that to happen the wind must be as devoted to you as these three are." She smiled as she reached down and stroked his hair, "Do not make the same mistake we did, you must complete the ritual, no matter what the outcome."

"Is that for your sake or mine?" he asked her.

"For all of us," she answered as she wrapped him in a ghostly hug.

When Mortimer woke in the morning he found he had fallen asleep sitting up, and he had some bruises as if he had been held a bit too tight on his arms. With a smile and a sense of purpose, he woke the women, "Come ladies, it's time to go look for some fun."

Scarlet looked at him and smiled, "I'm sorry we fell asleep without tending your needs."

He shrugged, "that doesn't matter, we have things to do. First, we'll talk to the merchant, and then we will most likely need a ship and a crew to sail it."

"Are you sure you're alright?" Scarlet asked as she got closer to him and stared into his eyes.

He smiled and took her in his arms, "I am fine, why do you keep asking?"

Clarice chuckled, "Maybe because the last time you said something like that you went crazy with power."

Mortimer laughed and kissed Scarlet so deeply she was left breathless and weak kneed when he released her. "I promise I will make it up to both of you tonight," he glanced at Tara, "if you would like to join us, I'd be happy to include you in that promise."

Tara tried to hold herself back, but couldn't, she suddenly found herself in a tangled mess with the other three, laughed and said, "I would love to be included in your promise."

"Great, then let us get cleaned up and be on our way," he said with a dry chuckle.

# A dead crew

The four of them bid farewell to the old witch, and headed into the village. They didn't have to go far before the merchant found them, he looked terrible, as if he hadn't gotten a wink of sleep the night before. "You have to help me," he said as he ran up to Mortimer, "these spirits won't leave me alone, please do something about them."

Mortimer laughed, "you brought them on yourself," he said. "From what they are saying they will not stop harassing you until justice is served. In other words, I suggest you publicly admit to your crimes and pay the penalties for those crimes, otherwise the dead will never leave you alone."

Tara took great pleasure as she watched the merchant squirm as he thought about his choices, "Don't worry, if I die before you decide, I will be sure to bring you the greatest of misery," she said with a grin.

The merchant looked at her and took a step back, "What happened to you? You've changed."

Mortimer laughed, "We removed her bonds and freed her power, if I were you I'd think about where you might be able to go where the earth can't reach you."

"That's impossible," the merchant replied.

"Then if I were you I would hurry up with writing a confession and submitting it to the merchants court," Scarlet said, "because we are going to go after your pirate friends, and I can guarantee more spirits will be coming to haunt you if we don't see that confession sent off before we leave the village."

The color drained from the merchant's face, as he scrambled back from them and ran towards his home.

The four of them continued towards the docks, "One question," Tara said, "where are we going to get a boat?"

Clarice laughed, "I am certain we can find one in the water, after all if I can fill a ship with water I can just as easily empty it of water."

Mortimer smiled, "Is anyone opposed to a ship salvaged from the sea and crewed by the dead? There are many ships which can be brought to the surface, if you don't mind patching the holes while we travel." He looked at Scarlet, "there are many men and women at the bottom of the harbor very willing to take us across the sea to the pirates stronghold. There are even a few pirates who are willing to guide us in exchange for being sent on to the spirit realm."

Clarice laughed, "There are many spirits in the sea who would give anything to be released from its watery depths, most of them are seeking forgiveness for their crimes in life, or wish to know their loved ones are safe."

"So how do you intend to find the right ship to raise from the sea floor?" Tara asked as they approached the docks.

"Leave that to me," Clarice replied, as she turned towards Mortimer she asked, "Would you mind assisting me with my dress?"

"Sure," he replied with a smile, "you might want a little privacy to change though."

Scarlet laughed, "You can easily provide her with cover, deer."

"You take all the fun out of life sometimes," he teased as he raised his arm and a wall of shadows surrounded them.

Tara watched curiously as Mortimer helped Clarice disrobe, and was quite surprised as she dove into the sea from the dock.

Once Clarice was in the water, Mortimer waved away the shadows, "Find us a good one with a decent kitchen please," he said as her head broke the surface.

"I will," she replied as she turned and dove deep into the water.

Tara stared in shock, "where did she get that tail from?"

Scarlet tried to hold back a laugh, but couldn't, "I forgot you didn't know she is half mermaid," she said laughing. "When she is in the water her legs fuse into a powerful tail. It will take her a while to revert to having legs though when she gets out of the water."

"Why is that?" she asked.

Mortimer smiled, "In order to be completely human she has to completely dry out. I have heard rumors that with enough practice some half-merfolk have learned to change shape whether they are wet or dry."

Scarlet smiled, "That could be interesting."

Tara shook her head, "You two are a very strange couple."

"Oh?" Mortimer asked, "why do you say that?"

"The way you just speak your minds is great," she answered, "but your sense of humor is rather convoluted and hard to follow sometimes. Then again I rather enjoy being with you three, so what does that say about me?" she sighed softly.

Scarlet started to giggle, "It means you belong in our twisted little group."

Mortimer just smiled as he watched her giggle, he rather enjoyed the way her body jiggled when she was laughing or giggling. He watched as Tara started to laugh as well, she didn't jiggle as much, but then again he hadn't seen her truly let down her guard and relax yet.

The three of them sat there for a while, chatting about various things, until a villager let out a yell of surprise. Sure enough, in the distance you could see the tattered sails of an old sailing vessel coming towards the dock.

"I hope it doesn't scare everyone away thinking ghost pirates are now attacking," Scarlet said with a serious expression on her face.

"I hadn't quite thought about that," Mortimer replied with a frown.

Tara suddenly burst out laughing, her shoulders shook, and it took her a moment to compose herself, "I'm sorry, but I was not prepared to hear you say you hadn't thought about how the townspeople would react to a sunken ship coming into the harbor."

Mortimer shrugged, "Even I can forget about things now and then." He smiled at her, as her shoulders still shook, "It's nice to see you let yourself laugh, and I'm happy I could be the cause of your merriment."

Scarlet smiled, "You just like the way she bounced, I honestly didn't think she had it in her considering how tight her muscles are."

Tara looked at her and frowned, "Just because my assets aren't as prominent as yours, doesn't mean they aren't soft."

"Are you jealous?" Scarlet asked. "If so, don't be, you're very beautiful yourself."

Looking flustered, Tara replied, "I'm sorry mistress, I just feel like I am less feminine compared to you sometimes."

Mortimer laughed softly, "I appreciate both of your beauty, but let's prepare to leave once Clarice gets the ship to the dock."

Scarlet smiled as she watched Clarice pulling the ship into the harbor, "Now that is a thing of beauty," she said.

"Which one, the ship or the mermaid pulling it?" Mortimer asked.

"Both," Tara replied, "but then again you already knew that."

As the ship pulled into the dock, Mortimer laughed, "Looks like it's missing a figurehead."

Scarlet laughed, "Are you suggesting we strap Clarice to the bow?"

They both had to dodge, as a small wave of water shot up at them, "You'd like that too much," Clarice replied with a chuckle. "Now hurry up and get on board so we can go find some more girls for you to surround yourself with."

Tara laughed as she jumped across to the ship, "Sounds like she's got you pegged."

Mortimer frowned slightly as he and Scarlet leapt aboard, "You two think so little of me," he said as he burst out laughing.

"That or they know you too well," Scarlet said as she started to look around the ship. I don't see much damage, what caused this ship to sink?"

Clarice laughed as she swam up to the side of the ship, "A storm, the wind and rain caused it to fill with water and it sank. It floated to the surface on it's own once I removed all of the water." She looked at Mortimer, "It's up to you to supply us with a crew, I'd rather not have to pull this thing all the way across the sea."

Mortimer noticed she was breathing slightly heavy, "Why don't we pull you up, and get some rest?" He looked around the ship's deck, ``we shouldn't need a large crew."

"Sounds good to me," she replied as Tara threw her a rope. It didn't take long to pull her up the side of the ship, and soon Clarice was sunning herself on the deck.

Mortimer looked out at the harbor and smiled, there were a lot of spirits just wishing for a chance to redeem themselves. With a sigh, he lifted both hands in front of him and pointed at various misty spirits, "Serve me and move on to the afterlife," he said to them, "fail in your duties to me and be doomed to the sea forever."

Immediately dozens of pirate ghosts manifested on the deck of the ship and knelt down before him, "We are yours to command," they said as one.

"Very well," he replied, "we need to find where all of the kidnapped girls are being kept, can you get us there?"

"Yes," they answered.

One spirit with a nasty scar through its eye raised a hand, "Allow me to steer the vessel and I will get us there within three days."

Mortimer smiled grimly, "Very well, you shall be the captain of our ghostly crew." He looked at the rest of the crew and said, "We should get moving."

The spirit captain smiled a twisted smile and yelled, "You heard him boys, let's get this beauty moving."

The rest of the spirits knew exactly what to do, without a word they dispersed to various parts of the ship and started adjusting ropes and sails.

Mortimer and the girls were surprised at how quickly they got the ship moving and that they appeared to be singing in unison as they worked.

Tara went to the ships wheel and asked the spirit captain, "Why are they singing?"

The captain laughed almost joyfully, "They sing in order to coordinate their movements. This was my crew when I was alive, and this was my ship. We know every inch of her, and since you folks brought her back to life, we are intent on keeping her afloat."

"What are those two doing over there?" she asked him.

"That is my gunner and his mate, they are cleaning and preparing the ships armament in case we have to fight," he answered. "After all, every pirate knows our ship sank, and seeing it come into port may start a fight."

"You are very dedicated to your vessel," Mortimer said as he approached the captain. "I promise you, after we get through this, you will all be sent on to the spirit realm, and this ship will be well cared for."

"While I appreciate that, sir," the captain said, "my crew and I are happy just being able to sail her one more time, and having a mermaid aboard is a good sign for this job." He grinned at Mortimer, "All my life I dreamed of spending a night with a mermaid, and now I actually get to meet one. Do you think she'd be willing to speak with me?"

Tara laughed, "Clarice will probably come up and talk with you once she's dried off."

Mortimer chuckled, "The two of you will have a great time swapping sea stories I'm sure."

Scarlet came up to the helm and smiled, "I got the fire in the stove started so we can have a hot meal tonight, and most of the deck is dry." She winked at him, "I will start working on the inside of the ship next, I would rather not sleep in wet blankets tonight."

Clarice came up behind Scarlet, "Thanks for helping me dry off," she said. "If we have a working stove, then we should catch some fish for dinner tonight."

"Won't the sea water on the fish cause you to change back into a mermaid?" Tara asked.

"Not likely," she answered, "it takes more than just a few drops of water to force the change." She smiled at her, "If you like though I can always fish naked just in case."

Tara blushed, "No, that's alright, I'd rather you not distract the crew too much."

The captain laughed, "You know since we died none of us have had any desires of the flesh, you could say that is one of the benefits of being dead. All of our greed, lust, hunger, and thirst simply vanished once we died, it left behind a huge amount of regret in its place."

Mortimer laughed, "It takes a truly evil person to become an evil spirit, only at the time of their death do they still have those desires, but given a few years those desires cease to exist and the only ones to stick around tend to be regret and remorse."

"You forgot love," Scarlet chimed in, "it is one of the strongest feelings, but not one that many people truly get a chance to experience."

The captain laughed, "Very true, when I first went to sea it was in search of love, and found myself captured by pirates. When given a choice between joining them or dying, you can guess which one I chose." He waved a hand towards the crew, "Most of them are the same, we all had various dreams of adventure on the high seas, but ended up becoming pirates just to survive, and that started a downhill spiral of our morals."

"That's a sad story," Clarice replied with a slight frown.

"Not all pirate stories are sad," the captain replied, "there are a few who grew up in the life, their parents were pirates and so they just sort of expected to become pirates." He shrugged, "To be honest, if I hadn't become a pirate who knows what sort of life I might have led, it's not like there are many options available for boys who don't fit in."

As the women went back to the deck, in order to see about catching dinner, Mortimer asked the captain, "So what do you think of mermaids now that you have met one?"

"Not quite what I expected," the captain answered, "to be honest, I'm kind of disappointed, she's just like any other woman in the world."

"Out of curiosity, why did the pirates in this area turn to enslaving women?" he asked.

"Oh, that's a long story," the captain replied, "Let's just say that at some point several ships got together under a single commander, and realized the best way to control the local villages was to control their access to women. She figured if she provided the wives for the commoners, she could then control the commoners. Without any real army in the area, she was correct and it has been that way for the last hundred years. Her granddaughter runs the fleet now, and is trying to find a way to safely get out of the trade, if you know what I mean."

"Oh, why is that?" Mortimer asked.

"She finds it disgusting," he answered, "it's one of the reasons there are less raids on the local villages, that and the villagers not having as many children as they used to for some reason."

Mortimer laughed, "It could be that the villagers have been sending their daughters to the cities to live, which explains the recent influx of young girls in town." He smiled at the ghost captain, "Either way this information may make our job easier, let me know if anything comes up, I'm going to go assist the gals in catching dinner."

"Aye aye, sir," the captain replied, as he wondered if the tattered sails of the ship would continue to pull them through the water. He had never during his life imagined being on a ship crewed by the dead whose ragged sails billowed in the breeze as if they were whole, and yet here he was captain of just such a ship. "Not a bad afterlife," he said to himself as he watched his living passengers tossing grappling hooks covered in dried meat into the sea.

# Zephyr

The next couple of days passed rather peacefully for them, they spent the days fishing and talking with the ghostly crew. Mortimer found the crew's stories of how they became pirates to be very similar, most of them had gone to sea as fishermen or young kids with dreams of finding buried treasure, only to be attacked by pirates and given a choice between becoming a pirate or dying.

"Sail on the horizon," the lookout called down to them on the third day.

"What colors do they fly?" the captain called back.

After double checking his spyglass, the lookout replied, "Black with a Red harpy, looks like we've run into the pirate queen herself."

Mortimer smiled, "This will be fun, I've never done battle on a ship before. Can you do anything to increase our speed," he asked Clarice.

"I can provide a little more push from the water behind us," she answered, "but be advised it won't be so easy to slow us again."

"Go ahead and do it," he answered. "Scarlet, can you handle firing the cannons, provided the crew loads them?"

Scarlet smiled back at him, "my pleasure. Tara, can you assist the crew with the heavy lifting?"

Tara laughed, "I was wondering what I was going to be doing during a battle since there is no earth nearby."

"Just remember, we keep our abilities secret until we are in close range," Mortimer said as he headed for the bow, "no sense tipping them off that we have magic on our side."

"She's hoisted sails and is heading straight towards us," the lookout called down.

In less than an hour they could all make out the outline of a ship heading in their direction. An hour after that they were close enough to see the crew on the decks, and in the rigging.

"Expect no quarter," the captain called out, "prepare to engage."

The crew laughed cruelly as they moved about the rigging and dropped to the decks to load the cannons

"She's a bigger vessel, but we're faster," Mortimer said as he turned to Clarice he continued, "give us a burst of speed and then let the sea rest."

"As you wish," Clarice replied as she sent her energy out to the water asking for it to assist them.

A huge swell came up behind the ship, and propelled it towards the larger vessel, before it sank back into the calm water. They shot forward like a cannonball, aimed at a spot shortly in front of the other vessel. As they passed the other ship's bow, Scarlet dropped her arm and all of the port side cannons fired into the hull of the ship.

The captain turned them hard to port after the cannons fired and they pulled alongside the pirate queens ship. Mortimer saluted the captain and leapt across the three feet of water separating the two ships and pulled himself onto the railing of the larger vessel.

He dropped to the deck and rolled, as several pirates with axes and knives charged towards him. As he regained his feet, he laughed and drew two short curved swords he had found on his ship from their scabbards. "Since you asked for no quarter, none shall be given," he said as he deflected a hand ax and with a twist sliced through a pirate's neck.

Mortimer loved it, they were trying to surround him, and at the same time they were being distracted from their duties and hadn't noticed his ship had come around and was in the process of grappling them from the other side. "Oh what a beautiful day it is," he said as he killed another pirate. "One of you is bound to get a hit on me," he said as he deflected a thrown ax, and in return sliced open a man's arm, "only then will you get to see how dangerous I truly am."

Out of the corner of his eye he watched as the ghost crew leapt between the ships and deftly slit the throat of nearby pirates. One ghost actually laughed, as a pirate swung a dagger through his neck just before the ghost gutted him, "I guess there's an advantage to being dead," the crewman said with a smile.

A woman's voice rang out over the noise of battle, "You fools, they swung around behind us and boarded from the other side, he's just a distraction," she yelled as she pointed at Mortimer.

Mortimer looked up at the woman and smiled, "Now you look like my kind of distraction," he said as he took in her black and red leather armor. The wind blew her blue/blonde hair back from her face, and her eyes were steely gray like a storm cloud.

With a growl, the woman leapt from the upper deck and landed before Mortimer, "I'll deal with this one, go push back the others."

He couldn't help but smile at her, "Mind if I ask, but what do you use to get that bluish tint to your hair?" He kept one eye on the cutlass she carried, but bowed slightly to her as he continued, "If you'd rather not say, then I may have to take some of it with me as a souvenir."

She stepped back a half step and looked at him as if not sure whether or not he was mocking her, "If you can beat me in combat I will tell you anything you wish to know," she answered.

Mortimer shrugged, "Very well, then I guess I better stop playing with these toys and take this seriously." He dropped the two short swords, and raised his right hand, with a whistle his black blade flew from the bow of his ship where he had left it and spun through the air, cutting ropes and sails as it flew into his hand. "Come dance with me," he sang as he stepped sideways.

The pirate queen was no coward, but she was smart enough to recognize a spirit sword when she saw one. With a slight movement of her right foot, she launched herself into the air and attacked him. If she could maintain the higher ground she should be able to beat him.

He continued to smile, as he dodge and blocked her attacks, "Aeromancy, very nice," he said as he deftly avoided another one of her attacks. "You realize this only gives you the advantage of height, but against my power that isn't really an advantage?" He waved a hand, and the shadow of a nearby rope lashed out and wrapped around her ankle.

He watched as she slashed at the shadow to no avail, before another one lashed out and wrapped around her sword arm.

Scarlet saw what was going on from the other side of the ship and yelled, "She is the only one we need alive." In her moment of distraction, a small knife managed to cut her, before a ghostly crewman killed her attacker.

"Sorry mistress," the crewman said, "I didn't think that one was still alive."

Mortimer saw the strike, and his eyes flashed from the dark blue they had been to a deep black, "This ends now," he hissed as he swung his left arm upwards in a circle. The shadows everywhere on the deck of the ship leapt upwards and wrapped themselves around the pirate queen. He could feel her fighting against his magic with her own and chuckled, with the amount of death that clung to this ship, he could hold her in there for the rest of his life.

Putting her behind him, he clutched his sword tightly and went to join his wife's side. Every pirate that came within reach of his blade fell to the deck, the power emanating from the blade prevented any weapon from reaching Mortimer. Once at Scarlet's side, he simply raised an eyebrow in question.

Scarlet laughed, "What, you aren't the only one allowed to get injured on occasion." She waved one hand lazily in front of her, and a line of fire appeared on the ships deck between them and the pirates. With a smile she turned and kissed him, "You know, I kind of like the taste of blood on you." She looked back at the pirates, now backing towards the center of the ship, "So should we slaughter the rest of them, or just restrain them until we can talk to their captain?"

Mortimer laughed and his eyes reverted to their normal blue, "I suppose that depends on them," he answered. "If they surrender then they may live, but if they don't drop their weapons, kill them all."

There was a great rush of noise as the remaining pirates dropped their weapons to the deck and held their now empty hands out before them.

The two of them wandered over to where the pirate queen still struggled, as the ghostly crew cheerfully bound the wrists and ankles of the pirates. "How long do you intend to make her suffer in there?" Scarlet asked him.

"Until she stops struggling," Mortimer answered.

"You do know how terrifying it is to be encased in shadows, correct?"

"Of course I do," he answered, "but I am not the one powering this spell, it is being powered by all those who have died on this ship and at her orders. Once she stops struggling, I will gladly exert myself to settle them down. There are a lot of very angry spirits on this vessel, I let them loose on her with one condition, they were not to harm her, only to contain her."

Scarlet watched the shadowy cocoon as it writhed around the pirate queen, "What is up with those little flashes of color which keep appearing now and then?"

Mortimer snorted, "I think we'll need a blanket when this is over, it appears they are destroying her armor, and I highly doubt she is wearing much beneath it."

"Why would they do that?" she asked.

"To embarrass her most likely," he replied, "or they are checking her for any more hidden weapons." he pointed to several fancy knives and daggers lying in a pile nearby. "Oh look, she has stopped struggling," he said as the shadowy mess slowed its movements. "I believe we'll move her to her cabin before we release the shadows," he smiled at Scarlet, "you coming?"

"Of course I am, do you think for a moment I would trust you alone with her?" she said with a smirk.

He laughed, as he led the way into the captain's cabin, situated next to the stairs leading to the upper deck. The shadowy mass followed directly behind him, and Scarlet followed behind it. They both were surprised to find very little extravagance in the cabin, it had a simple hammock in one corner, a table and chair in the middle of the room, and a single bookshelf along one wall.

Once the door was closed Mortimer waved away the shadows, to reveal the pirate queen, stripped completely naked kneeling on the floor, looking like nothing more than a scared young woman.

Scarlet grabbed a simple blanket off the hammock and threw it around the pirate queen's shoulders, "Are you all right," she asked her.

She nodded her head, but couldn't hide the tears she was holding back.

"We're alone," Mortimer said gently, "it's alright if you cry."

She relaxed, and a few tears ran down her face, "I've never been so terrified in my life. The shadows wanted to kill me, but others kept saying you would destroy them if they did. I wasn't sure if they would kill me or not, and the things they were saying they could do once I was dead, is it true?"

"Some of it," he answered, "I told them they would be allowed to punish you provided they did not physically hurt you. As for what they could do to you if you died, yes they could have taken revenge upon you, but they would have doomed themselves for all eternity in doing so. Those were only the spirits who refused to leave this world when they died, most spirits move on after they die and only watch us from the afterlife."

"Then I owe you my life," she replied.

"Not really," he answered, "your life was only in danger because I lost my temper. If my wife hadn't been injured I never would have summoned that many spirits that rapidly and with such open directions."

Gently, he reached down and lifted her chin up, "You know it's difficult to have a conversation when you can't look into the eyes of the one you're talking to."

"It is irrelevant," she answered, "you defeated me, and as such I and my ship are now yours to do with as you please."

Scarlet raised an eyebrow, "We do not require a slave, we require an ally."

The pirate queen laughed, "It is too late," she raised an arm and they could both clearly see a blue ribbon wrapped around it which traveled up towards her shoulder. "As you can see, I was bound at birth to be the pirate queen and as such I was required to maintain my post until defeated. Now I am a servant to the person who has defeated me, just as I was a servant to my predecessor," she stood and dropped the blanket, so they could see how the ribbon wove its way around her body. It was similar to the binding Tara had, but a ribbon instead of metal.

Mortimer frowned and turned to Scarlet, "Go get Clarice and Tara. I want the ship anchored for the remainder of the day, and the captain to patrol around us making sure we are not disturbed. This is going to be painful for her, and I want as much backup as necessary in case her crew tries to rescue her."

He looked at the pirate queen, "Lie down please, so I might examine your bindings. Also what should I call you?"

"Whatever you want, master," she replied as she lay down on the floor.

Mortimer laughed, "I meant, what is your name?" He picked up the blanket and draped it back over her before kneeling beside her and taking her hand in his own. "Interesting bonds," he said softly as he picked at the edge of the ribbon with a fingernail.

"Zephyr," she answered, "all of the children are bound in these bonds of servitude, in order to guarantee they will not betray the fleet. It has been this way for three generations."

"Who cast these bindings?" He asked, "Also, are they still alive?"

"My mother," she answered, "and no she is not, or she would still be queen."

"I notice you aren't even trying to ignore my requests, why?" he asked.

"To disobey an order is to endure excruciating pain," she answered, "you have not given me an order yet that would be worth the pain to disobey."

Mortimer raised an eyebrow and out of curiosity asked, "What kind of order would be worth the pain?"

"I have never heard of one," she answered, "I have seen people walk into a fire and burn to death as it is less painful than disobeying an order."

"What if I ordered you to lie still and be quiet as I ripped these bonds from your flesh," he asked, "which pain would be greater?"

"I do not know master," she answered, "but I will do so if that is your wish."

"When the others return," he answered, "there is a side effect to doing so, since you obviously are a witch, it will cause a bit of a mess with both of our magics and you will find yourself pulled into a very confusing magical mess."

"In other words you are saying I will still be bound to you but not as a servant," she replied, "my mother once described it as a partnership between witches."

Mortimer laughed, "you could say that. Tara would be a better person to ask about it, as it was in removing her bonds that I found out about the side effect."

"Mind if I ask, master, but why do you travel with three witches?" she asked.

He laughed, "That's a confusing story, Scarlet is my wife and is bound by a blood bind spell cast during a moment of battle madness, Clarice is a friend and mermaid, who got magically entangled with our bond when she tried to undo the blood bind, Tara is an earth mage, and as I mentioned she got entangled in the magical knot when I removed her bonds. Strangely her body changed when I released her bonds, her muscles got harder and more defined, as if she took on some aspect of the earth itself."

At this point they were interrupted as the three women came into the room, Tara raised an eyebrow and chuckled softly to herself, "Now isn't this a surprise, you yourself have slave bindings."

"I recognize you now," Zephyr replied, "my mother said you were a tough one to bind." She looked at Mortimer, "She took on that form because she is a half earth elemental, and the bindings prevented her from showing her true nature." She looked closely at Scarlet and laughed, "I'm in for a world of hurt, so I'll tell you this now, your wife has the look of a fire elemental, you will eventually need to remove that binding if you don't want your children to inherit it."

Mortimer laughed, "I figured out her fiery nature back when we first danced, as for her bond I will gladly remove it if she wants it removed. Sadly the blood bond cannot be removed without killing her, but it is something my family has had for many generations." He looked at Tara, "How do you feel about the bond between all of us?"

Tara smiled, "At first I was nervous and scared of it, but now I really enjoy it and wouldn't give it up for anything. It is strange feeling your emotions, and knowing the bond grows stronger the more we're around each other, but at the same time it provides a source of energy when at other times we would run out. All in all I would gladly go through all that pain all over again knowing how I feel now." She winked at him, "Thank you for setting me free, and allowing me to join your family."

"Thank you for joining the family and being honest," he replied. "Now the question is does Zephyr here want to join the family and be free, or would she rather remain in these bonds and be a servant?"

Zephyr looked up at him and smiled ironically, "It is up to you master, I will endure the pain if you order it, or if you prefer I will be your willing servant. Although," she said with a chuckle, "no matter how you look at it I will be bound to you for the rest of your life."

"Very well," he replied, as he let his own shadow slip under the ribbon and started to peel it away from her body.

She closed her eyes and grimaced, but refused to scream as she felt as though thousands of needles were being drawn through her body. As he worked she felt the tears leak from her eyes, the pain was almost too much, it now felt as if her flesh was on fire, her bones ached and she thought for sure she was being ripped to pieces. Suddenly the pain was gone, she opened her eyes to see him looking into her own eyes, and then the world went black.

Mortimer sagged from exhaustion, "That was a tough one, so many dark spirits here didn't want the bonds removed and fought hard to keep them in place." He smiled at Scarlet, "remind me not to do something like that again in an area filled with angry spirits." He too collapsed in exhaustion and landed atop Zephyr.

Scarlet laughed gently, "He knew it would be tough, that's why he had them drop anchor and set up a patrol around this ship." She pushed him off Zephyr, and threw the simple blanket over the two of them. "Shall we get the crew whipped into shape while we wait for them to wake up?" she asked the other two.

"Do you think they will side with us?" Tara asked.

Clarice laughed in response, "That is where I come in, they can either join us or swim back to shore."

"Spoken like a true pirate," Scarlet muttered, "let's go see if they're willing to work for us.

The three of them stepped out onto the deck, and were surprised to see several of the pirates had been cut loose and were busy lowering the sails and binding them to the mast. One pirate spotted them and bellowed "Captain on deck!" Immediately all activity ceased and the crew turned to watch them.

"You come here, the rest of you continue with your tasks," Scarlet called out. Immediately the pirate dropped what he was doing and ran to stand before her, as the others went back to their work.

"Your orders ma'am?" the pirate asked as he approached them.

"We were planning on questioning all of you to see who would side with us and who wouldn't," Scarlet explained. "Since you obviously have sided with us, I would like to know who else you believe we can trust to work the ship if we release them."

The pirate smiled, "Honestly ma'am, I wouldn't trust any of us to stand by your side. We are all here in order to stay alive, so if a more powerful enemy were to arrive most of us would switch sides in a heartbeat." He blushed slightly, "Having told you that, let me add, after seeing you in battle we can't imagine a more powerful adversary."

She chuckled softly, "I appreciate your honesty," she replied. She turned to Tara and Clarice and said, "I guess it's a good thing I have you two to watch my back."

Tara smiled back at her, "I'll keep watch here until Mortimer is done, while you two go and talk to the ones who are still tied up."

Scarlet smiled darkly, "Of course, I hope he doesn't have too much fun with her." She led the way towards the crowd of kneeling pirates, Clarice and the one pirate directly behind her.

The group of pirates looked at Scarlet and Clarice half in fear and half in relief as they approached.

Clarice smiled at them, and they visibly relaxed, "Funny, I'm the one who wanted to just throw them all overboard to begin with," she said to Scarlet.

As they visibly tensed up, Scarlet laughed and said, "It's not nice to tease." She looked at the group and smiled, "While it is true when we saw your flag our first thought was to wash the decks clean of the crew and burn the vessel to the waterline, it is not our intent to murder all of you." She watched as they tensed up and then relaxed a little while she spoke. "You can all thank my husband later for convincing us not to just sink this vessel and move on."

Scarlet looked around at the bound pirates and simply asked, "Is there any person here who is not willing to join us in our adventure?" None of them reacted to her question, so she continued, "Those who join us will be rewarded, those who do not will have to find their own way back to shore, as I will not keep anyone aboard whom I cannot trust."

One pirate chuckled, and said, "There is no land nearby, and you wouldn't just throw us out into the sea. Even the pirate queen is not that cruel."

Clarice started to laugh evilly, "We are not as soft as the pirate queen," she said as she waved her hand and a ball of ice appeared in it. "This represents my heart when it comes to pirates," she tossed the ice ball over the rail of the ship. "I don't think there is anyone on this ship who will be able to defrost it regarding any pirate."

Scarlet smiled, "I think this is the first time I have ever seen you this upset dear, maybe you should leave this to me."

Clarice laughed, "why should I let you have all the fun? First you get your husband, and now you get to play with these folks, when do I get to have some fun?"

Scarlet wrapped her arms around Clarice and kissed her on the cheek, "You realize dear that you are married to him too, so you can have fun with him any time you want. I didn't realize you were feeling left out. As for these guys, I would like to have enough of a crew to manage the vessel without having to raise them from the dead."

Clarice leaned into the hug, and gave Scarlet a quick kiss, "I'm sorry, I'm just being emotional, being on the sea does that to my people. Our emotions tend to run hot or cold with the tide. After all, I'll try to be better." She looked at the pirates and blushed, "That's a bit embarrassing to be so emotional in front of such a crowd."

Scarlet smiled at her, "why don't you go for a swim, I can throw anyone overboard who doesn't want to work with us."

One of the kneeling pirates spoke up, "that wouldn't be a good idea ma'am, there are usually sharks in the waters near our ship."

Clarice looked at that pirate, "What is a bad idea? Me going for a swim, or throwing people overboard?"

The pirate blushed, "You're going for a swim, I'd hate to see you eaten by a shark."

"I like him," Clarice said to Scarlet, "he can live." With that she turned and slipped out of her dress as she dove overboard.

Scarlet turned to the kneeling pirate and with a touch burned off the rope around his wrists, "If you would be so kind as to retrieve her clothing and have it ready for her when she is done with her swim."

"You have to get her out of the water," he said as he scrambled for her clothing, "it's not safe."

Clarice's voice came from over the side, "The water is quite nice actually, and as for the sharks, they don't bother me at all."

The pirate looked over the rail and almost ended up falling overboard as he saw the change in her appearance, "She's a mermaid," he gasped as he slumped down next to the railing.

"So," Scarlet said loudly, "who's joining us and who is going for a swim? Those who wish to go for a swim raise your hands above your head." Nobody moved a muscle, "alright then, those who wish to join us raise your hands." Every pirate on the ship raised their bound hands over their heads. "Cut them loose and put them to work," she said to the one pirate still standing behind her.

"Yes, ma'am," he answered as he stepped forward.

Scarlet walked over to the railing and looked down at Clarice, "Sorry hun, nobody wanted to swim to shore. How long do you think you'll be down there?"

"Just a little longer," Clarice called back, "I am going to see about catching some dinner while I'm in the water, do you think we have a large enough kitchen to cook a shark?"

A nearby pirate laughed, "If she can catch a shark, we can cook it, I believe we still have some lemon down in the ship's stores."

"Then you're in charge of dinner," Scarlet called back to Clarice, "and this young man just volunteered to cook it for you." She looked at the pirate still holding Clarice's clothing, "You sir just became her personal assistant, anything she wants you get for her, understood?"

"Yes ma'am," he choked back as several other pirates rushed past in a hurry to show they were busy working.

Scarlet stood back and watched as the crew went to work repairing sails and ropes in the rigging, others worked hard at scrubbing the deck, a couple of them brought instruments up onto the deck and started to play a lively jig.

"We hope you don't mind captain, but since we are not going anywhere for a while we thought we would relax with some music after our work is done," a pirate with a set of pipes said as he walked past her.

Scarlet smiled, "Here I thought you were all a bunch of bloodthirsty brigands, of course I don't mind provided it doesn't get too rowdy."

"Never," he replied with a bow. As soon as he started to play, everyone stopped what they were doing for a few minutes and listened raptly. Once he stopped, they went back to work with a will, even more motivated than before to get the ship into shape.

Clarice arrived on deck amidst a wave of sea water, a grin on her face and a large shark in tow. "He put up a great fight," she said as she wrung the water out of her hair.

Her now assistant, ran up to her with a towel in one hand and her gown draped over the other, "Ma'am," he said as he approached, a slight look of fear in his eyes.

"Thank you," she said as she took the towel and started to dry off. Once her tail was dry, she changed back into a woman and put on her gown, "That was a very refreshing swim," she said. Noticing her assistant blushing, she laughed, "Don't worry I am not concerned about you seeing my body, I'd probably be more offended if you didn't appreciate it."

The pirate's blush deepened, and he looked at his feet nervously, "If I might say, you are absolutely beautiful."

Clarice gently touched his cheek with her hand, "Thank you for saying as much, I promise I won't eat you, after all I already have a man in my life."

The poor man looked like he was going to pass out with relief.

"I have to admit though for pirates, most of these people are pretty nice," she said.

Scarlet laughed, "No surprise really, when you take into account the stories we heard on the other ship, most of them never set out to be pirates."

"True," Clarice replied, as they watched a group of pirates haul the shark down to the galley so it could be cooked. The two of them returned to where Tara stood guard, and informed her of the crew's decision.

Tara laughed, "We were told about the pirate queen's desire to get out of the family business, it's no surprise she would have a fairly decent crew. Should we change the flag, or do we sail under her banner until we complete our mission?"

Clarice's assistant stepped forward and said, "If I might interject, if you fly her grace's banner other pirate ships will avoid interfering with you, but if you change the banner they will most likely attack in retaliation for taking her ship."

Scarlet smiled, "Good advice, I believe we will listen to it. How many officers are still alive?"

"None," he answered, "the man you were with killed them all."

Scarlet laughed, "Mortimer would target the officers first, standard mercenary tactic. Very well, you have just been promoted to second mate, find the man who cut everyone loose and inform him he is now first mate."

"Aye, Captain," the new second mate replied with a bow, before he turned away in pursuit of finding the soon to be first mate.

The three of them spent the next couple of hours wandering amongst the crew and finding out their stories and what they would do if they could escape the pirate life. Almost all of them would be more than happy to settle down to almost any other life than piracy, but it had to be a life where they didn't have to worry about starving to death.

As the sun was setting, Scarlett entered the cabin to see how Mortimer and Zephyr were doing, she was only mildly surprised when his eyes snapped open at the sound of the door closing. "Good evening love," she said softly, "are you enjoying her as much as you do me?"

He sat up, and looked down at the sleeping Zephyr, "No, and you know we didn't do anything." He smiled at her and continued, "Although I can think of a few things I'd like to do to you right now."

"I could say the same to you," she replied, "but right now you should come on deck and meet the crew. I assigned a few new officers to keep everyone in line, but didn't want to step on your toes since you are technically the new captain."

Mortimer laughed, "You know we don't hold well with titles right?"

Scarlet laughed in return, "I know, otherwise you would have chosen one of those other witches to be your wife. Oh and before I forget, according to the crew you are also married to Clarice and Tara, understand?"

"You know that's not a very good joke," he replied with a frown. "It has been known to become real when jokes like that are played."

She smiled, "My dear sweet husband, haven't you figured out that you are only one step away from being married to Zephyr as well?"

Mortimer fell flat on the floor again, "The magical entanglement, coupled with sleeping together. Ugh, I totally forgot about that when we got together with Tara and Clarice." He sat back up and shook his head, "my sister is going to kill me."

Scarlet saw Zephyr's eyes open and a grin appear on her face, "Not if she kills you first." she said to him.

"Least I'm still dressed," he said with a sigh, as he looked down at Zephyr's face. "How are you feeling?"

She grinned darkly at him, "That it is unfair that you get to see me fully exposed and are not willing to return the favor master." As he started to scramble away, she grabbed the front of his shirt and pulled herself onto him, "You will finish what you promised when you ordered me to lay naked on the floor." Her grin softened to a smile, "I will though wait until after you have eaten, I can't have you passing out on me now can I?"

Mortimer shook his head slowly, "She listened better when she was still bound by the slave bonds."

Scarlet laughed, "She is just feeling the residuals of the battle lust, you will need to satisfy that before it drives her mad. I'll explain to the other two, and let me be the first to congratulate you on your fourth witch and the completion of your collection," she said with a sarcastic smile.

He knew she wasn't kidding, and even though he felt the desire, he wanted Scarlet too.

Scarlet felt his emotion, and smiled as she shrugged out of her clothes, "I thought you would never ask my love."

Zephyr looked confused at first, until Scarlet ran a hand down the center of her back.

"Welcome to the family," Scarlet said, as she helped Mortimer remove his armor, "You'll understand completely afterwards."

In the corner, the crimson witch manifested and smiled, "No spell should ever be left unfinished, only love can truly break the bonds of slavery, and apparently this family has an over abundance of love," she said softly as she watched Clarice and Tara slip into the room and join the fun.

The black blade manifested its own spirit and chuckled, "He has completed the circle in a way neither of us thought to, and as much as he cares for each of them, he is really not enjoying himself as much as one might think."

"I know," the scarlet witch replied, "you didn't enjoy it either after your second wife."

"I was satisfied with my first, the second was nice to have when you weren't available, but beyond that I always felt as if I couldn't truly show anyone how I felt about them without creating a problem with the others," he replied, "and I think that is exactly what our great grandson is feeling right now."

The crimson witch laughed, "I always wondered why you spent so much time talking to all of us and less time taking pleasure with me. If I had known I would have simply told them as first wife my pleasures come before theirs." She stuck her tongue out at him, and he smiled, "Anyways, we have another battle ahead of us before she can provide us with a shortcut home."

The black blade spirit smiled, "I know my love, and then I get to spend eternity showing you how much I missed you. I can't wait till I can touch you again."

"Neither can I my love," she replied as they both faded away back to their respective blades.

# Powers

Zephyr was completely worn out when she realized how many people were in the room with her. "Well, that was very interesting," she said with a slight smile.

Scarlet laughed, "I'm sorry, but ever since he removed your bonds, the three of us have been feeling his desire for you. It is a slight side effect of removing that type of magic, unless you are the one who originally cast the spell, it tends to warp and eventually bind both parties together."

"So you knew this was going to happen?" she asked.

"Yes," Tara answered, "we all did, it was something we learned after he removed my bonds."

Clarice chuckled, "my circumstance was different. I tried to remove his blood bond, and instead ended up getting wrapped into it."

Mortimer chuckled dryly, "Basically you are permanently bound to us, my family has a priestess who knows how to break this bond, but that is only if one of us wishes for the bond to be broken when we speak to her." He smiled at her, "it was not what I was planning on doing when I came to your ship, but at the same time I couldn't bear the idea of having a slave."

Scarlet smiled, "she knows deer, she can feel it already, just as I did shortly after the blood bond took effect between us."

He shrugged in response, "I still feel guilty about it all, all I ever wanted was you and now look what happened." He smiled at Zephyr, "As much as I love the feathery look of your hair, my heart will always belong first and foremost with Scarlet."

Zephyr smiled back at him, "Thank you, my lord, and no apologies needed. It is as it should be, she is your first wife and all others must defer to her." She bowed her head to Scarlet, "Mistress you are the same as my master in my eyes."

Scarlet raised an eyebrow, "are you saying that because you wish to, or because you feel you have to?"

She smiled at her, "It is how I feel, you are his first wife and thus none of us can be jealous of his attention towards you. The master/mistress, well that was because I am unsure how to address you two."

Scarlet burst out laughing, "However you wish, by name, or pet name, it's all the same to us. You can call him husband and myself your wife if you're comfortable with that. Might be best actually, considering you are now part of a very complicated family." She smiled to herself, "As far as the crew is concerned Mortimer is married to all of us anyways, so might as well tell them that was the terms of your surrender."

More and more, Mortimer couldn't wait to get home and get this all untangled.

Zephyr's smile broadened, "Very well, then shall we get dressed and join the crew before they eat everything in the ship's stores? Knowing them they already broke out the alcohol and will have drunk all of it before we can get a drink."

Clarice laughed, "Not likely, I specifically ordered no alcohol until after I returned, and that shark I caught was large enough to feed triple the number of men you have on this ship."

Zephyr got up from the floor, and walked over to her bookcase, on the bottom shelf was a green gown, "Well, I guess I'll be wearing formal clothes until we return to port."

Scarlet smiled and put on her leather armor, while Tara and Clarice both put on their gowns, before assisting Mortimer with his battered armor.

Zephyr looked at Mortimer's chest plate and asked, "Were you wearing that when that cut was made?"

He smiled at her, "Yes, it was a pretty nasty wound, but thanks to Clarice I survived it."

"I'm surprised you got hurt considering how powerful your magic is," she replied.

Mortimer laughed, "It was in a duel against a witch hunter, so I was avoiding using my magic. I won't make that mistake again."

Zephyr's eyes got huge, "I heard someone destroyed the witch hunter's power, don't tell me it was you."

Scarlet laughed as he blushed, "It was him," she said.

"Now I feel honored that he would choose me to join your family," Zephyr replied, as she buckled her belt. "These claws are going to become a nuisance, oh well, I guess it's part of the harpy inheritance."

"Oh?" Scarlet asked.

"Yes, as you guessed earlier I have the powers of the wind, but that is mostly due to being part harpy," she answered. "Part of the binding spell is to hide our natural appearance, I am part harpy, an air elemental. Similar to how Clarice is part mermaid, and Tara is part nymph even if she doesn't know it. I am just not sure what you are, if he ever removes the bindings it would be interesting to find out."

"Why don't my bindings show up like yours did?" Scarlet asked.

"You haven't done anything yet to remind you of the bindings," she answered, "or it is entirely possible that your family did not put restrictions on it."

Mortimer laughed, "Or it could be that they are simply inherited bindings, and as such there are no restrictions other than hiding your natural appearance. Eventually though you will become powerful enough that the bindings will appear and then I can remove them if you want."

Zephyr smiled at him, "Well said, my question is who removed your bindings?"

"I never had any," he answered, "my power was realized on the battlefield. I was stabbed, and should have died, but instead my power manifested itself."

"Ah," she said, "then the book is correct, death removes the bindings, or at least anything that would normally result in death. Based on that, if Scarlet were to throw herself into a volcano, her bindings would be released, but because she is part fire elemental it wouldn't kill her."

Scarlet laughed, "How about we not test that theory out."

"Oh, I wasn't suggesting you die," Zephyr said rapidly, "it's just a theory I read in a book about magic. You see the original witches received their powers from their parents, seducing elementals as such only those who are of the proper lineage can become witches."

"And how did warlocks gain their powers?" Mortimer asked out of curiosity.

"The theory is that a group of men offered up their lives to protect their loves, and the spirits in the afterlife took pity on them and gave them the ability to borrow a spirit's energy. The more spirits that are about, the more energy they have to manipulate." She answered, "That's why I find it strange you try to do so much without using your power."

Mortimer laughed, "It's not as easy as it sounds, first of all when we borrow a spirit's energy, we also receive their emotions and if we're not careful those emotions can overpower our own will and do great harm. A good example is the amount of will power I had to exert to keep those spirits from tearing you apart, not just your armor, there are a lot of spirits who want you to suffer greatly on this ship."

"What I don't understand," Zephyr said, "is why they aren't able to affect this world unless a warlock allows them to."

Mortimer laughed, "Because it was my will that summoned them, without it they lose cohesion and can't see clearly into this world. It's kind of like looking at the bottom of the sea from the deck of a ship, everything is fuzzy, but with the right tools you can see it quite clearly."

Clarice laughed, "That sounds like how we see the surface world, from under the water it is blurry, but when you break through the surface it comes into focus."

"Exactly," he replied, "as such when we send them back to the spirit world all they can do is watch until we call them to our world, unless they can muster enough power to break through on their own."

Zephyr nodded in understanding, "That makes sense, will they follow me when I leave this vessel?"

He shrugged, "That I do not know, I do know many of them are quite exhausted now, but they may follow you. It is the curse you bear for being responsible for so many deaths."

The five of them finished adjusting their clothing, and headed out on deck together, the crew was quite surprised to see Zephyr still alive and many came over to see what her new standing was. She simply told them Mortimer was now in charge of the vessel, and she was to be his next wife. They accepted this easily and many of them cheered for the new leader and for her to be happy in her new life.

About an hour into the celebration, a lookout called out that the ghost ship was returning, Mortimer went to the rail and called out to the ship, "What news?"

Instantly a ghost pirate stood next to Mortimer, "Several sails heading this way, the captain wants to know your intentions."

"Well Zephyr, do you think they'll be friend or foe?" he asked.

"Most likely foe," she answered, "the only ships out here would be ones plotting to overthrow me."

Mortimer smiled, "You heard the lady, we will send them to the depths."

The ghost bowed, "Aye sir, we shall do our best."

Clarice laughed, "Remember good spirit, I made your ship unsinkable, and you can fight better in the dark than your enemy can."

"Thank you ma'am," the spirit replied with another bow as it vanished from sight.

"The ghost ship is turning," the look out called down to them.

"Good," Mortimer said softly, "pass the word, I want lights out about the ship and the cannons loaded and ready to fire." He turned to Zephyr, "Take the helm and follow on their port side, I want silence about the decks until we engage. Clarice, you are responsible for our forward movement, I don't want to risk them hearing the sails in the breeze."

"Yes sir," they both said as they headed up to their posts.

Everyone moved silently about the dark deck, Mortimer smiled at Scarlet and Tara, "If all goes well, this will make our next move even easier," he whispered.

As they drifted in silence, Mortimer moved to the bow of the ship and watched as torch light appeared in the distance. They were moving fairly fast without using their sails, and he knew it had to be wearing Clarice out, but he didn't want to show their magical advantage, just in case anyone escaped.

He waved over a crewman and whispered, "Have us brought around the rear, I want to cut off the possibility of retreat."

The crewman nodded his head in understanding and ran off to the helm, in order to relay his orders.

Sure enough, upon seeing the ghost ship, the group of ships converged on it, and rapidly surrounded them.

As they passed behind the pirate ships, Mortimer waved his arm and signaled the canons to fire. One after another they fired, the crew reloading right after firing. "Let's have some light to destroy our enemies by," he cried as he leapt onto the bowsprit and moved as far out as was feasible.

Scarlet smiled and with a wave of her arm over the side rails each cannon started to glow, "Fire at will," she yelled and watched as the cannons fired flaming metal balls at the enemy.

Mortimer laughed as three of the enemy ships caught fire as the magically imbued cannonballs struck them. "Bring us in close and prepare to board," Mortimer called out as the crew cheered.

Zephyr knew how to handle her ship, and turned it hard to starboard. As they approached the enemy she yelled out, "Brace for impact." A few seconds later the underwater ram in the bow punched through the side of another ship.

On impact, Mortimer leapt from the bowsprit and landed with a roll on the deck below. As he rose to his feet he drew his black blade and prepared to engage the enemy. Soon he was joined by several of his own crewmen, who went to work immediately pushing the ship away from them.

One of the crewmen yelled over to him, once she is loose we will be on our own as they maneuver to strike another ship.

Mortimer smiled, when faced with multiple enemies it is best to eliminate them as quickly as possible. With a groan the two ships came apart, and the ship he was standing on started to list to the port side as it filled with water. "To the next ship, quickly," he called to the crewmen as they drew daggers and axes to fight alongside him.

It was a long several minutes as they battled across the sloping deck, but eventually they made it to the railing. Mortimer was the first to leap over, his black blade cutting smoothly through a pair of enemies while in mid-air.

With his now level footing, he threw a rope back to the other ship for the others to use if needed to cross over. Here the fighting was not as bad, many of the pirates already had their hands full as grapnels flew at them from the ghost ship and before long there weren't any survivors aboard the ship.

Mortimer paused to take stock, and started to laugh, two ships were sinking after being rammed by his own, three were burning uncontrollably from canonfire, and the one they stood on was devoid of enemies. On the other side of the ghost ship were three more ships, two with lines attached to the ghost ship, and the third was pulling away from them to engage his main ship. "Do not let them disengage," he called to the crew.

"Zephyr has them," one crewman called out as he pointed off towards the side.

Sure enough when he spotted his ship, he could see a good sized swell behind it and it was gaining speed as it lunged towards the ship trying to disengage. "Then we best clear these other two ships and send them to the bottom."

"Aye captain," came the reply from his crew, as they leapt over the rails of the ships and ran across the deck to leap onto the next ship.

They rapidly swept the decks of the two ships tied to the ghost ship, and Mortimer watched as the crew cut them free and sank both of the ships. "Let's get over to the ladies, and help them take on the last ship," he said to the ghostly captain as the enemy ships started to list to one side.

"Aye sir," the captain replied as he gave instructions to the crew.

The battle between the ships was fierce, even from a distance Mortimer could see the damage being done to each of the ships. As they approached, he watched his ghostly crew load the cannons with the aid of his crewmen from Zephyr's ship. "Fire when in range, then pull alongside and prepare to board," he called out.

"Aye captain," came the raucous reply from the crew, many of them drawing their weapons, while others prepared grapnels to pull the ships together.

The first wave went off perfectly, as the enemy ship was not prepared for an attack from this side, the second one was a bit trickier as the decks of the other ship sat higher above the water.

Mortimer rapidly climbed the rigging, and raced along the yardarm in order to leap across to the other deck. He barely made it across, and went to work defending the ropes his crew were throwing up onto the rails in order to lash together the two vessels. The enemy was well trained and kept him on his feet, as much as he was defending he couldn't get in a clean strike until more of his crewmen climbed over the railing.

One of his crewmen laughed as he clambered onto the deck, "these guys, they're always talking so tough in the pub, guess now's our chance to teach them a lesson."

Mortimer laughed, "Watch each other's backs, and defend the ropes. Once everyone is aboard we'll take them down."

The fighting was fierce around him, but he also knew they were only fighting a small part of the crew, if the bulk of the crew didn't continue their fight against Zephyr, the ship would be sunk in no time.

Mortimer laughed as two men feinted an attack towards him, while a third tried to come in from the opposite side. Deftly he blocked their feints, and with his other hand pulled a dagger and deflected the third. "Big mistake," he said as he reversed his dagger and stabbed the man in the chest. As the man fell to the deck, the other two backed up and a worried look suddenly appeared on their faces.

"You should never hesitate in battle," he said to them, as he leapt forward and swung his sword with two hands in a wide arc before him. The first man was cut in half, and slowed his blade just enough for the other man to block it. The force of the swing was hard enough the second man dropped his blade a second after the impact and his eyes opened wide as Mortimer turned and thrust his sword through his chest and ripped it savagely upward.

A quick glance around told him his crew was all on the deck, and pushing back the enemy. With a shrug, Mortimer looked at his next several opponents and smiled, "I can't remember when I've had this much fun."

A feminine voice called back to him, "Probably when we took Zephyr's ship, or was it when you killed the witch hunter general?"

"Ah, the good old days," he replied with a laugh, as he saw Scarlet standing on the far side of the deck. With a grin in her direction, he started to lash out with his sword, every strike was hard and fast either disarming his opponent or outright killing them. His crew gave him lots of room and stayed close enough to engage any enemy which might get too close to him.

Soon the nearby deck was clear of enemies, and they paused once more to look around. The bulk of the enemies were backing towards the rear of the vessel, where a big bearish looking man stood with two swords in his hands.

Mortimer smiled and said, "He's mine, kill everyone else."

With a roar, his crew leapt forward into the enemy, cutting, slashing and thrusting their weapons into the enemies. One crewman, his blade knocked out of his hand, simply punched an enemy and then picked up the man's shortsword and stabbed him with it.

Mortimer calmly walked around the edges of the battle striking enemies down every so often, gradually getting closer and closer to the enemy captain.

The man grinned darkly and yelled, "You must be the queen's champion, too bad you are supporting the wrong person." He lifted up a pendant, "I have protection from her magic, and will be taking over her fleet, surrender now or you will die."

Mortimer laughed and struck down two more sailors, "I am not her champion, I am the one who defeated her, she is now mine and I will not allow any who would attack her to live." He leapt up the stairs towards the helm, as he spoke, his sword in a defensive position.

The large man barely gave him time for his feet to touch the deck, before he launched into a rapid two sword attack.

Mortimer parried blow after blow, his sword singing through the air, for several minutes before he felt the sting of a blade slipping along his left arm. "I grant you first blood," he said with a smile as he tucked and rolled across the deck.

The man laughed, "You have some good speed, I will grant you that, but you will tire out long before I will."

Mortimer started to laugh maniacally, "I highly doubt that," he could feel the energy around him as more and more of his enemy's crew died, and suddenly he launched himself at his opponent. His black blade sang loudly as it whipped through the air, it twisted and turned as if all on it's own. His strikes wove this way and that, while his opponent countered them with both his swords. Suddenly there was a resounding crack, he pulled back and noticed one of his opponents' swords was shattered.

The big man looked a bit surprised, but with a shrug tossed the hilt of the broken sword aside. "I may have underestimated you," he said as he wiped sweat from his forehead, along with a little blood.

Mortimer grinned back at him, "You know, this charm you were wearing wouldn't really work against anyone's magic." He swung the charm in the air casually, before he tossed it aside, "Shall we finish this now?"

It was at this point he noticed how quiet it had gotten nearby, a quick glance around told him his crew had been victorious and that the enemy had been defeated. "It looks like it is just you and I," he said to the big man, "Your crew is all dead, you cannot win."

The man grinned, "At least I will take you with me to the afterlife," he said as he lunged at Mortimer.

Mortimer twisted to the side and felt the man's sword slide along his side, "I think not," he replied as he slammed his sword point first down through the man's ribs and into the deck. With a twist and a tug, he ripped his blade back out of the deck and his opponent. The spray of blood directly from the wound covered him, and he staggered to the ladder way. "Return to the ship and send this beast to the depths," he called to his crew.

By the time he made it to the bottom of the steps, Scarlet was at his side, "You just can't resist getting hurt when in a duel can you?" she asked. She waved over to Zephyr, who with a wave of her hands was at their side.

He smiled at the two of them, "That was fun, he was actually a better opponent than the general." His knees buckled, and he held on tightly to the rail in order to stay on his feet. "I guess I won't be able to finish my mission after all."

Scarlet looked at Zephyr and said, "Get everyone back to the ship and cut the tethers. Tell Clarice to get in the water she will know what to do and when."

Yes mistress," Zephyr replied, and proceeded to hurry everyone off the ship.

Scarlet looked at Mortimer and smiled, "Child of death, you shall be reborn with fire at your side." She raised her hands above her head, and began to chant in a strange hissing tongue, slowly the deck around them began to smolder and then burn, suddenly the entire ship was engulfed in flames. She wrapped her arms around Mortimer and said, "I will not let you die here, the fire has come at my command and now I command it to save you even if it costs me my own life."

She felt the blood bond awaken, it was angry, there was also another bond, a bond of fire, it felt as if fire danced in her veins and thousands of fiery daggers were piercing her flesh. Scarlet felt as if her body was being ripped to pieces and as each tiny piece was torn away fire was applied to the raw flesh beneath it. She ignored the pain and continued to command the fire to heal the man she loved, the fire continued to rage around them, but finally it settled down and she watched as it entered his body and burned out the toxins within.

Finally exhausted she collapsed along with the flames, they had consumed the entire vessel, even the sea had not been able to put out the flames. As she collapsed and they fell into the water, she felt scaly soft arms wrap around her and pull her to the surface, where she floated on a piece of ice. The last thought she had before she blacked out was, she had to save Mortimer.

# Sea Dragon

Mortimer woke instantly as his body struck the cold water of the sea, his side was on fire, and something was trying to pull him down into the depths. "Scarlet," he tried to yell, only to have water enter his lungs. Unable to breathe, he gave himself up for lost, when a set of soft scaly arms wrapped themselves around his chest, and a beautiful and yet terrifying woman's face appeared before him.

The face pulled in close as if about to kiss him, and instead it sucked the water from his lungs and filled them full of air. It pulled away for a second and then came close and gave him a passionate kiss.

He could feel her entire body along his own, as she pulled him towards the surface, he was momentarily confused as he felt her body sliding across his own from side to side, until they broke the surface. As the water cleared from his eyes, he saw it was Clarice who held onto him, "Thank you," he said to her and kissed her back.

Clarice giggled and smiled at him, "You had me worried, I got Scarlet to the surface first, I knew that's what you would want, but I wasn't sure if I could get to you in time."

"As long as Scarlet is alright, I don't really matter," he replied, "Although I greatly appreciate your saving my life."

She gave him a dirty look and pushed him back under the water for a second, "I should have let you drown, she is not the only important person around here you know."

Mortimer spluttered some more water out and laughed, "Actually you are all very important to me, much more important than I am. I am sure you and Scarlet would finish my mission and figure out some way to convince the other two to help you do so."

Clarice's eyes got dark and she whispered, "That's it, I think it's time you realized how important you are to us." She pulled him in with surprising strength, kissed him as she dove with him down into the water.

Mortimer suddenly found he was pretty much helpless, she dove so rapidly that by the time he thought to fight back, he couldn't tell which way was up.

Eventually they surfaced in an underwater cavern, and she let him go. "Now," she said, "I have you all to myself, what are you going to do?" She was circling him slowly as if she were a predator preparing to strike.

He shook his head, he was not about to fight her, he didn't even know if he could. He could also smell her pheromones filling the air of the cavern, and realized this was a dangerous trap for any man.

She grinned at him as she saw the realization dawning on him, "Yes, this is a breeding cave, mermaids come here when they wish to breed and if there is a receptive male nearby he will meet with them here."

Mortimer frowned, "So I am important to you as breeding material?" he asked, wondering if that's the only reason she had wanted to accompany them.

"You idiot," she exclaimed, as she flipped around and smacked him with her tail, "if that's all I wanted, I could have just asked you. I brought you here so you would understand how important you are to all of us, listen to the bond, I know you are still struggling with the battle madness, but that doesn't mean it isn't still there." She swam up close to him again and placed both her hands on his chest, "Go sit on that shelf and let me see your wounds, I will tend to them while you deal with the conflict within your mind."

He couldn't see the point in arguing with her, but at the same time it was hard to think about anything with the feelings being stirred up within him. He felt her hands on his side and looked down at her, such a wonderful creature, he couldn't resist, he grabbed her and pulled her up out of the water more and kissed her. She returned his kiss easily enough, and then pulled away slightly.

"You are horrible," she whispered to him, "but this should tell you how important you are to us, we would give you anything you desire, even if it hurts us to do so." She smiled at him, "But, now is not the time for us to behave this way, your wounds aren't too bad, but we should get you to the ship so they can heal."

Mortimer sighed, "As you wish," he replied as he slipped into the water next to her. "What happened to my armor and sword?" he asked.

"I'll let Scarlet tell you," she replied as she wrapped her arms around his neck and pulled him underwater.

It took longer to reach the surface than it had to reach the cavern, and he realized it was because she was taking her time so she could continue to kiss him and give him air to breathe. Once they reached the surface, they spotted the ship nearby, and she swam him over to it.

The crew must have spotted them, because they lowered a small boat to the water for them to climb into. They huddled together under a wool blanket, as the crew hauled the small boat up to the deck. Mortimer picked up Clarice and set her on deck, before he himself got out of the small boat, his side hurt, and he knew he shouldn't have picked her up, but that didn't matter to him.

Tara and Zephyr were waiting for them, Tara simply picked up Clarice and carried her off to the cabin, while Zephyr took in his injuries and offered him a shoulder to lean on. "Never thought I'd fish a naked captain out of the water," she said to him with a smile.

Mortimer rolled his eyes, "First how is Scarlet?" he asked.

"Sleeping in the cabin," she answered. "Did the mermaid steal your clothing?"

"No," he laughed and winced, "Second question is where are we heading?"

"Wherever my captain orders," she answered, "but for now I think my captain is heading for the cabin."

"Are you going to tuck me in?" he asked with a smirk.

Zephyr shook her head, "I guess it takes more than nearly dying to dampen your humor, besides I'd say Clarice has plans for you."

Instantly his head whipped up, and he looked around to see the reaction of nearby men, "Good, none of them smell it."

Zephyr chuckled, "I caught wind of it when she dove into the water, I ordered the crew to keep satchels of incense under their noses in order to block her pheromones. It's not my first time meeting a mermaid in heat."

Mortimer relaxed, as they entered the cabin, and Zephyr locked the door behind them. Clarice looked sullen, still in her mermaid form lying on a blanket on the floor, while Tara stood nearby with her back against the wall.

He kissed Zephyr on the cheek and said, "Thank you," before he pushed himself away from her and fell to the floor next to Clarice. Gently he reached out to touch her face, and as she looked at him, he smiled at her.

She started to reach for him, and stopped, out of the water in this form she was nervous and scared.

Mortimer smiled at her and gently pulled her body close to his and kissed her, "You are important to me, you are all important to me."

Clarice smiled and wrapped her arms around him, the scales scraping slightly now that they were drying off, as she kissed him deeply and passionately. "Even though I am like this?" she asked with a nod towards her tail.

"Especially when you are like this," he replied. "I understand now, you are most vulnerable both physically and emotionally when you are in this form out of water. I would love to have you in any form, whether we are in the water or not, but it is always going to be a decision you will have to make as well."

She smiled at him and said, "Let me show you what my decision is."

Zephyr smiled, "Just be sure to leave some of him for the rest of us."

Tara laughed, "Should we devise a calendar to decide who gets him on what days?"

Mortimer sighed, "You know once you're free of the magical entanglement, you'll all leap at the chance to be with someone else."

"No," Zephyr replied, "I don't think so. A magical entanglement just allows us to feel each other's feelings and to make a deeper connection, it means yes we can feel each other's emotions and occasionally get wrapped up in them, but it does not mean we have to act on them." She winked at Tara, "I have already moved most of their feelings aside into another portion of my mind, so when I say I want to be here with you, I mean it and it's not their feelings, but my own."

Tara laughed, "I learned to hide my emotions long ago, a slave doesn't live long if they show their true feelings, I too choose to be here with you because I want to. I would ask though that you focus on being happy with the person you're with, instead of trying to include all four of us all the time."

Clarice grinned, "Are you saying I can have him all to myself then?"

Zephyr laughed, "Only until Scarlet wakes up, or he chooses to be with another person."

Mortimer opened his mouth to say something, but forgot all about it as Clarice kissed him and he got the full force of her pheromones.

Zephyr and Tara stepped out of the cabin with a smile on their faces, "That captain will be fine," Zephyr said, "She wouldn't be so aggressive if she was worried about his health."

Tara nodded in understanding and saw several relieved faces amongst the crew, "Mind teaching me how to steer the ship while they rest?" she asked.

"I'd be honored," she replied, as she leapt up the stairs to the helm.

Mortimer was awoken in the morning by Scarlet's hand touching his shoulder, he opened his eyes and found Clarice in her human form with her arms wrapped tightly around his chest. "How are you?" he asked quietly.

Scarlet smiled at him, "Better, but we need to talk."

Carefully and with some help from Scarlet, he extricated himself from Clarice's arms and stood up. "I'll need to get some new clothes, whatever happened after I passed out, mine are gone."

Scarlet dropped the blanket she had wrapped around herself and smiled, "You're not the only one, and that's one of the things we need to talk about."

Together they walked over to the table and sat down, "Okay, do you want to go first?" he asked.

She smiled, "First thing first, I'm glad you finally have started treating us all as individuals instead of as a collective, and on that note I'll be direct. You have enough wives, please don't go out of your way to get anymore, I'm not jealous of any of them, and I don't mind sharing you with all of them, but I am afraid you might be moving too fast in collecting more wives." She continued to smile at him, as she reached out to gently touch his cheek.

Mortimer frowned, "To be honest, I hadn't intended on taking a second wife, much less a third or fourth. I am sorry about upsetting you, and will try to be a better husband to you."

Scarlet laughed, "It is not me you need to be a better husband to, you need to be a better husband to all your wives. Spend some time alone with each of us, and should you find a potential fifth wife, let's get to know her before she joins the family, agreed?"

He smiled at her, "Agreed, but I seriously hope we don't find a fifth wife." He leaned close to her and gave her a kiss, "Now, what happened after I passed out and where are my clothes and weapons?"

She frowned, "That leads to the second half of our conversation," she answered. "Basically when you passed out I tried to cast a very powerful spell to seal your wound until we could get you to the ship, in the process I summoned a very hot fire and it kind of incinerated the ship, along with everything on it. The black blade and the crimson blades fell into the sea, when our clothing was destroyed by the fire. It also destroyed the bond that concealed my magical ancestry, very painfully I might add, and modified the blood bond."

"Oh?" Mortimer said in curiosity.

"Yes," she continued, "once the fire bond was removed, I was able to direct the fire into your body to clean and close the wound. With the blood bond, the flames followed the magic, and as such you received some dragon's blood into your body."

He slowly started to laugh, "So basically we now need to retrieve the spirit blades from the sea, buy some new clothing, and my wife is now a dragon."

"It's not funny," she replied, "I have claws now, and my teeth are sharper, and my skin itches something fierce."

Mortimer stopped laughing and stared her straight in the eyes, "I love you, and you know what I want to do with you right now, so what's the problem?"

"Really?" She asked, "you would want to be with me like this?"

In answer, he leaned across the table and kissed her, "Yes," he answered. We can get new clothing, and I'm pretty sure Clarice will help retrieve the blades, so the only real issue is how you feel about the changes to your body."

Clarice spoke from behind him, "I will get right to work on my part, why don't you show her how you feel while I'm out."

"Thank you Clarice," Mortimer replied, "I appreciate it."

After she left, he looked at Scarlet and said with a smile, "If I catch you, you're mine."

Scarlet didn't try to run, instead she met him with open arms, "You realize you are creating one hell of a scandal for your family."

"Who cares," he replied as he pinned her to the wall and kissed her.

"True," she mumbled back as she returned his kiss and then pushed off the wall bearing him to the floor with her weight.

A while later, they had to open the windows and door to the cabin to let the smoke out, there were scorch marks here and there on the floor and walls. Even the ceiling had a few scorched claw marks in it.

The two of them laughed happily as they exited the cabin wrapped in wool blankets and a small cloud of smoke billowed out the door with them.

Zephyr frowned, "I guess it would be a good time to remodel the captain's cabin."

Tara laughed, "You knew we would eventually need something that is flame proof with her around."

Scarlet and Mortimer laughed, "Is there anywhere nearby we can put in to get some new clothing?" He asked as they all stopped laughing, "Once Clarice has returned I would like to purchase new clothing, since I seem to have run out of things to wear."

The lookout called out, "Mermaid in the water," and pointed just off the bow.

In just a few seconds Clarice was drawn up out of the water, "I found your blades," she said with a smile. "I can easily retrieve the crimson blades, but the black blade is nearly impossible for me to reach."

Mortimer shrugged, "If you can get me close enough, I should be able to summon it to me." He spoke with much more confidence than he felt, he had never tried to use magic underwater before.

"I can get you fairly close to it," Clarice replied, "if you're alright with my breathing for you."

He laughed softly, "We've done it before, let me know when you're ready."

Clarice shrugged, "I'm ready whenever you are, being in the water is very revitalizing for me."

Mortimer smiled and gave Scarlet a kiss, "I'll be back soon."

"Take good care of him," she said to Clarice.

"I will protect him with my life," Clarice replied, "oh, congratulations on breaking your bond, it must be so liberating to be free."

Scarlet smiled to herself as Mortimer dived over the side of the ship, she was correct, in a way she felt free to be herself, something she had never really dared to do before.

Clarice pulled Mortimer deep under the water, occasionally turning and exhaling a lungful of air into his mouth as they dove down further and further. Soon they could see the crimson blades scattered about the seafloor, and they started to retrieve them. Mortimer felt like a fool when he realized he had no way to carry all five of the blades and call his own sword while swimming.

Clarice watched him struggle for a moment, before she pulled up some strands of seaweed and brought them over to him.

Together they fashion a crude seaweed belt with loops for holding all of the blades together, Mortimer felt even more foolish wearing seaweed and weapons, but at the same time it was necessary.

Once all of the crimson blades were retrieved and strapped to him, Clarice led Mortimer off to the side, where at the bottom of a deep, narrow ravine he could just make out the hilt of the black blade.

Mortimer stretched out his hand for it and it twitched as if it wanted to come to him, but couldn't. He tried again, and got the same result, something was preventing him from calling the blade to him.

He looked around the area for something to extend his reach, but there wasn't much nearby, about the only thing he found was a long metal ramrod from a ship's cannon. Picking it up, he thought about it and decided to see if it could be used to loosen his sword.

With a little effort, he was able to use the ramrod and loosen the sword a bit in the crevice, and finally he was able to call it to his hand.

As it came out of the crevice, a small cloud of blackness came up with it and Clarice gasped. She darted forward, grabbed his other hand and started to swim as hard as she could away from the area.

A quick glance back and Mortimer understood as a huge head rose from the seafloor, apparently his sword had embedded itself into the head of a sleeping sea serpent. There wasn't anything Mortiner could do but hold onto Clarice's hand as her powerful tail propelled them through the water and towards the surface, the serpent following closely behind.

When they broke the surface of the water, they flew a good couple of feet through the air before splashing back into the sea.

"Go get help," Mortimer told Clarice, "I'll distract it until you return."

Clarice laughed, "You should swim for the ship, I can outswim it." She said as she darted underwater and to the side.

He didn't have much choice as the creature changed direction to chase after the mermaid and the side of its body struck him, sending him flying through the air. Swimming with the black blade in hand was not easy, but he struck out for the ship as best he could.

They were in luck though, the lookout had spotted them when they surfaced and the ship was already under sail heading towards them. Mortimer felt a disturbance in the water and glanced down, the serpent was coming back towards him. He knew it would get to him before the ship, and he didn't see Clarice, with a low growl, he dove down towards the monster, his sword directly ahead of him.

The monster saw him coming towards it and actually stopped moving, it cocked its head sideways as if puzzled.

As he got closer, the serpent lunged past him and circled rapidly around him, before it pulled him up to the surface of the water with its coils.

Mortimer found himself staring at a huge scaly brown head with black eyes, the serpent's fangs were about as long as his arms, and it's body was easily thicker than he was tall. He glanced at the ship and frowned, there was no way it would reach him before this thing could crush the life out of him.

"Why did you disturb my sleep?" a soft voice asked in his head.

Mortimer couldn't help but chuckle, "I am sorry about that, but I was trying to retrieve my sword and didn't realize it was stuck in your head. Now, mind telling me what happened to my mermaid companion?"

The serpent cocked it's head sideways so that a single eye was focused on him. "I simply stunned her, she will be alright, you though are quite the curiosity I must say," the voice responded. I have never had a human charge at me before knowing I could swallow them in a single gulp."

Mortimer lowered his arms to the serpent's coils and laughed, "Not the brightest idea was it? If you don't mind though, we had no intention of waking you and really would like to continue on our way if possible."

"Be that as it may, I have more questions." The voice replied, "I have been asleep a long time, and this is the first time a sword has pierced my scales, so if you answer my questions I will be happy to let you leave in peace."

"I'll be glad to answer your questions," he answered. "I will say though my companions need to know I am alright before they decide to try and rescue me."

"Feel free to stand upon my surface," the voice replied. "Your mermaid friend should be waking shortly and she can let them know we are just talking."

Mortimer pulled himself out of the coil and stood up on the serpent's body, "I really wish I had my scabbard right now," he mumbled as he realized he had no place to put his sword.
The serpent's body shook slightly as if it was laughing, and the voice asked, "Is this not how you normally look?"

"No," Mortimer answered, suddenly realizing how cold the air felt. "Normally I am wearing clothing or armor, as our skin does not offer much protection from the weather."

"Ah, that makes sense," the voice said in his head. "How is it that your sword was able to pierce my scales?"

Mortimer frowned, "I believe it may be because it is a magical blade, it has been known to cut through metal."

The serpent nodded it's head as if this was something new for it to think about, "Do many people have blades like this?" it asked.

"No," he answered, "it takes a huge personal sacrifice to make one of these blades, and very few people can properly use these blades as they tend to have a will of their own."

The serpent seemed to like this answer as the muscles in its body relax a bit. "Where is your current journey taking you?" the voice asked.

"We are hoping to put an end to the pirates in the area, and then I plan to go home to put my ancestors spirits to rest," Mortimer answered. "It is why it was so important for me to retrieve this sword."

"Explain," the voice replied.

"One of my ancestors' souls is tied to this sword, another is tied to the other blades I am carrying," he answered. "When I get home I will be able to perform a ritual which will release their spirits to the afterlife, in the process it will destroy the magic within the blades themselves."

"I commend your devotion to your ancestors," the voice said. "Allow me to grant you a gift from my hoard that others may know that you pass through my territory with my permission. Is that your ship approaching?"

"Yes it is," Mortimer answered.

"Very well, if you will hold on tight, I shall put you on board your ship and return shortly with my gift to you," the voice said.

He found it a strange sensation as the serpent began to move through the water, it was as if he stood on the back of a giant horse as it wove between trees at a gallop.

In no time at all he found himself standing alongside the railing of his ship, and jumped onto the deck.

One of the crewmen laughed and said, "Crazy man on deck."

Mortimer started laughing and replied, "Please slow our movement, the serpent will be back shortly."

"Aye aye captain," the crewman replied as he ran off to give orders to the helm.

A few minutes later, the serpent returned with Clarice wrapped loosely in one of its coils, "I believe she is sleeping," it's voice said in Mortimers head.

Mortimer chuckled, "well it has been a busy day for her," he replied. "Do you mind if I come over and retrieve her?"

"Not at all," the serpent replied, "you should move quickly though, I smell a dragon nearby."

"That's probably just my wife," Mortimer answered, "she is a descendant of the dragons."

"Humans have certainly changed over the last few centuries," the voice replied. "Before I went to sleep humans were slaying dragons and any other magical creature they came across."

Mortimer picked up Clarice and carefully carried her to the ship's deck, "Things haven't changed all that much, many people still go out of their way to kill magical creatures, but there are some of us who would rather work with magical creatures for the benefit of everyone."

The serpent nodded his head as it thought about his information, "It is good you woke me else I might have slept through another century or two and missed even more changes in the nature of man." It lifted its tail up out of the water and dropped a small bundle on the deck of the ship, "This is a piece of my shedded skin, you should be able to fashion it into some new clothing for yourself. Now I bid you pleasant travels my new friend," the serpent said as it slid back beneath the water.

Scarlet walked over to his side after the serpent had left and looked at the bundle of shedded skin, "Interesting," she said, "it is believed that when worn, the skin of a water dragon grants the wearer the ability to breathe underwater."

A nearby crewman laughed, "It also is supposed to be naturally resistant to fire."

Mortimer shrugged, "Well, I have repaired armor many times, so I should be able to make myself some out of this. After all, it would be an insult to refuse such a noble gift."

Scarlet laughed, "Dragon hide is hard to work with, you will have to first find someone who knows how to work with it." She picked up the bundle, "You should put Clarice in bed, I will check with Zephyr to see if she knows anyone who can fashion this into clothing."

Mortimer nodded his head in agreement and took Clarice to the cabin, even though the walls were slightly charred, it was still in good shape. After he tucked her in with a couple of blankets, he decided to go and see what Zephyr knew about the dragon skin. He didn't want to admit it, but he felt very self conscious running around with no clothes on.

Mortimer made his way to the helm, where Tara, Zephyr and Scarlet stood in conversation, "Well, what do you think, can it be made into clothing?"

Zephyr winked at him, "Yes, the hardest part will be designing the panels and then cutting them. This stuff is very resistant to blades, too flexible to make a decent armor, but if worn with armor it would prevent just about any blade from piercing it."

He reached out to feel the material and was shocked, one side felt as if it was the softest satin he had ever known, but the other was coarse like rock. "Interesting," he said, "this is pretty thin material for such a varied texture."

Tara chuckled, "I can sew you an outfit, but I don't have the tools to cut this type of material, and I'm not sure if a needle will go through it."

Mortimer smiled at her, "Let's keep it simple, shirt and pants. I would like to use as little of the material as possible." He looked at Scarlet standing nearby with a blanket fastened around her and added, "If possible make something for Scarlet to wear."

Tara bowed her head thoughtfully and said, "I believe I can make something for each of us, there is a lot more material here than you realize. That dragon gave you a treasure worth more than you can imagine."

"Then I leave it in your hands," Mortimer replied, "My sword can cut the material, so I am pretty sure the crimson knife should be able to punch holes in it if needed."

"Thank you, for this opportunity," she said, as she headed down the stairs towards the cabin. It was obvious she had left something unsaid, but something told him it was best not to pry at this time.

Scarlet chuckled, "she loves to sew, and you just gave her permission to experiment with the rarest material she's ever seen."

Zephyr laughed, "That would be an understatement, I have never heard of anyone being given such material. According to the stories it took an army to take down a dragon, and even then most of the material would have been destroyed in the process."

"How did they take down a dragon?" Mortimer asked.

"A lot of magic and muscle," she replied. "The weapons they had back then were not as advanced as what we use now, and thousands of swords would be broken just to create a small hole in the hide of a dragon. Eventually people learned to use dragon teeth and claws as weapons, but most of those have since been destroyed in the making of various spells. The few that are left are highly sought after, and are never brought out in public."

Scarlet chuckled dryly, "It was a sad time in our history, the guard has records of a few dragon weapons, but only the highest ranked witches are allowed to see those records."

Mortimer shook his head, "Weapons taken from a living being tend to have a piece of that being attached to them, they should be given a proper burial by their people to release them fully to the afterlife."

"Now now," She replied, "don't go getting any funny ideas, we have enough to do already. We can look into that journey after we finish our current task."

They were interrupted by the return of Tara, "M.., I need your body for measurements sir," she said with a strange tone in her voice.

"As you desire," Mortimer replied and followed her down the stairs. As they entered the cabin he asked, "Is something bothering you Tara?"

She turned to look at him and said, "Yes and no. I am very happy that you are letting me work with such a rare material, and even more excited about the fact you are letting me do all of the designing, but at the same time I am wondering what it is going to cost me."

He was puzzled by this answer for a moment, "What do you mean by cost you?"

"What are you going to require me to do in order to repay you for the privilege of working with dragon skin?" She answered with tears in her eyes.

"Nothing," he answered, "You owe me nothing, if anything I am in your debt, after all look at how silly I appear wearing a seaweed belt and all these weapons." He spread his arms in a how can you take me serious gesture.

This was more than Tara could stand, she flung herself into his arms and started to cry. "You know you are still my master even though you have claimed me as a wife, and yet you treat me as an equal, why?" she cried into his shoulder.

He wrapped his arms around her and held her close, "Nobody is superior to anybody else. We each have our talents and when it comes to sewing, I firmly believe you are the master." He held her until she stopped crying, and let her go when she started to step back from him.

"I am so sorry," she said, "do you think the others will be upset if we spend some time alone together? In order to sort out my emotions," she added quickly.

"I am certain they will be fine if we are alone for a while," he answered. "They will probably be glad that I am spending some time with you."

They spent a good hour talking with each other, as Tara took the measurements she needed, and at the end of the conversation she said, "I know when we get back to your family, they will find a way to break the magical entanglement, and you will need to choose between us all." She smiled at him, "I know you will choose Scarlet, I could never compete with her for your love, but if you don't mind I would like to have the illusion that you might choose me."

Mortimer was a little surprised, he hadn't expected her to actually want to be with him of her own will, "You are correct that if forced I would choose Scarlet, but right now I do not think I am willing to let any of you go, so until things change you are my wife."

# Revelations?

It was another hour before Mortimer left the cabin, but when he left Tara was humming happily to herself as she worked with the dragon skin. He climbed the stairs to the helm, Zephyr looked at him and asked, "Are you alright? You appear a little thoughtful."

He gave her a sort of half smile, and noticed Scarlet leaning against the rail watching him. "Just thinking," he answered, "out of curiosity, what is your desire when we complete our task?"

Zephyr laughed musically, "We have a few days before we reach my, now your, little kingdom so I'm not entirely certain what task you are referring to."

Mortimer grimaced, "Freeing the slaves and ending the pirate kingdom will be a fairly simple task in my eyes, returning home and bringing an end to the magical entanglement may prove a bit more complicated."

She laughed again, "Why worry about that? Thinking of finding something to delay the destruction of your harem?" She winked at Scarlet and said, "I believe he is having a crisis of conscience."

"Something like that," he replied, "I don't want to see anyone get hurt."

Zephyr's face suddenly turned serious, "Tara told you how she feels I take it."

"You knew?" he asked.

"As did I," Scarlet said suddenly, "I don't blame her either, but I believe Zephyr is better able to explain it than I am."

Zephyr laughed heartily, "Naturally, harpies love to screech about everything, we are natural talkers, unlike dragons." She smiled at Mortimer, "You see you have a major flaw, and you need to get it under control before we get to port." She paused and winked at him, "You see you're a nice guy."

Mortimer started to argue, but she interrupted him by placing a hand over his mouth, "No my dear it's my time to talk and your turn to listen," she pulled her hand away and continued, "you are always sacrificing yourself for others, you don't judge anyone based on their appearance, and you give everyone a chance to do the right thing, even if you know they won't." She paused for breath and then continued, "Normally nobody would notice these qualities, but at the same time you have this unnatural ability to survive anything thrown at you, and you are a decent leader. When you put all of this together you get the perfect mate, the funny thing is you keep it hidden from everyone, except those who need you." She winked at him and said, "Yes I too want you for my own, but it is in my nature to wait for the winds to change before I worry about where I'm going."

He shook his head and said, "Maybe I need to talk to someone who is not entangled with me."

"Good luck," Scarlet said, "as far as the crew is concerned you're the luckiest man alive, they'll just tell you to stay at sea the rest of your life."

"Not a bad idea," he muttered. "How is the scout ship doing anyways?"

Zephyr laughed, "They're fine, they are going to reach port a day before us, so will anchor off shore and wait for us to arrive."

"Thank you for taking charge," he replied, "You make a much better leader than I do."

"Not true," she replied, "Part of being a good leader is recognizing your people's skills and utilizing them in the best capacity. I take it Clarice is still sleeping."

"Yes," he answered, "she used up a lot more energy today than she realized."

Scarlet chucked, "Sleep sounds like a good idea, I think I will join her for a bit. I trust the two of you will not decide to embark on some crazy side mission."

Zephyr laughed, "Go ahead mistress, we shall be sure to wake you if anything of interest arises."

"I'm pretty sure you can handle just about anything that comes up," Scarlet replied with a smirk.

Mortimer frowned, "Why do I get the feeling you mean a lot more than you are saying."

As Scarlet descended the step to the cabin, Zephyr whispered, "I wouldn't mind spending more time alone with her."

Mortimer raised an eyebrow and said, "Oh really?"

"Yes, she is an interesting woman," Zephyr answered, "but you already knew that. She has a lot of knowledge about magic, and a lot of passion. Now that her bonds have been broken, she is going to find spells that are difficult for a human will be simple for her."

"Have you always ridden the winds of change so easily?" he asked.

"No, it took me many years to understand the winds and how it affected me," she answered. "Now that my bonds are broken, thanks to you, I find it much easier to feel those winds and chooco my path."

"And what path would you choose if you hadn't gotten caught in the magical entanglement?" he asked.

Zephyr laughed, "You mean if I had the choice would I want to be with you?" She suddenly stepped around the tiller, wrapped her arms around him and pulled him close to her. "I would keep you all to myself if I could, but not being able to do so, I am willing to share you with the others." She kissed him passionately and gently bit his lip, "I would die to be with you, and I wish to be with you forever, even if only as a friend."

Mortimer frowned, "How much of that is you and how much of it is the bond?"

She waved over the first mate, "Take the helm and keep us on course, the captain and I are going to have a private conversation."

"The cabin is being used, so where do you wish to talk?" he asked.

Zephyr laughed, "There are other rooms on this ship, the boatswain's locker will do for now." She led him down the stairs, and then down a ladder into the hold, once there she lit a lantern and escorted him to a small room in the bow of the ship filled with extra ropes for both the anchors and the sails.

Inside the room, she turned and bolted the door, "Everything I have said is what I believe. The entanglement is interesting, but I found a way while you were asleep to block the emotional sharing in the entanglement, so now you know that everything each of us tells you is our personal feelings." She put a hand on his chest and licked her lips, "I told you I wanted you all to myself, and for now I have that wish. Scarlet knew it, she even suggested it while you were with Tara."

"And what about my feelings on the matter?" Mortimer asked nervously.

"You see that is why we are doing this," she replied, "to see what your feelings are on the matter." She stripped out of her clothing, "The question is do you want me as a part of your life, or will you simply cast me aside? You are the only man to see my true form, and you have not pulled back or shown any sign of disgust, so again I ask, do you desire me in your life?"

Mortimer looked at her naked body and smiled, as he reached out to stroke her arm. The tiny little feathers on her arms were so soft, he gripped her arm harder and pulled her closer to him. "You are beautiful, I don't know any man who wouldn't desire you, but your body does not define you." He slid his hand down to hers and pulled it up between their faces, her bird-like claws glinted in the lantern light as he gently kissed them. "You know that when I broke the spell on you I knew the consequences and accepted them, so yes I do want you."

It was as if he had been caught in a wind funnel, he was picked up and thrown to the floor. She kissed him deeply, it sucked the air from his lungs and he soon found himself gasping for breath. He felt her claws dig into his back in almost the exact same place as Scarlets had, it was an experience like no other, as half the time they floated in the air and the other half he was pinned against a hard surface, or she was. When they were both satiated, they settled back to the floor and sat facing each other.

"Let me see your back," she said with an apologetic smile.

He turned and she laughed, "You have all left your mark on me," he said as he turned back to face her.

"You could say that again," she replied. "You realize you have marks on your back from each of us?"

"Yes," he replied, "I'm surprised you didn't see them earlier."

Zephyr laughed, "You kidding they are magical, Clarice left blue/white marks, Scarlet left bright flaming red ones, Tara left what looks like brown roots, and mine are bright blue like the sky." She smiled, "They make for a very interesting pattern."

"You say they're magical," he said, "does this mean only people looking for magic can see them, or anyone who practices magic can see them?"

She smiled, "Only those looking for them can see them, but they wouldn't show up if you didn't truly care about the person who left them either, so this answers another question I had. When Scarlet and Clarice wake up we should have a family meeting."

Mortimer laughed, "What about this time?"

"How are we going to resolve this when we get back to your home," she answered. He frowned, "I suppose in the middle of the sea is as good a place as any for such a conversation."

"What better place," she asked, "This way if there is any major fallout there are less innocent people around to get hurt."

Zephyr got dressed, led him out of the room, and back to the helm, she was only mildly surprised to see Clarice and Scarlet waiting for them. "Nice nap?" she asked.

Scarlet shrugged, "I've had worse."

Clarice frowned, "It could have been better, apparently I missed quite a bit while I was out."

Mortimer shrugged, "You needed the rest after trying to evade a sea serpent."

"Water dragon," Zephyr corrected him, "and a very ancient one at that." She looked at the first mate, "can you handle the helm for a bit longer?"

"Yes ma'am," he answered.

"Good, we'll be in my cabin if anything should occur." She said as she turned and waved for the others to follow her.

Inside the cabin, she surveyed the scorch marks and laughed softly, "I do believe this place has seen better days." Turning to them she continued, "Please find a comfortable place to sit, preferably out of reach of anyone else."

Mortimer noticed how they all picked a wall and leaned against it, so he sat in the middle of the room.

Zephyr laughed and the other girls all smiled, "Well, that figures, you would sit an equal distance from each of us." She shook her head, "Just as well. So we all have the same thoughts and feelings in regard to our family situation. The question is how are we going to handle it when we meet Mortimers family?"

Scarlet raised an eyebrow, "Not beating around the bush I see."

Mortimer frowned, "Zephyr and I talked quite a bit about the situation, and we have a couple of choices and based on the group's decision we will proceed." He took a deep breath and continued, "We could rescue the prisoners from the pirates, and return home, completing my original quest. Or, we could rescue the prisoners and decide to go off and find more adventures together, delaying my return home."

Tara was the first to speak, "Returning to your home will be painful for some of us, but at the same time it is the right thing to do, as you have a promise to uphold regarding your ancestors, as such I vote for that path."

Clarice spoke up, "I agree with Tara, as much as I know it will end our relationship, I can't ask you to forsake your honor for me."

Scarlet laughed, "I am of two minds on this and would ask Zephyr her opinion before I speak."

Zephyr frowned, "Yesterday I would have said to run with the wind and stay at sea as much as possible, I don't understand this honor thing too well, but I do know I would sacrifice everything I have to make him happy." She nodded her head towards Mortimer, "Thus, I have to say we head to his home and deal with the consequences."

Scarlet returned her frown, "I agree with you, but I feel as if I am being selfish in wanting to return to his home and see what his family decides."

Mortimer frowned, "Then after we rescue the prisoners, we will focus on completing my quest. Now we just need to decide if we accept the resolution of the magical entanglement when we get home, or if we simply return the blades and leave town."

Scarlet's head whipped around and she stared at him, "Is that even possible?" she asked. "Wouldn't your family hunt us down?"

Mortimer frowned, "My sister might, she is really looking forward to hosting my wedding, but I believe my father would order everyone to leave us alone if I left the order completely."

Zephyr laughed darkly, "Not likely love, nobody has ever successfully left the order that I have heard of."

Clarice looked thoughtful and asked, "Would my grandfather know?"

"Yes, he would," Mortimer answered, "but that would mean having to summon him through his sword."

She frowned back at him, "Damn, I left it with most of our possessions on the other ship."

Mortimer laughed, "Well, that can't be helped, we will just have to discuss it with him when we catch up to them."

Zephyr shrugged, "We are only a day or two away from them, we can wait that long."

Scarlet frowned, "Why not ask your great grandfather?" she asked.

"I could try, but I am not too sure he would be willing to provide an answer," he answered. "Besides, it's hard to summon him when I have the crimson blades on me as well, it's almost as if they are competing to respond."

"So, give the crimson blades back to me and then try to summon him," she replied.

With a shrug, he pulled the crimson blades from his seaweed belt and handed them over to her. He then sat back down and placed his black sword across his lap, "Spirit of the blade, I request you to present yourself, in the name of your heir and the lives we have taken together."

The shadowy form of his great grandfather drew itself out of the blade and smiled down at him, "I was wondering how long it would take for you to summon me again. You do know you don't need to go through all that ritual speech to summon me correct?"

Mortimer frowned, "In a mood to give away secrets today?"

The spirit laughed hollowly, "I am not giving away anything they won't learn in time anyways, since they are now members of the family." He looked around at all of them and frowned, "First and foremost, the magical entanglement cannot be broken, this is why professional curse breakers are such heartless bastards. When you broke their curses, and yes that is what the bonds really are, you did so with love in your heart, and love magic cannot be broken even by the most powerful curse breaker." He looked over at Scarlet, "You should let my wife out, she can explain it better than I can."

Scarlet raised an eyebrow at him, and picked up the crimson dagger, "Will you please present yourself in order for us to get your advice?" she asked.

A crimson shadow appeared before her and smiled, "You drop me in the water again and I will charge you double what I normally charge for manifesting. Darling you have nothing to fear from returning home, nor do the rest of his wives, although I must warn you, you will forever be bound together when everything is said and done." She looked around the room and smiled at all of the women, "All of you will get your desire, but at the same time all of you will need to learn to share everything with each other, and I do mean everything. I can't tell you what is going to happen, but I can tell you this, the family will be very excited when they discover he is bringing home the four of you, it will save them a lot of work."

The black shadow laughed, "I still can't believe they thought this would fail, all because you never brought home a girl when you visited. You should have heard the dismay in your fathers voice when his spy's told him you refused to date when out on campaign. Anyways, we have told you too much already, just know your family will accept any number of wives you bring home." With this the shadow dissolved back into the black blade.

The crimson shadow frowned, "Don't take that as permission to go around breaking bonds every chance you get, each bond will put a strain on you, and if you get too many they will destroy you." She looked at Clarice, "You are so beautiful, you remind me of your great grandmother." With Tara she smiled and said, "The power of the earth runs through your veins, and I am sure you will soon discover how to change yourself as your ancestor did." She looked at Zephyr and laughed, "Oh you are a fun one harpy child, never has a harpy's blood mixed with that of the order, I can't wait to see you when your plumage shows itself fully."

Zephyr blinked in shock, "Wait, you mean I am not done changing?"

She laughed in response, "My dear when your feathers thicken, give or take a few months, you will no longer be able to wear anything that is not custom made, your wings will be glorious." She looked at Scarlet and smiled, "your scales will harden in that time too, and become thicker, you too will find normal clothing to be irritating, but loose robes will be quite comfortable."

She started to fade away and whispered, "your true forms have not yet been realized, so please be patient with each other."

Mortimer laughed softly to himself, "She is tired, I guess fire spirits lose a lot of energy when they are immersed in water."

Scarlet blushed a deep dark red, "I hope she will forgive me in time."

Zephyr laughed, "I believe she already has, as she probably gave us much more information than she was supposed to."

Scarlet glared at her and replied, "At least you're going to have nice pretty feathers, I'm going to end up with ugly thick scales."

Mortimer didn't even see Zephyr move as she leapt across the room and slapped Scarlet, "Do you really think any of us are going to think less of you because you have scales? You know how jealous people are going to be when they see you together with our husband?"

At first Scarlet didn't move, and then suddenly her hand snapped up and she slapped Zephyr across the face, "How dare you?" she demanded as she stood up, her face contorted in rage.

Tara simply picked up her sewing and left the cabin, Clarice in hot pursuit.

Mortimer stood up as Zephyr laughed and said, "Is that the best you can do?"

Enraged Scarlet swiped a clawed hand at her, only to have Zephyr catch it in her own claws. She stared at the claws, and started to cry, "I'm sorry, I don't know what just came over me."

Zephyr laughed, "Jealousy, it happens to the best of us, just remember you're not in this alone. I have a ship to sail, and I think you need to spend some more time with our husband, I know you didn't believe him when he told you how beautiful you are this morning, but I think it's time you let it sink in through that tough exterior of yours." With that she let go of Scarlet's hand, turned and left the cabin.

Mortimer stepped in before she could move, and wrapped his arms around her, "As passionate as you are, sometimes you need to slow down and smell the burnt wood," he said with a smile.

She couldn't help it, she collapsed into his arms laughing and crying at the same time. "I knew what was going to happen leaving you alone with her, she's too attractive for you or any man on this ship to turn down, but at the same time I was afraid you would prefer her over me, and after what the crimson witch said, I know you will prefer her over me."

He snorted, "I would argue the opposite, especially since she mentioned she really wanted to spend more time alone with you, but I know I can't win that argument when you're upset." He pushed her back a little and looked her in the eyes, "Have you seen my back yet today?"

She shrugged, "You have a few scratches on it, why?"

"Look at it as if searching for magic, and tell me what you see," he replied.

She stepped back and turned him around, "Oh my," she gasped, "did I do that?"

"Some of it," he replied, "you can guess who did what by the colors according to Zephyr."

Scarlet started to laugh, "you know there is a distinct design in those claw marks?"

"No, I did not know that," Mortimer answered, "she only told me that they were of different colors."

She smiled at him, "I owe her an apology, hopefully she is willing to wait for one. In case you're wondering, it's a rose, it has blue, white and red petals, and a green stem with brown thorns."

"Interesting," he said as he turned back around to face her and put his arms around her again, "come sit down with me and tell me all of your worries."

After a while, there was a gentle knock at the cabin door, "Is it safe to come in?" Tara's voice came from the other side of the door.

"Yes," Scarlet answered.

Mortimer smiled down at her, and tightened his arms ever so slightly around her.

"You squeeze much harder and you'll crush my arms," Scarlet said as Tara opened the door.

"I thought you said it was safe to come in," Tara said with the door half open.

Mortimer laughed, "It's safe, we were only sitting here talking."

Tara gave him a half smile, "You do that a lot, I don't think it's normal for people to have a conversation before or after sleeping together."

He laughed, "You must have known some pretty low class men."

Tara laughed, "That's for certain, the men I know get done and get out. Anyways, I have some pants ready for you to try on."

"That's great," Scarlet said, "let's see how they look on him."

Mortimer frowned, "It's a sad day when your wife is more eager to get you dressed rather than undressed."

The two women laughed as Tara threw a bundle of cloth at him. "I believe the crew will take you more seriously if you at least have some pants on." She smiled at Scarlet, "I am taking the crimson witches advice and making you a robe, it will be sleeveless, but once I get your measurements it will compliment your figure nicely."

Mortimer pulled on his new pants and smiled, "They fit like a glove, you are an amazing seamstress Tara."

"I'm glad you like them," she replied, "now would you be kind enough to give us ladies some privacy while I get Scarlet's measurements?"

Scarlet smiled at him and added, "Oh, please ask Zephyr to come down here, I need to have a word with her."

Mortimer bowed to the two of them and replied, "As you wish." Tara's face grew pale at these words, but she didn't say a word. He left the cabin and climbed the stairs to the helm, "Zephyr, Scarlet wants to have a word with you," he said as he reached the top of the short set of stairs.

Zephyr's eyes flashed at him, "If that is your wish, but I am not sure the ship will survive another confrontation between the two of us."

"There will be no fight," he replied, "Tara is in with her now, and if anyone can keep you two from fighting it is her."

She suddenly burst into laughter, "you have a point there. Alright, I'll go talk with her, please don't wreck what's left of the ship."

He watched as she climbed down the stairs and gave a shake of his head, he hoped Zephyr would be willing to listen to Scarlet, but he wasn't sure, wind was known to make a fire burn brighter after all.

After about half an hour Tara came up to the helm and laughed, "I got both of their measurements while I had the opportunity, I'm not sure what you said to Scarlet, but thank you for calming her down."

"I didn't say anything to her, I simply showed her the artwork you ladies left on my back, and let her vent her emotions," he replied.

"What artwork?" she asked.

"Look at my back as if you are trying to see a spell," he answered.

She walked around behind him and started to giggle, "Sorry, but I didn't realize I had dug my nails in so hard."

"Don't be sorry, it doesn't hurt, and I like the image that it portrays," he replied.

She gave him a quick kiss on the cheek, "You're a strange man, but it's the reason we all love you. I'll take the helm for a bit, you should show that to Clarice."

"I will," he replied as he let her take over the ship's wheel.

It took him a while to find Clarice, she was sitting on the bow, singing softly to herself. Mortimer listened to her singing for a bit, before she noticed him.

"Oh, sorry," she said embarrassed, "I didn't hear you come up."

He chuckled softly and smiled, "You have nothing to be sorry for, you have a nice voice."

Clarice laughed in response, "That's part of the mermaid's magic, the siren song used to lure sailors to their deaths." She returned his smile, "My song is not nearly as powerful, as I am only half mermaid, but it can still be dangerous. That's why I don't sing around other people."

Her eyes ran the length of Mortimers body for a second and she said, "Those pants look good on you, now you'll find it much easier to move around underwater."

"Thank you," he replied, "do you by any chance know if there are any other special properties with dragon skin?"

She laughed, "Only a few things, it is believed that it enables the wearer to breathe underwater, and that it provides protection from water based magic." She giggled slightly, "There is a rumor that it will allow you to turn into a dragon, but that has never been confirmed."

Mortimer laughed, "I'll let you know if that happens." He paused for a moment before he asked, "Did you know about the design you and the others put on my back?"

She simply raised an eyebrow at him and said, "Turn around please." As he turned around, she laughed, "That's interesting, you have certainly been touched by my magic, and it is very fitting it should take that shape."

"Oh?" he asked as he turned to face her once more.

Clarice's answering laugh was like the waves rolling into the beach, "Well, yes, it is fitting since you are from the order of the rose. What I find more interesting though is that I know I didn't scratch you there, meaning my magic moved the scratches to take on that appearance."

"You're sure you never scratched me there," he asked.

"Yes," she answered, "even at our most passionate moments I have never broken your skin with my fingernails, only my teeth."

Mortimer frowned, "If that is the case, then we may have to find a more experienced witch to find out what is happening."

"Ask the crimson witch, she'll know," she replied, "but something tells me she won't give you an answer."

"I doubt she will too," he replied, "she is definitely hiding something from us."

"Do you blame her?" Clarice asked, "It must be hard knowing what is needed and knowing that in the end someone has to suffer one way or another."

"Yeah," he replied, "she already told us how they couldn't complete the ritual the last time and how it created a mess of problems for them."

"There is one difference though," she said, "all of us are willing to sacrifice ourselves for you if necessary."

Mortimer laughed, "Your mother is going to kill me if I allow you to do that."

Clarice laughed, "I doubt that, she would be upset, but she would understand it was my choice."

He looked out over the sea for a moment, before he said, "I am going to head back to the cabin, hopefully Zephyr and Scarlet haven't destroyed the remainder of it."

"You left those two alone together?" she asked, "I better come with you just in case."

As they entered the cabin together, they were surprised to see Scarlet and Zephyr laughing together, "Everything alright with you two?" Mortimer asked.

They both smiled at him, "Yes, we had a very good talk," Scarlet answered.

Zephyr gave him a sinister smile and added, "We have come to the conclusion you are hopeless when it comes to people who need help."

"Oh?" he asked.

"Yes," Scarlet answered, "you just can't help yourself, as much as you dislike people in general, you can't help but to step in and give aid to those who need it."

Clarice laughed, "It sounds like the two of them have figured you out pretty good."

Mortimer shrugged, "Be that as it may, I do know that we can't delay our return home forever, besides I'm not nearly as nice as you girls would like to believe."

The three women looked at each other and burst out laughing, "You are not nearly as evil as you think," Scarlet replied as she gasped for air. "If you were, we wouldn't be here right now."

"She's got a point," a voice said in his head, "your powers may be inherently dark, but you yourself shine as bright as the sun."

He jumped at the sound of the voice, and looked around as he drew his sword. "Who said that?" he asked.

The voice giggled, "Oh, this is an interesting side effect of the dragon skin. I'll be down in a second to explain, and I have gowns for both Scarlet and Zephyr."

A few seconds later, Tara walked in wearing a dragon skin vest laced tightly around her torso. "Sorry about startling you like that," she said, "when I put on the vest and thought about you, I was suddenly able to hear the conversation in the room." She handed a bundle of dragon skin to Clarice and then walked over to Scarlet and Zephyr, giving them each a bundle, "I made these gowns for you two, they should fit you both quite nicely." She smiled at Clarice, "In your case I made you a vest like mine, so you won't need to remove it when you change form."

Zephyr smiled as she stripped off her clothing and put on the gown, "Oh, this feels very nice, I'm sure you caused quite a stir amongst the crew changing up on deck." Tara laughed, "Not really, I simply turned my back to the crew and changed, it probably helped that I was able to create a dust curtain to change behind."

Scarlet slipped the gown on and smiled, "Oh, this feels nice and soothing against my skin. I wonder if we could talk the dragon into giving us more discarded skin in the future."

Tara smiled, "who knows, we'll have to ask him the next time we see him." She turned to Mortimer, "I will have a shirt ready for you in a few more hours, the more I work with this material the easier it gets to manipulate."

"When I left you were at the helm," Mortimer replied.

"Oh, the first mate took over the helm, while I sewed," she smiled, "he dreams of one day having his own ship."

Zephyr laughed, "I bet he does, and if he keeps working as hard as he has been, I will give him this one."

"But then what ship will you command?" Tara asked.

"I am ready for a change of pace," she answered, "so most likely I will travel with you to the city and then see what it's like having a more relaxed lifestyle."

Mortimer laughed, "I wouldn't exactly consider my family as having a relaxed lifestyle, but it is certainly a lot less risky than your current lifestyle."

At that everyone laughed, and headed out on deck to make certain there were no issues which needed their immediate attention.

The rest of the day was pretty slow, towards evening Tara finished the vest she was making for Mortimer, it fit him very nicely and had holes placed strategically to allow for him to add sleeves to it in the future, and pleats in the sides so that when he wanted to he could wear it over regular clothing. "You are an impressive seamstress," he said to her when she gave it to him.

She blushed slightly and said, "Thank you, I should have some sleeves made out of the scraps tomorrow, it is vital we have you well protected since you spend so much time fighting."

"Hopefully I won't be spending so much time on the battlefield," he said with a slight frown. "To be completely honest I am getting tired of fighting all the time."

Scarlet chuckled and said, "You know, Tara would make any man the perfect wife, I'm glad we found her before somebody else did."

Mortimer smiled, "All of you make good wives, you each have your talents. Clarice is an amazing healer, Zephyr is a great scout and conversationalist, Tara is a great homemaker, and you Scarlet are a great cook. The four of you balance each other out very nicely."

Zephyr burst out laughing, "In other words, he needs us as much as we need him."

"Oh, I don't think you need me," he replied, "I believe you want me to be a part of your life. I can't picture any of you ever needing someone."

Clarice laughed as well, "You are a fool if you believe we don't need you, everyone needs someone at some point in their life."

Tara smiled, "I believe the truth is we complete each other, us women are the four elements, but without a central bonding point we would all go our separate ways, and he is the pin that keeps us all together."

A sailor approached them and interrupted, "Pardon me, but we have sighted the scout ship, and are approaching our meeting place. What are your orders?"

Zephyr grinned at the sailor, "Proceed to the meeting place and retrieve all personal effects from the other vessel, in the morning we shall dock and put an end to the enslavement that has been going on."

"Yes ma'am," he replied as he scurried off to relay the orders.

174

"I'm not sure if there will be a war or not," she said as she turned towards Mortimer, "but you better be prepared either way."

Mortimer shrugged, "It's better to be prepared for war and not have one, then the other way around."

Scarlet laughed, "I just can't picture you living a calm life."

"Same can be said about you," he replied with a smile.

They all laughed, as the only one who appeared comfortable with a calm life was Tara.

Once they caught up with the scout ship, the crew spent the night preparing for battle, and getting what rest they could. Mortimer learned one important thing on this sea voyage, a ship at sea never rested, there was always a portion of the crew working.

# Pirate King

The morning came quickly, and with the promise of a beautiful day. The sky was clear and the sun rose brightly as if to say let me show you the way. Ahead they could see a large island with many ships moored off the coast, through the spyglass they could see a single long pier devoid of any vessels as if waiting for a particular ship.

"That pier is where we will dock," Zephyr said, "My ship is the only one allowed to dock there, all others drop anchor further out and use the longboats to ferry their wares to the shore."

As they approached the island, Mortimer noticed several buildings built against cliff sides, "Why are they built against the cliffs?" he asked.

"They are only the fronts of the buildings," she answered, "we built into natural caves and then dug out tunnels into the cliffs. This way if the buildings are burned, we will only lose a small portion of our wares."

As he looked at the other vessels, Mortimer started to calculate the number of potential enemies and frowned, "There are a lot of men we could be fighting against."

Zephyr laughed, "There are almost an equal number of women who will be likely to side with us, but first let us dock and we shall head to the council of captains. If we can convince them to join us, then their crews will side with us as well."

"You make it sound like a walk in the park," He replied.

"I wouldn't know, I've never been in a park," she retorted.

Mortimer laughed, "Oh, it is going to be very interesting taking you girls to the city."

Zephyr laughed as well, "It's going to be just as interesting introducing you to the council of captains."

As they neared the island, the ship's crew raised two flags, the topmost was a multi-colored rose on a black background, and the other was a harpy with a golden crown over its head on a red background. "Well captain, should I put her into port or will you?" Zephyr asked.

Mortimer frowned, "If I tried, I would most likely wreck the ship, so please feel free to bring her in."

Several ships noticed the flags, and the crews on board could be seen standing and staring at their vessel, they received almost as much attention as the ghost ship which sailed in alongside them. A large number of men and women gathered on the dock as they drew closer and quickly pulled them alongside the dock as the sailors threw mooring lines to the crowd.

Zephyr threw a loop of rope around the ship's wheel, and led the way down the stairs and to the gangplank. It wasn't until Scarlet, Clarice and Tara joined them at the gangplank, that she allowed it to be extended to the dock. Once the plank was in place, she turned to Mortimer and said, "As you are the captain, you must descend first." She then turned to Scarlet, after that we will descend in order of rank, so you will follow him, then Clarice, Tara and finally myself. The rest of the crew shall remain here and await word from the captain."

As Mortimer descended the gangplank, he heard a slight hiss of surprise from the crowd, it was joined by murmurs when Scarlet and the others followed behind him. When he stepped off the gangplank, he noticed many in the crowd had their hands on their weapons, but none of them attacked.

When Zephyr stepped off the gangplank, the crowd got silent and watched as she bowed slightly to Mortimer and said loudly, "Captain, allow me to escort you to the council of captains."

Mortimer bowed his head slightly to her and replied, "I would appreciate it if you would."

The crowd parted slowly to allow them through, a couple of men made comments about the women as they parted, until Scarlet waved her hand and a ball of fire appeared in it. Instantly the crowd moved to the sides of the dock and was quiet.

Zephyr laughed, "Now, now mistress, they meant no harm and were only trying to pay you a compliment."

Scarlet blushed slightly and shook out the fireball, "Sorry dear, it was only meant to be a warning should any think it would be a good idea to board our vessel uninvited."

"Oh, such a warning is not necessary," Zephyr replied, "the last to do that was skinned alive and then left to die of exposure in a cage. The people here know better than to mess with a vessel on this dock."

Mortimer chuckled dryly, "You realize I will do far worse than skin someone alive for boarding my vessel without my permission, but here and now is not the time to discuss such things."

"Yes captain," Zephyr responded, as she slipped her arm into his and escorted him down the dock and towards a large building at the back of the small city. Once on land she smiled sweetly at him, "Well, that went better than planned, I wasn't expecting to get this far without a fight."

Tara laughed, "Well now that we are on land, I can be much more effective if it comes down to it."

Zephyr grinned, "That's good to know," she said as she led them to the entrance of a two story building which appeared to have arrow slits in the second floor. "We have a unit of archers stationed on the second floor at all times, along with four cannons on the first floor behind the curtains. It would cost a lot of lives for an army to get inside the council."

As they approached the doors, two guards lowered a pair of poleaxes across their path.

"Has the challenge been answered?" asked the guard on the left.

The guard on the right looked over at Mortimer and his eyes widened slightly, but he said nothing.

In answer, Zephyr threw a torn and burnt flag on the ground at the guards feet, "now, let us pass that I might speak with the council."

Mortimer chuckled as the guards raised their poleaxes to let them pass, "Good to see you again," he said softly as he passed the guard on the right, "if it comes down to it I will kill you this time."

The guard smiled back at him, "My loyalty is to my queen first and foremost, so I hope we are on the same side."

Zephyr laughed, "As long as you are on my side, you shall not face my husband on the battlefield."

Both guards' jaws dropped at this comment, and they watched the group enter the building. They heard the guard on the right saying to the other guard, "I'm glad I don't have to fight against him, he wiped out an entire regiment by himself the last time I saw him fight."

Mortimer laughed, "So much for discipline."

"We've never been big on discipline," Zephyr replied, "we always found loyalty to be more important." She led them down a narrow hallway for about fifty feet, before it opened out into a large cavern with chairs lining the walls.

Mortimer noticed that about half of the chairs sat empty, the rest were filled with an odd assortment of men and women. In the center of the room sat a throne, it was positioned as such that anyone walking in would be seen immediately. Zephyr led him directly to this chair and with a wave of her arm indicated he should be seated. When he sat down, a gasp arose from the people in the room.

One older gentleman wearing very fancy clothing with lots of gold jewelry stood up and asked, "What is the meaning of this?"

Zephyr turned to them and said, "As is customary I must surrender my position to the person who has bested me in battle. Allow me to introduce you all to the man who spared my life after subduing myself and my crew, Captain Mortimer DeRose, the new pirate king, and my husband." She took a deep breath and continued, "Also permit me to introduce to you his wives, Lady Scarlet, Lady Clarice, and Lady Tara. If any would like to challenge this transition let them do so with blade and blood in the confines of this court."

One woman stood up and asked, "Am I to understand that you are willingly submitting to being his fourth wife, and his subject?"

"That is correct," she answered, "he bested me fairly in battle, and as custom dictates I became his servant when he spared my life."

The woman laughed, "Talk about irregular, this could set a bad precedent for captains ordering their crew to marry them if they want."

Mortimer laughed, "I would never order a woman to marry me," he said, "it was simply something she agreed to after speaking with my other wives." He smiled at Zephyr, "Besides, I doubt any man here would survive ordering her around."

The woman smiled and winked at him, "You mean any man other than yourself, after all you bested her before in battle." After she spoke, she sat down with a contented look upon her face.

Mortimer watched as the captains talked among themselves for a few minutes, before one strong young man stood and said, "I would challenge your right to be king, choose the time and we shall meet here for a duel to see who is king."

Zephyr sighed, as Mortimer stood up and stepped down from his seat, "How about now?" he asked, "or are you merely peacocking in the hopes of getting a woman tonight?"

The captain who had challenged him removed his coat and drew a cutlass as he advanced towards the center of the court.

Mortimer smiled as he simply stepped forward, and drew his sword, "Rules of engagement?" he asked Zephyr as he passed her.

"Kill him," she answered, "he is one of those who enjoys hurting others."

Mortimers smile widened as he heard this, "Ah, it has been a while since I have fought on land, so forgive me if I don't kill you quickly enough."

The man facing him growled at him and rushed forward, he tried to slash Mortimer and continue past, only to have Mortimer deflect the blow.

Mortimer kept a smile on his face, as he blocked each strike. "You lack imagination," he said as the man tried once more to cut him as he ran past. As the man charged at him, he dropped his sword to his left hand and said, "Try something more creative, like this." He deflected the strike and drove his right fist directly into the man's face. As blood erupted from his nose, Mortimer gave a flick of his left wrist and lunged, his sword drove into the man's thigh and out the other side. He grimaced and the man screamed in pain, as he twisted his sword and ripped it out of his leg, slicing a chunk of flesh off at the same time.

Mortimer noticed he still held his cutlass and smiled evilly, "This could take a while."

The man swayed on his feet for a minute, before he collapsed to the ground and dropped his sword, "I" he started to say, when Mortimer's sword whipped around in an arc and removed his head from his shoulders.

"The only way to leave an enemy is in pieces," he said as he sheathed his still bloody sword and returned to his seat. "Anybody else have a problem with me?" he asked.

Zephyr laughed softly as the captains started talking amongst themselves again, "He would have been my replacement if I had died at sea," she said to him. While the captains are voted in by their crew, the queen or king is decided by who is the most powerful among the captains."

"So what happens with the fallen captain's crew now that he is dead?" Scarlet asked softly.

"In this case, they will be given the choice of joining the crew of the captain who killed him, or voting for a new captain," she smiled, "his crew will most likely vote to join us, as he was known for being extremely harsh to his crew."

A young man walked calmly into the court and approached Zephyr, "Permission to speak with the king."

She in turn looked at Mortimer and winked, Mortimer nodded back and she said, "He grants you permission to approach."

The young man bowed as he approached and said, "As you have defeated our captain, would you like me to spread word to the rest of the crew and have them take a vote?"

Mortimer frowned for a second, and the young man winced, "Normally I would have to send a messenger, but I believe this method might work out better. Please take the message to his ship, and be sure to deliver it with a barrel of grog at my expense, in compensation for killing your captain."

The young man straightened up, "Right away sire." As he turned to leave, Zephyr handed him two gold coins for the grog.

After he left one of the nearby captains laughed, "Well, I guess you just gained an extra crew and ship. They will not forget your generosity."

He looked over at the captain and raised an eyebrow, she was dressed more like a tavern wench than a pirate, but the cutlass on her hip and the daggers in her boots spoke of her ability to kill. "Thank you, I believe in dealing fairly in all things."

"Well you know if you're looking to increase your fleet, I wouldn't be opposed to a mutually beneficial marriage," she replied.

Mortimer laughed gently, "You would have to speak with my wives about that, for we have an agreement, they have to approve of any new wives before I marry them."

She returned his smile, "Well said, you are a much smarter man than I first thought." She stepped closer to him and smiled as she leaned towards him, "Would you at least like to spend the night on my ship, so that I might get to know your lovely wives?"

Mortimer frowned, he could see the waves of magic emanating from her, but was unsure how best to deal with it, without starting another fight. Then it dawned on him, "Let me introduce you to my first wife," he replied, "and if she agrees, then I will spend a night with you." He turned his head slightly and said, "Scarlet, can you come closer, there is someone you need to meet."

Scarlet turned towards him and instantly saw the web this lady was casting, with a smile on her face she stepped right next to Mortimer and replied, "Did you find a new playmate for me dear?"

Mortimer smiled at Scarlet, "Yes I believe I have." He got a deep whiff of the scent of an open fire from her and felt the powers of the captain back away. "This captain would like me to spend the night on her ship tonight, what do you think?"

"Sounds good to me," she answered, as everyone looked shocked, "provided she spends the night with me, and should she leave my presence she forfeit her ship and crew to us."

The captain smiled, "I concede mistress, I can see you are not one to take lightly." She turned back to Mortimer and said, "Myself and my crew are yours to command."

Mortimer saw the waves of magic fade away and smiled at her, "Good to hear, my wives will fill you in on our objective. Oh, you probably should be more careful who you try to use magic on, if I had accepted your offer, it would not have turned out as you expected."

Scarlet smiled at the captain and said, "Come let us talk, you should meet the rest and we'll explain exactly what you just avoided."

The captain nodded her head and waved to a young lady who ran off out of the chamber, to report the change of alliance to the rest of the crew.

Mortimer noticed a subtle shift in the room, all of the women had moved over to speak with his wives, while the men continued to argue amongst themselves. "What is happening?" he asked Zephyr softly.

She smiled coyly at him, "They are debating whether they will follow you, or stage a rebellion. Many of the older men are willing to side with you, but some of the younger captains feel they should put up some form of resistance."

"That makes sense, my next question is what is going on outside?" he asked.

"That I don't know, but as of now you have half of the council on your side," she answered. "You could speed things up if you demand they make a decision. Those who support you will sit to your right, those against you will choose seats to your left. I should warn you, that is a power play that could backfire."

"I will let them continue to argue amongst themselves for now," he replied. "Why did all the women make such a decision so rapidly?"

She chuckled, "The women have always stood together, and when you didn't fall to Lorelei's spell, they knew they couldn't defeat you easily and their lives and freedom would be forfeit if they tried."

Mortimer laughed, "All her magic did was irritate me, if she hadn't tried to use it I might have agreed to spend a night on her ship, on condition my wives accompany me."

Zephyr couldn't resist, she burst out laughing, "That would have terrified her, she's very innocent in regards to certain things."

Mortimer noticed some of the older men had stopped arguing and came over to talk with the women. After another hour or so, he cleared his throat loudly and asked, "Is it possible to get a drink while you gentlemen converse?" At this point he noticed he had more than half the captains on his side of the chamber.

Zephyr suddenly turned a deep crimson color, "Oh my lord, I have been so remiss in my duties, I shall get you some wine immediately." She turned and headed out of the chamber at a brisk walk and returned in mere moments with a sealed bottle of wine and several goblets. "I inspected each and every goblet myself to be certain there was no sign of poisoning sir, and the wine is from my own stock. Several more bottles will be brought in a few minutes." She quickly uncorked the bottle of wine, filled the goblets and handed them to him, Scarlet, Clarice and Tara.

"Thank you," he said as he took the wine. He waited while she poured herself a goblet from another bottle, and together they lifted their goblets and drank. "This is very nice wine," he said with a smile.

"Did you see that?" one of the women said, "He waited until all of his wives had been served before he drank himself."

One of the men across the room laughed, "What a fool, how does he know she didn't poison it herself?"

Mortimer raised an eyebrow at the man and asked, "Do you challenge my ladies honor?" He turned to Zephyr and asked, "Would you like for me to deliver his head to you?"

The color drained from Zephyr's face, "No thank you captain, I would rather collect it myself." She hoped the insult of a crewmate challenging him would cause the captain to back down; she had heard about how Mortimer could go into a battle frenzy when protecting his wives.

Scarlet stepped forward, "Captain, if it pleases you, allow me to retrieve his head, my blades are thirsty after all."

Mortimer looked at Scarlet and smiled as he saw her hand resting on the crimson sword, "Very well, provided he accepts the challenge."

The captain snorted at this and stepped forward as he drew his sword, "Very well wench come forward and learn your place in our ranks."

Scarlet didn't hesitate, with a wave of her hand a wall of fire sprung up around the two of them. "To keep things fair, anyone who tries to step over the ring of fire shall be burned to death, but don't worry it will go out when one of us is declared the victor." She drew the crimson shortsword and stepped towards the captain, "I should warn you, I have killed many men before you and am certain I shall kill many more."

This captain wasn't a fool, he stepped towards her cautiously and made a few quick slashes, as she dodged them he grinned. "You are light on your feet, that is good, but fancy footwork won't keep you alive in this battle."

Scarlet returned his smile as she spun like a dancer and her sword whistled in the air. There was a collective gasp from the crowd, as a thin red line suddenly appeared on the captain's arm.

"First blood to you," he said with a grunt.

"And last as well," she replied as she slipped inside his sword arm and thrust the crimson sword up under his chin and into his head. "That wasn't much fun dear," she said as she removed the man's head and brought it back to give to Zephyr. "Maybe we should just kill them all and call it a day."

Zephyr frowned, "And here I thought he was the bloodthirsty one."

Mortimer laughed, "It's her sword, it is very bloodthirsty, and if it isn't fed often it tends to affect her personality."

Everyone who heard this started to laugh nervously.

"Don't worry though, she has never killed anyone who hasn't deserved it." He added with a smile.

Zephyr laughed, "I'm glad she's on my side."

At this point more of the men came and sat down on his side, Mortimer frowned, "I do believe we have waited long enough, it is time for the captains to make their decision."

Once everyone had sat down, Mortimer looked around and smiled, "What will those in the minority do?"

One of the captains stood up and said, "My crew and I would like to find a nice safe place to retire."

Mortimer smiled, "Anyone else have this desire?"

Several captains raised their hands.

"Granted," he replied, "I have just the place for you to move to, provided you are willing to sail under my banner to get there. I'm not entirely certain how some of the villagers will receive you, but if you're willing to help protect them in the future they should eventually accept you as neighbors."

With that being said, he watched as several more captains moved over to his side of the room. "Anyone else looking for a way out of the pirate's life?" he asked. He was surprised by the number of hands that were raised on both sides of the chamber, "Very well, then I would have you write down suggestions as for what you would like to do other than being a pirate. Anyone who insists they only want to be a pirate, please stay put for now."

Zephyr sidled up next to him and asked, "What are you planning on doing once you have the list?"

He winked at her and replied, "You mentioned most of these folks were only pirates because that is the only life they know, and if given a chance would leave and live a more legal life. I am going to give as many of them that chance as possible."

She shook her head, "They are bound by magic to serve the pirate throne, they cannot be released unless the throne approves of it."

He chuckled softly, "Just as you were bound to adhere to the life of a pirate and unable to escape it?"

She nodded her head.

"I am not bound by any of that," he said softly, "I am bound by my oath to protect my home and family, as such I am going to protect them by eliminating the pirate threat." He watched the captains for a moment before he asked, "How many of them do you think would be willing to become privateers for the order? The pay is decent and they would be allowed to raid ships and towns of our enemies."

Zephyr's eyes widened for a moment, "That would subvert their bonds easily."

He smiled at her, "Circulate the idea, we will review the list of desires the captains have tomorrow. Right now I would like to visit the slave pens and see how crowded they are."

She bowed her head respectfully and slipped back into the crowd of captains as they wrote down what they wanted from the new king.

# Shar

Mortimer chuckled as he slipped away from the throne and across the chamber, he approached a woman who watched him warily from the sidelines and said, "Would you kindly show me the way to the slave pens?"

She raised an eyebrow at him, but bowed her head, "As the king wishes, are you seeking a new playmate?"

"Oh, you think so little of me," he replied. "No, if I wanted a playmate I'd ask any number of the women back there. I just wish to see what their living conditions are and be certain they are still in good health."

"Very well," she replied as she turned and led the way to a door, "follow me."

He followed her to a small doorway into a side tunnel with several locked doors in a row. Once they passed through and she unlocked the third door, she turned to him and said, "We take very good care of the people down below, sometimes better than the homes they have come from."

Mortimer chuckled, "That is to be expected, after all weak or sick slaves don't bring in much money. Now, take me to the pens, I wish to see for myself how they are living."

The woman frowned at him and replied, "You try so much as to harm one of them and I will kill you, king or not."

"You would be remiss in your duties if you did not attempt it," he replied, "but fear not I have no intention of harming them."

She led him down the tunnel until they came to a split in the tunnel, "To the right are the bound slaves, to the left are the ones not yet bound, which do you want to see first?"

"Let us go to the left," he answered. "Maybe I can find a way to prevent them from getting bound into slavery." He noticed the guard had tensed when he said this, and he dropped his hand to the pommel of his sword, "Don't make me kill you," he hissed at her.

The guard didn't move, but stared him directly in the eyes. "I am not sure who would win in this tunnel, but if you don't draw a weapon neither will I. Why do you wish to prevent them from being bound?"

"Because then I will be forced to break the bonds, and that is an extremely painful process for them," he answered. "Not to mention it really complicates matters for me, as I apparently end up causing an entanglement."

Suddenly the guard burst out laughing, "Come, I will show you the new arrivals, they are not scheduled for processing until tomorrow."

"Processed," he asked as he followed the guard.

"Yes," she replied, "basically we keep them for about a week, before they are taken into a separate room, and are magically bound to us, after which they are moved to the other tunnel where their training begins. Those who show a willingness and aptitude for the pirate's life we keep, the others we train and sell to the villages." She stopped for a second, before she continued, "I have never been a fan of this process, but I am bound to my duty to the throne just like everyone else on this island."

"Then knowing what I intend to do, how can you lead me to them?" he asked.

"I felt no recoil from the bond when you told me your intent, actually it felt like it loosened a bit," she answered.

Mortimer started to laugh softly, "Because it recognizes me as the throne." He thought about what Zephyr had said about the magical bonds put on her as a child, and suddenly he could hear the conversation going on in her presence and grinned, she was getting oaths of loyalty to him from some of the captains.

"Are you alright?" the guard asked, interrupting his thoughts.

"Yes," he replied with a shake of his head, "I was just checking on Zephyr's progress, that is all."

"That must be one strong marriage bond," she said as she started to unlock a door in the tunnel.

Mortimer couldn't help but laugh, "It's what happens when one uses a blood bond in order to break the bond on another, it creates one hell of a magical entanglement, as all of my wives are now tied to me through the same blood bond."

"How does a blood bond work, and how can it be used to remove a seritude bond?" she asked.

"It is a very dark art, in which my own blood is used to attack a person and take control of their body. Normally it is for a brief time, after being injured, and the black blood from the wound basically will kill the person it strikes." he chuckled darkly, "I have learned how to use mine to basically rip the bonds of others out of their bodies, it is the battle between the two bonds that creates the entanglement. The stronger the bonds are, the stronger the entanglement."

"What would happen if their bond was stronger than yours?" she asked in awe.

"Then I would be bound by its requirements," he answered.

"So your wives are bound by the same bonds as you are?" she asked.

He thought about it for a moment and laughed, "I never thought of it that way, but yes."

She opened the door for him and smiled, "You must be very powerful if you can break that many bonds and are thinking of breaking even more."

He looked around the room, inside there were maybe a dozen naked girls of various ages, but they all appeared healthy and well fed. "They need clothing and to be relocated to my ship immediately."

The guard looked shocked at this statement, but bowed her head, "Right away." She shivered for a second and frowned, "You must have quite the hold on the captains, the bond reacted before I could react on my own, and it hurts when it does."

He looked at her and smiled darkly, "That's nothing compared to the pain of disobeying it, or having it ripped from your flesh, just ask my wives."

"I will," she replied, "Now let me show you the ones who have already been bound." She led him back up the tunnel after locking the door, and down the other tunnel to another door. This door was not locked, and when she opened it he saw a huge cavern behind it.

In this cavern about a hundred girls and young women sat at tables and worked on various projects, none of them looked up when they entered.

"The tables on the left are all of the girls who have had their bonds for more than a year, they will be the next lot taken out and sold, on the right are the girls who have only just recently received their bonds, and they will be here until they are of an age for us to sell them." The guard said, "I have prevented any underage girl from being sold for the past five years, through the doorways are their sleeping areas, each room dedicated to a particular age."

"Don't let Tara see this," he advised her, "I am not sure how she would react since she was once kept here."

The guard gasped, "You are truly powerful if you broke a slaves bonds. Do you mind if I speak with her about it?"

"Not at all, but please try to be circumspect when you talk to her," he replied. "Come, we should get back to the council chamber, I am certain people have noticed my disappearance by now."

"Yes sir," the guard replied as she led him back up the tunnel and through all of the doors. "One can't be too careful when it comes to protecting these girls," she said as she locked the three doors at the entrance to the tunnel.

"So you lock the doors to keep people out, not to keep the girls in?" He asked.

"Correct," she replied, "when Zephyr took over she forbid any man from going down there, as such you are the first man to see the slave pens in the last six years."

"Thank you," he replied, and bowed his head slightly to her before he headed back to the throne.

Zephyr spotted him as he approached and smiled, "Did you have a good inspection?" she asked.

"You assigned a good woman a horrible job," he replied, "but in all it was a good inspection."

She chuckled, "Honestly she asked for the job when her captain died at sea. She is a tough woman, and brought many of the soldiers here. I am surprised you didn't ask her to join us."

"I left an open invitation for her to speak with you and the others, it is up to her if she decides to accept," he replied. "If you wish to spend some time with her, you may, I am sure I can handle the remaining captains."

Zephyr smiled, "I will go talk with her, the captains will be done soon enough, only a few do not agree with your assumption to the throne, but they are willing to accept you as our leader."

He nodded his head in understanding and watched her walk over to speak with the guard woman. Running a fleet of pirate ships was not something he had ever intended to do, but now that he had taken charge, he didn't have much of a choice.

One of the captains noticed the look on his face and laughed, "Better you than me," he said as he signed his name on a scroll. Afterwards he looked at Mortimer and continued, "It takes one hell of a tough man to beat her in combat, and an even tougher one to make her his wife. If you must know, the simple fact you were able to defeat her in combat and not kill her persuaded many of the captains to vote for you, and when you offered to let us lead the lives we want to lead, that persuaded the rest of us. Well, there are a few hold outs, but they won't last long."

Mortimer chuckled dryly, "She was a fun fight, I will admit, but if you really want to feel the heat, go a few rounds with Scarlet."

The captain raised an eyebrow at him, "You're saying if someone wants to be with her they can?"

He laughed, "Not quite, I'm saying if they want to try to win her over they had best be prepared for a very tough fight. In case you hadn't noticed, she doesn't hold back, and she'll use every tool she has to win."

"That could be a very painful death," the captain replied with a nod. "What about your other wives?"

Mortimer chuckled, "Clarice is as cold as ice and will make your blood run cold, Tara on the other hand is very nurturing and gentle but she will crush your bones to dust in a fight."

"So, how do you describe Zephyr then?"

He could tell the captain was trying to see if there was any weakness in his relationship with his wives and chuckled, "She is a great person to talk to and can take your breath away, quite literally." With a smile he continued, "Honestly all of them are quite beautiful and very deadly, the perfect match for a child born of death."

"So you're not a warlock," the captain replied, "you're a necromancer. You gain power from death, whether recent or in the past. The last I heard there weren't any of them left outside the Order of the Rose."

"Correct," Mortimer replied, "so now you know who the fleet will be working for, any problems?"

"Not at all, you just made us into honorable men," he answered.

"Once we eliminate those who won't give their oath," Mortimer replied, as he turned and walked over to Scarlet's side.
"You look frustrated," she said as he approached.

He shrugged and gave her a hug and a quick kiss, "No more so than usual, I am eager to return the slaves to their homes and then to return to my own."

"I know, we have a present for you tonight, when we return to the ship," she said softly, "It may help alleviate the darkness you've been collecting since we got here."

"Oh? Who did you manage to spirit away?" he asked.

She chuckled, "A certain captain who caught your eye, apparently she isn't very well trained in her art, and when she gave her oath, the bond had a very nasty reaction to the spell she tried to use on you." She chuckled softly, "it was still in effect when she took her oath, so you can imagine the outcome. As it is, I had a pair of guards take her to the ship, but you are going to have to teach her how to properly cancel her own magic."

"No," he replied, "I can't teach her unless you girls are in the room as well. Her magic is similar to Clarice's mating scent, and I withstood it because I had you near me."

Scarlet laughed, "So you're saying you think she's got mermaid blood?"

"Yes," he replied, "not nearly as much as Clarice, but she definitely has it in her ancestry."

"Then it's simple, Clarice can teach her proper control," she answered, "but we are going to need to first loosen the bonds on her."

"It'll have to be a team effort then," Mortimer replied, "I can command the bonds to loosen, as they are tied to my wishes as pirate king, but if her spell activates they will automatically kick in again."

Scarlet laughed, "This is promising to be fun, especially since you aren't planning to use her to release the darkness, which means you will probably use me."

Mortimer frowned, she was definitely feeling what he was, and he wasn't sure if he wanted her to feel everything he felt inside.

She suddenly looked at him with a serious expression and said, "We have shared blood, I feel your hunger and look forward to satisfying it with however many bodies you wish to consume."

He frowned, "Let's go," he said as he grabbed her hand and dragged her over to where Zephyr was talking to the guard woman. "Zephyr, you are in charge, be sure to get the materials we need to remodel the captain's quarters on our ship."

Zephyr took one look at him and bowed, "Yes sir," she replied and headed back over to the remaining captains as Mortimer and Scarlet went down a side corridor.

"That's not the way out," the guard woman said, as they went through the tunnel.

Zephyr stopped and smiled, "Don't worry, they're not looking for a way out, they're looking for a safe place to blow off some steam. Come with me, I'll introduce you to Clarice and Tara."

"Will they be alright?" she asked.

"They will, whatever is in the cavern they end up in probably won't be," she replied. "Almost all of my belongings were destroyed the last time this happened, there are still scorch marks on the walls and ceiling as it is."

"Scorch marks?" the guard asked.

"Yes," Zephyr replied, "as you know I am part harpy, well Scarlet is part dragon." She approached Clarice and smiled, "This young lady is Clarice, and she is half mermaid. As you can see Mortimer has an affinity for the exotic."

"So then what is Tara?" The guard asked cautiously.

Zephyr laughed, "She is part earth elemental, but we are not sure exactly what type. Now are you sure you really want to be our personal guard?"

"To be honest, I'm not too sure you ladies need a guard now," she replied.

"Well, for the last couple of years, the throne guards have been more of an honor guard than actual guards." She smiled at the guard, "Don't get me wrong, you take your job very seriously, and train hard, but we really haven't had a need for you in recent years. However, I do believe we will need you in the near future, as some of the king's plans may not sit well with some of the captains."

"How many have not sworn loyalty?" the guard asked.

Zephyr handed her the scroll of those who had sworn loyalty to Mortimer, "These are the ones who stand with him, the others I am sure will try to attack us when they feel they may have the advantage."

"None of their ships will be allowed to leave the area," the guard replied, "that should make it easier for you to challenge them to battles here in the council chambers."

Clarice frowned, "They have chosen their side, tomorrow we shall destroy them, that is why he needs to release his tension." She looked at Zephyr and Tara, "I know you two feel it as well."

The guard bowed her head, "Very well, I will serve in whatever capacity the king requires of me."

Zephyr laughed, "How far are you willing to go to serve your king?" she asked.

"I would give my life, you know that," she replied.

Clarice and Tara looked at each other and laughed, "Are you willing to endure extreme agony?" Tara asked.

"Are you willing to become one of us?" Clarice asked.

The guard stared at both of them and replied, "I would walk through the fires of hell to protect my king, and gladly I would become one of you but I am nothing special compared to you."

Zephyr looked around and said, "Show yourself witch, I can hear you whispering."

A crimson mist rose slowly from one of the pools of blood on the chamber floor, and thickened until they could make out the form of the Crimson Witch. "Oh, she fed me well today, and her power is extraordinary right now. I didn't realize their bond had gotten so strong, they share power. It is amazing."

Zephyr laughed, "They're not the only ones who feed off his power, all of us do, it's just some of us have more subtle ways of releasing it. Now what were you saying about the pieces coming together?"

The Crimson Witch laughed, "The ritual requires a body per blade, as my soul was split into five pieces, so must there be five people willing to sacrifice themselves to restore me. Mortimer can't be one of those people, as he has to be willing to sacrifice himself to restore my husband." She saw the reaction from all of them and laughed, "Oh come now how did you think we would untangle the magical entanglement?"

The guard woman stepped forward, "I will take Mortimer's place, it is my duty and my right as his guard."

"I'm sorry child, but that is not possible, at present." the witch replied, "I will say though you would be a welcome addition to the family." She smiled at her, "you would be quite a unique addition I would have to say."

Clarice looked the Crimson Witch in the eye and laughed, "You are correct, in that we are prepared to die for Mortimer, but I get the feeling you are not telling us something."

"You are correct, descendant of my best friend, and I cannot give you that information until after the point of no return. I will say I wish I had done things differently, and that I had included her in the ritual instead of another." She smiled darkly, "I do recommend that he bring both the guard and the innocent hussy into the family, just to be safe." She turned to the guard and her smile softened, "You are far more special than you know child of war." With that she faded back into a mist and vanished.

Zephyr frowned slightly, "Just as ambiguous as always, is it possible for her to give us a straight answer?"

Clarice laughed, "Oh yes, when she is in a particularly good mood she will joke around a bit and answer many questions straight forward. I'm wondering how she manifested here without Scarlet and the crimson blade here?"

Tara frowned and pulled a small red knife out of her pouch, "I was using it when I made our clothing, and forgot I still had it."

Zephyr laughed, "That's alright, I assumed it was because Scarlet had given me one of her daggers when we had our chat the other day." She looked at Clarice and smiled, "I'm surprised you didn't notice the knife she gave you the other day was a crimson blade."

Clarice shrugged, "I hadn't thought about it, I haven't pulled it from its scabbard since she gave it to me."

"My question is why she would want a backup water witch for the ritual?" Tara asked.

"Because of my great grandmother," Clarice answered, "they couldn't use her and had to use a stand in, but with all the problems that created with the ritual I could never do that to him, or the rest of you."

Zephyr chuckled dryly and turned to the guard woman, "So are you still interested?"

"How does this sound for a pickup line? My name is Shar, but you can call me Honey." She replied, "Do you think it will work with him?"

"No, but it works on me Honey," Zephyr said as she laughed, "you don't need a pickup line, we'll introduce you."

At this point she noticed smoke billowing out of the tunnel Scarlet and Mortimer had gone into, "Well, I guess now would be a good time to check on them. I think we should all go, we may need Tara's walls, and they may need Clarice's healing."

Shar followed the three of them into the tunnel, after several twists and turns, they came to a room, which used to contain unused furniture, but currently was filled with the charred remains of wooden furniture and two completely exhausted people asleep in the middle of the floor.

Zephyr waved her arms in the air and mumbled something softly, and the smoke cleared out of the room. With the smoke gone you could clearly see scorch marks all over the walls and ceiling, along with what appeared to be claw marks from some sort of animal. "They did a lot less damage than I had expected," she said as she surveyed the room.

Tara laughed, "It was a good test for their clothing, it appears to have survived it, but can you feel that energy coming from him?"

Clarice laughed, "Yes, it would be a good idea to move them to the ship, it will help him to decompress. It's going to be a fun night tonight, I wonder if he'll sleep for very long."

Mortimer chuckled dryly, "No, I won't, you are correct I have an over abundance of energy right now, I'm not sure if I can burn it all off by morning though even with the three of you."

"Four," Shar said.

Zephyr chuckled, "We'll let you start with her first, just remember to go easy on her, she isn't a witch and we don't want you to break her."

"You'll have to check with Scarlet first," he replied, "I'm not exactly looking for another wifc aftcr all."

Tara shrugged, "Given the information the Crimson Witch gave us you need two more than you have, and she wants them to be Shar, and that hussy captain, her words not mine, that's on our ship right now."

"Any particular reason?" he asked.

Zephyr smiled, "One for each piece, and a spare just in case one backs out."

"And what do you three think?" he asked.

"We all agree on Shar," she replied, "the other one we will need to discuss."

"Very well," he said, "but you get to tell Scarlet." With that he leaned over and whispered in her ear, instantly she sat up.

"What did you say?" she asked him with an arched eyebrow.

Zephyr smiled at her and said, "I'll explain on the way back to the ship."

It was a very interesting conversation, but in the end Scarlet agreed to the idea, if only to see the captain go through a ton of pain for trying to seduce Mortimer. She agreed to Shar based on the simple fact that Zephyr trusted her and she had not tried anything on Mortimer when she was alone with him. "Shar first though," she said, "I want that bitch captain to see what is going to happen to her."

Zephyr smiled, "Wow she really rubbed you the wrong way, you weren't even this mad when he added me to the family."

Scarlet smiled at her, "None of you actually had designs on him, I don't trust that bitch."

Zephyr laughed, "Just think though when those bonds come off, her true nature will be revealed."

Clarice laughed, "I am used to my nature, and being able to switch forms means it doesn't show up in my human body, in her case she will freak when her skin turns scaly and she develops webbed toes and fingers. That will depend on how long ago her mermaid heritage was though."

Shar shook her head and asked, "What exactly does this wedding ritual entail?"

Tara shrugged, "Oh the usual, ripping the magical bonds from your body and replacing them with new ones, followed by ritual sacrifice of your body to your husband's desires, and his sacrificing his body to yours." She smiled, "You will hate it, but at the same time you will find yourself willing to do it all over again if he asked you to."

Everyone laughed at the look on Shar's face before Mortimer said, "Tara it is good to see you in such a playful mood, I look forward to our time together tonight, that goes for all of you. Please don't tease her too much, she need not fear what is going to happen tonight, but please feel free to torment the other one."

"True," Scarlet replied, "in all honesty it is a simple removal and replacement of your bonds, the removal part hurts the most, usually followed by sex although with us it was quite rowdy, with you I believe he will be much more gentle. Honestly he only gets as rough as his partner, the more you get into it the more he does."

Shar shook her head and laughed, "Well that will make three firsts in one night then for me, first time having my bond broken, first time getting bound to a man, and a first time to sleep with a man, I've pretty much stayed away from romance after all the abuse I witnessed to others."

"Well, if anyone tries to hurt you once you're part of this family, they will find out hell is a real place," Mortimer said with a grimace.

Once they reached the ship, they went directly into the cabin, and Shar was shocked by all of the scorch marks on the walls, "It's a miracle you didn't catch the boat on fire."

Clarice laughed, "A well placed wave prevented that several times."

Mortimer looked at Shar and smiled, "You can back out at any time before I start removing the bonds."

Shar shook her head, "No, I can do this."

"Then remove your armor and clothing," he replied. "After that lie down on the floor."

She followed his instructions, part of her ashamed of the scars she had on her body, but she lied down as instructed and tried to relax.

Mortimer chuckled to himself, her bonds were not nearly as difficult as the others had been. He placed his fingertips on her wrist, and let his own magic slip between the bonds and her flesh, with a wry smile, he gave a sudden jerk and she arched her back in pain. He worked quickly, using his magic to replace the bonds that had originally bound her to the pirate throne and in only a few minutes he was done.

Shar lay there on the floor panting and staring up at him, she didn't know why, but she reached up and pulled him down to kiss her. The next thing she knew was that she was comfortable and his arms were wrapped gently around her. "Are you asleep?" she asked softly.

"No," he answered, "but you fell asleep quickly afterwards. I didn't hurt you did I?"

"No," she answered, "I enjoyed myself, thank you for accepting me, now we should probably get to work."

Mortimer chuckled, "I see you have already connected to the others."

Zephyr laughed from the corner, "I told you captain, she would be a great fit in the family."

Shar looked around, "you mean you were all watching us?"

Clarice laughed, "Yes, we wanted to make certain you didn't hurt him."

Scarlet laughed, "Welcome to the family," she said as she handed her a dagger. "Take good care of this, she gets really upset if she gets misplaced."

Shar stood up, and put on her armor, the crimson dagger strapped to her side directly above her own short sword. "I will carry it with honor and pride," she responded to Scarlet.

"I know you will," a voice came from the shadows, "after all I picked you."

Mortimer laughed, "I know you're full of energy right now, but you should try to conserve it until tomorrow."

"Very well, but don't forget about the other one," the crimson witch replied as she faded away.

"I won't," he replied as he turned back to his wives. "Any theories as to why it was so easy to remove Shar's bond compared to the rest of yours?"

Zephyr frowned slightly, "It could be that control of the pirate bonds was given to the pirate rulers, but I am not quite certain that is the case or mother and I both would have released several good people from their bonds."

Clarice laughed, "It's the magical ability of the person with the bond, the greater their magic the more difficult it is to remove their bonds."

"Next question," Mortimer said, "is there a way to remove all of the bonds at one time without replacing them with new ones?"

Zephyr laughed, "There is a rumor, that the throne is what sets the bonds, and should the throne be destroyed all of the bonds would be released. Nobody has ever tried it though, for fear of the reprisals from the other captains and the slaves."

"It is something we should look into," Tara replied, "since the throne is stone, maybe I can find out more tomorrow morning."

Scarlet laughed, "it would be nice if for once it was something as simple as destroying a stone chair, I am pretty certain it will be a bit more complicated than we think."

"Besides," Zephyr chimed in, "as the pirate king," she nodded at Mortimer, "you are bound to the throne as well. It gives a great deal of leniency to the ruler of the pirates, but I am pretty sure you won't be able to attack it directly."

Mortimer shrugged, "I doubt it requires us to destroy it, the crimson witch probably knows more about it than we do, and I am sure once we have done as she asked, she will be willing to provide us with some information regarding it." With that he looked around and said, "Come let us deal with Lorelei."

# Lorelei

Mortimer followed Zephyr, as she led him through the ship and to a small cabin in the bow where Lorelei was staying. "No guards?" he asked as they approached the door.

Zephyr laughed, "I thought it best not to allow her an opportunity to seduce one of our sailors."

"Probably a good idea," he replied. As he opened the door, his senses were assaulted by the perfume of the sea, and the sound of waves crashing on the shoreline. Stepping into the room was like stepping into a waterfall, the magic in the air came crashing down on him with terrible force, and yet he knew he would not back away from it.

In the corner of the room a woman was curled in a ball and whimpered in pain beneath a blanket.

Mortimer turned and with a great deal of mental effort closed the door to the room, there was no sense in letting the magic spread to the rest of the ship. He noticed the runes on the inside of the door when it was fully closed and laughed, they were designed to prevent magic from leaving the room, obviously this room had been designed to contain witches.

He turned back to face the woman and smiled, "I am not going to hurt you, so please relax."

She lifted her head and looked at him, the colorful makeup she had worn when they had first met was now a wash of colors all over her face, her eyes were red and swollen from crying, and at the sight of him she groaned and curled into an even tighter ball.

Mortimer shook his head slowly, so much for the plan of having Clarice teach her how to control her magic, Lorelei was already showing signs of madness from the conflict between her own magic and the bonds. He moved closer to her and crouched down, "Well, I guess we have now learned what happens if you try to use magic against the pirate throne." He pulled the blanket from her, and lost his balance in shock, her once smooth looking tanned skin was covered in lumps and swollen with dark purple bruises. The dark chains of the bond fought against the white chains of her magic, and her flesh was getting crushed randomly in the conflict.

He had seen many atrocities in war, and suffered many painful injuries, but what he saw happening to her body was brutal, he could almost feel her pain as he watched the bonds fighting.

Suddenly there was a loud crack, and Lorelei let out a high pitched scream as one arm suddenly bent backwards, the bones in it clearly broken. It was soon followed by another crack as her arm folded back into itself, the same bone broken again.

With a growl, Mortimer grabbed her by the shoulders and held her still, as he attempted to control the two different bonds of magic.

After several minutes, Lorelei let out a ragged gasp and her body relaxed a little. As she opened her eyes and looked up at him, the bonds contracted once more and she writhed in pain until they relaxed again.

"It's a good thing I have so much energy right now," Mortimer whispered, as he let his own power creep along the magic bonds that held her. He focused on her broken arm first, with the intention of immobilizing it before it got any worse, but every time she saw him, her magic went out of control and triggered the pirate bonds.

After several hours, Mortimer was able to intertwine his magic with the pirate bonds surrounding her body; they were pretty strong bonds, but he knew he could remove them if he moved fast enough. "I'm sorry," he said softly to her, "but this is going to hurt even more than what you've felt so far."

Lorelei opened her eyes at these words, and suddenly it felt like her entire body was being ripped apart and set on fire. She saw her magic flood out before her, as it tried to seduce the man before her, at the same time she could see his magic as it dove deep within her flesh and tore through her body, getting stronger as it consumed her own spell. Her crystalline magic was being consumed by his blood red magic, and she could feel the barbed hooks on the black chain as it ripped and tore itself free from her body.

Mortimer's growl deepened and grew louder, the chain did not like being pulled from its prey, never before had anyone challenged it once it had been triggered. Gradually he pulled the last of the bond from her flesh, and it turned towards him. It tried to impale him, but he blocked it, it tried to entangle him, but he broke free from it, finally it dropped to the floor and lay still. He watched as the chain gradually faded away, and he felt something lift from his shoulders, a strange weight that he had not realized he carried.

He almost passed out from relief, until he saw the red cocoon encasing Lorelei, "can't stop yet," he growled.

Lorelei watched him through the red haze that covered her face. She wasn't sure who he was anymore, but she knew he had just done something nobody had ever tried to do before. She smiled, the pain was gone, so was the feeling of always being held back. "You have done enough," she whispered, "you don't need to save me."

Mortimer started to laugh, "I'm sorry, but I have to at least try to save you." He looked at the crimson cocoon and smiled as it sank onto her body and gradually into it.

She watched him closely until all of the red haze was gone, before she threw her good arm around his neck and kissed him. Loroloi forgot about the bruises and broken bones in her body, as she clung to him and drew him closer to her.

He didn't fight it, but gave into her desire, ever mindful of her injuries. It was always the same, something about the use of blood magic always made the people near it very lustful. "Welcome to the family," he whispered when they were done. "Scarlet is going to want to have a word with you."

At this point Zephyr opened the door and said, "She's not the only one." She looked around the room and smiled, "At least you didn't try to burn the place down." One glance at Lorelei and she whistled, "dang you were a lot rougher than even I expected."

Mortimer winced, "I was trying to be gentle, the bonds did a number on her body, and I am pretty sure they did a number on her mind too."

Zephyr shook her head, "and yet you still had your way with her."

He frowned, "I couldn't help it, it's what she wanted."

Lorelei smiled, "It was worth the pain, and he is telling the truth, something in the way our magic interacted made it necessary, I could feel it."

"Clarice will need to tend to her wounds," Mortimer said, "I know her left arm is broken in at least two places, not sure about any of the other bones."

Lorelei grimaced, "It feels as if all of my bones have been pulled out of place, but other than that I think just my arm."

Zephyr smiled, "Let's get you dressed and we can take you to our cabin to get healed." She picked up Lorelei's shredded clothing and frowned, "Did the bond do this or did you?" she asked Mortimer.

He chuckled dryly, "It was shredded while I was removing the bonds, apparently the magical struggle was too much for it."

Zephyr frowned and wrapped a blanket around Lorelei's shoulders, "This will have to do until we can send a runner to your ship to get you some new clothing."

Lorelei smiled, "If it will make him happy I will run around in a sack." She winced as she crossed her arms over her bruised chest, but still smiled at Mortimer and said, "I'd do it again if you asked me to."

Mortimer frowned as he helped her to stand up, "I doubt that will be necessary."

Zephyr led them back to the captain's cabin, where the other wives were waiting.

Scarlet frowned at Him when they walked in, and said, "I know I said I wanted her to suffer, but you didn't have to be that brutal."

He forced a laugh and replied, "You don't realize just how close it really was, her bonds had a mind of their own and were more than eager to go after the person removing them."

Lorelei stepped between him and Scarlet and said, "Don't you be mad at him, he did everything he could to prevent my suffering."

Scarlet bared her teeth at Lorelei, "Oh? I can't wait until you're fully healed so I can break you myself. You brought this upon yourself by trying to seduce him with magic, and I fully intend to see you suffer for that."

Lorelei dropped the blanket and smiled back at Scarlet, "I doubt you can make me suffer any worse than I already have. I still feel the burn of the chains as they were ripped from my body, every inch of me feels as if it is on fire. Do you really think you can do worse than what was done to me?"

Scarlet's eyes appeared to flicker for a moment, and then she relaxed, "True, nothing compares to having the bond ripped from your body." She eyed Lorelei's naked body and smiled, "At least I know that he will enjoy your body, and you won't be able to use your magic on him anymore."

Lorelei smiled back at her, "I am pretty certain he won't be with me all that often, after all I knew when he introduced you to me, he would rather have you than anyone else." She frowned slightly, "I do believe though I still owe all of you a dinner and a chance to get to know you." She gave Scarlet a twisted smile, "Your emotions are as chaotic as the fire you yield, I look forward to further conversations with you."

Clarice laughed, "You hide your pain well, but now you need to come lie down and let me work on healing your body. I am very curious about your ancestry and it will give us a chance to talk privately."

Mortimer visibly relaxed as Clarice led her over to a sleeping mat and started to cocoon her in ice. "The crimson witch should be happy now," he mumbled under his breath, "even though I would have broken the bonds without her telling me to."

"I know, child," a voice said beside him, "you remind me of my husband." The crimson witch manifested next to him and smiled softly, "Don't worry the bonds will end when the ritual is complete, and only those who truly love you will stay married to you."

He smiled at her and replied, "So your demand was not for my sake, but for Scarlets?"

"Correct," she replied, "although I would prefer you use Lorelei instead of Clarice for the ritual. She should be allowed to return to her mother."

"I have to agree," he replied, "I promised her mother she would return, it was a stupid promise to make at the time."

The crimson witch smiled at him, "You are growing so quickly now, I am very proud of my descendents."

"There was something different about the bond she had on her," he replied, "it was as if it was alive, can you explain that to me?"

"I can," she replied with a slight frown, "since this is not something directly related to my imprisonment I can share my knowledge of this matter, which isn't a whole lot." The crimson witch drifted gracefully up to him until her figure started to overlap his body. "You may experience some discomfort," she whispered into his ear.

His body felt very warm when it made contact with her spirit, different from when he interacted with other spirits, it was as if he was facing a large fire at first, and then he felt her step into his body and it was as if he had just stepped into the sun. The room around him looked different, he could see the others, but they appeared as a fog, each of them had a blood red ribbon that ran from them to him and to each other. At the same time they each had their own different colored ribbons wrapped around their spirits and tangled up with the red one.

"The red is your bond to them, made with your own blood it is one of the darker bonds," a voice whispered in his head. "The other colors are the bonds of their nature, or elemental bonds every witch has them." His head turned towards Shar, and he noticed she did not have a colorful bond other than his red one, "She is not a witch, she does not have an elemental bond, but if you look closely you will notice a transparency that entangles your bond. This is called a hollow bond, and the less elemental ancestry one has the emptier it is."

He felt a hunger come from deep within, and wondered why.

"It is the desire to fill that emptiness," the voice purred in his mind. "All bonds have a form of life, whether it is from an element or from an individual. The bond you

removed from her was and still is to some extent full of life. You broke a piece of it, but you did not entirely destroy it, to do that you must confront it at its source."
He could feel a sort of excitement emanating from the spirit of the crimson witch, "This is a confrontation you wanted to have when you were alive, isn't it?" he asked silently.

"Yes," the voice answered, as he felt a coolness come over his body.

Mortimer opened his eyes as the crimson witch pulled herself completely out of his body, "thank you for the information," he said with a half smile.

She returned his half smile, "let's not do that again anytime soon, I'd rather not risk getting caught in the web you have cast about you."

"It was good to see the world the way you do," he replied, "it has taught me quite a bit."

The crimson witch nodded her head, "it has also taught me a lot as well," she started to fade away as she whispered, "good luck against the source of this bond, dragons are very tough creatures."

Mortimer's smile faded, he wasn't sure if he could handle a dragon, but then again he had never been sure he could handle the witch hunters. He found the one chair in the room and brought it over to what remained of Zephyr's desk. As he sat down he absently grabbed a piece of coal and started to write a list:
        Deal with renegade pirate captains
        Track down the source of the pirates bond
        Either deal with or eliminate the source of the bond
        Return home and prepare for the ritual to free the crimson witch

Scarlet wandered over to where he sat, "You look a bit stressed."

He looked up at her and smiled, "A little, I'm not entirely sure of the best way to deal with each of the items I need to complete." He looked at the list and laughed, "I'm not even sure if I'm doing things in the correct order."

She smiled at him, "The captains, I say we just burn all of their ships to the waterline and kill any who try to leave the ships, however it might be better to deal with their bond first and see if that convinces them to leave us alone."

Zephyr laughed, "As long as the bond is in effect, they cannot coordinate an attack against you, but must instead challenge you individually." She grinned evilly at him and continued, "You have already proven to be too strong to take on directly, so they are probably plotting against you in other ways. My mother once put down a possible rebellion by challenging them all at the same time with the rule that all combat had to be done in the rigging, they lost their desire for rebellion rapidly after that, as the bond enforced the rules, you could do something similar."

Mortimer chuckled, "That could be interesting, especially if they try to wear me out by challenging me back to back."

Zephyr laughed, "They tried that before with me, and I created the rule of allowing a champion to fight in your stead."

Scarlet shook her head, "it would be much simpler to deal with the source of the bond and then slaughter them all at one time."

Tara smiled, "I agree, it wouldn't be hard to deal with the bond and then simply sink our enemy's ships with boulders before they have a chance to react."

Clarice frowned as she approached the table, "You three are so destructive, it appears my healing abilities will be sorely needed in the next couple of days." With a slight grin she added, "I have already taken the liberty of summoning large chunks of ice to block the harbor, no ships will be entering or leaving it until the spell ends."

"How long will it last?" Mortimer asked.

"Until I cancel it," she answered, "should I die the ice will melt slowly until it is completely gone."

"You have grown quite powerful since we first met you," Scarlet replied.

Clarice smiled at her, "Not really, I am simply drawing on his power, and currently he has an overabundance."

Zephyr laughed, "That can't be helped, the amount of death that has occured on this island, it will continue to feed his power for a long time."

Mortimer laughed, "If Clarice can draw on my power to increase her own, maybe the rest of you should as well, that way we can start looking for the source of the pirates' bond right now."

Lorelei laughed softly from her cocoon of ice, "If you are going after the source then I am coming along."

"Not until you're strong enough to break free of the healing magic on your own," he replied.

She shrugged her shoulders and grimaced in pain, "My arm may be broken, but I am healed enough to be of assistance to you."

Clarice waved her arm dismissively and the cocoon of ice melted away, "she may be useful, besides it is best to have our rivals nearby so we can keep an eye on them."

"I am not your rival," Lorelei replied, "I tried something stupid and paid the price. I leapt before I looked, if I had bothered to check for magic first I could have avoided a very painful lesson." She smiled at Scarlet, "When the pirate bond is broken, if you still wish to break me, you may do so, I will not stop you, but until then I am bound to aid my king in any way he requires of me."

Scarlet raised an eyebrow at her, "In other words, you knew he would let me do whatever I wanted to you, and yet you still stand by his side."

Lorelei laughed slightly, "I never had any designs on your husband, only on his throne, if my magic worked on women, I would have tried the same thing on the queen."

Clarice started to laugh, "Funny, since I have been bound to Mortimer my power works on both men and women."

Zephyr looked at her and said, "Really, care to demonstrate?"

Mortimer chuckled, and he recognized the scent of the sea, it called to him, at the same time he found he could resist it as Clarice winked at him. After a moment, he saw all of them being drawn to Clarice fawning and pawing at her.

Clarice smiled at Mortimer and nodded her head at him, "Come, I know you feel it, play with us."

Mortimer smiled, "In a moment darling, I want to see if I can resist a bit longer." He took a deep breath and caught the musty scent of a deep dark cave, the acrid scent of a super hot fire, the electrifying scent of the air during a thunderstorm. But there to one side was a scent that was different, it was the bitter scent of metal and it came from Shar. He closed his eyes for a moment and focused on the magical energies around him, and through them he found it, it emanated from her mixed gently with his own blood bond. He laughed softly to himself as he opened his eyes, "As we share our power, so too can we share our abilities," he said as he relaxed and let himself fall into the siren call of his second wife.

# Egg

Shar woke before the others and winced, she was sore and had a few bite and claw marks on her body, but she felt truly happy for the first time in her life. Carefully she extricated herself from the pile of women and got dressed.

"No need to rush," Mortimer said softly from the corner, "you should get washed up before putting your clothes on."

She turned and looked at him, "Do you even sleep?"

He shrugged, "Yes, but in order to sleep I have to expend the energy I have collected from the dead, so I sleep very little."

"I guess that makes sense, since people have probably died everywhere," she replied.

"Correct," he replied. "I would wake everyone, but honestly I feel you all needed the rest more than I did."

Shar blushed slightly, "And here I thought we were supposed to be taking care of you." She glanced at Lorelei's broken arm and noticed it had turned a silvery blue color, "What happened to her arm?" she asked.

Mortimer chuckled, "Her true nature was awoken last night, and her innate magic created a healing cast over it. Her arm will be fine in a couple of days, I'm not entirely sure how her mind will be though after she sees the other changes it brought to her body."

Shar looked closer at Lorelei's body and frowned, it was covered in scales for the most part except for sections that looked as if claws had dug deeply into her flesh and torn them away. "What caused those marks?"

He smiled, "We all did," he answered, "Most of the claw marks are from Scarlet and Zephyr, although you, Tara and Clarice caused some as well. As did I, it was a very wild time and it will come back to you soon enough."

The entire pile of women woke up, when there was a knock at the door, "You have the clothing I asked for?" Mortimer asked.

"Yes captain," the muffled response came from the door, "Just letting you know they are outside your door captain."

Mortimer laughed as the women untangled themselves from each other, "Apparently the crew is now afraid to enter the cabin, something about it being safer not to know what's in here."

Zephyr laughed, "Sailors are a superstitious lot, and I'm sure it sounded like demons were having a party in here last night."

Mortimer chuckled to himself as he opened the door and retrieved the pile of clothing that was sitting outside it, "I am not sure how flattering this will be with your new body Lorelei, but your change of clothes has arrived from your ship."

Lorelei looked down at her body, and cried softly, "What did you do to me? You destroyed my body."

Clarice laughed, "No, he didn't, he unlocked your true nature."

Scarlet nodded her head in agreement, "Magic comes at a price, and you were going to have to pay that price at some point in your life. You are actually lucky it was Mortimer who broke your elemental bonds and released your true nature, at least he won't turn his back on you and walk away." She frowned slightly, "although, sometimes I wish he would stop helping damsels in distress."

Mortimer couldn't help it and burst out laughing, "I had nothing to do with breaking the bonds that concealed her elemental nature, that was all you."

"What do you mean?" Scarlet asked.

"In the midst of all of the passion Clarice decided to incite, you decided to help her understand her nature better, by breaking the elemental bond she had," he smiled darkly. "I was going to wait a while longer so she could experience the pain of having a bond ripped away all over again, but instead you burned it away last night." He started laughing, "I have never seen a bond destroyed so fast in my life, I don't think she even noticed it."

Scarlet looked at Lorelei and frowned, "I'm sorry, I didn't realize what I was doing."

Lorelei returned her frown and replied, "I told you I would let you break me, I thought you would kill me not destroy my appearance and let me live."

"You are still quite beautiful, even if you do not see it," Mortimer said solemnly, "after all it is your true nature that attracted us to you in the first place, not your body."

Scarlet grinned at Lorelei, "See even now you are trying to take my place with my husband."

"I'm never going to make you happy, am I?" Lorelei asked Scarlet.

Mortimer laughed, "She's teasing you, quit worrying about how you look, we have things to do today."

Scarlet laughed, "Honestly once you joined the bond, any dislike dissolved, the only way for one of us to hate you would be for us to first hate ourselves. Yes, I was jealous of you, but that was for the same reason I am jealous of Shar, Tara and Clarice, you could venture into the city with Mortimer and people see you as human, whereas with me they see a demon."

Tara frowned, "You don't need to be jealous of me, I can't stand the way they stare at me due to my muscles, almost as if they think I'm some sort of freak."

Shar laughed, "People don't stare at me not because I blend in, but because they are afraid I might kill them if they did. So don't go around being jealous of me."

Clarice just shrugged, "I can't help my nature, but I really don't want you to be jealous of me, after all I was jealous of you first, you have a man who could resist the lure of the merfolk."

Lorelei smiled slightly, "Well if you can do it, then I suppose I can let people see my true nature too." She looked at the pile of clothing and picked out a tight fitting pair of blue trousers, a bright red low cut top and a pair of knee high boots. "Let's go find the source of the bond."

Mortimer laughed gently to himself, yes they were a chaotic lot, but now he had one of the most powerful groups of people working with him. "I have a feeling it involves a dragon, so we had best be prepared," he said as he picked up his sword.

Once they were all cleaned up and dressed, they headed back to the meeting hall, the people on the docks watched them as they went past, most of them surprised by Lorelei's transformation. Inside the hall a couple of ship captains stood in the middle of the room arguing about who would challenge Mortimer first.

"Before you decide to make a challenge, I would recommend finding out how powerful your enemy is," Mortimer said as he walked past them.

Tara walked up to the throne, and placed her hand on it. There was a kind of popping noise from the ground and it fell to the side and exposed a hole with a ladder in it. "I believe what we seek lies below."

Mortimer smiled, "I figured as much, any traps that you can feel?"

"None," she answered.

With a nod to her, he started climbing down the ladder, Shar came directly behind him followed quickly by the rest. Tara came last, and sealed the passageway above them with rock, "No sense having unwanted guests follow us down."

Mortimer chuckled to himself, as a single line of flame ran down the tunnel wall behind them to the floor. "Thank you Scarlet," he said as he finished the descent into a small circular room with a single door in the wall.

Shar laughed slightly when she reached the bottom, "I've run across a few of these doors in some of the older tunnels, give me a second and I will have it open." She pulled a small pick from her belt and inserted it into the lock, in a few minutes they heard a click and she opened the door.

Immediately Zephyr waved her arm towards the door, and they heard a clunk sound just on the other side of it, "Bolt trap," she replied, "I heard a second click after the lock and realized someone may have set a trap on the other side."

Sure enough when they opened the door fully, there was a crossbow aimed directly at it, the bolt lay just inside the door having struck the stone wall and fallen to the floor. "Careful, it may be poisoned," Mortimer said.

"I'm the most expendable, I should go first," Lorelei said.

"No," Scarlet and Mortimer said together.

Tara shook her head, "I don't sense any more traps, but if they aren't made of stone I wouldn't feel them."

"Then we shall proceed cautiously," Mortimer replied, "Shar you and I together, the rest of you I want you to be alert for any changes to our environment as you follow."

The passageway seemed to wind back and forth for a very long time, before it came to an end before a pair of steel doors.

Mortimer pushed against the door on the left and it gently swung open, "I'm surprised it's not locked," he said as he drew his sword and stepped through it. Three steps into the room and he suddenly felt as if he had just stepped into a large fire.

Scarlet leapt forward as she saw the flames start to sprout from the floor, and with a wave of her hand she forced them up and over Mortimer and Shar.

Quickly everyone stepped through the hole in the flames and Scarlet let them drop to the floor and burn as they pleased.

"Thanks," Shar said, "for a moment there I thought I was going to be cooked."

As their eyes adjusted to the brightness of the flames, they could see the source of the pirate bond, the huge skeleton of a dragon lay on the floor of the chamber as if it lay there protecting its nest.

The floor of the chamber was covered in gold and gems, weapons, armor, statues and paintings lay everywhere, and in the middle was a large reddish gold egg.

Scarlet frowned, "That egg should have hatched centuries ago."

Mortimer shook his head, "It would have if someone hadn't used it as the focus of the binding spell."

Scarlet frowned, "I can't destroy a dragon egg, it would be like killing a baby."

"Agreed," all of them said together, "but how do we stop the spell."

"Wait here," Mortimer said as he started to climb the mountain of treasure towards the nest, "we may be able to stop the spell if we remove the focus from the spell's boundaries."

Scarlet laughed, "Then we had better start looking for the pentagram, a spell this size will require a lot of focus, so we need to find the runes and destroy them."

"Couldn't the mother dragon have done that?" Lorelei asked.

"Not if they were a containment spell," Scarlet answered. "They probably put up a spell to keep the dragon from the egg, and another to keep the dragon in the room. If the runes were on the opposite side of the pentagram from the dragon it would not be able to reach them."

Clarice laughed, "I bet they are just outside the fire wall," she said.

"Most likely," Scarlet replied, "I just hope they are elemental protection. For now though we should look for the runes around the egg."

Climbing the mountain of treasure beneath the egg proved to be a difficult task, every step Mortimer took the coins and gems beneath his feet would shift and slide. Several times he found himself on all fours scrambling to find a solid spot to put his feet. Eventually he reached the egg and discovered it was on a solid golden pedestal in the shape of a pentagram with symbols engraved along the inside of it. "I found the inner seal," he said as he stepped onto the pedestal.

The egg itself was about two feet tall, and a good eighteen inches across, it appeared to be quite heavy, and up close he could see a slight movement inside it.

"If you can destroy some of the symbols, it should break the seal," Scarlet called to him.

Mortimer looked at the symbols and drew his sword, he tried to smash one of the symbols with the pommel, but his sword passed right through it, "That won't be very easy, they are engraved in the floor."

Tara closed her eyes and frowned, "I can feel them, you are going to need something much more powerful than your sword, let me come up there and try."

Mortimer sheathed his sword and watched as she deftly climbed the mountain of treasure, he had never heard of an earth witch being able to affect metal, but he was sure she had some sort of plan.

When she reached the top, Tara looked more closely at the symbols and laughed. "Scarlet would not have been able to come up here, they are definitely elemental seals meant to keep a dragon out." She pointed to one of them and continued, "That one there is the key, they were engraved by a dwarf, and based on the ragged cuts he was not too happy about placing this ward."

Mortimer watched as she walked a complete circle around the egg, as if she was searching for something, "What are you looking for?" he asked.

Suddenly she let out a laugh and replied, "This, everyone knows if a seal is unwillingly made, then the maker will always forget one of their tools." She picked up a small iron chisel and showed it to him, "Give me something I can hammer with, preferably a stone or piece of iron."

Zephyr waved her arms in a quick circular motion and a decent sized rock flew up to land next to them, "Will this work?"

Tara picked up the rock, "Yes, thank you." She set the chisel at the edge of one of the runes and smashed the rock down on the edge of it several times. It took a little while and by the time she was done hammering, Tara was covered in sweat and gold dust, but eventually she picked up a piece of the pedestal with a single rune etched in it. "The runes themselves are almost indestructible, but the pedestal can be broken," she said as she tossed the chunk of gold out of the pentagram.

There was a loud cracking noise from above, Mortimer grabbed Tara and threw her against the egg as a huge chunk of the ceiling came crashing down where they had stood.

Tara forced a laugh and gave him a kiss, "Thanks, but now is not the time for pleasantries," she said with a smirk.

Immediately they were both covered in ice cold sea water. Mortimer laughed, "I agree," he looked around and saw Clarice and Lorelei holding hands and chanting as the water looped back upwards in mid air and turned into a sheet of ice closing off the roof of the cavern.

"Well, that was a bit of a surprise," Tara said, "I hadn't thought of setting a trap for whoever removed the runes, but it's obvious that it was designed to kill the dragon should it find a way to break the seal."

"Are you two alright?" Scarlet called out to them.

"We're fine," Mortimer called out, "Thanks for being so alert you two," he called to Clarice and Lorelei. "Now to figure out how to move this egg," he said, "it's a bit big to try and move it myself."

Tara looked at him and said, "We could try and just drag the entire nest down the pile of gold."

He shook his head, "No, it might pick up too much speed and break when it hits the bottom."

"What about building a ramp and stairs by melting the gold?" Scarlet asked.

"We can try that," he replied, "but it will take quite a bit of energy."

Zephyr laughed, "Scarlet you melt a ramp, I can use the wind to slow down the nest."

Immediately Scarlet waved her hands and a sheet of white hot fire came out of her hands. She moved them very slowly and carefully up the mountain of gold, walking on it once it was cool enough to do so. Soon she stood a few feet from them and with a flick of her wrist the fire went out. "That should work," she said with a smile.

Mortimer smiled, "Thank you, my love, now comes the fun part."

Tara shrugged, "The three of us should be able to pull the nest down the ramp and use our bodies to keep its descent at a safe pace."

Scarlet shook her head, "Dragon eggs are not nearly that fragile, just roll the egg itself out of the nest and down the ramp. Zephyr's wind walls will slow it down enough to keep it from breaking."

"Are you sure?" Mortimer asked

"Yes," she replied, as she walked to the far side of the egg and started to push it.

Mortimer and Tara quickly stepped up to help her, and together they were able to get it to roll over the lip of the nest and towards the ramp. Once on the ramp, the egg took off on it's own and picked up speed rapidly, occasionally it slowed down and then picked up speed again as it passed through each of the barriers Zephyr created in front of it.

The three of them searched through the rest of the nest and found nothing but a few more runes, but they started to fade once the egg was removed from it.

Once the egg rested comfortably at the bottom of the pile of treasure, the three of them followed it down. "That was fun," Mortimer said when they reached the bottom of the ramp, "I haven't slid down a hill since I was a child."

All of the women started to laugh, "It's good to see you having some safe fun for once," Scarlet replied.

Shar laughed, "I highly doubt there is such a thing as safe fun with you around Scarlet."

Scarlet started laughing again, "true, what I consider safe many would consider dangerous."

Mortimer chuckled, "and what I consider fun is usually called deadly."

At that Clarice burst into laughter, "that is true enough."

Mortimer looked at Lorelei, and let his vision shift in order to see the lines of magic around them. The black thread was completely gone, and his blood red one was completely entwined with her own icey blue power. As he watched, her body started to crumple, and he rapidly stepped in to catch her, "You alright?" he asked.

She grimaced slightly at him and then smiled, "Yes, I was just dizzy for a moment, but now I feel stronger than ever."

He smiled back at her, "That is because my bond has completely replaced the bond of the pirate, if you weren't bound to me, you would be completely free to do as you please."

"Then we need to get back to the ship," she replied, "before an all out war starts."

Scarlet turned and pointed at the wall of fire, "We'll have to deal with the other seal first."

Zephyr laughed, "That is easy enough, Clarice please melt the ice and direct the sea water at the fire."

Clarice shook her head, "No, we would end up cooked as the water turned to steam."

Tara laughed, "That one is easy to deal with," with a wave of her hand, the ground in front of them erupted upwards sending chunks of rock to slam into the walls. "The seal is broken, if the mother dragon had seen the runes before entering the circle she could have easily destroyed the trap that imprisoned her."

Zephyr laughed, "I hadn't thought of that, what do we do with the egg?"

"Take it with us," Mortimer answered, "we can't risk it falling into the wrong hands."

"Agreed," Shar and Scarlet said in unison, "but how will we get it up the ladder?"

Clarice shook her head, "We don't have to, if we circle the egg and hold hands, I can let in the sea water and use it to push us out through the ceiling."

Zephyr frowned, "You forget dear not all of us can breathe underwater."

Clarice winked at her, "you can while you are wearing the skin of a sea serpent." She looked at Lorelei and continued, "You had best stay close to me so I can assist you if necessary."

Lorelei nodded her head and moved next to Clarice, as everyone formed a circle around the egg.

With a roar, water suddenly poured in from the ceiling, tearing chunks of rock down with it. Mortimer blinked in surprise as the rock floor beneath their feet suddenly rose from the ground and started to float.

"Good idea," Clarice said, as the water rushed beneath them and filled the cavern. "Get closer together," she said as they approached the ceiling.

"Best to sit down," Zephyr said, "this could get a little bumpy."

As a group, they sat down and huddled even closer together, as piece of stone chipped away from the edges in the torrent of water, then suddenly their makeshift raft entered the waterfall and they could feel the bubble of air around them getting smaller as they floated through the ceiling against the current.

In mere moments they found themselves floating in the harbor, as Zephyr passed out from exhaustion. Clarice too was showing signs of exhaustion, but she focused her energy and got them alongside their ship. Crewmen immediately threw ropes over the side and pulled them up to the deck.

# War

Mortimer waited until all of the women were aboard the ship, before he made a sling out of some rope for the dragon egg, and climbed up a rope himself. On deck things were a little crazy, the crew was fully armed, and some showed signs of having been in a fight. "Let me guess, you were attacked once the bond was destroyed," he said to the first mate.

The first mate smiled, "Yes Captain, only minor injuries though and no deaths. They haven't been able to move their ships, so we have only had to defend the dock side and once we pulled up the gangplank, it stopped the fighting."

"Good job," Mortimer replied, "who wants to join me for a little fun?"

All of the nearby crewmembers cheered in response.

"Very well, lower the gangplank," he cried out, "it is time to teach them the meaning of fear." He drew his sword as he crossed the deck, Scarlet pulled the crimson sword and followed him with Lorelei, Shar, and Tara right behind him.

The five of them walked down the gangplank once it was set in place, the pirates in the front rows held back until someone in the back threw something towards them, even though it missed them it served to launch the mob forward.

In seconds Mortimer was covered in blood and laughing as he cut down opponent after opponent, Scarlet laughed next to him as her blade twisted and turned, each cut no matter how small bled profusely as the magic of the sword made every wound deadly.

Soon enough the dock was clear of enemies and all around them was a pile of corpses. Mortimer saw several groups of pirates charging towards them from different ships, only to be intercepted by more pirates from other ships. "This is insane," Lorelei said, "nobody knows who is on what side."

Mortimer laughed, "I see your crew over there, they and three other ships have taken control of that entire dock. If they work together they should push the others towards us."

Lorelei smiled, "That should sort out some of the chaos," she replied as she waved over to the group of pirates.

Almost immediately the large group started to push their way towards them, and grew in size as more people were able to join in with them. Soon enough they had control of half the docks, and more than half the pirates.

Mortimer merged his crew with the larger force and said, "We only fight those who resist, those who don't will be given the opportunity to join us."

A rowdy cheer went up from the crowd, and it continued to grow in size as they pushed forward, Mortimer was surprised for a moment when a man wearing the emblem of one of his enemies was fighting alongside him, "Just wanted to say thank you for freeing us," the pirate said as he impaled a particularly large and vicious enemy.

Mortimer laughed and replied, "Glad to have been of service."

It took several hours, but eventually the battle was over, the harbor waters were red with the blood of the dead and dying, but every enemy had been eliminated.

"I'm not looking forward to dealing with those inside the keep," Mortimer said as he surveyed the carnage. He was full of energy, and enjoyed the fight, but he knew many good people would die getting into that place.

Shar laughed at the look on his face and said, "Don't worry I can get you inside undetected."

"Alright, Scarlet and Tara will come with us," he replied. "Lorelei, you Clarice and Zephyr will organize this group and tend to the wounded." He smiled at Lorelei, "Zephyr and Clarice should be awake soon, until then I am counting on you to help as many of the wounded as you can."

Lorelei returned his smile, "Understood, please be careful."

Mortimer laughed softly, "I'll try. Let's go," he said as he turned back to Shar.

Scarlet chuckled softly to herself, and licked some blood from the back of her hand. "This should be fun, are we going to use magic or continue with blades?"

"We'll make that choice when we see how things stand inside," he answered. "Magic can be a great weapon, but a sword is much more precise."

Tara shook her head, the two of them were having way too much fun.

Shar led them quickly along the cliff face outside the doors, and gestured up to a small opening about thirty feet up the cliff, "We can climb up here and get in through that window. That room contains a ballistae and weapons storage. There was a minor cave in, a few weeks ago in the hallway beyond, but we can squeeze through easily enough."

Tara nodded her head in understanding and with a wave of her hand, little holes appeared in the cliff face, "This should make climbing a bit easier for everyone."

Shar led the way up the cliff and laughed softly, it was as if someone had built a ladder into the rock.

Inside the room was crammed full of crates although there was a clear walkway through the center of the room. A giant crossbow-like ballistae stood about two feet from the window, loaded and ready to fire.

Mortimer shook his head as he inspected it, it was not in the best condition and would be dangerous to fire at this point. "I'm not really impressed with the way this equipment is being taken care of," he said to Shar.

Shar couldn't help but laugh, "Many of the guards have gotten lazy, I can't remember the last time any of this stuff was inspected. I was more concerned about maintaining my personal gear than all of the stuff they kept in storage."

Scarlet picked up a sword from one of the crates and laughed, "I'm not a smith, but even I can tell these are poorly made." She said as she tossed it back into the crate.

Tara shook her head slightly, "I will stick to throwing stones, as I'm not trained in using a sword."

Shar led them through the doorway and into the hall, sure enough about twenty feet down the hall a pile of rubble was blocking most of the passageway. "This was on the list of things to clean up, but other projects kept taking priority."

Mortimer laughed, "You were in charge of the slaves, so I'm pretty sure feeding and educating them was more important."

Tara shook her head slowly, "Give me a minute," she said as she laid her hands on the rubble. In a few minutes, it piled itself up neatly against one wall, "it's safe to proceed now," she said with a smile.

Shar led them rapidly through the corridors, stopping at every turn and intersection, to check for guards, "It's strange we haven't run across anyone yet." She said after the third empty intersection.

At the fourth intersection they found a couple of dead bodies, and at the sixth one they ran into their first guard.

"What's the situation?" Mortimer asked when he saw the guard.

"My lord," the guard replied, "we have pushed back the rebellious pirate captains, they are currently contained in the central chamber."

"Loyalties and numbers?" Shar asked bluntly.

The guard laughed, "They have us outnumbered two to one, but all of the guards stand with the last pirate king."

"How did you manage to contain them?" Mortimer asked.

"Sire, we know these tunnels better than they do and used that knowledge to restrict their movement and push them back," the guard answered.

Shar grinned, "I'm glad to see not all of my advice was ignored."

The guard laughed, "Those who ignored it died quickly, but that is always the case when you refuse to listen to those with more experience."

"There is only one more turn in this tunnel between us and the central chamber," Shar said to Mortimer, "Now would be a good time to determine battle tactics."

"Are there any allies inside the central chamber?" he asked the guard.
"Not that I know of," the guard replied.

"Is there a way to seal off the other exits from that room?" Mortimer asked Shar and the guard.

"Not really," Shar answered, "the doors all lock from this side, in case invaders made it into the central chamber."

"There might be a way," Tara said, "but I would have to go to each door and seal it individually."

Mortimer nodded thoughtfully, "We can't seal the main doors, but the army outside will take care of anyone trying to get out that way. We can't guarantee there aren't enemies in the tunnels, after all even the best troops occasionally miss a single enemy."

Scarlet laughed, "I will go with her to protect her as she seals the doors, between myself and the guard we should be able to keep her safe."

"Very well," he replied, "you two will go with the guard and start sealing doorways." He turned to the guard, "Is there a way to send word to the other guards to seal off doors as best they can?"

"Sire, we were already planning to seal off all but two doors and then to attack as a group through those two doors," the guard replied.

"That's a good plan," Mortimer responded, "You'll take Scarlet and Tara with you to seal off doors rapidly, while Shar and I go the other direction to seal off other doors." He smiled at the guard, "I want all of the guards with your group, I will serve as a distraction while you attack from the opposite side."

Tara frowned, "You will be careful?" she asked.

Scarlet laughed, "No, he won't be, but he will be fine in the end."

The guard shook his head and led them down the hall, around the corner and to an intersection with a door opposite the hallway. A group of about ten guards were busily trying to wedge the door shut with wooden wedges.

Tara looked at them and whispered, "Step back from the door." With a few pulling gestures with her hands, two great big stone spears rose up out of the floor and drove into the stone ceiling above the door. "That door isn't opening any time soon," she said softly.

With that, the guards headed off with Tara and Scarlet down the hall to the right.

After they left, Shar looked at Mortimer and said, "There is only one more door down the left side, you are not planning on waiting very long for them are you?"

"No," he answered, "Just long enough for them to get to the opposite side of the chamber. When we attack, Scarlet will prevent them from being able to escape through any unsealed doors."

She shook her head with a half chuckle and led him rapidly down the hall to the next door, where a dozen guards stood with spears wedged to hold the door shut.

"You can remove those spears," Mortimer said as they approached.

The guards looked at him and jumped, "Yes, sir," one proclaimed as he moved forward and pulled a spear off the door.

The other guards followed his example.

"Thank you," Mortimer replied, "In a couple of minutes I am going to go through that door and have a talk with them. I would like for you folks to back me up."

Shar drew her sword with her right hand and the crimson dagger with her left, "Whenever you are ready my lord."

Mortimer chuckled as he drew his own sword, "You don't have to call me that dear, you are a part of the family now."

The guards all seemed a bit surprised by this statement, but remained silent as one of them prepared to open the door for him. "Ready when you are sir," the guard holding the door replied.

Mortimer waited a few more minutes, then nodded his head towards the door. As the guard pulled open the door, Mortimer leapt through the doorway and swung his sword in an upwards arc before bringing it back down and into a nearby pirate's shoulder. With a twist and a jerk, he ripped the sword free of the pirate and swung it completely around taking off two peoples heads with a single strike.

Shar followed directly behind him, and when she saw him start to spin, ducked under the whistling black blade. She deflected an ax blow from the left and sliced under her own sword with the dagger. The cut was just deep enough to draw blood, and the man fell screaming to the ground as the wound burst outward with a gush of blood.

Mortimer laughed, as he charged across the room towards the bulk of the enemies, the guards following directly behind him. His blade was alive with the power of death, and gave off a strange shadowy presence as he charged.

Once Shar was clear of the area around the wall, the room was suddenly alight in a giant circle of fire. She could hear the dagger in her hand singing, calling out for more blood, with a shrug she gave into the dagger's desire and charged into the battle.

It was a rather short battle all things considered, Scarlet and the guards easily surprised the pirates after Mortimer had charged into them, and her group managed to take out several pirates apiece before they even realized they were being attacked from behind.

Once they saw they were outnumbered by the guards, most of the pirates surrendered and only a couple of captains continued to fight.

Mortimer shrugged and ordered those who had surrendered to be bound so they may be given the opportunity to make their own decision without the influence of the captains. He then addressed the captains, "You have made your choice to continue as pirates, as such your fate will be the same as that of bandits." He smiled at them, "Death by hanging."

As he said this, three out of the four captains charged at him with weapons raised. A crimson blade flew past Mortimer and impaled the captain on the left right through the heart, as Shar charged past him and slammed her shoulder into the next captain's chest.

The third captain hesitated for a second, only to have a flaming spear thrust through his back.

Shar was brutal in her fight with the captain, her initial strike knocked him back a couple of steps, and as she thrust her sword forward and up, he dodged to one side. He swung downward with his own sword only to have her twist and block it with the pommel of her blade. The two of them traded blows repeatedly as they circled, until suddenly she dropped down to one knee and thrust her sword upwards under his ribs and through his heart and lungs. As he stood there with a look of shock on his face, she twisted the blade in a circle and ripped it back out of him.

The captain dropped to his knees coughing and choking on his own blood as Shar went over and retrieved her dagger. "Oh, are you still thirsty?" she asked it as she calmly walked back and slit the captains throat with it. "Treacherous swine," she spat on the captain as he fell dead to the ground.

Mortimer smiled, "Red looks good on you my dear," he said as he walked past her. "So, what is your decision?" he asked the remaining captain.

"I would prefer a clean death," the captain answered, "but given the choice I would rather not die at all."

"That is not a choice I can give you, but if you are willing to be bound, you can make that request of the townsfolk whom you have wronged." Mortimer answered, "That is the best I can do for you."

The captain dropped his sword and bowed his head, "Thank you, I accept your proposal and surrender."

Tara laughed, "I believe most of these pirates never truly went up against a trained warrior and now that they have seen the true brutality of war they are ready for a peaceful life."

Mortimer laughed with her, "Truth be told this is nothing like war, war is much worse. Of the hundred men and women who signed up when I did, only a handful are still alive, and of those I believe I am the only one who still fights."

Scarlet smiled, "That is because only a few can truly appreciate the beauty and the horror of the battlefield."

Shar shook her head slowly, "I can see all of your points, but Scarlet you only see beauty because you love the color red."

"True," Scarlet replied with a smile, "if blood was any other color it would not be beautiful."

Tara frowned, she didn't see any beauty in war, even though she too had felt the desire to fight and kill, maybe she truly didn't belong with them.

A soft voice whispered in the air, singing the praises of the dead and dying, as the Crimson witch rose out of the pools of blood. She placed a hand gently on Tara's shoulder and said, "My child it is exactly that gentleness that makes you a valuable part of this family." She turned to the others and frowned slightly, "You folks are filthy, now have you decided what to do with the egg you found?"

Mortimer shrugged, "Keep it quiet for now, we'll make that decision when we get home."

The witch laughed deeply, "Oh, this shall be interesting, most hero's slay the dragon, but you go out and rescue the dragon. It is not that important a decision to make just

221

yet, for now you need to start heading home, you have everything you need for the ritual."

"Then I suggest you rest for now," Mortimer replied, "you know the ritual is going to take a lot of energy to perform." He turned to the guards and smiled, "Please take the prisoners to the holds of the largest vessels. We will leave no ships behind, if we don't have the bodies to sail them, then they are to be sunk."

"Yes sir," the guards said in unison and got to work escorting the prisoners to the main door.

Mortimer turned to the women and smiled, "As much fun as this has been, I believe it best if we follow the witches advice and head home soon."

Scarlet laughed gently, "Yes it is, Zephyr should be fully recovered by the time we get back to the village and that old witch there might be able to teach her how to create a travel portal."

Mortimer laughed, "I totally forgot about those, I've never seen one outside of shadows, although I have heard they are possible."

"Only those with strong air magic can create them," she replied, "and the few that I've seen were small and covered only short distances, the longer they are the more magic they consume. Centuries ago though they say there were witches who could create permanent portals between cities."

It didn't take long for them to return to the docks, where several ship captains waited for them. "What are your orders sire?" one asked as they stepped through the main doors.

Mortimer glanced at the carnage around him and frowned, "Prepare to set sail, we leave in the next couple of hours."

"What about the dead?" another captain asked.

"We leave them where they are," he answered, "let the birds have them."

A musical voice from behind the captains chimed in, "You are ever the cold hearted one." Clarice, pushed her way through the captains with a smile, "I have dropped the ice blockade, most of the wounded have been treated, and Zephyr is eager to return to the open sea."

Mortimer returned her smile, "I'm glad to see you on your feet already, take us to our ship and have Zephyr start preparations to move the fleet."

With that, the captains disbursed to their own ships and prepared to set sail, at the same time those ships without a crew were set alight and allowed to burn.

Tara chuckled as they left the docks, "The sooner we get to sea the better," she said to Zephyr, "soon enough that island will be overrun by molten rock."

Zephyr looked at her and laughed, "Let me guess the water that rushed in when we destroyed the seal, ended another spell?"

Scarlet walked up onto deck and laughed, "Yes, it did. Lava is a strange crossover between my element and Tara's, we both can command it, but it is difficult." She looked at Tara, "it is the reason he wanted you to go along for the battle, if things took too long we would have had to work together to stop the lava flow."

Tara nodded her head in understanding, "I have never seen anything quite so brutal, and I thought Shar was a sweet and gentle lady, until I saw her in battle covered in blood and smiling."

Scarlet hugged Tara close, "we are all sorry you had to experience that, and we will do our best to make certain you never experience it again."

"Where is Shar now?" Zephyr asked.

Scarlet smiled, "In the cabin with Lorelei and Clarice getting cleaned up, I offered to burn the blood from her clothes like I did my own, but she turned me down."

"I'm not surprised, she is embarrassed about her bloodlust, and worries she may have ruined your opinion of her." She sniffed the air, "I see he is in his own darkness again, I wonder what it is he is constantly worried about that he refuses to share with the rest of us."

Scarlet laughed, "He thinks about death often, he has already died twice, and he wonders why he has not stayed dead and what it could mean for those around him. I wasn't there for his first death, but I witnessed his second, and it took all of my power to bring him back to us, it changed him both physically and emotionally."

Zephyr shook her head sadly, "I wish I could help him with his problems."

"Go to him, and speak with him," she replied, "but if he lets you in, also know you will never be free of him."

She laughed gently, "I can never be free of him as it is, what could possibly be so different than it is now."

Scarlet laughed, "Once you have seen inside the darkness, you can never unsee it, and you will truly understand why he is the way he is."

"Who else has he let inside?" Zephyr asked.

"Only myself and Clarice," she answered, "and he fought hard not to let Clarice inside, but it was a bad time and he couldn't help it."

"Very well," Zephyr replied, "I will go speak with him, Tara, you have the helm until I return."

Tara frowned at Zephyr, "be careful," she said.

# Death's realm

Zephyr just smiled and headed down to the deck, she knew exactly where he was at, the air carried his scent to her and guided her as if it was on a mission. She went below deck, and into the hold where a single room had been built with a magical lock. "Can I speak with you," she asked as she entered the room and closed the door.

Mortimer frowned slightly, "Planning on locking me up for a bit?"

She laughed gently and said, "No, it is to ensure our privacy, the lock only prevents people from using magic to get free, and nobody will open the door if it is closed. I built it as a safe room so Scarlet could practice her magic without catching the ship on fire."

He laughed at this, "It sounds to me like you enjoy her company, considering how much you two fought just a few days ago."

"Yes well, in Scarlet's case she isn't really happy unless she feels she has won, it doesn't matter what it is, she just needs to feel as if she earned it," Zephyr replied. "In my case, I just kind of go with what the energies around me direct, as such when she would get upset I would get drawn into her anger. It makes for a very dangerous situation when you think about it."

Mortimer laughed slightly, "Air feeds fire, fire hardens earth, earth moves water, and water pushes air. When all four elements are applied correctly you have a force that continues to grow stronger the longer it is applied."

Zephyr chuckled, "That explains the need for some of us, but what about Shar and yourself? What are your elements?"

He looked at her and replied, "Shar is the empty vessel that will be filled by those elements, and I yield the power of death. I do not fit into the elements, and neither do the elements fit into myself."

"Do all warlocks have such a bleak outlook on life?" she asked.

"I was a warlock in my younger days, and fed off the power of the soul, my own actually, but then I turned to the darker path and now I am a necromancer," he explained, "I feed off the power of the dead. I kill a chicken and I gain a little power, I kill a cow I get more, I kill a human and I get a lot of power. With every kill my wounds heal and my strength grows, but at the same time I pay a heavy price."

"How did you become a necromancer?" she asked.

"A battle as a mercenary," he answered, "a sword was driven through my heart, I knew I was going to die, but I also heard the soul trapped in that sword and knew I had to help it. I killed the man who impaled me, I literally threw my body forward and drove the sword clean through myself to remove the man's head. It was then I saw the souls on the battlefield and one woman charged across the battlefield to protect me with a shield. It was at that time I drew upon the power of the dead around me and leapt into battle. I paid dearly at that time, as I died shortly after the battle was over, and when death came for me I told him I did it to save the soul trapped in the sword. After which he told me he would grant my life to me, but I was required to use that life to free the soul from the sword. Since then I have been a necromancer, using the power of the dead to serve me."

"So, this darkness you fall into, is it your fear that when you free the soul from the sword you will die?" she asked.

At this Mortimer laughed, "In a way, I do not fear death, but I fear not being with you ladies. Another part of it is every time I borrow power from a soul, I also take in some of it's emotions, that which ties it to this realm, and that means I gain visages of their lives and deaths."

"How does one enter this darkness in order to help you?" Zephyr asked, more than a little afraid.

"If one is smart, they don't," Mortimer answered. "If one truly desired to though, they could simply follow the blood bond back and they would experience the darkness themselves." He looked her straight in the eye, "Please do not do this to yourself, let me do it alone."

She gave him a crooked smile, "Sorry, but I cannot let you suffer in your mind by yourself, allow me to take some of the pain from you."

"I don't want others to suffer on my behalf," Mortimer growled softly.

"You have no choice," Zephyr replied as she pushed him back against the wall. "You will let me in because I am asking, and because I care about the others and will sacrifice myself to protect them."

"Very well," he said as he slumped down to the floor.

She sat down in front of him, and took his hands. She was mildly surprised to find they were shaking, he was afraid of letting someone in, she wondered why, and it was that curiosity that let her see the blood bond between them. She let her thoughts turn to that red ribbon of power and felt it wash over her and draw her into his consciousness.

It was a dark and smoke filled space, in the distance she heard screams of agony. Body parts littered the ground all around her, and she felt a searing pain start at her shoulder and crawl slowly down her arm. She looked down and watched as a single line of red appeared as if a knife had cut her. She walked forward through the landscape of madness, the few times she spotted someone, they would die horribly. A man ripped to pieces by wild dogs, a woman brutalized by a gang of bandits, who were in turn impaled one at a time by a man in blood soaked armor. She approached this man and as she got closer she recognized him as Mortimer. His face was twisted in rage as he buried his blade up to the hilt into the last bandit's back and slowly twisted it upwards and ripped it out. He looked at her and pointed to her arm, she looked down and saw several more cuts had appeared, but could not determine from where.

He smiled at her, it was a twisted and evil smile, unlike any she had ever seen before.

For the first time since meeting him, she felt true fear of him, something she never thought she would feel, and then Mortimer threw his sword past her and she heard a scream. When she turned around, she saw what had been causing the cuts to her arm. She even recognized the man who stood before her, Mortimers sword having impaled his shoulder.

Zephyr found herself paralyzed with fear, he had hurt her as a child, and when her mother found out she ordered him whipped to death. Suddenly she felt a searing pain on her back and other arm, and she knew she was experiencing his death. This was the true price of his power, anger exploded within her, anger that he suffered so much just for the sake of helping others.

She ignored the pain that now spread throughout her body, and lunged towards the man. She wrenched Mortimers sword from his shoulder and felt the power it contained, fueled by her rage she attacked the form of the man who had hurt her. She lashed out with the sword and her own power, the wind cut like a thousand knives at both her and the man she attacked. In minutes the figure was nothing more than a pile of little tiny pieces of flesh and bone, and her own body bled from hundreds of tiny cuts.

Exhausted, but feeling better, she turned back to Mortimer. It was strange, his sword appeared back in his sheath as she collapsed sobbing in his arms. "I'm so sorry," she cried, "I never knew I caused you so much pain."

Mortimer laughed softly, "Nobody knows the pain the dead carry with them when they refuse to leave the material world. I work very hard to send them on to their final resting grounds, or to get them reborn into new lives," he nodded towards the corpse of the young woman brutalized by the bandits. "Now, you have seen the darkness that I live in, are you ready to return to the mortal realm?"

"No," she replied, "not until I meet death and barter for your freedom."

He smiled at her, "Sadly you will not see him here, you will have to wait until your name appears on his list and then you will be negotiating for your own survival."

"Then at the very least, will you come back with me?" she asked him.

"I will always come back from the darkness when my wives ask me to," he answered.

Zephyr blinked, and suddenly found herself sitting in front of Mortimer, her body ached, but he had a smile on his face. She tried to return his smile and burst into tears, "Scarlet was right, once you have seen the darkness you are forever changed." She wrapped her arms around his neck and cried softly, "I am yours do with me what you will."

Mortimer frowned slightly and replied, "No my dear, we are as one and as such we do what we will with ourselves."

He held her closely for quite a while, before he realized she was undoing the straps to his clothing. He did not argue, but let her go at her own pace, she had seen something that he would have preferred she not know about.

A couple hours later Scarlet walked into the room and smiled at the two of them cuddling together and sleeping, gently bringing a blanket over and laying it on them. She knew the cuts on Zephyr's body would heal when her mind was ready to accept everything it had just been exposed to. "Now you know the truth about him, and understand why I fight so hard for him."

She walked out of the room and the sword on her belt whispered, "I hope we don't have any more large battles ahead, I am running out of people to distract him."

"You're a conniving bitch," Scarlet growled softly to the blade.

"Not nearly as much as my husband," the blade replied, "after all he killed his own grandchild to make it happen."

Scarlet felt her temper flare and dashed up to the deck, once there she fired off a fire ball into the air that made everyone jump.

Clarice walked over to her and asked, "Everything alright?"

She smiled at Clarice, "Yes, they're sleeping together."

"What was the fireball about?" Clarice asked directly.

Scarlet laughed, "Just something the witch said, you don't need to worry about it."

"You really shouldn't let her get to you," Clarice replied, "we both know she only gives partial information depending on her mood."

"I know," she said, "but at the same time what she said really upset me. Oh, before I forget, let's try to avoid any more large battles, I don't want to send Tara into the darkness and I dread sending Lorelei."

Clarice frowned, "What about Shar, could we send her?"

Scarlet shook her head, "I doubt it, he would have to take her into it since she isn't a witch, and you know what that would entail."

Clarice nodded in understanding, "A fight similar to the fight with the witch hunter general, and on a similar battleground." She thought for a moment, "I wonder if grandfather has any advice?"

"Highly doubtful, I know he would appear if you asked him to, but I doubt he has any experience with the darkness a necromancer deals with."

"Then it is best we avoid any conflict for a while," Clarice agreed, "Could you get close enough to see how his mindset is?"

Scarlet laughed, "He is calm for now, but I believe that is because she distracted him and helped him burn off some of his energy. I feel a little guilty using her that way though."

"Next time send me," Shar suddenly said from behind her, "that way you don't have to feel guilty about anything."

Scarlet jumped and instinctively took a swing at Shar only to have her catch her hand, "Sorry, but you shouldn't sneak up on people. How much of our conversation did you hear anyway?"

Shar chuckled dryly, "Only the last couple of sentences. Look I'm not innocent when it comes to violence, and if my actions during that last battle caused any problems with him, then let me clean up the mess."

Clarice laughed, "Honestly we would, but he would have to let you in, and I highly doubt he would do so. If you want to try though, feel free, he is in the new room down in the hold with Zephyr right now."

Shar nodded to the two of them and headed down to the hold.

"Do you think that was a good idea?" Scarlet asked Clarice.

Clarice shrugged, "Who knows, if not, I'm sure the Crimson witch will manifest and let me know."

The crimson sword just laughed and said, "I am curious to see what happens, I'll let you know the details."

Shar easily found her way to the room where Mortimer and Zephyr were at, and was surprised to find them both awake.

Zephyr smiled at her, "We were informed of your coming, so decided to get dressed."

Shar smiled at Zephyr, she had to admit she was a splendid looking creature, her feathers really suited her. "Thank you, can I speak with him alone?"

Zephyr laughed, "certainly, you're a part of this family after all, and you have as much right to him as we do."

She frowned at Zephyr, "No, I have no magic, so I am less than all of you."

"No, you are as much a part of this family as I am," Zephyr growled at her, "don't ever discount your importance or our desire to have you by our side."

"I'm sorry my queen, I forgot my place," she replied.

"I am no longer your queen," Zephyr said with a sigh, "I see you more as a very close friend than anything else. Please come see me when you are done with him, I think we need to talk."

"As you wish," Shar replied, as Zephyr walked out the door and closed it.

Mortimer raised an eyebrow and waved her over to him, "What's bothering you?" He asked, "besides being the only non-witch in the family."

Shar walked over and knelt down in front of him, "My lord, I did not know that my battle lust would lead to problems for you, and I wish to try and undo any pain I may have caused you."

He frowned slightly, "First, I am not your lord, I am technically your mate or husband. Secondly any pain you inadvertently cause me is already forgiven, and is not your fault so you need not worry about it."

"If I am truly your wife, then let me into your mind that I might perform the same duties as your other wives have done," she said, for some reason she was terrified he would say no, but at the same time slightly afraid he would say yes.

Mortimer took a deep breath and finally replied, "If that is what you desire."

Afraid to speak, Shar nodded her head yes.

"Then get comfortable," he said. Once she had sat down in front of him he continued, "I want you to take my hands and focus your attention on my eyes."

She stared into his eyes, and relaxed until she could feel the bond between them pulsing beneath her skin. She could hear his breathing as she breathed, she could even feel his heartbeat as if it were her own. Gradually the room faded out and she found herself standing in the middle of a smokey battlefield covered in body parts. She was alone and at the same time she wasn't, her battlefield experience kicked in and she moved sideways as a large ax came down from behind her.

Shar spun to face her attacker and laughed, it was the old guard captain who had laughed at the idea of a woman soldier. "You know I bested you in combat when you were alive, what makes you think you will win this time?"

The figure smiled at her and relaxed his grip on his ax, "You can't blame me for trying, besides I told you I would win one of these days."

"You didn't die in the battle, why are you here?" She asked.

"He doesn't just draw in the energy from those who died in the battle, he draws in the energy of all who had died in the area. Did you forget I was poisoned in the council chamber, so my spirit was bound there until he freed me," he explained. "Since you came here to help him, you will find your opponent over there," he pointed towards the left. "I must warn you though, once you engage with them you will feel what they felt when they died so you must brace yourself for the pain before you take up his sword."

"I am prepared for any pain I must face," Shar replied, "I cannot allow him to suffer for my actions." She turned and headed in the direction he had indicated, as she walked she made out a group of pirates getting closer and frowned, she would have to battle the same people she had killed in the battle.

Suddenly less than a few steps ahead of her a sword appeared, without thinking about it she grasped the handle, and instantly knew it belonged to Mortimer, and even here he would protect her. She smiled inwardly as she felt the weight of the blade and a voice inside her head told her how to use it to destroy the soul. With a scream, she charged into battle, the common pirates were cut down quickly and easily, their heads separated from their bodies. The two captains fought back, she knew she was at a disadvantage as she didn't have a second weapon, when suddenly a familiar ax swept in and pushed the captains back.

Shar was amazed when Mortimer stepped in from the right and the old guard captain from the left. She realized Mortimer had no weapon and when one of the captains lunged towards him, she threw herself forward. She winced as the captain's sword cut deep into her side, but instead of falling back, she thrust her own weapon deep into the captain's chest and ripped it upward in an arc cutting his head in two.

With him out of the way she turned to the other captain, the pain was intense, and she felt as if a blade had just plunged into her chest. The pain was almost unbearable, but she pushed on and attacked the captain. She knew he wasn't much of a swordsman; he had poisoned many people when he was alive and now it was time for him to pay for those poisonings.

She let the rage overtake her, she welcomed the berzerker power her family had been known for. All pain ceased to be felt as she attacked over and over again, she would not stop until all enemies had been destroyed. Anything that moved was cut to pieces, first an arm, then the other arm, followed soon by the legs. She stood over his mangled body and grinned as she cut his head from his shoulders and cleaved his chest in two.

The rage didn't stop, soon she turned on the next thing to move, if it had a weapon she attacked it, if it was a threat she attacked it. She no longer saw a dark smoky battlefield, but instead she saw a field of enemies and the sky was filled with the spray of blood. Suddenly strong hands grabbed her own, and she found herself unable to swing the sword.

"Easy," a voice said in the red haze, "easy," it said again.

Slowly she came back to herself and found Mortimer standing before her, "Oh my," she said as she let go of the sword, it didn't even fall, but vanished to appear in his scabbard. "I'm so sorry, I didn't mean to attack you."

He smiled at her, "you didn't, I stepped in before you attacked a friend."

She looked past him and saw a young child standing there, a child she had tried to protect, but had died anyway of some disease.

"Thank you, for trying to help," the child said as it faded from view.

Mortimer smiled at her, "Not every spirit is in pain, some stay behind because they wish to watch over the ones they care about. She stayed because she never got a chance to thank you."

Shar stared at where the child had been and started to cry.

"Your time here is done," Mortimer said to her, "come back to the real world now."

She opened her eyes to find herself in the room with Mortimer, and she had a dreadful pain in her side.

Mortimer chuckled, "injuries in the world of the dead carry over to the world of the living. Please remove your armor so I might tend to your wounds."

Shar looked down, "You don't have to ask, you know you can do as you please," she said as she started to unbuckle her armor.

Mortimer sighed, "Actually it's the other way around, our custom is that a married couple is as one, and as such what you do to one you do to yourself. So if I disrespect you, then I disrespect myself."

She looked at him puzzled for a moment and then lifted away her breastplate, underneath her padding was soaked with blood and carefully she peeled that up and over her head.

His hands, although covered in calluses, were strangely gentle and warm as he inspected the wound. "It is not deep," he finally said, "it should heal in a couple of days. Try not to do anything too strenuous or you might make it worse."

Shar looked at him and grinned, "What would be considered too strenuous?"

"I'll let you know," he answered. "In the meantime you should get some rest, the realm of death can take a lot out of you and you are very active."

She looked at him and smiled, "Not yet, I want to be active a little longer."

He raised an eyebrow at her, but didn't say anything when she removed the rest of her clothing, "Are you sure?" he asked.

"Yes," she answered, "provided you want to be with me."

Mortimer didn't question her, but removed his clothing and pulled her in close to him. "Never doubt my desire," he whispered as he pulled the blanket over the two of them.

When Shar finally woke up, she was surprised to find her armor stacked in a neat little pile, and Mortimer was sitting a little ways away with a plate of food.

Clarice brought it down to us, "She figured we might be hungry."

Shar smiled at him, "How is it you are so cheerful all of a sudden?"

Mortimer laughed, "I draw energy from the dead, so when I release them, it releases their emotions, basically you just released two of the most hateful spirits that were hanging around in my little energy store. The rest of them are really fairly easy going and a couple of them are really quite gentle."

"So, when do we get to meet the real you?" she asked him.

He frowned slightly, "That's my greatest fear, that the real me will get consumed eventually. Scarlet could tell you when it's the real me."

From the doorway Scarlet laughed, "That would be the one who didn't hesitate to sacrifice himself to save a stranger's life, and that person is still here, I see him all the time."

Shar started and asked, "When did you get here?"

"Just a few minutes ago, mind if I join you for breakfast?" she asked.

"Please do," Shar answered as she blushed slightly.

Mortimer laughed, "Do not worry about your state of undress, we certainly aren't."

Scarlet laughed, "Most definitely, oh Clarice wanted me to tell you no armor until that wound heals, and Zephyr still wants to talk with you when you feel up to it. Word of your wound spread quite rapidly and we are all worried about you."

Shar's blush turned crimson and traveled from her face to her neck, "Please don't be worried about me, I'll be fine."

Scarlet shook her head, "I'm sorry, I shouldn't have let you hear my conversation with Clarice, if you hadn't you would not have felt the need to prove yourself."

"Stop," Shar said sharply, "it is not your fault I got injured, you tried to warn me and I refused to listen so I only have myself to blame." She dropped the blanket and pointed to several scars on her body, "I earned every single one of these scars, and this will one day be the one I am proudest of because I earned it protecting my family, don't ever think it is your fault."

Scarlet winced slightly, "Sorry, I didn't mean to offend you."

Mortimer laughed, "Wow you did something no one has ever done before, you got Scarlet to apologize twice in one day."

Scarlet threw a mock punch at him and laughed, "What can I say, it shows how rarely I am wrong."

At this all three of them burst into laughter until Shar winced, "Okay that's enough laughing for me," she gasped.

Mortimer and Scarlet were instantly at her side and checking her wound, "It would be better if it was cauterized," Scarlet said, "at least then the bleeding would be stopped."

Shar nodded, "That's probably a good idea, can you do it without getting any dirt in it?"

Scarlet smiled, "Of course dear, have you forgotten who you are talking to?" She raised her hand and a small white hot flame appeared in her hand, "this is going to hurt a lot," she said as she ran her hand over the wound.

Shar felt the heat and clenched her teeth, Scarlet hadn't been kidding, it burned like hell, but she had cauterized her own wounds before and didn't scream, "Thank you," she gasped when it was finished.

"Now eat," Mortimer said to her, "you too," he said to Scarlet. He sat back and watched the two of them, he wasn't sure what it was, but he had a suspicion he was missing something.

Scarlet watched him closely as she ate, she could feel everything he felt, hers was the strongest bond with him. There was something definitely wrong, but he wasn't saying what it was and every time she tried to push into his mind he blocked her. Finally she gave up trying to be subtle and said, "What are you worrying about?"

He couldn't help but smile at her directness, "I am worried about a lot of things, but I am mostly worried about whether or not we are making the same mistake as my ancestors."

Shar looked at the two of them and asked, "Is this a conversation I should be here for?"

Scarlet smiled at her, "Of course, you are part of this mess now." She turned back to Mortimer, "I wondered the same thing, but I'm not sure if we are even capable of changing the ritual."

"Neither am I," he replied, "although I have to wonder why go through all of the trouble to put me in a position of creating this convoluted bond, when they could have simply sent me to collect the crimson blades and return." He smiled at Shar, "don't get me wrong, I love all of you ladies, but wouldn't it have been easier to send me out with a

233

bunch of knights to retrieve the pieces and then simply order a bunch of witches to perform the ritual?"

Scarlet was shocked at the simplicity of the idea and at a loss for words.

He looked her directly in the eyes and smiled, "better yet, why did they set you up to go through hell just to arrange our meeting?" He saw the anger on her face and continued hastily, "I love you, I have since the moment I first laid eyes on you, so why not simply introduce us to each other like normal people?"

Shar remained very still, as she watched Scarlet closely for any signs of danger.

Scarlet sat there with her eyes closed and her hands clenched, "I do not have the answer to either of those questions, but I can surmise the answer to the reason behind our meeting the way we did." She took a deep breath and very softly said, "It is because I wanted nothing to do with being paraded around as a wife of some rich brat. I was only attending that party at the order of my teachers, and fully intended to disappear immediately after they introduced us to the young prince they wanted us to entertain." She opened her eyes and looked at him with tears in them, "I don't know why they thought a trick like that would work, but I am very thankful they thought to do so, as I got to see who you really were and fall in love with you." With a frown, she continued, "You know I would do anything to see your eyes turn that brilliant blue once more."

Mortimer smiled at her, "I know you would, I just wish we could be given all of the information up front instead of being put through so many tests."

"Really child?" a voice said from behind him. The crimson witch stepped around him and slowly sat down next to Scarlet, "if you truly wish to know, then I will explain." She looked at Scarlet and smiled, "you know, you are from another branch of my family and you two are distant cousins?" Before anyone could say anything she continued, "Your great great grandfather was my brother, so no you are not that closely related."

She smiled slightly as Clarice and Tara walked into the room, "Children, come sit and join us for breakfast, the others will be along soon."

Mortimer looked at her and frowned, "I take it you are overfed?"

"Correct," the crimson witch answered, "I need to burn off some energy before we return home."

Lorelei and Zephyr arrived shortly, "The first mate has the helm," Zephyr said as she entered, "I instructed him to follow the ghost ship."

The crimson witch smiled, "That is the best way to go about it, when this conversation is over Mortimer and you will need to create a portal to speed things along and burn off some of his excess energy."

"Traveling a shadow portal is something best done with your eyes closed," Mortimer whispered.

The crimson witch laughed, "Oh sweet child if she creates the portal it will not be nearly as bad as if you were to create it." She gestured for the others to sit, "You all have wondered why I have put you through all of these challenges, and I intend to explain. I am not sure you are truly ready to hear everything, but I have realized that by not knowing it has made things more difficult." She looked directly at Mortimer and smiled, "First of all we made the mistake of replacing a bonded witch with a regular one back when we united the last crimson blade and that created a loop which forced us to share the same destiny as that previous witch. I became the crimson blade because there was a hole in the bond and thus the curse was passed on to us."

She looked around the circle and they were surprised to see a small red tear appear in her eyes, "Your life my child was cursed because of my husband and I selfishly trying to save Clarice's great grandmother from being consumed by the ritual. All who are bonded must participate in the ritual, or the cycle will continue." She smiled slightly at Scarlet, "I was not counting on you destroying the witch hunter's power, and am not sure how that would affect the next cycle, but I also don't want to see you go through what we did."

They all stayed quiet as she looked around the circle, "All of you have one thing in common, all of you are connected to the order of the rose. You see each and every one of you is related to one of the witches who sacrificed themselves to destroy the last crimson blade, descendents of siblings, but still related, as such you have the greatest chance of breaking the cycle."

"All of you had your powers bound at birth," she smiled, "this has become a common practice to prevent accidental deaths, and all of you have broken through those bonds." She smiled at them, "None of the witches in the guard presently have managed to completely remove their bonds, but you have all surpassed their abilities. If we had used just any five witches to release me from my prison, the backlash would have destroyed the entire town and all who live in it, if not the world. The bond serves as a sort of path the power will travel through and it will keep the power contained and allow Mortimer to channel it into the realm of the dead releasing both myself and my husband." She looked around the circle and asked, "Any questions?"

"Yes," Shar replied, "there are six of us and only five blades, how will that work? And, how am I connected to all of this since I am not a witch."

The crimson witch smiled, "Very good questions, you my dear are the vessel into which all of the power will flow. There is a very special item you will need during the ritual, and it is waiting for you at the order."

Mortimer nodded his head thoughtfully, "What will happen to them during the ritual?"

She hesitated a moment before she answered with a deep sigh, "They will die, but they will be reborn so you will not lose them."

He shook his head slowly, "I swore an oath to free you, but I cannot demand they sacrifice their lives for yours. Is it possible for you to take my life instead?"

She shook her head slowly, "Sadly you know that is not an option, you already tried to sacrifice yourself for her," she nodded towards Scarlet, "and you saw how that turned out."

"And what happens if we do not perform the ritual?" Tara asked.

"If my blades are sealed away without access to blood, I would be trapped forever, or until someone is willing to perform the ritual," she answered.

Zephyr shook her head, "honestly if that were to happen someone would eventually steal the blades and use them for evil, we would just be passing our responsibility onto someone else." She looked at the witch and her face turned very serious, "I want a promise from you though, I want you to swear that we will be able to be with Mortimer after the ceremony is complete."

All of the women nodded their heads in agreement, Lorelei smiled darkly, "I know I am not a wanted addition to this mix, but I have to agree if we cannot continue with Mortimer after the ritual then I see no point in the ritual."

The crimson witch smiled darkly, "I promise you will all be with him afterwards, if you still wish to be."

Mortimer frowned, "What happened to the other witches who performed the ceremony with you?"

The crimson witch smiled and her face took on a different appearance, her hair turned dark brown and her eyes sparkled, "I was wondering when you would ask that question, we are all part of the one. Trust us when we say our husband never had a desire to stray because he always had whatever kind of woman he wanted." She smiled as she suddenly transitioned through several different faces and bodies, "We discovered all of us were missing something and when we came together all of those missing pieces created a feeling of being complete."

Scarlet laughed, "I was wondering about that, but was afraid I wouldn't like the answer. Why are you telling us this now?"

She smiled at Scarlet, "because he is having second thoughts and I am hoping the truth will convince you to see it through."

"That explains a lot," Scarlet replied, she looked at Shar and asked, "Is that why you took the forefront at the battle?"

Shar bowed her head, "Yes, she told me he intended to die in that battle, and I couldn't let that happen."

Scarlet's eyes narrowed as she stared at Mortimer, "You let her get injured in the realm of death, you could have protected her and you didn't."

"He couldn't," Shar growled at Scarlet, "I had his sword, I felt his power trapped within his sword."

The crimson witch put her hand between the two, "it was not his fault," She said, "He stood on the edge of a cliff when Zephyr went in, my husband watched her pull him back from that ledge. When she went in he was lost and not able to focus, so he was unable to use his own power to free himself. If anything she saved him from himself, if she hadn't gone in there he would have not been able to return to us."

"I should have been the one to go in, I never should have let another enter that horrible place to retrieve him," Scarlet growled.

The crimson witch laughed, "you don't understand, if you had gone in there he would have thrown himself over the cliff, he was there trying to protect you from any further harm. Although you might have been able to save him, you might have also destroyed a part of him in doing so."

"Then why didn't you go in and save him?" Zephyr asked.

"Because I am not allowed to go there yet, I have to rely on information from spirits who can come and go as they please," she answered.

Mortimer shook his head, "Enough, we can talk about it more later, right now I need to think."

The crimson witch bowed her head, "As you please, but you remind me a lot of my husband." She turned to Scarlet, "Do not leave him alone until you see blue in his eyes again oh and get rid of that ridiculous black hair, he needs to be true to himself." With that she faded into a crimson mist and vanished back to her blades.

Scarlet glared at the spot the witch had been in and said, "in that we can agree." She looked at the others as they all nodded their heads in agreement, "He is not to be left alone until I determine he is alright," she said.

Clarice looked at Scarlet and said, "Everyone can go back to what they were doing, I am going to stay and keep an eye on him and Shar." She smiled at Scarlet, "you are great at cauterizing wounds, but honestly you should leave the healing to me, and I would like the opportunity to try and heal his spirit before the rest of you tear it apart again."

Zephyr and Scarlet both looked as if they were going to say something, before Tara interrupted, "agreed, all of this anger cannot be good for him right now, he needs calm and stable energy. When it is time to change watches I will take the next watch," she looked at Scarlet, Zephyr and Lorelei, "whichever one of you is calmest can take the watch after that."

Lorelei smiled at Tara, "I have no reason to be upset, so unless those two can unwind before the third watch I will take that one."

Scarlet and Zephyr both huffed up for a second and then Zephyr burst out laughing, "My word, she is right we are feeding each other's anger, why don't we head on deck and try to relax?"

Scarlet couldn't help but laugh a little, "Fine, but if he goes back into that realm again I'm going to kill someone."

Clarice looked at them all and said, "Then go, I'll be fine tending to these two for a while." She turned to Mortimer, "You know what I am going to do, so for Shar's sake would you please relax and let me work my magic so she can see what is happening?"

Mortimer knew better than to argue at this point, so he lay down and closed his eyes, "Very well, but I am not sure if it will help."

Clarice bent over and kissed him, "For me please it reminds me of how all this got started." She then turned to Shar and guided her into a sleeping position, "you too dear," as she bent over and gave her a kiss, "I don't want you struggling just relax and let it happen."

Shar was confused for a moment, until she saw the icy cocoon encase Mortimer and then felt a cold sensation along her back as she found her own limbs quickly encased in ice.

Clarice smiled at them both, "you two look absolutely delicious, I do hope the others will be able to resist the temptation to break the ice prematurely."

Mortimer chuckled softly to himself, "Let's just hope this doesn't end up the way it did the last time you did this to me."

"It shouldn't," she replied, "this time you're actually cooperating instead of struggling." She smiled to herself as she relaxed and allowed herself to follow the bond lines into his mind.

Clarice instantly felt a nearby presence, "So you know how to follow the magic," she said to Lorelei.

"How did you know it was me?" Lorelei asked.

"You aren't very good at masking your scent."

"That can't be helped, it got so entangled with his magic I can't turn it completely off, why do you think I have been staying close to the rest of you?"

Clarice smiled, "and here I thought it was because you loved us. When do you plan to tell Shar and Zephyr you desire them?"

"You know too much about me," Lorelei replied.

"Not really, I felt it the first time you got near them, it's the real reason your scent was so strong, you weren't trying to attract Mortimer, you were trying to attract Zephyr since she was no longer queen." She turned and smiled at Lorelei, "the only problem is that type of magic doesn't work on women very well."

"How did you figure out about Shar?" she asked.

"Oh, you gave it away when you noticed her injury and this morning when you were so concerned about her safety," Clarice replied.

Lorelei sighed, "At the same time I am confused because I desire him as well."

"Don't worry about it," Clarice replied, "give yourself time you'll eventually discover exactly what it is you want in life."

"To make them all happy," she answered, "I already know my desire, just not how to obtain it."

"Then you are a step ahead of everybody else," a voice said from the shadows of the battlefield. "What are you two doing here? You do not belong here."

"Searching for you," Clarice answered. "I have questions and you are going to give me answers."

"She's gutsy," a softer voice said from behind the first.

"She looks good enough to eat," another chimed in.

Clarice shook her head and laughed, "I should have known he trapped you guys here. Do you remember what happened the last time we met, or do you need a reminder?"

"You can't harm us here," the first voice replied.

"I wouldn't be so sure about that," she replied. "If you don't mind, I would like to finish my conversation with my wife."

"I have no intention of fighting you," the first voice answered, "these others though might. Please feel free to finish your conversation, it is the best entertainment I have had in a long time."

Clarice smiled, "thank you, for the lord of this domain you are quite respectful." She turned to Lorelei, "How did you get past the wards in the room?"

Lorelei laughed, "Easy, nobody closed the door, so it meant the wards weren't complete."

"That was foolish of me," she replied, "I need you to go back to the realm of the living and close the door. After that, tell Tara to check on us in an hour."

"Are you sure you'll be alright?" she asked.

"Yes," she answered, "I came here for a conversation nothing more." She watched as Lorelei faded away and then turned back to the speaker, "It's been a while since we last saw each other."

"Yes," the first voice replied, "Mortimer was quite adamant back then that you would not be harmed. So, I have to wonder why you would put yourself at risk by coming here."

"Like I said earlier," she replied, "for some answers to my questions."

"I am not bound to answer your questions, only to be sure no harm befalls you, but feel free to ask and if I am inclined I will answer," the voice replied.

Clarice smiled at the shadowy figure, "Thank you, that is all I can expect from you. Is it true Mortimer defeated you and that is why he doesn't die?"

"No, he made a deal with me, he would retrieve two lost souls and return them to me in exchange for his life," the figure chuckled. "I only saved him once, all the other times it was one of you women that saved him."

"Then why did you agree to protect me here?" she asked.

The voice laughed a deep and booming laugh, "That is because I have a great respect for all of you and until you are whole it would do no good to take your souls."

"So you intend to collect us shortly after the ritual is complete?" She asked.

"Oh, you are such an innocent young thing," the voice said, "I do not cause people to die, I only collect their souls to take them to their final resting place. This place is neither good nor bad, I promise you if you do not change your ways you will forever be in a place much better than this."

"What about Mortimer?" she asked, "Where will he go?"

The figure stepped close to her and stooped down to look her in the eyes, "I do not know, but based on his actions he will most likely go to a nice afterlife. Unlike most necromancers, he uses my power with permission, not by stealing it."

Clarice took a deep breath to steady herself, seeing the skull up close like that terrified her, but she knew she had to protect her husband. "Final question, what will it take to convince you to guarantee his happiness?"

The skull laughed once again, "Oh, you truly are a sweet one, I cannot guarantee his happiness, only he can do that. Do you have any more questions?"

"Just one more," she replied as she reached out and grabbed him, "Are you allowed to accept a token of my thanks?"

The figure pulled back slightly a look of surprise on its skull face, "Nobody has ever offered me a token of thanks before," it looked at her arms around its neck and chuckled, "I believe you are the first person to even touch me in all time."

Clarice smiled at the skull and suddenly gave it a kiss on the cheek bone, "Thank you very much for not only enabling Mortimer to come into my life, but for taking the time to answer my questions. There will be a few more visitors to your realm in the next day or two, please forgive us for trespassing, we are only trying to help him."

"How could I refuse such a wonderful request," the skull replied, "he is truly a lucky man to have such a beautiful person in his life and I am glad I was able to help."

Clarice smiled at the skull and released his neck, "Thank you again, I look forward to seeing you at the ritual."

The skull laughed, "I am looking forward to it."

As she returned to the world of the living she chuckled, Mortimer was correct death was not such a bad person after all.

Clarice checked on her patients and smiled as she kissed them both.

"You have the smell of death on you," Mortimer said, "what did you do?"

She laughed and replied, "I had a conversation with an old friend of yours and invited him to the wedding."

Mortimer laughed, "Only you would invite death to a wedding. How long do I have to stay in this cocoon?"

"Until I determine it is safe to let you out," she replied.

"You know I could break out on my own."

Suddenly Tara spoke from the doorway, "If you try that I will encase you in stone." She turned to Clarice, "I got your message from Lorelei, my turn to watch him?"

"Yes," Clarice answered, "it is also your turn to enter the realm of death. In there you will find some people who have hurt you in the past, feel free to use whatever means necessary to destroy them." She turned to Mortimer, "he has already given permission for a few more visitors to his realm, so no complaining it is for your own good." With that she turned and left the room, being very careful to close the door all the way.

Tara looked at Mortimer and Shar, "How are you two doing?"

Shar smiled, "It's a strange sensation, but I am finding it rather nice."

Mortimer frowned, "I do not like being restricted, so let's get on with it. You can follow the bond to enter the doorway, but remember your magic will not affect the creatures there unless you have a weapon blessed by death himself."

Tara smiled at him, "don't worry, I'm pretty tough or have you forgotten?" She followed the bond lines easily enough, and found herself in the middle of the slave pens from when she was a child, "I guess everyone sees something different," she said to herself.

"That's right honey," a voice said from behind her. "Now that you're all grown up I can do whatever I like to you."

She spun around and instinctively brought her arm up to ward off a blow. It stung something fierce as several welts appeared on her arm. She recognized the slaver before her, he had been known for brutalizing the female slaves before Zephyr's mother caught him and beat him to death. She felt more blows to her body and saw more welts rise on her skin, "that's right, mortimer always said he felt their deaths when he took in a soul."

She jumped as a heavy blow doubled her over, "how does he deal with all this pain?" she asked aloud.

The slaver laughed at her, "It's too bad you were sold off before I had a chance with you, I guess now I get that chance."

She fell to the ground as a fist punched her hard in the jaw, as she tried to get up a foot found her stomach and her eyes spotted Mortimer's sword lying on the ground just out of reach. With a surge of energy, she slammed her hand on the ground and felt it tilt.

The sword slid towards her and she grasped the pommel with her left hand, there was a powerful jolt of energy from the sword and she rolled sideways as she lashed upwards with the blade.

She got to her feet and looked around, it wasn't just one person she faced, but several, the brute squad, they had always taken pleasure in breaking the strong willed slaves, or those who refused to listen.

"What are you going to do with that thing sweety," the leader asked, "you should put it back down before you hurt yourself."

Tara smiled, "I am not going to hurt myself, my husband would be upset if I ever did that." She turned her right hand palm up and extended it towards them, suddenly she made a fist and swept her hand upwards.

The entire brute squad let out a horrific scream as they were impaled by the earth beneath their feet.

"You're being too loud," Tara said to them, "you will disturb my husband's rest." She stepped forward and took the leader's head in a single sweep of the blade. "That's much better," she said as she turned towards the others. "Who's next?" She asked as she walked towards them. "You see I came to eliminate whatever was causing my husband so much pain, and I found you here, so I guess it is best that I eliminate you."

The brute squad started to struggle, trying to get off the stone spears and run from her, but she simply twisted her hand and watched them squirm as the spears turned inside their bodies. She looked at the next one and smiled darkly, "I am starting to understand his pain, it's not just your death he feels, but also what you did to others. Now I will get to do it to you," she said as the spear suddenly developed hooks.

Tara watched as more stone spears erupted from the ground and impaled the men in different places. "You know the irony is, you can't die unless I use this sword to kill you, do I have any volunteers?" she asked.

All of them tried to raise their hands as they were getting pierced over and over again.

Suddenly she noticed a single figure watching her, it was larger than any man she had ever seen before and it was walking towards her.

"I sense you have a lot of pent up anger," the figure said as it approached her. It snapped its fingers, and she found her clothing ripped from her body.

Tara gripped the sword with both of her hands and prepared to charge, but found she couldn't move her feet.

"Oh don't worry child, I mean you no harm, I just wished to see where that anger is coming from," the figure said. "You should put them out of their misery, for their destination is a hell far worse than this."

Suddenly she found she could move again, she turned to the impaled men and rapidly removed all of their heads, "Who are you?" she asked.

"You already know," the figure answered. "Release your husband, and walk with me."

Tara found it hard not to obey this figure, but she stood her ground, "I am not sure whether or not I should trust you."

The figure laughed again, "Oh you are so much more grounded than the other one, you trust a man who ripped the bonds out of your body only to replace them with his own, and yet you do not trust the person who gave him such power."

Tara felt true fear all of a sudden, "What are you going to do to me?" she asked.

"Nothing," the figure answered, "I have been watching all of you come and go through my realm, but you are different. I felt your rage and had to see for myself what was causing it, and now that I see the marks on your body I understand it. You are free to return to the mortal realm, but you must leave the sword here."

The figure snapped its fingers again, and she was once again fully clothed.

Tara released the sword, and felt a slight tug on her shoulder, and suddenly was staring at Mortimer's face, "That was horrible, how do you handle it?"

Mortimer chuckled, "I don't, but thankfully I have you and the others in my life to remind me how lucky I am." He looked at the bruises that were visible, "Are you alright?"

"I'll be fine," she answered, "but I can't believe anyone would go through that willingly."

He laughed, "You should have seen it when I took Scarlet and Clarice in the first time, it almost destroyed them both."

Lorelei came in through the door and said, "You look like crap Tara, Clarice will be down in a minute to tend to your wounds, she is bringing Zephyr down as well, apparently the former queen tried to hide her injuries and Scarlet found out." She grinned, "It was one hell of a fight, but Scarlet won in the end."

"Oh?" Tara asked, "how badly did they get hurt?"

Lorelei laughed, "From their fight, no injuries, but Zephyr's pride took a beating. The best part was when Scarlet threatened to tie her up and lick her wounds clean if she didn't consent to being treated by Clarice." She winked at Mortimer, "Scarlet's forked tongue scared Zephyr worse than a fireball."

Mortimer chuckled, "Well you should ask her to show you what she can do with that tongue."

Lorelei looked at him strangely and said, "Just how wild are you?"

Tara laughed, "He's wild enough that even death respects him."

Clarice walked in followed by Zephyr and Scarlet, "I see you had a rough time of it," she said to Tara.

"Not really, they just surprised me."

Scarlet laughed, "I should have warned you, death's realm changes depending on who enters it, so you have to always be prepared to deal with issues from your past."

Tara shrugged and winced, "I figured that out rapidly enough, I just hesitated for a moment and paid the price." She turned to Clarice, "I am ready when you are."

Clarice smiled at her, "Good it's a lot easier to heal someone who doesn't struggle." She walked over and looked at Mortimer, "I see you are starting to recover quite nicely. Lorelei, you are next, once you have dealt with your demons, we might just have him back to normal."

Lorelei smiled at her, "Okay, just do me a favor and have one of those cocoons ready for me when I return. I have a feeling I am really going to need it."

Tara and Zephyr lay down next to Shar, as Clarice said, "I will be ready, watch your back in there."

Lorelei took a deep breath and sat next to Mortimer, "Please don't fight me on this."

"You don't have to do this," he replied.

She smiled down at him and replied, "Of course I do, it is the only way to prove to myself I belong."

Before anyone could react, she reached out mentally and grabbed onto the bond between them. She raced along it and into the realm of death. "Interesting," she said as she looked around, she was on a ship and a huge figure stood before her."

"Welcome back," the figure said in a deep voice, "I have never seen anyone rush so headlong into a painful experience."

Lorelei laughed at the figure, "There is no point in delaying the inevitable, I know I will die here, but I will take as many of those who are hurting my husband with me."

"You will not die here," the figure replied, "not if you give me what I want."

"What is it you want from me?" she asked cautiously.

"I will wipe out all of his pain, if you give yourself to me," the figure replied.

Lorelei looked at the figure and grimaced, "I would do so in a heartbeat, but he would hate me for it."

"You would sacrifice your life for him," the figure replied, "and now you are saying you would sacrifice your body for him. I am amazed at the loyalty you women show to him. Very well, I shall allow you to do what you came here to do, but know this I will not allow you to die here," the figure said as it turned and walked away.

Almost immediately Lorelei felt a burning sensation all over her body, when she looked down she saw hundreds of wounds open up and she screamed in agony. After a few moments the pain subsided and she gasped for breath, "I had a feeling you would be here," she said as she forced herself to turn around.

Before her stood a man whose arms were dislocated, his entire body torn up and bruised, he didn't try to speak and simply stood there staring at her.

"You never should have tried to mutiny," she said, "better yet you should never have tried to rape me when you tried to take my ship." She felt more pain and saw more wounds appear, and laughed coldly. "I came here to take this pain from my husband, I will not allow you treacherous bastards to continue to exist."

The man before her tried to step back as Mortimers sword appeared at her feet, there seemed to be an ominous presence within that sword.

Lorelei knelt down and retrieved the sword, "I see, even here you would protect me," she said to the sword and felt a wave of warmth come from it. Her wounds no longer hurt as much and she knew she had to return to him alive.

She smiled wickedly and moved rapidly, three quick swings and the men before her fell. A quick spin and those behind her stopped moving closer, "Here I can let loose with all of my power for I do not have to worry about drawing those I care about to their death." The acrid air suddenly filled with the smell of the open sea, she could taste the coppery flavor of blood as the waves rose up around the side of the ship and fired frozen needles into the crew.

The air was filled with screams of the wounded and she reveled in the pain she drew from each of them as they were ripped to shreds. When they were all destroyed, she looked down and saw her entire body was a mass of wounds, her skin hung from her body as if someone had peeled it from the bones. Her clothes were rags and her once firm breasts were torn and shredded, but she didn't care, she was ready for more. "Is that the best you have?" she screamed, "I will not retreat and I will not surrender."

She looked around her and frowned, there was nothing but chunks of human flesh everywhere on the deck. "Well, now where do I go?" she asked as she felt the energy drain from her.

"Back to the mortal realm where you belong," a deep voice said from behind her. "I am very impressed with your tenacity, but what you have done to your own body is far beyond even my expectations. Go home and heal up the best you can, you will not die this day."

She turned to try and see the speaker only to find the sword gone from her hand and the world spinning around her. She opened her eyes and smiled at Mortimer, "I won," she gasped as she collapsed.

Clarice having seen the wounds appearing on her body quickly wrapped Lorelei into one of her healing cocoons, she wasn't sure if it would be enough though, her magic was being stretched thin with this much healing.

Scarlet saw Clarice swaying and said, "Focus on Lorelei, the others can survive without immediate attention."

Mortimer pulled himself out once the cocoon was soft and leapt to Lorelei's side, "What the hell was she thinking? I was dealing with them one at a time."

Scarlet laughed, "While you might be immune to the physical damage caused by that world, you are not immune to the emotional. She was thinking the best gift she could give us would be to allow you to return to us completely as quickly as possible."

Zephyr laughed, "It is more than that, she has felt out of place with us and wanted to prove she belonged." She stared directly at Scarlet, "you pretty much told her how much you disliked her being a part of the family, I would say her true goal was to go out in a blaze of glory."

Mortimer shook his head, "Enough you two, the fact is she chose to take on more enemies at one time than she should have. I face them one at a time because it takes much less of a toll on the body. Taking on the pain of a single death is a lot easier than taking on the pain of a dozen or even a hundred deaths." He turned to Clarice and said, "She is to be your primary focus, let me know immediately when she can talk." As he stood, the others rapidly scrambled out of the room, there was a look in his eyes that even Scarlet had never seen before.

Mortimer smiled at Clarice as he drew his sword, "I'm sorry, take good care of her while I am away." He slowly muttered something under his breath and drove the point of his sword into the floor. A thick black smoke curled up from the point of his sword and wound its way around his body as he continued to chant, his words became more ominous and suddenly the smoke was gone and he stood still as a statue suspended a foot from the floor.

# Judgment

He wasn't sure where he was at first, until he heard the high pitched screams of agony nearby. "Show yourself," he called out, "you and I both know neither of us will win if we get in a fight."

"I have no desire to fight you, old friend," a booming voice came from a short distance away. "Come give me a hand if you want to talk."

Mortimer frowned, this was not the greeting he had expected, death normally did not tolerate anyone forcing an entrance into his domain. He walked towards the voice, prepared for an attack at any moment, but was surprised to see death running around catching pieces of flesh and putting them in a sack.

Death looked at him and laughed, "You don't need your sword, I can't believe you actually used that spell to come here instead of just entering the normal way."

"I wanted to make full use of my powers," he replied, "besides this isn't my territory in your realm."

"True, this is another's domain and not truly of my realm," he replied, "which is why we need to act quickly if that young lady is going to survive and maintain her sanity."

Mortimer sheathed his sword, "What are you collecting?" he asked.

Death laughed, "These are the pieces of her soul she left behind, the parts that were ripped from her body while she fought. As you know only a soul can enter into my domain, but when you lose a body part here that is a piece of your soul that is removed."

"You once told me that the soul is what powers our will and to destroy a man's soul would be to destroy his mind," he said as he caught a few pieces of flesh out of the air. With each piece he collected he felt a sense of growing urgency. "Why are you concerned about her?" he asked.

Death looked up from his task for a moment and for the first time ever he looked happy, "Your wife gave me a present and thanked me for my help. I have never been given anything from a mortal without a formal contract being created, so since this one is bound to her through you," he paused as if in thought for a moment as his hands moved rapidly to catch more pieces of flesh. "I don't want her to be saddened by losing this person from your lives," he finished.

Mortimer smiled to himself, only one person he knew of would thank death for his help. "Why do I feel this sense of urgency?"

"Because the owner of this domain is near, and he has never been known for negotiating," death answered.

"Can he be defeated?"

"Not in his own realm, and don't even think about testing his power, you won't survive."

Mortimer laughed as he sensed a blow coming from behind and drew his sword, "It looks as if I have no choice," he replied as he blocked the blow. "I will hold him back while you finish collecting the pieces of her soul."

A cold wind blew around him on one side and a warm breeze blew on the other, "You do not belong here mortal," a strange voice said from either side. To his left the voice had a slight hissing sound and to his right it was musical.

He laughed slightly, "I walk often through the realm of death so why can't I walk here," he asked his sword at the ready in case of another strike.

Sure enough he sensed a strike from behind him, but as he turned to block he also noticed a shield appearing directly in front of his sword. "One of you attacks, and the other protects, how interesting."

Death suddenly stood next to him, "Done, you can take this bag and leave now."

"No," both voices said from the wind, "we are not done with him yet." Suddenly death vanished as the voices said, "You can be gone though until you bring us more pieces for sorting."

Mortimer laughed, "You are stronger than death, how interesting. If you wish to speak with me then let's cut through the games and show yourself."

"As you wish mortal," the voices replied as a figure appeared before him. The figure that appeared was both beautiful and horrendous at the same time, one side had smooth pale skin with a bright blue eye, the other was covered in dark red scales and had a flat black eye. One side had a pure white feathered wing, the other a black leathery twisted wing.

"Amazing," he said as he stared at them, "you two are absolutely amazing."

"We are one," the figure said, "give us the soul that is our due and we will let you leave in peace."

Mortimer shook his head, "Sadly I cannot do that as I need these pieces to help a woman who sacrificed everything for me."

"You are foolish, if you do not give them to us we will rend you to pieces and keep your soul as well." the figure replied, "Once a soul reaches our domain it can never escape."

"Considering the number of souls I have sent to you, I would think you'd be a little more willing to negotiate," he said as he lifted his sword.

"Do you think that thing can even hurt us?" the figure laughed.

Mortimer smiled, "No, it is the key to unlocking the realm of death," he answered as he slammed its point into the earth and released his spell.

He woke to Clarice shaking him, his body was stiff and sore, but he ignored it and sat up, "How is she?" he asked immediately.

"She is awake," Clarice answered, "I don't know what you did, but suddenly her flesh started to grow back and she woke up. I have been trying to wake you for the last couple of days and when I tried to follow the bond death blocked me." She started to cry as she held him, "I was afraid we had lost you, but you kept breathing."

Mortimer gave her a hug, "Death had his reasons for blocking you, where I was at even he could not help me. I am glad I was able to help her." He got to his feet and winced, his entire body ached, definitely not a spell to use without good reason. He staggered to Lorelei's side and gave her a half smile.

Lorelei looked at him and returned his smile for a moment and then reached up and slapped him, "Why did you do that?" she asked. "Why did you save me?"

He couldn't resist a slight laugh, "it's what I do," he replied. "How bad are her injuries now?" he asked Clarice.

"They are on par with Zephyrs, no longer life threatening, but they'll definitely leave a few scars," she smirked slightly, "that seems to be par for the course when it comes to the people around you."

"I knew when I went into death's realm I would no longer be pretty, I knew who would be waiting for me and how they had died," Lorelei said softly, "I understand completely if you cast me aside, I know how hideous I look."

"Clarice does amazing work," Mortimer replied, "have you looked in the mirror yet."

"She refuses to," Clarice replied, "she has also refused to have any visitors."

He nodded his understanding and waved her out of the room, before he turned back to Lorelei, "You impressed death with both your loyalty and courage," he said to her as he bent over and kissed her gently on the lips.

Somehow her arms wrapped around his neck and she returned his kiss, "I'm sorry," was all she said as they parted, "I'm sure you can't stand me now."

He smiled at her, "you have a lot to learn, and the first thing you need to be aware of is the truth."

"Oh?' she asked, suddenly curious.

"Yes," he replied, "you look good enough to eat, and I am very hungry."

"Now you are just teasing me," she replied, "I know you don't desire me anymore."

Mortimer sighed deeply, "If you truly believe that, then you have no qualms with letting me show you my desire?"

She rolled her eyes, "I'm pretty sure" she was silenced by his lips on her own, and this time she realized she couldn't pull away from the kiss. She felt his hands on her, and then she felt the rest of his presence, but he was holding back.

"May I continue?" he asked as the kiss ended.

"No," she answered, she could feel his energy even though he was physically inches from her, it felt as if she were held down by him.

"Very well," he sighed as he physically moved farther from her.

"Stop," she said, she could still feel his presence on her body, all over her body, she was confused, "please don't move," she said.

250

Mortimer froze, "are you alright?"

She hesitated a moment, as she realized he respected and cared about her. "Are you using magic?" she asked.

"No, why do you ask?"

"Because I still feel you," she answered "I feel as if you are pressed against my body."

"That is because your soul still feels the presence of my own," he answered, "I held it close to my heart when I brought the pieces back from the realm of the dead. It will fade with time, as you become distracted with other things."

Lorelei couldn't help but smile as a warm feeling came over her, suddenly she threw herself at him, wrapped her arms around his neck and kissed him. She was embarrassed at her sudden loss of control, and forced herself to pull back from him for a moment, "Are you sure I am not hideous to look at?" she asked.

For an answer, he pulled her in close and kissed her deeply, "I am very sure," he answered when she pulled back again.

"Then do with me what you will," she replied as she rolled off of him.

She was surprised when she awoke several hours later and he was still sleeping next to her, "It must have been a dream," she whispered to herself.

"It was not," someone said softly behind her.

Lorelei jumped slightly and felt Mortimers body tense up. Slowly she extracted herself from his arms and turned to see who was there. She was mildly surprised to find all of them sitting there staring at her.

"Breakfast?" Tara asked, offering her a plate of fruit.

"What are you doing here?" she hissed at them.

"Shhhh, you don't want to wake him," Scarlet said with a smile. "I haven't seen him sleep like this since before we left home."

Lorelei felt her muscles tense, "Why are you here," she asked a touch of fear seeping into her voice.

Scarlet sighed, "Are you still afraid of me?" she asked.

Lorelei let her eyes find the floor, "A little, I know how much you hate me."

"Hate is too strong of a word," Scarlet replied, "yes, I admit I didn't like you trying to seduce my husband, but I don't hate you. To be honest I don't really know you, but I do know you tried to sacrifice yourself for my husband."

Zephyr reached out and playfully smacked Scarlet upside the head, "our husband."

Scarlet smiled, "True," she looked at Lorelei, "look, you are a part of us, and like it or not we are not always going to get along, especially since you have a much nicer body than I do."

"Not anymore," Lorelei replied, "I don't need you to remind me how ugly I have become."

Zephyr laughed softly, "Honey, you really should look in a mirror some time, trust us when we say a man would prefer you over either of us."

"You can include me in that thought," Shar added, "people don't exactly clammer to sleep with someone in armor."

"Why do you tease me?" Lorelei asked.

"Why don't you look in a mirror?" Scarlet retorted.

"Fine," she replied, "give me the mirror." As she took the mirror from Clarice's hands, she braced herself for the worst. She had been avoiding looking at her body ever since Mortimer broke her bonds, but now she forced herself to look in the mirror. Lorelei almost dropped it, her face had healed almost completely, her hair was much shorter and had strange white streaks in it. She had lines on her face, but they didn't really detract from her appearance. In surprise she looked down at her arms and legs, they were lean and muscular, "but, I should be missing chunks of flesh, I saw them fall off in the realm of death." she said in shock.

"Mortimer went back in and retrieved the missing pieces," Clarice said.

Lorelei looked down at her stomach, and felt it, "I seem to have lost weight, I have no fat on my body."

Scarlet laughed as she stood up and approached Lorelei, "Oh, you have fat on your body," she said as she reached down and stroked her shoulder. "Would you like me to show you where it is?" she asked mischievously.

Lorelei looked at her confused for a moment, this wasn't like Scarlet, she almost felt like a child as she said, "Yes, please."

Scarlet's eyes widened and she burst out laughing, "Well I certainly wasn't expecting that." She reached down and cupped Lorelei's breasts, "right here silly."

Lorelei's eyes twinkled mysteriously and she grabbed Scarlet by the hair and pulled her face closer, "he loves you, you know," she said as she gave her a deep kiss. She was very surprised when Scarlet dropped to her knees in front of her and returned the kiss just as passionately as Mortimer had.

"I know," Scarlet said as they separated, "he loves you too, you know." She moved in close to Lorelei again and whispered, "If you want her, then take her, otherwise she is going to believe you're only teasing her."

"Does everyone know?" she whispered back.

"No," Scarlet answered, "Clarice told me, but Shar is off limits for now."

"The hell I am," Shar said loudly, "this little scratch is not going to stop me from doing anything you can do, physically."

Everyone winced at the loudness of her voice and Mortimer snorted, "Well, I guess everyone knows I'm awake now, just when things were getting interesting."

Tara chuckled and asked, "Out of all your wives who is the most beautiful?"

He snorted, "what kind of question is that? You're all beautiful."

"Alright," she continued, "fair enough. Which one of us do you desire the most?"

"Again you ask a question with no answer," he replied, "I desire all of you, why do you ask?"

"If you could change anything about any of us, what would it be?" Scarlet asked, an acidic tone in her voice.

Mortimer smiled at her and suddenly wrapped his arms around her and Lorelei, "Nothing," he answered. "Sometimes I wish you all would get along better, but at the same time it is those little disagreements that strengthen our love," he said as he kissed her.

Lorelei squirmed for a second, then said, "Hey where's my good morning kiss?"

Scarlet laughed and said "I already gave you one."

"No, I took one from you, you didn't give it to me willingly," she retorted.

Scarlet grinned and said, "Oh really?" She pulled Lorelei in close and gave her a fiery kiss, "Morning sweety, was that good enough?" she asked her.

"I forgot how hot you are," Lorelei laughed, "I think you burnt my tongue. If you ever get tired though you're welcome to warm my bed," she teased.

"Anybody else want to give her a good morning kiss?" Scarlet asked, "get them while her lips are still hot."

Zephyr swooped in, and gave Lorelei a hug and a kiss that literally took her breath away, "I've been wanting to do that for a while now."

Tara and Clarice both came over and gave her a kiss on either cheek, "Never forget you are a part of this family again," Clarice said with an icy tone in her voice, as she gave her a deeper, colder kiss.

Tara followed up with a strong and hard kiss, "We are yours and you are ours, forget again and I'll bury you."

Lorelei smiled at Clarice, "you taste of the sea, I understand why he is addicted to you." She turned to Tara, "you are hard as rock and as calm as the earth, thank you."

Shar knelt down in front of her, "Part of me wants to beat the crap out of you for putting yourself in danger," Slowly she kissed her, and as she ended the kiss, she slapped her, "Don't make me worry like that again."

Lorelei smiled and started to cry, as she nodded her head in understanding. She had never felt this way, these people actually accepted her, whether she had anything to give them or not.

Mortimer laughed from behind her, "I suppose we should have warned you, we don't like it when people try to get themselves hurt." He shrugged his shoulders, "Besides, soon enough you will get the opportunity to sacrifice yourself, we'll see if you still want to when that time comes."

Mortimer stood up and reached for his clothing, "What is the status of the fleet?" He asked Zephyr.

Zephyr smiled at him, "Nice bruises, she do that?" she asked.

"No," he answered, "it's the price I pay for bringing the rest of her soul back to her. You didn't answer my question."

She laughed, "I had all prisoners transferred to this vessel, and the others have all broken off to various villages to make amends. It will help that the freed slaves will attest they had very little choice but to follow my orders." She winced slightly, "My head is going to end up on a platter when this is all over."

Scarlet laughed, "Not likely, you are currently in the custody of the order, worst case we have to shackle you whenever we are in town."

"Very well," Mortimer replied, "how long until we reach our destination?"

Tara laughed, "With the winds as they stand, two to three more days." She poked him in the ribs, "And, quit being so snappy all of a sudden."

"Ow," he replied, "believe it or not I do feel pain."

Shar chuckled, "Those bruises are from an internal injury, chances are he is in a hurry because he knows he is likely to die from them."

Clarice frowned, "I was afraid of that, once more you are trying to hide your injuries from me, why?"

Mortimer tried to step back from her, but suddenly found himself surrounded. "I don't want you wasting energy on my injuries," he said as he tried to step between Lorelei and Scarlet.

The scent of a thousand wildfires filled the air, as Scarlet blocked his path, "You are going to let her tend to your wounds, or you may find yourself with a few new ones." She then turned to Lorelei, "You should stay too, long enough for Clarice to be sure you're fully mended."

As Scarlet turned towards her, Shar took a step backwards, "I will stay as well Mistress, no need to order me to."

Scarlet turned towards Zephyr and Tara, but Clarice suddenly said, "Those two are fine, they can return to their duties."

Scarlet smiled at Clarice, "Very well, if you need me I will be with the dragon egg."

Lorelei chuckled, "and what if we desire your presence to keep us warm?" she asked.

Clarice shook her head slowly, and asked Mortimer, "Are you sure you didn't slip a little of your soul into her?"

He returned her look and frowned, "Some of it may have rubbed off on her, sorry."

Scarlet looked at the two of them and replied, "Once you have a clean bill of health I will be happy to make all your fantasies come true, but not until then." She never saw two people move so fast in her life, even Shar looked surprised or was she seeing something else in Shar's eyes. With a confused shake of her head, she walked out of the room and closed the door, this was turning into a wild day for sure.

# Heat

Scarlet sat down in front of the dragon egg to think, it was recovering nicely now that it was no longer having its life energy drained from it. She knew it hadn't created the bonds, she also knew its parent had died trying to protect it, what she didn't know was what to do with it now.

Zephyr and Clarice both wanted to throw it overboard, but then again dragons were the natural enemies of large birds and the merfolk. Tara suggested cooking it for breakfast, Shar said she would go along with whatever Mortimer decided. She hadn't had a chance to talk to Lorelei about it yet, and suddenly Scarlet started to blush. "Oh god, am I seriously trying to seduce her so she'll agree with me?" she asked herself.

A cough behind her made her turn to find a sailor standing there with a rag in his hand, "Pardon me Mistress, but if you need someone to talk to I have a few minutes available."

Scarlet smiled at the sailor, "Thank you, I am just trying to decide the best action to take regarding this egg." She took a step towards him and noticed he backed away slightly, "why did you back away?" she asked, a little irritated.

He took a deep breath and then took a step towards her, "I didn't mean any offense, it's just that we have all heard rumors about your temper and to be honest most of us are terrified of you."

Scarlet thought about this for a moment and started to laugh softly, "I always dreamed people would fear me, but now that they do I wish they didn't," she said with a chuckle.

"Whoever it is you were trying to seduce," the sailor started cautiously, "do you think they might be afraid of you as well?" He paused as she turned serious.

"Go on," she urged.

He gulped for breath and continued, "Maybe you should start by just talking to them and letting them see you don't mean any harm, if you move too fast, you may scare them even more."

Scarlet couldn't resist, she lunged past him and put an arm around his shoulders, "You mean like this," she breathed softly to him.

The sailor's body stiffened, and for a moment she thought she might have scared him to death, but eventually he turned his head and looked her in the eye. "If I die here and now I will die a happy man."

"Why am I doing this," she suddenly snapped as she stepped back from the sailor.

"How long have you had scales?" the sailor asked.

"You noticed them?" she asked.

"Well, yes, you were quite close to me just now, and I really wish you hadn't pulled back," he answered.

"Remember that idiot who sought to challenge Zephyr for the crown at sea? Well I broke my bonds in that battle, why?" she asked.

He counted the days rapidly and said, "Come with me mistress, there is a book I have been reading from, it mentions witches and their ancestry."

"Hold on," Scarlet said with a laugh, "moments ago you were terrified of me and now you suddenly want to be alone with me?"

"Well, yes and no," he answered, "I would love to be alone with you, but I am terrified by the thought of what would become of me afterwards."

"What would become of you?" she asked.

He laughed a little forcefully and answered, "Yeah, I'm not sure if you will kill me during the deed or if your husband would kill me afterwards."

"If you can provide me with the answers I need, I will protect you while you ask for permission from my husband," she replied.

At this the sailor turned into a doorway and walked smack into the door, "Damn, forgot to open it, you distracted me," he said as he opened the door.

Inside the room was a small library of books, a quick sniff and Scarlet detected the scent of magic. "Where did you get all of these?" she asked.

He chuckled, "I found them in a cave and when I showed them to Zephyr she said I could have them." He smiled, "she was even so nice as to have this room built for them. She can read some of them, but these ones," he waved to the top shelf, "I am the only one able to read them."

Scarlet looked at the top shelf and smiled, "Then you were well educated," she picked one of the books and read the cover, "How to enjoy life with the fae?"

"Great book," he said, "it tells how to shape trees into houses without hurting the tree, and also how to help heal wounded animals along with fairy creatures." He paused for a moment "you can read them too?" he asked.

Scarlet laughed, "Yes I was taught how to read the ancient writings when I was part of the guard."

The sailor froze all of a sudden, "You are part of the dreaded witches guard?"

"Not anymore," she answered, "I have learned a lot since leaving them."

He visibly relaxed and reached for a book, "This is the book I was thinking of," he said as he handed it to her.

She took the book from him and looked at the cover, "The proper breeding of witches," she read. "What, does the author think we are some sort of animal or something?"

"Yes," the sailor answered, and then stepped as far away as the cramped little room would allow.

It wasn't far enough, Scarlet stepped in close and trapped him in the corner, "Do you think I am an animal?" she asked him.

"Yes and no," he answered hastily, part of him wanted her to back up, the other part wanted her to come closer. "Oh god," he said, "I think I have an addiction to you."

"You what?" she asked as she stepped back.

He laughed, "Please don't go, you smell so good." The sailor slapped himself, "Sorry, but you do smell good, honestly the book describes it better, it is about halfway through. Let me find it and then I truly have to get some distance from you before I lose my senses completely."

She handed the book back to him and watched as he sniffed where her hand had been holding the book. It took her a moment before she realized where she had seen behavior like this before. "Oh, god," she said, "I'm in heat aren't I?"

"I believe so," the sailor replied, "just let me check the book."

"Hold tight to the book and come with me," she said as she suddenly grabbed his free arm and dragged him out of the room. She sniffed the air in the hallway and followed her own scent back to the hold, past the dragon egg and to what was now being used as an infirmary. She burst through the door and practically flung the sailor across the room at Clarice. "Show her what you were trying to show me," she gasped as she tried to catch her breath.

The sailor simply handed the book to Clarice and turned back to Scarlet and said, "Mistress, please come closer. It hurts to be this far away from you."

Clarice looked at her and asked, "What is going on?"

Scarlet laughed, "Remember the little problem you had when we first met?"

"Yes," she paused, "oh, what caused you to go into heat?"

"I believe it was the dragon egg, but I can't be certain." She gestured to the book and continued, "The book may contain the answer, but the longer he is close to me the worse it gets for him." She grimaced, "he doesn't even care if Mortimer kills him if he can just be close to me for a little while."

Mortimer laughed, "So, are you going to fulfill his wishes?"

"No," she answered.

"Thank you," the sailor said, "I know it sounds stupid, but as much as I enjoy the feel of your body against mine, I really think it best if we don't let things progress. At least from this distance my mind is starting to clear up again," he turned to Clarice, "how long since your last heat?"

Clarice looked as if she was about to slap him and then started to laugh, "It was not so long ago, but it will come again soon. Why?"

"According to that book a mermaid in heat can cause an entire ship's crew to dive overboard," the sailor answered.

She smiled, "That is true, my mother has done that once or twice, but don't worry, we can contain it to this room."

"I'm in big trouble aren't I?" he asked.

"Not at all," Clarice answered, "there is a reason we married a warlock. Once the effects of her heat wear off you, I will shuttle you through the door and you can go about your business. I would ask you not to mention any of this to the rest of the crew though, some of them might get ideas."

Scarlet took the hint and stepped away from the doorway, keeping as far from the sailor as possible. Once she was in a corner, she turned her back on the door and waited until she heard it close.

Clarice calmly walked the sailor to the door, opened it for him and closed it behind him.

Scarlet heard the bolt slide shut, and Clarice said, "It's safe to turn around, I need you to read this book anyways, I don't recognize the language."

"I would be surprised if you did," she replied, "he's got quite a few books written during the time that the druids were powerful." She pointed to the book and continued, "That particular one is titled 'The Proper Breeding of Witches', I'll let your imagination run for a bit while I peruse its contents."

"Well, this is quite interesting," she said, "the name is a bit offensive, but once you start reading it, it makes sense. The book starts out by explaining how witches all have magical creatures as ancestors, and how to determine what type of ancestor they might have had based on their physical attributes and magical powers. From there it breaks down the ancestry based on element, earth, fire, water and air, and inside each of those sections it has specific creatures associated with that particular element."

"What does it say about mermaids," Clarice asked.

Scarlet flipped through the pages and laughed, "it says mermaids are sensual creatures, their breeding cycle depends on their sexual activity levels, if you wish for your witch of mermaid decent to get pregnant, to keep her away from men yourself included for several weeks. The sight of a male will trigger her to go into heat at that point and her chance of conceiving are at their peak."

"I don't know if I should be offended or not," Clarice replied, "what does it say about the Naga?"

Scarlet turned a few more pages and whistled, "This rare magical descendent is truly dangerous, she will use a combination of her voice, her appearance, and her perfume to lure men to their deaths. She will only breed with the strongest male, if she is able to get the upper hand she is likely to crush the life out of you after having her way. They tend to go into heat suddenly and without warning especially when a man proves his strength in combat."

Clarice laughed, "It's wrong on one account, it happens when a man or woman proves their strength in combat." She pointed towards Lorelei, "She's been in heat for a while now, if I released the three of them from their cocoons, they would all be trying to breed in seconds." She chuckled, "Poor Mortimer is the only person in the room not immune to her scent."

"Not true," Scarlet replied, "Shar and Zephyr both felt it before, but out in the open, and I definitely felt it earlier. Why me though?"

Clarice laughed, "The first day on the island you took out that captain, you also drowned out her perfume, and even today you took a dominant position on her. Her fear of you is triggering her desire to breed with you, and thus it is altering her perfume so that it affects you."

Scarlet frowned, "Fair enough, let's see what it says about dragons." She flipped several pages and then laughed, "It says here, you have to be insane to attempt to breed with a descendent of a dragon. Their tempers are out of control, prone to burning down the house before they even think of looking at you or helping with chores. They are consummate hoarders of shiny objects and they are prone to bouts of jealousy. Anyway, you wouldn't be looking at this section if you hadn't already made the mistake of getting mixed up with one. Dragons being violent creatures tend to love a lot of violence and shiny objects after a violent outing just throws them into a breeding cycle that won't leave you begging for more. Shredded skin from their claws and teeth, the occasional broken bone from being slammed about. Seriously, if you are reading this before choosing a wife, stay away from the dragon descendents. She will break you."

Clarice looked at Scarlet, "She, as in singular? I am beginning to wonder if whoever wrote this book had personal experience with all of them and if so, how did he survive it."

"I don't think he survived it," Scarlet said when she flipped to the back page, "it says here he died writing this book shortly after he was caught with a nymph descendent by the dragon descendent."

"Can you keep it together for another day or two?" Clarice asked. "I really would rather he be fully healed before you put him back into my care."

Scarlet laughed, "I will try, I'm curious to read more of this anyways. I wonder what it says about earth and air."

"What does it say about harpies?" Clarice asked.

Scarlet flipped to the book and whistled, "It says, harpy descendents tend to be attracted to shiny objects and love to live a free life not constrained by the city. To truly awaken a harpies spirit, provide her with a home where she can come and go as she pleases with lots of access to the air, large windows, open ceilings, and a good breeze. When supplied with such a nest as they call it and presented shiny objects they become quite docile with their chosen mate and will defend their family to the death. They can be some of the most passionate lovers, but also can be very creative in their love making." She chuckled, "I am almost jealous of her now, I can't even imagine what Zephyr will come up with to try with Mortimer."

"Well, we have a good week until we find out," Clarice replied, "I wonder what type of earth creature Tara is."

"I do not think she has fully broken her bonds yet, but let me see what I can find out," Scarlet replied as she flipped through the pages."

After a minute, she chuckled, "Earth descendents all share a single quality, and that is their stability. Loyal to a fault, they will never betray those whom they share a deep connection with, always supportive; they are known for sacrificing themselves to protect their loved ones. This one has two sub sections, one is titled stone the other titled plants, I believe Tara is definitely stone."

"Agreed," Clarice replied.

Scarlet continued to read, "Stone types are far more durable than plant types, and their moods do not change with the season. They tend to be resistant to most elements and are tough creatures to get to know. Trolls tend to be tall, gangly and greenish gray colored skin, Goblins are short, wiry and rough spoken, Dwarves are short of stature, broad of shoulder and very muscular." She paused reading and said, I think she might be a dwarf descendent.

Clarice laughed, "That is the only race I can think of that lives in the ground and doesn't have a mangled body."

"Well there is a race of elves that live in the ground, they tend to be shorter than humans, very pretty and agile warriors, they prefer to keep their distance and are very aloof from others."

A knock at the door startled them both, "Come in," Clarice said cautiously.

The sailor from earlier opened the door cautiously and said, "I thought it best since you had that book to bring his other wives down. I wanted to also offer my services if you need any further research materials."

Clarice laughed, "It may be safe for the others, but it is not safe for you in here, unless you want to become a dragons toy."

"I would be whatever she wished me to be," the sailor said, and then slapped his hand over his nose. "Oh god, I have to go, call me if you need me." He looked at Scarlet and for a moment they thought he would throw himself at her feet, but a hand grabbed him by the collar and pulled him out of the room.

Zephyr and Tara stepped into the room and locked the door, "That was interesting," Zephyr said with a frown, "he has never once shown an interest in anyone but his books."

Tara sniffed the air and asked, "What's burning?"

Scarlet sighed, "I am, and it's starting to get out of control."

Zephyr laughed, "Better you than me, feathers smell horrible when they burn."

Clarice frowned, "Well, your time is coming, your ancestry now that it has been unlocked will cause you to go into heat eventually and when it does watch out."

Zephyr looked puzzled for a moment until Scarlet read the passage to her about Harpy descendents. "That explains a few things," she replied calmly, "How long do you think I have before this heat kicks in?"

Scarlet laughed, "That's a good question, has he given you anything shiny recently, or your freedom, or a nest with lots of air flow?"

Zephyr laughed, "I have lots of shiny objects, and I have an open nest here on this ship, and he gave me more freedom than I ever, oh my," she said, "He has done far more than my father ever did for my mother."

Clarice started to laugh, "It smells like now that you realize what he has given you, you are going into heat, this can't be good as your kind tends to like freedom and containing you will do a lot of harm."

"I'll be fine," she replied, "I can be happy in my nest as you called it for weeks at a time."

"Not with all those tasty sailors running around," Scarlet replied.

Tara laughed, "What does the book say about me?"

Scarlet frowned, "we are trying to decide what type of descendent you are, stone obviously, but we are trying to determine if it is a dwarf or subterranean elf."

Tara chuckled, "I am not sure either, I am shorter than the rest of you, but I am not sure what else would help you to find out."

Clarice laughed, "what does it say about unlocking ancestry for stone witches?"

Scarlet fumbled through the book, not sure if it had the information or not, finally she found a note in the back of the book. "Stone types are the hardest to identify until their powers are fully released, in order to do this you will need to separate them from the earth and force them to bring the earth to them."

Zephyr laughed, "Well that shouldn't be too difficult, we'll simply hang her from the bow of the ship and threaten to drop her in the sea if she doesn't summon a path to the deck."

Tara shook her head, "that wouldn't work, I would simply hang there until we came to shore, I can endure quite a bit of pain."

Scarlet looked at her and frowned, "What if I told you I could accidentally kill Mortimer when in heat and you could be the only one capable of stopping me."

Tara looked at Scarlet to see if she was serious, "You are joking correct?"

Clarice shook her head, "She is not joking, dragon descendents have been known to kill their mates when they go into heat."

"I'll be back," Tara said as she unlocked the door and walked out of the room.

"Her emotions are so hard to read," Zephyr said.

"She most certainly is," Scarlet replied.

"Is Lorelei ready to be released?" Zephyr asked.

"She is more than ready," Clarice replied, "I am only keeping her locked down due to realizing she may be in heat as well." She frowned, "Things could get really ugly between her and Scarlet, both of their ancestors are very violent when it comes to a mate."

"Let her loose," Zephyr replied, "it will only make it worse if she is trapped."

Clarice nodded in understanding and waved her hand towards one of the remaining cocoons. "Be nice," she said to Lorelei as she wriggled her way out.

Lorelei laughed hysterically for a second before regaining her composure, "Nice? After being trapped and smelling her?" she swung her head at Scarlet and grinned, "I didn't know your scent worked on women."

Clarice stepped in and placed a hand on Lorelei's chest, "it doesn't, that is the effect of the pieces of Mortimers soul he gave you in order to save your life."

Lorelei looked down at Clarice's hand and paused, "You probably shouldn't touch me there," she whispered with a strange look in her eye.

Zephyr stepped around behind Lorelei and grabbed her by the back of the neck, "You know better than to threaten one of my family, my ancestors have hunted your kind for centuries."

Scarlet suddenly grabbed Zephyr by the wings, "Mine have hunted yours for just as long, you are starting a bad situation."

Clarice moved closer to Lorelei and kissed her, "Sister you must resist the urge for now, I wish only to help you."

The tension ran like a ripple out of Lorelei, and from her it ran through Zephyr and finally Scarlet, "Oh my, I can't believe how angry I was just now," Scarlet said, "Are we all good now?"

A sudden jolt knocked all of them off their feet, "What the hell was that?" Zephyr asked, "It felt like we ran aground, but I don't recall any island in this area."

The four of them picked themselves up from the floor and sorted themselves out, the first thing they noticed was the mixture of odors in the room, it was as if a lightning storm had just hit amidst a forest fire along the shore of the sea. "Crap," Clarice said suddenly, "none of us can leave this room at this point."

A few minutes later Tara came back in and locked the door, she looked different, soaking wet, her face was more angular, her body leaner and her figure more pronounced. She walked with her eyes half closed and moved with a surefootedness of someone who thought they would never fall. "Sorry about that,' she said. "I jumped overboard and thought about Scarlet hurting Mortimer and suddenly an island rose up out of the sea, it was quite painful and yet I feel much more free now than ever before." She smiled at Zephyr, "I patched the holes in your ship with stone, so it wouldn't sink, I hope you don't mind." She walked over and picked up the book from where it had landed on the floor, and threw it at Scarlet, "Now tell me what it says of my ancestors."

Clarice frowned, "I think she's mad at you."

"What was your first clue?" Scarlet asked. She turned to Tara, "you do know I would never hurt Mortimer right?"

"Honestly, I don't know," she answered, "but I am pretty sure you would do everything in your power to not hurt him. I didn't do this for you, I did this for him, I realized he needed a strong earth witch for the ceremony or it could fail and the only way to become stronger was to break through the seals that kept my powers contained."

Scarlet wasn't sure she liked this new version of Tara, but picked up the book and flipped to the section on stone types, "I believe you are a subterranean elf," she said. "Let's see, subterranean elves are one of the most dangerous of the stone types, slow to anger and slow to relax. They are fast and agile and appreciate the beauty in an agile mate. Although the most beautiful of the stone types, they are also the most deadly. Do not worry about taking care of the home, they are perpetual home makers and amazing mothers. These women do not go into heat as others do, or at least we have not discovered a way to cause such a heat, treat them right though and they will provide you with many children and make for a perfect mate."

Tara laughed, "So that book basically calls all of you animals, but then refers to me as almost human." She shook her head slowly, "I guess you are the lucky ones, you get to have him whenever you want."

Clarice laughed, "Not necessarily, we don't have control over our bodies reactions, at least now that we know what triggers the heat, most of you can avoid it, unlike myself since I go into heat if I am not sensual enough."

"So you have to have it all the time, and I want him, but all of you take priority over my desires," Tara laughed, "it's a bit ironic really."

"What's odd is that this is happening now, when he is incapacitated," Clarice replied, "I really wish I could read magical energies better."

Scarlet frowned, "What do you mean? I can read the bonds alright if I try, but what am I looking for?"

"Try and find the blood bond between us all and see if there is anything strange about it," Clarice answered.

"It's brighter than normal," she replied, "it also appears to be stronger than it has been in a while and there is a black line mixed in with it."

"So it's coming from him, but why? He usually doesn't let his emotions travel along the bond."

"Let him out and let's find out," Zephyr replied.

"I would, but that might be dangerous considering our current desires," Clarice replied.

The crimson witch suddenly appeared, "Well this isn't good, this wasn't supposed to happen until after the ritual."

"What do you suggest we do? Tara asked with a smirk.

"Good to see you finally shed that damn bond," the witch said with a smile, "now you are ready for the ritual. You need to find that sailor and have him look in his books for a way to delay the breeding of animals. Druids dealt with life, and he should be able to find a spell or potion in there that will mute your desires for a bit. Oh, and move those two to a different room, you need to put the dragon egg in this one, it's latched onto one of you and is boosting the bond." The witch shook her head and as she faded out said "children need a better education."

Tara shook her head, "You folks stay here, I'll go talk to the sailor." With that, she bounded across the floor and out the door.

Scarlet found herself licking her lips, and when she turned to the others and saw them doing the same, "Oh god I hope there is something in those books."

Lorelei chuckled, "so do I, I really want to sink my fangs into her."

Zephyr frowned "yes, the sudden desire to dig my claws into her flesh and pin her down." she shook her head, "damn our ancestors were violent."

Clarice shook her head, "I only wanted to teach her how to ride the waves of love. This is getting harder by the minute, part of me wants to remove the cocoon and take the risk of hurting him."

"I just can't see you hurting him," Zephyr said with a smile.

"Oh, you'd be amazed," she replied, "that first time I drew blood and well I'm not sure what happened."

"We all blacked out," Scarlet replied, "but it was definitely a satisfying night."

Lorelei chuckled, "Maybe Tara would be willing to be his stand in for a while."

Clarice chuckled, "I forgot, your ancestors were known for partaking of both sexes indiscriminately."

Lorelei laughed, "true enough, and it explains why I am drawn to women as easily as men, quite possibly why I feel an attraction to Zephyr and Shar."

Zephyr laughed, "you could be fun, I was going to ask you about that earlier, as you seemed to always be so shy around me when I was the queen."

Lorelei blushed slightly, "you wore my target when you lost your position, not him, but with your bond it kind of hit you both. I knew the pirate bond would have caused my magic to backfire if I used it against the throne, and I paid the price for underestimating the bond you had with him."

Scarlet raised an eyebrow at her.

She smiled at Scarlet, "You scared me off, to be honest you still terrify me, the power of your ancestors is strong, nothing has ever been strong enough to defeat an angry dragon."

Scarlet laughed and grabbed Lorelei in a hug, "Don't worry, if I hurt you I will be sure to lick your wounds clean."

Trembling in fear, Lorelei kissed Scarlet, she felt her forked tongue on her lips and opened them slightly, the next thing she knew they were on their knees and she could feel the terrible strength that lay beneath the soft arms holding her. "Please, hurt me if you must, but know I give myself freely."

When they pulled away from each other, neither was completely satisfied, but both felt much better, "Is it sad that I want to feel your tongue in me again so soon?" Lorelei asked.

Scarlet smiled and licked her lips, "Not as much as I want to taste your flesh again," she said with a glint in her eyes.

Zephyr and Clarice both laughed, "You have to wait until it is your turn again," Zephyr smiled with a grin, "I am curious to see if a dragon can match the wind."

Scarlet moved faster than anyone thought possible, pinned Zephyr to the wall, and knocked the air from her lungs. Quickly she seized Zephyr's arms and held them over her head, her tongue flicked rapidly from her mouth and she tasted the tender flesh of her neck.

Zephyr could not stay tense, her body reacted before she realized it, and she found herself struggling to reach Scarlet's lips with her own. Scarlet held her firmly against the wall and slowly licked every inch of her body as she squirmed, it was too much, with a groan she succumbed to the desire within and soon found herself lying on the floor with a smoky aftertaste in her mouth. "We have to do that again some time, when not in heat," she said softly in Scarlet's ear.

Clarice smiled at Scarlet and said, "I know it won't help, but come to me and satiate your hunger, at least I will be able to quench your thirst long enough for your heart's desire to finish healing."

Scarlet got up slowly and looked at Clarice, "I hurt you last time, I do not wish to do so again."

"My deer, with me you do not have to hold back, I survived it last time and I will again this time," She replied.

The others watched as Scarlet pounced and took Clarice straight to the floor, Clarice did not struggle, she simply kept her eyes locked on Scarlet's. They watched in silence as Scarlet's claws drew lines in Clarice's flesh, as her teeth drew blood when she bit into her thigh, and her tongue slid into her, deeper than one would think possible. Clarice groaned in pleasure once and her body spasmed, before Scarlet lifted her head and began to lick the wounds she had made. Then with surprising ease Clarice pushed Scarlet aside and straddled her, her mouth found Scarlet's, red with her own blood and kissed her deeply before she proceeded to explore her body.

Scarlet and Clarice were both exhausted after a while, and Scarlet smiled sweetly at Clarice, "I'm sorry I hurt you, but once I tasted your flesh I couldn't control myself."

Lorelei chuckled, "I thought for sure you were going to kill her the way you were biting."

Clarice laughed, "Not likely, my blood is a sort of aphrodisiac for humans, but for dragons it tends to cool their heat, besides this was mellow without Mortimer feeding into the passion."

Lorelei frowned slightly, "I am slightly jealous she didn't bite me like that, but I am not sure if I would have survived."

"If you like, we could find out," Scarlet said at this roundabout invitation.

Lorelei crawled towards her, "Would you really be willing, nobody has ever shown me a desire like that."

Scarlet couldn't resist, Lorelei's perfume was still strong in the air, and she turned and pounced on her. She met no resistance, as she drove her to the floor and sank first her claws and then her teeth into Lorelei's breasts. She tasted amazing, not as salty as Clarice, but definitely tougher and a stronger predatory taste. She pulled her lips from her breast and kissed Lorelei as she cried in both pain and pleasure. "Im' sorry for the pain," she whispered as she raked her claws down Lorelei's body and let herself explore the woman beneath her thoroughly.

Lorelei lay gasping for breath as Scarlet once more kissed her deeply, "I told you I would break you," Scarlet whispered in her ear.

Lorelei flexed and rolled over on top of Scarlet, "I'm not completely broken," she whispered as she kissed Scarlet and started to explore her body with hands and tongue. She paused for a moment when Scarlet groaned as her fangs sank into her flesh, but when she pulled her closer, she relaxed and gave into her desires.

Zephyr couldn't stand it, she wanted some attention, and found herself drawn into the two, next thing she knew she felt a burning sensation along her body, as claws scraped through her flesh and teeth sank into her shoulders and breasts, each time it drove her more and more crazy. Eventually they lay in a pile, Scarlet slowly licking the wounds of the others, it felt strangely good, and at the same time it had a sort of healing effect as the blood stopped flowing.

"We shouldn't have done that," Lorelei said to Scarlet as she lay with her head on Zephyr's breast lazily licking at a bite mark.

"I know," Scarlet replied, "but you have to admit she tastes very good, like a summer storm."

"Yes," Loerlei answered, as she nipped gently at Zephyr's breast again.

Scarlet finished licking the wounds and moved up to Zephyr's face, "May I?" she asked.

"Do what you will," Zephyr replied, "it is not like I could stop you."

She almost screamed as Scarlet bit down deeply on her shoulder, the pain was intense and the feeling of her forked tongue pressing against her flesh as Scarlet drank deeply of her blood felt strange.

Lorelei chuckled, "That one is going to leave a mark."

Scarlet pulled at the wound as she bit deeper, she was starving, and needed to eat, she felt Zephyr tense up, she also felt another presence at the back of her mind. Slowly she eased up and settled for licking the wound clean. "I'm so sorry, I am starving right now and you just tasted so good, why didn't you struggle?"

Zephyr winced, "I would have if I could have, but you still have my arms pinned and Lorelei is on my legs."

Scarlet loosened her grip instantly, "Oops, I didn't realize."

"It's alright, it was an interesting experience, I'd like to do it again sometime if you don't mind," Zephyr replied. "Provided I still have all of my body parts."

Lorelei chuckled, "You do, we didn't bite anything off, but you have definitely been marked." She turned to Scarlet, "Once again you beat me to it."

Scarlet gave her a strange grin, "Come closer and I'll mark you too."

Lorelei found she couldn't resist this side of Scarlet, and slid over Zephyrs body so that she was right next to Scarlet, "Do it, and remember I am yours to punish for trying to take your man."

Zephyr gasped, she knew that was a trigger for Scarlet, and that Scarlet still resented Lorelei for it, but she could do nothing as Scarlet turned and bit Lorelei.

Scarlet's teeth connected with the side of Lorelei's breast and she bit down, deeper, deeper than she had ever bitten before.

Lorelei did not make a sound as the burning sensation started, it was the most horrible pain she had ever felt, it wasn't just the bite, it was the burning, it ran deep into her body and she felt the blood drawn through her flesh and to that warm mouth, but she knew she owed it to her, she would let Scarlet rip chunks of her flesh out until she was satisfied, she owed it to her.

Scarlet found it satisfying to bite, she hadn't thought of it before, but it was in her nature to taste flesh and this one had given permission for her to do anything she wanted to to her, this one wanted her to punish her. That thought caused her to stop, why did she want to be punished, did she think that little of herself. Slowly she let up on the pressure, and she heard Lorelei gasp in pain for a second before she started to lick the wound, this one was deep she wasn't sure if she could heal it with her tongue. She opened her eyes to see Clarice next to her,watching and waiting. She released and watched as Clarice tended the wound. "I shouldn't have done that, I am truly sorry."

Lorelei winced and then smiled, "I am not, this means I am marked as well by you, now I truly feel like a part of the family."

Zephyr sat up, and Scarlet leaned across her to give Lorelei a hug, "You have always been a part of the family."

Tara walked in and paused, "I guess that's one way to reduce your desire, but why couldn't you wait for me to return?"

Scarlet laughed, "It isn't exactly safe to be in here right now." she said.

"It is for me," Tara replied as she walked over and put a hand on Scarlet's shoulder. "I see you have gotten a little rough, she should heal." she said as she saw Lorelei's wound.

Scarlet shuddered at the touch, "I wish you hadn't done that she said, as she spun and tackled Tara. Tara was fast, but Scarlet got a good grip on her waist and dragged her to the floor. She tried to bite and claw at her but found her skin was too tough to penetrate. She managed to pull herself along Tara's body until she found her face, and she suddenly kissed her, it was like kissing a statue at first, and then suddenly the flesh softened and Tara allowed her tongue to slip into her mouth.

"Oh my," Tara said when the kiss was over.

Scarlet didn't hesitate, but kissed her again, now she could feel her claws sink into flesh she had known Tara was teasing her, and would not stop her, but she hadn't realized how much desire Tara had either. In seconds she was on her back and she felt Tara's hands exploring her body, she was quick and limber, her fingers did things she had never thought possible. Soon Scarlet was in the throws of ecstasy and flipped Tara onto her back once again. She clawed and bit, licked and sucked until Tara cried out in pleasure, then she settled down to lick the wounds of her passion, she smiled at Tara as she licked the last wound.

"Do it," Tara said, "You won't be satisfied until you do."

Scarlet smiled at this and wondered what she had meant by that, as she bit down hard on Tara's shoulder, she tasted earthy, as if she was made from the very heart of the earth itself. Her teeth sank deeper and deeper, until Tara started to struggle with the pain, Scarlet let up slightly and slowly drank in the taste of this creature. She felt her muscles tighten, the taste of iron and copper came to the forefront, and she backed off even more, slowly licking the wound. "Oh my, you are absolutely delicious," she said to Tara.

"Thank you," Tara replied, "I wasn't expecting you to bite quite so deep, but I get the feeling you held back, that is a good sign."

Slowly Tara sat up and grimaced, "I take it you didn't hold back on Lorelei."

"Not at first, but then I realized what I was doing," Scarlet answered.

"At least you realized it before killing her. Dragon saliva can be very acidic, and will consume anything it comes across if the dragon wills it." she smiled at Scarlet, "Don't worry once you break contact the acid starts to weaken, soon it will have no effect."

"It's a good thing mermaid saliva counteracts dragon saliva," Clarice said as she wiped a bit of blood from her lips. She turned to Loroloi, "You have an interesting flavor though I must say."

Tara laughed and rubbed her shoulder, "This isn't exactly what I had planned when I walked in here, that is for sure. I was going to suggest partnering up until Mortimer is fully healed, and then take turns in order of who's heat was going the longest. That sailor has some interesting books, and I would like to take him home with us if you don't mind, he might be able to restart the druid line." She smiled, "he informed me he would go through all of the books to see what he could come up with, and will leave them outside the door each day."

Zephyr laughed, "that one is a smart one, not cut out for a sailors life mind you, but a smart one, I brought him on board as a ship's doctor due to his knowledge, and since he wanted the books brought along I agreed."

Tara smiled, "As it stands, we get through this part of the journey, drop everyone off who wishes to stay in the village, and then set sail for home, hopefully we can figure out how to create a portal to move along a bit faster. I don't think a shadow portal would be good, as they go from shadow to shadow across short distances, we'll need to learn how to create an actual portal for long distance travel."

"Agreed," Scarlet replied, "we can't keep traveling at this rate or who knows when we'll get home."

Zephyr laughed slightly, "It is funny we all talk about going home, but Lorelei and I have never truly had a home to go back to."

Tara laughed, "Neither have I, I just assumed Mortimer and Scarlet would share theirs with us."

Clarice chuckled, "I am not sure I will ever truly go back home, more than likely I will visit my parents, but I too assumed Scarlet would make room for me in her home."

Scarlet frowned slightly, "You know Mortimer and I never discussed where we would live, but I have always had a feeling he meant for us to live with the order. As for the rest of you, you do have a home, and it is with us."

Lorelei chuckled, "As much as I enjoy the thought of you tearing chunks of my flesh off, I am not sure if I want to endure that for the rest of my life."

"Wait, you enjoyed that?" Tara asked.

"Part of me deep down inside did," she answered.

"I'm not surprised," Clarice said, "your ancestors were known for some very violent mating rituals."

Scarlet nodded her head, "I understand the feeling, part of me was thrilled to bite and leave a mark, but part of me further down panicked when I did."

Tara laughed and tossed a small book at Scarlet, "This should explain it."

Scarlet looked at the cover and laughed, "Mating rituals of dragons, I bet this was the first book he showed you in his room."

"No," Tara said, "at first he wanted to convince me to try some things he had found in a book titled how to woo and keep an elf. Apparently I too am attracting the attention of males all of a sudden."

Zephyr laughed, "Maybe I should go talk with him, I'm curious to see what he would do with his former queen."

"No," Scarlet and Tara said in unison.

"He has been traumatized enough as it is," Tara added.

Scarlet licked her lips, "Are you sure about that?"

"Stop talking about men," Clarice said suddenly, "it only makes things worse and Scarlet is already losing control."

Tara rolled her eyes, "great, who's turn is it next? Cause I know the longer she goes the more violent she is going to get."

Scarlet laughed as she read through the little book, "Good news, that little bite marks you as mine and warns other dragons to stay away, and apparently it is part of the mating ritual, no wonder dragons don't breed very often, a lot of this is quite brutal."

Clarice frowned, "I'm next, Lorelei and Zephyr already had two rounds with little miss savage over there."

Tara nodded her head thoughtfully, "I will keep a close eye on you two and if she gets too wild I'll intervene."

Scarlet grinned evilly, "Why wait, it's been a while since Clarice and I had you last."

Tara shook her head, "You have an exhausting appetite, you know that right."

She shrugged, "Blame Mortimer, he woke it up when I first met him."

"First met or first slept with him?" Tara asked.

"Met," she answered, "although I didn't realize it until now."

"Interesting," Tara replied, "did it occur to you that it could have something to do with how alike you two are?" She looked Scarlet directly in the eye, "I agree though, it has been a while, but that also depends on how you view time."

Clarice grinned at Scarlet, "Oh this should be fun since he's asleep right now."

"Out of curiosity," Tara said, "why is it taking so long for him to heal?"

Clarice frowned, "Internal injuries, they can't heal until he let's my magic do its work, it took a while to get him to relax and let the magic in. I'd hate to wake him now and have to start all over."

Tara laughed slightly and suddenly tackled Clarice, "then I guess we get to have some fun for a while," she whispered as she let her primitive side take over.

Clarice and Tara were very gentle in nature, and this drove Scarlet crazy, but at the same time they were willing to play rough when it came to her. In the end all three of them had wounds to lick, but they were all happy with the rough play. "I can't wait until he awakens and I can really cut loose," Scarlet said finally.

Lorelei looked at her in disbelief, "You mean you've been holding back all this time?"

Zephyr laughed, "Yes, she has, last time she cut loose she almost burned the ship down."

Scarlet chuckled, "I miss having him here beside me."

Clarice shook her head, "If this is how you are after only a little time without him, I dread the idea of how you would be should he die."

Lorelei shook her head at this thought, "I can't imagine how any of us would deal with that situation."

"There would be a lot of bloodshed," Zephyr answered, with a strange solumness in her voice.

"If he rests all night, he should be up in the morning. In the meantime I would like for Scarlet to teach us how to read some of these books." Clarice replied.

# Convergence

Scarlet started to teach them to read the books in ancient druidic, with the occasional knock at the door letting them know there were more books waiting for them. The sailor was good to his word, he only dropped off books that they might be interested in, and would put slips of paper between pages where he thought important information was.

One of the books caught Scarlet's eye immediately when it arrived, "The foul art of necromancy and how it can be good," she read on the cover. "This might be useful," she said as she opened the cover.

It was prefaced with the statement, "Although my colleagues do not like necromancers, they asked me to study them and their powers, here are my findings, please do not judge them based on where they get their powers."

"See what the chapters are titled," Clarice said enthusiastically.

Scarlet read through the names of the various sections of the book and paused, "Healing with necromancy" she looked at the others in shock.

"Well, what does it say?" Lorelei asked eagerly.

Scarlet let out a low whistle, "A necromancer is impossible to kill unless he allows it. Why you ask, because even their own death can be used to heal themselves. As I explained earlier they get their powers from those who die around them, this is both a good and a bad thing as they often have to battle both the living and the dead when on the battlefield. Not only can they raise the dead as servants, but it appears they can craft potions and cast spells that heal the wounded if there has been a death nearby. If a loved one sacrifices themself for the necromancer, and their blood spills on his corpse, it will also resurrect the necromancer. I must warn you though from what I have learned it sounds as if the necromancer will come back to life in a rage and will kill every living thing around it until it feels the death of its loved one has been avenged. Likewise do not kill the necromancer's love interest, or you will surely incur a wrath that will transcend generations, the order of the rose is a prime example of this."

Scarlet let out a low whistle, "Hundreds of years they have been seeking out and destroying the witch hunters, I never knew it all stemmed from the death of a single witch."

Clarice frowned, "true but apparently to heal him one of us must sacrifice ourselves for him."

"I volunteer," Lorelei blurted out instantly.

"No," Scarlet replied, "there is more." She continued to read, "There is a way for a loved one to heal a necromancer without losing their life, it is a potion necromancers use to heal allies in war. First you will need the blood of those who love him, mixed with the tears of those who love him. Mix equal parts of these together, and then the dead must bless this mixture with their essence. The final step in giving him this potion is what is called the kiss of life, be warned though whoever gives the kiss forever binds their soul to his and will share in his fate, this warning is even more important for witches whose blood is in this mix, you will be tied to him and unable to die unless he dies and then you shall die with him."

"Getting the blood is easy," Zephyr said, "we have plenty of that, but what about the tears, can any of us bring ourselves to cry on demand?"

Clarice laughed, "Some of us can, but whether or not you and Scarlet can I don't know."

Scarlet smiled, "I don't know about Zephyr, but the idea of dying with him makes me happy enough to cry."

Clarice pulled out a small bottle and handed it to her, they watched as a couple of crimson teardrops fell from her eyes and landed in the bottle. She then took and bit her own arm and let a couple of drops of blood trickle into it. Lorelei nodded and added her own green tinted tears and blood to the bottle.

Tara smiled and remembered how he freed her from the merchant and found herself crying as well, "At least this way we know he will heal," she said as she handed the bottle to Zephyr.

Zephyr took the bottle and thought about all he had done to help the people around him, and she too found herself crying, a large clear teardrop fell into the bottle and she quickly scratched open her breast and added a drop of blood before she handed it to Clarice.

Clarice smiled at Zephyr, "That was dramatic, maybe you should become a performer." She herself merely touched her eye with her finger and pulled out a single white teardrop which she placed within the bottle, then she too scratched her breast and added a drop of blood. "From my heart to yours," she said softly.

"Talk about dramatic," Zephyr laughed.

Scarlet drew the crimson sword and asked, "Do you wish for my blood or will you manifest willingly?"

The crimson witch slowly appeared, "Oh you all smell delightful," she said, it's like a battlefield after a rainstorm, by the beach. I can just picture the sand covered in blood, thunderclouds in the sky, the cliffside wet from rain and the water trying to wash away the blood "

Scarlet smiled, "You are feeling poetic I see, can you please grant us some of your essence?" she asked.

The crimson witch looked at the bottle and her eyes widened, "You did not tell me he was badly injured, I am barred from death because of my curse, what happened."

"He went beyond death's realm to retrieve pieces of my soul I had left behind," Lorelei answered.

"Silly girl, why did you go to death's realm? It is a place for the dead and necromancers only." the witch replied.

"He was suffering because of those I killed so I went to stop them from hurting him," Lorelei answered.

"And left a piece of yourself behind," the witch concluded, "so he went to retrieve it from the land of judgment. Stupid boy, he could have been destroyed there." She looked at all of them, "let me guess internal injuries and water magic is having little effect."

"Yes," Clarice replied.

"Then I have no choice," the witch replied, "I will give you some of my essence if only for the love you show by taking this chance. Where did you find that recipe though, it was lost a thousand years ago, or I would have used it to bind my husband and I together." She reached up to her cheek and brought down a single ghostly tear which glistened as it entered the bottle along with a drop of clear crimson blood.

"We discovered it in an ancient druid book," Scarlet answered.

"Do not take the spells in those books lightly," The witch said, "Magic back then was much more powerful than what you see today, and a single mistake can have very dangerous consequences." She faded from sight after giving this warning, a very worried look on her face.

"She has no idea," Scarlet said, as she looked at the next paragraph in the book. "Apparently necromancers also have the ability to kill off entire cities if they have a large enough source of dead energy."

Clarice whistled, "You mean like that battlefield where my magic got entangled with yours?"

"Exactly," she said, "I was lucky he was so stubborn, he could have destroyed me in a heartbeat, along with every living thing within a few miles."

Zephyr gave a low whistle, "That's dangerous, so are we going to do this or what?"

Scarlet grinned and took the potion from Clarice, "Let me wake him."

She quickly applied the potion to his lips and then her own, slowly she leaned over his face to kiss him when his eyes opened. She didn't hesitate, but wrapped her arms around him and gave him a long deep kiss, it was as if a piece of her was sucked inside him and a piece of him came up and jammed itself down her throat. As she pulled away she Motioned for Clarice to continue.

Clarice followed her example and found herself sitting back gasping for air as she waved to Lorelei.

Lorelei was surprised, but did as they had done, her head was spinning when she pulled back from the kiss and waved Tara over, "Continue the application," she gasped.

Tara nodded in understanding and gave Mortimer a passionate kiss that caused the floor to drop out from under her, soon she staggered back and waved to Zephyr, "finish it," she gasped as she stumbled and fell to the floor.

Zephyr flew across the room and quickly applied the remainder of the potion to her lips and gave Mortimer a strong deep passionate kiss, she used her magic to hold them together as long as possible until she finally released him and had to brace herself as the room spun around her. "What was that?" she gasped.

"A piece of his soul," a voice said from right next to her ear. "I hear your request and agree to the terms of the contract once it is fulfilled."

All of them looked and saw the bottle with a little left sitting next to Shar. Instantly Clarice removed the icey cocoon from her and went to wake her.

"I heard," Shar replied, tears running down her face as she grabbed the bottle and let them drop into it. She looked for a blade, as her nails and teeth were not sharp enough to tear her own flesh like the other had, when Scarlet suddenly grabbed her wrist and dug a single claw into it.

"I'm sorry," Scarlet said, as she withdrew her finger from her arm.

Shar didn't respond as she let the blood drop into the jar, and then applied it to her lips. She pushed Scarlet aside, and dragged herself over to Mortimer, and gave him a slow deep kiss.

At first everyone thought she had passed out, but eventually she rolled aside and gave them a smile. "Is it my turn now?" she asked as her eyes rolled up into her head.

Scarlet leapt to her side, "Is she going to be alright?" she asked as she felt how cold her limbs were.

"She needs warmth," Clarice replied, "I dropped the spell too fast and her body is still half frozen."

Scarlet nodded and lay down on Clarice, she was freezing, but Scarlet could feel her body warming rapidly beneath her.

"What about Mortimer?" Lorelei asked.

"I'm fine," he replied, "I am fairly resistant to the cold after all."

Clarice waved at his cocoon and let it start to melt around him, "Better safe than sorry," she said.

Mortimer chuckled, "Very well, but after Shar gets a turn, then it's my turn," he replied, "actually I believe you owe her two turns, then I will get my two turns."

Clarice frowned, "You were listening the entire time."

"Yes, not much else I could do if I didn't want to hurt you by breaking your spell," he grimaced, "You wouldn't believe how difficult it was for me not to break free and join the fun."

Scarlet chuckled, "You're planning something aren't you?"

"Oh yes," he replied, "I might make you wait a week locked away in this room, maybe two weeks all by yourself."

I'll kill you," she growled.

Mortimer laughed, "I don't doubt it, that's why it's an empty threat, provided you never do that to me again."

Scarlet laughed, "Fine, I promise any time I feel a heat coming on I'll jump your bones right off the bat." She suddenly yelped as Shar wrapped her cold arms around her and bit her on the shoulder.

"Me first," Shar said through a mouthful of shoulder.

Scarlet's eyes darkened as she lowered her head and licked at Shars exposed neck, "Let go, and let me show you what I did to them," she whispered.

Shar let go with her teeth and grinned, "Don't hold back or I'll bite you again when you least expect it."

Scarlet tried to hold back a little, Shar wasn't descended from an elemental like the rest of them, but soon she regretted that decision as Shar grabbed her hair and pulled her head up to her own and kissed her with all the savagery of a young dragon.

After a while they lay panting next to each other, Shar had a fistful of Scarlet's hair still in her hand and dozens of claw and bite marks on her body. "Again," she suddenly said as she pulled on Scarlet's hair. This time Shar pinned Scarlet down and nibbled at her flesh, biting hard occasionally and even drawing blood once or twice.

Scarlet didn't mind, her hands were now tangled in her hair in some sort of knot, and Shar proceeded to explore her body most excitedly.

Finally Shar laughed and said, "that was a fun round, let me know when you're ready for round two."

"You can't be human," Scarlet whispered as she tried to untie her hands from her own hair.

"I am descended from a tribe of barbarians," Shar whispered back, "we were the original dragon hunters, until we learned to live with them."

Clarice laughed, "A direct descendent of the line that created the first witches, I should have known."

Finally Shar untied Scarlet's hands and smiled, "now are you ready for round two?"

Scarlet looked at her and smiled, "I am not fully satiated yet."

Shar returned her smile and this time she kissed her gently and stroked her back softly, it was different from what Scarlet had ever felt, and she melted like butter.

Once again the two of them found themselves lying on the floor next to each other panting heavily, Scarlet smiled at Shar as she stroked her breast, "that was very pleasant, I wasn't prepared for that."

Shar smiled, "I learned it from Mortimer," she replied as she gently stroked Scarlet's hair, "are you going to mark me like the rest?"

"I would love to," Scarlet answered, "but are you sure you want me to?"

"If you don't, I will mark you as mine," Shar replied.

"Your teeth aren't sharp enough," Scarlet whispered as she leaned over and bit down on Shar's shoulder. This time it was different, no struggle, no urgency, just a nice and simple bite as the recipient groaned in pleasure.

"Thank you," Shar said as Scarlet let go, "you are an amazing creature you know and I look forward to becoming one with you forever."

Scarlet raised an eyebrow, "You know something I don't?"

"The witch said I was a vessel that he needed to fill and you others would fill me," Shar smiled, "I believe she means I will be tied directly to you spiritually and to me that means I will become one with you."

Scarlet smiled, "I look forward to becoming one with you as well if that is what she means."

Mortimer chuckled as he was finally able to get up from his icey cocoon, "I am a bit curious, why did you all just use a spell from a thousand years ago? I would have healed eventually, my injuries were not that severe."

"Because something has triggered all of us to go into heat at the same time," Clarice answered, "and I would like to discover what that was, but can't do so while I am distracted."

He frowned slightly, "I don't think it's too complicated, the bond between us all has been breaking down our personal barriers, meaning that although you learned how to block out each others emotions, the bond is slowly forcing those emotions through so when one goes into heat it causes the others to as well. Given enough time, your various forms of magic will also blend and you'll all be able to use each other's magic."

Scarlet frowned slightly, "How much time before that sort of blending happens?"

He laughed, "Obviously the emotional part is already happening, and given a couple more weeks it will be complete. Normally it progresses in the order you were bound, but Zephyr, Lorelei and Shar caught up rather quickly due to already having had a bond which controlled the mind placed on them, the blood bond simply replaced that bond and thus they succumbed to it quite rapidly." He smiled at Scarlet, "You and Clarice were always allowed to think freely, so you took longer. Tara was always stubborn, but when she gave up that stubbornness she succumbed to the bond."

Mortimer surveyed the entire room and laughed, as he walked up to Scarlet and kissed her, "do you mind if I have a bit of fun?" he asked with a grin.

Scarlet couldn't help it, she melted in his arms and purred gently as he pulled her closer to him. He held her so tightly, she thought for sure he was going to break a few ribs, but she didn't care, her scales fluttered with excitement and bits of fire sparked up from her body.

At the same time a shadow slowly crept up from around Mortimer and the lanterns in the room were extinguished. The shadow wrapped itself around the flames and pulled them into a slowly spinning wall around them.

Inside of that wall, Mortimer gently stroked Scarlet's back as he lowered her to the floor, she gave no resistance to him, he was her everything and they both knew it. She returned his gentleness with a soft bite at his shoulder, and tasted his blood as her sharp teeth broke the skin.  He tasted different than before, as if he had just walked out of a fire and had been offered to her.  She couldn't help herself, she bit deeper and tried to get more blood from him, and he responded by licking her neck gently and biting down as well.  Scarlet released her teeth from his shoulder and growled softly, he was in control now.

Mortimer did not release her neck with his teeth, as he slowly let himself be taken over by the dragon he held in his arms.  He instinctively knew if he released his bite from her neck she would become more aggressive, her animal instincts had almost completely taken over, so he let them flow into his mind and take over his actions.  He released only for a second, as he flipped her onto her stomach and bit down on her neck once more, he could taste the smokey metallic flavor of her blood in his mouth and felt her push upwards against him.  Animal instinct completely took over, and when he was done, they collapsed on the floor, he was still on top of her, his face buried in her hair and his teeth latched on her neck, he wasn't sure if he would ever be able to let her go, but knew eventually he would have to.

Finally he released his bite on Scarlet's neck and rolled to the side, "Are you alright?" he asked as he sat up.

Scarlet smiled wistfully, "That was different than anything we've ever done, where did it come from?"

He looked at the swirling magic in the air around them and laughed, "Your basic animal instincts, and I let them guide me."

She looked around and frowned, "I hope we didn't hurt anyone with that magic."

Mortimer shrugged slightly, "Only one way to find out," he concentrated on the shadows for a moment and they faded a bit.

With the shadows gone, the flames dwindled as well, as if in disappointment.  Scarlet laughed, "I think they enjoy playing together."

The lanterns in the room flickered slowly back to life, as Lorelei and Zephyr went around the room lighting them.  "We're all unharmed," Zephyr said, "you kept it contained to just around the two of you.  I'm a bit jealous though, that looked like fun."

Mortimer shrugged, "It was, but you will have to wait."  He turned to Clarice and smiled.

She leapt instantly into his arms, "Maybe contain the shadows to just one corner," she whispered to him.

He laughed slightly as he moved her to a single corner and let the shadows rise around them, "this is your time, share with me what you desire."

Clarice gave him an impish smile and waved her hand in a grand circle. A globe of ice encased them and filled with water.

Her transformation into a mermaid did not bother him, nor did the water, he knew he could breathe normally provided she was touching him.

She couldn't resist her nature and she knew it, she took hold of Mortimer and kissed him deeply and passionately.  She pressed in close to him and felt the roughness of his skin against her own scaly flesh. She was nervous, for although he knew of her nature, she was half afraid he would reject her after this.

Mortimer felt a slight hesitancy from her as she kissed him, and wrapped his arms around her gently, and then more firmly. His body fit perfectly with hers and soon he felt himself inside her. That is when he felt her confidence come back, and her grip on him became stronger and more urgent.

She was done sooner than she had expected, but still she did not let go of him, and groaned slightly as he pulled her tighter against him, he wasn't done yet she could sense that. She groaned slightly as he turned her around with him in the water, he had total control of the situation now and she found it just as enjoyable as when she had control.

He kissed her and caressed her, he bit and he clawed on occasion and in the end, he lifted her to new heights and brought her down to the bottom of the globe of ice, pleasantly exhausted.

Clarice let the magic globe drop from around them, and lay there holding him, her wet body curled against his chest and her tail wrapped in his legs, "That was magical," she said with a smile, "Thank you."

Mortimer frowned slightly, "Thank you? Whatever for, almost anyone I know would gladly have taken my place."

She blushed deeply, and everyone in the room was amazed at how the blush reached all the way to her waist. "Not every man would stick around, or even desire to stick around with a mermaid," she said softly.

He laughed gently, "That is because most men are fools who do not realize what they had until after they have lost it."

Clarice laughed gently as well, and he admired the way it made her body move, he also noticed a few jealous looks from the others, "You should pick your next victim," she whispered to him.

Mortimor shook his head, "No, they should decide who is next," he replied, he wasn't sure yet what game the ladies were playing at, but he knew they intended to wear him out.

Tara grimaced and said, "Zephyr or Lorelei, I can wait and," she glanced at Shar who nodded, "Shar is still recovering."

He looked at the two of them and smiled, "So which one of you is first?" he asked, not sure he was ready for the answer.

Lorelei pointed to Zephyr, "Rank before desire," she said.

Zephyr laughed musically, "but if I break him, what will you do?" She pushed Lorelei towards him, "go on, I know I'm going to hurt him, so you might as well have some fun first."

Lorelei bowed to Zephyr and Mortimer smiled, it was apparent they were both afraid of something, a quick glance at Scarlet and he understood, both of them had been fighting with her in the past and they were afraid it would start another fight.

Mortimer looked directly at Scarlet and as if reading his mind she grabbed Lorelei by the shoulders and whispered in her ear, "All arguments aside, I am starting to appreciate you being part of the family, so go have some fun and tell me about it afterwards." She then kissed Lorelei on the cheek and pushed her towards Mortimer as she laughed.

Mortimer caught Lorelei as she stumbled towards him and laughed, "Don't worry, it's not like I'm going to hurt you."

Lorelei chuckled, "I'm not nervous about that, I am more nervous about hurting you, my ancestry isn't exactly known for being gentle."

He chuckled as he carried her to another corner, and caught a whiff of her perfume, "Let your own nature take over and we shall see who gets hurt and how badly," he said to her as he felt both of their magic start to circle around them.

She cuddled against his chest and smiled, "I am more afraid of what Scarlet will do if I hurt you." Lorelei heard his heartbeat.through his veins and relaxed a bit more, then she struck and her fangs were buried deep into his shoulder. She was surprised, she didn't even know why she did it, but she couldn't release as she tasted the blood that pumped beneath his flesh.

Mortimer waited a few seconds after she bit, before he nuzzled her neck and returned her bite, he was amazed she was able to gasp without releasing his shoulder. He bit down a little harder as he lowered her to the floor, she was moving fast, her serpent ancestry showed in her movements as she tried to wrap arms around him and crush his body. As their bodies pressed closer together, he felt her tense up and her mouth released from his neck as she screamed.

Lorelei couldn't help but let out an animalistic scream, she had let the beast out of the cage she had kept it locked in and now it had taken over. She tried to bite again, and he pulled her head back away from biting range, as he himself arched his back and bit her on the arms and chest, any part of her she put in reach of his mouth, he bit, and each time he did so it drove her further over the edge.

Soon the two of them were wrapped tightly together, and Mortimer bit her gently on the back of the neck, the beast within her subsided a bit, and he loosened his grip on her arms. She turned slightly and felt him inside her, and the beast came back, only this time in a much gentler way. His hands continued to trace lines between the bite marks on her body after they were done, and she felt a strange tingling sensation as his fingers traced their path.

"That was most violent," he said with a slight grimace.

Lorelei frowned, "I am sorry," she replied, "I will never let that animal loose again."

He could see the tears in her eyes, and gently wiped them away, "Nothing to be sorry for, the longer you keep an animal caged the more violent it is bound to become. I didn't say I didn't enjoy myself, I was just surprised."

She smiled slightly, "Honestly, my ancestors are known for killing their mates while breeding, so of course it means for me love is violent."

He smiled and kissed her gently, "I understand, it is like Scarlet and her passion, Clarice and her gentleness, our nature is our nature, and I accept your nature." He winced slightly as he moved his shoulder, "Although I will be more careful now that I am aware of it."

Lorelei returned his kiss and said, "Maybe next time just tie me up."

Scarlet suddenly burst out laughing, "He would enjoy that too much." She knelt down next to them and checked their injuries, "Not bad," she commented as she looked at the bite mark on his shoulder. "Although I believe you might need more tending to," she continued as she inspected Lorelei's wounds.

Mortimer frowned, "Sorry about that, I'm a bit hungry, mind if I have a bite to eat?"

Zephyr laughed as she tossed him an apple, "I am sure our sailor friend will be bringing lunch shortly. I for one would rather you not go too long without food," she looked at Lorelei and winced. "If I had known he would try to devour you, I would have gone first," she said to her.

Lorelei laughed, "Honestly I wouldn't have it any other way," she replied.

Everyone jumped slightly when they heard a knock at the door, "I'll get it," Scarlet said as she pointed to Zephyr and Tara, "you two go stand on that side of the room."

Carefully Scarlet opened the door to the room, and quickly caught a platter of food that slipped from the sailors hands.

"Lllllunch," he stammered, his eyes wide with shock while he visibly struggled to keep from looking at her body.

"Oops," she said, "I totally forgot I was naked." Carefully she took the platter and set it on a nearby table. "Have you found anything else of interest for us?" she asked the sailor.

"You are the most interesting creature I have ever seen," he said and then slapped himself. "I am sorry," he said, "I don't know what came over me."

She couldn't help it and laughed, "Thank you, that is quite a compliment for a woman of my nature." She started to open the door further and said, "You should come in and see if you find the rest of the women here just as interesting."

Tara suddenly pushed Scarlet aside, "Quit toying with the poor man, you know he would never survive our attention."

The sailor blushed slightly and replied, "I agree, I wouldn't survive, but I would die happy if it was with you."

She thought about letting him in, but instead closed the door a little further, "That's just the magic talking, you'll feel differently tomorrow, trust me."

The sailor bowed his head, "True most beautiful elf maid," he said as he backed away, "I better get back to work now," he said as he turned away from the door.

Tara closed the door and Mortimer started to chuckle, "You two probably should have thought about getting dressed before you opened the door, I'm not sure that poor man is ever going to be alright after that display."

Shar burst into laughter, "I think he would have been fine if it weren't for Tara shoving her way to the forefront and letting him get a whiff of that perfume."

Scarlet laughed, "yes, even I could smell that mountain meadow in the springtime scent coming from her."

Zephyr chuckled dryly, "He got a good whiff of more than that," she turned to Mortimer and said, "Hurry up and eat, I have a ship to run."

Tara picked up the platter and brought it over to Mortimer, "you should definitely eat, the rest of us have eaten far more than you the past day or so." She pushed past Zephyr and smiled coyly at Mortimer, "I am willing to let you have your fill of whatever you most desire, food or?" she balanced the platter on one hand and gestured with the other down the length of her body."

Zephyr smiled to herself, and went over to where Shar sat, "This should be interesting."

Shar looked at Zephyr and frowned, "You act as if you don't want him, but I sense from the tightness of your muscles you want to throw yourself at him."

Zephyr laughed softly, "It is not that I don't want him, it is that I want him fully worn out when I get him, part of me is afraid he might hurt me, he has become something of a demon today."

Shar shook her head and laughed, "He is merely reflecting their own energy back to them," she replied, "Scarlet told me about it while he was with Lorelei, what you let loose in that cloud gets channeled through him and his appetite matches your own." She smiled slightly, "He is going to have one hell of an appetite after this though, Tara has been holding back for a very long time and she is not used to this body and it's abilities."

"So you're saying I shouldn't have let her go first," Zephyr whispered as she watched Tara feeding Mortimer a bit at a time from the platter.

Shar shrugged, "No, I am looking forward to seeing what he does with you, it could be very educational."

Zephyr shook her head slightly, "You confuse me sometimes, you look like a normal young woman, but act like an ancient crone sometimes."

Shar shrugged, "I joined a mercenary company when I was thirteen, and until I hired on with you, I fought almost every day of my life." She laughed a little, "I actually considered working for you as my retirement, then he came along and ruined it all."

"Well, he did give you fair warning," Zephyr replied.

"I'm not complaining, but I will admit this is the most complicated my life has ever been, so I look to learn at every opportunity," she said with a smile.

"How old do you think Mortimer is?" Zephyr suddenly asked, as she looked around the room.

Mortimer almost choked on his bite of food as he overheard this question.

Tara shook her head and patted him on the back, "Late twenties, is my guess."

"Mid twenties," Clarice answered.

Shar laughed, "based on my life, early twenties."

Lorelei Smiled, "Late twenties."

Scarlet smiled, "What's your guess Zephyr?"

Zephyr frowned thoughtfully, "I respect Shar, so I will nudge my initial thought from late twenties to mid twenties."

All of the women looked at Scarlet and waited for her answer, "Late teens," she finally said with a smirk.

Mortimer chuckled, "that's not fair considering you know how old I am."

"Not exactly," she replied, "your family didn't exactly say you were a certain age."

"Well then how old are you?" Zephyr asked.

"You first," he replied, "if you want to know my age then you should disclose yours."

Tara smiled and breathed, "Twenty three."

Shar laughed, "Twenty."

Zephyr's jaw dropped at these answers, "Impossible."

Scarlet laughed, "Eighteen."

Lorelei frowned, "Twenty five."

Clarice grinned, "I don't know, my kind doesn't keep track of birthdays."

They all looked at Zephyr who frowned, "alright, that makes me the oldest at twenty nine."

Mortimer laughed, "You certainly don't look it," he replied with a grin.

Scarlet suddenly turned a little pale, "I just realized, you were killed before I met you, so you could physically be the age you were when you died."

The look of horror on all their faces made him laugh, "It doesn't work that way, the spell to remain young requires the blood of children, and I am not about to kill children to stay young." He watched them all relax and then said, "I am only a couple of years older than Scarlet, and the same age as Shar, as a matter of fact I may have fought alongside her in the past."

"Then where did you get all of your experience at your age?" Zephyr asked.

Mortimer laughed, "that depends on what you're talking about, combat, magic, or" he winked at her, "sexual?"

She couldn't resist blushing, "the last one."

"Oh, that is easy, I let you ladies guide me and occasionally just let my imagination go wild," he answered. "When it came to Scarlet, our first time was the biggest experiment I ever did, I had no idea what I was doing, just stories the soldiers told around the fire."

Scarlet laughed, "That goes for the both of us, I wasn't sure what I was doing, and just let nature take its course." She smiled slightly, "it's not like either of us really expected anything to happen between us that night, but after dancing with you, things just sort of happened."

Mortimer smiled at her, "That was definitely an interesting display of magic we put on in front of my family, wasn't it."

"Yes, it was," she replied, "I have never heard of anything like that happening."

"There is a lot of old magic in my family's home," he said, "more than likely it was some sort of spell in the room to show compatibility. My family doesn't like to leave anything to chance."

He finished eating and looked at Zephyr and Tara, "So which of you is next?" He asked, "there is a lot of ambient magic in the air and it could be interesting to see if we can expand on it."

Tara shrugged and looked over at Zephyr, "Who would you prefer?" she asked when Zephyr returned her shrug.

Mortimer rolled his eyes for a moment, and finally said, "Whoever is closer," and he grabbed Tara into his arms."

She wasn't expecting him to move so rapidly, and suddenly found herself pulled up against his body. It felt strange, different than before, there was an intensity between them, she couldn't quite describe.

He felt it too and smiled, she was trying to hold back her own power, gently he kissed her and let his magic envelope them. As the shadows started to swirl, he saw the dust on the floor and in the room around them gathered into a whirlwind, and surrounded them.

Tara was surprised by the reaction of her own power as he released his, and gradually released her own to match it. She returned his kiss and was pleased at how his lips tasted, slowly she let her lips wander to his neck and shoulders. She was surprised at how the dried blood from the bite marks seemed to call to her, slowly she dug her fingernails into his shoulders and pulled herself up into his arms.

As her fingernails broke the skin on his shoulders, she purred loudly and licked at the blood. She wasn't sure what had come over her, but she knew she wanted him and she wanted him now. She also realized that even though he was of average build, she felt small compared to him.

Mortimer gently held her close, he was worried, she was smaller than she used to be, and he didn't want to hurt her. He felt the pain of her nails digging into his flesh, but it didn't bother him, when she wrapped her legs around his waist he smiled and listened to her purring. He loosened his grip and let her decide how fast they would move.

Tara felt his grip loosen and frowned, she wasn't going to let him escape that easily. She let herself drop and felt him enter her body, with a gasp, she pushed herself down on him completely and leaned backwards.

Suddenly unbalanced, Mortimer was dragged to the floor and landed heavily on top of her, his reflexes saved him from crushing her as his hands snapped out at the last second to catch them.

She started to laugh slightly, "now this is more like it," she said as she thrust herself down even harder.

He couldn't help himself, he let her desire take over, and could only hope he didn't hurt her too much. "I'm sorry," he whispered as he thrust himself as far into her as possible.

"I'm not," she whispered back, as she grabbed his hands and brought them to her firm breasts, "Squeeze, pinch, bite, do whatever you want, just please don't stop."

Mortimer kissed her deeply, and enjoyed the earthy taste of her mouth, as he dug his own fingernails into her breasts, just enough to draw a hint of blood. As he licked the fresh blood from the wounds, she groaned in pleasure and rolled over on top of him.

After a while, Tara groaned and collapsed on top of him, "Can we do that again some time?" she asked with a smile.

"Any time you want," he answered, "I didn't hurt you did I?"

She laughed and kissed him on the shoulder, "No more than I hurt you, I am not used to the changes in my body, and even though I knew I desired you, I didn't know how badly until now." She smiled wistfully at him, "Sometimes I wish I could keep you all to myself, but that wouldn't be fair to the others."

"Your passion surprised me," he admitted, "you have always been so reserved, it is good to see you break out of your shell a little bit." He kissed her deeply and felt the magic as it swirled around them, intensifying slightly, before it settled down to the floor and swirled in its own little pattern.

"Take good care of Zephyr," Tara whispered to him, "I think she is still scared of what will happen between you two."

Mortimer looked across the room at where Zephyr sat in the only space along the walls that didn't have a little whirlpool of magic spinning in it, "Your turn," he said as he stood up.

Zephyr looked around at the elementally charged whirlpools and opened her arms towards him, she knew he would treat her the same as she treated him, but she wasn't sure how she would treat him. As it was she was holding back a desire to launch herself at him, sink her claws into his arms and carry him off to the crows nest for some aerial love making.

He entered her reach cautiously, he could already feel the air about her gathering and moving rapidly. He saw her twitch slightly, as if trying to make a decision, so he stopped and waited.

She knew he was waiting, but at the same time she needed to feel as if she had caught him. Suddenly she launched herself from against the wall, her arms outstretched like giant wings. She struck him directly in the abdomen, and her legs wrapped tightly around his waist. Her arms snapped shut around his neck, and she kissed him deeply, she felt her tongue enter his mouth, and then thrilled when his own tongue entered hers. She couldn't pull away as he stepped forward and let the air lift their feet from the floor slightly, the shadows began to dance around them.

Zephyr lost complete control as he stroked her back and gently pulled her face from his, she dug her claws into his back and lunged at his ear. She was surprised though when he twisted and turned and somehow pulled free of her embrace. Next thing she knew he held her from behind and nipped at her neck a few times until she stopped struggling. His legs wrapped around her own and she felt him enter her, and she screamed in pleasure, she couldn't help it, it was as if her very nature required her to scream.

Mortimer let himself feed off the animalistic energy she tried to keep bottled up, and continued to hold the back of her neck with his teeth as he gave into her desire. As she screamed it drove him to even greater heights of passion and soon they disengaged and he watched her turn and offer her body to him, he smiled as he discovered how flexible she truly was.

All she wanted to do now was to impress him, she spread herself out as an offering and was ecstatic when he accepted it, as he entered her, she arched herself backwards and angled her body to try and get as much of him into her as possible. She was willing to do anything to make him happy, and she was going to prove it.

"You have nothing to prove," he suddenly whispered in her ear as he gently pulled on her breasts.

"To myself I do," she whispered back and she did the splits and rotated her body so her legs went down the length of his.

"Then what is it you're trying to prove?" he asked as he turned her further and squeezed her breasts a bit harder.

"That I am every bit as tough as they are, and that I'm not too old to make you happy," she answered with a slight groan.

Mortimer bit her on the back of her shoulder, and let his teeth sink in as he squeezed her breasts tightly, until she groaned even more. Slowly he released his bite and licked at the wounds, as he said, "You do make me happy, and you are just as tough as they are or you wouldn't be here with me at all."

She groaned again, "Leave your mark on me, let me feel everything you felt from my demons, whip me, beat me, but whatever you do make me yours," she started in a whisper and ended in a scream.

He now knew why she had been so nervous, and he took her, he knew he would leave bruises, and he knew she would be proud of them, he just didn't know why. He refused to whip her or beat her, but he did hold her down and take her until she was satisfied, and then he lay down next to her and gently kissed every mark he saw on her body. "I am sorry," he said as he kissed each one, "but I am very confused as to why you desired this?"

Zephyr smiled at him and answered, "because now I know you truly desired my body, I never truly knew if it was just a duty to you, or if you desired it." She frowned slightly, "my only regret was that you held back, I saw the demons you faced, and I felt some of the pain you felt, the least you could have done is punished me for causing you pain."

"If I made everyone suffer the pain they endured on others, nobody will still be alive," he replied. "Besides, you didn't deliberately cause all of the pain, sometimes you had no choice."

She gave him a slight grin, "I was hoping for a few deeper marks, just to show the others I'm not as fragile as they think I am."

Mortimer laughed and shook his head, "sometimes you women are very silly," he said as the magic once more settled to a whirlpool on the floor. He looked around at the room and laughed, "The question is, is everyone satisfied?"

"No," Shar replied, "I want a shot at you now. I'm pretty sure I can break you now that the others have softened you up."

He stepped towards her, and glanced around the room, all of the circles of magic where now connected, and he realized they created a sort of pentagram, "This could be interesting," he said to himself as he took another step and saw the energies around him speed up.

Shar noticed the other women all sat in the center of where they had been with Mortimer, and she too noticed the pattern it would form if you drew a line between all of them. She wondered if this was deliberate or just by chance, but she felt as if she was missing something important.

Mortimer stopped when he stood directly in front of her and watched her eyes for any clue as to what she was thinking.

She smiled at him, "You know I never got to fight alongside you as a mercenary, but I had heard about you." She chuckled, "I always pictured you a lot bigger in my mind, and dreamed of meeting you on the battlefield to see who was a better warrior." She grimaced slightly, "Now that I have met you though, the only thing I really want is to be one with you, does that make sense?"

He smiled, "In a way it does, but are you really sure you want to do this with all of the energy in this room?"

Shar laughed nervously, "No, but I am the vessel, I cannot break." She stepped in close to him and whispered, "I also don't want to disappoint the others by not claiming a piece of you."

He wrapped her in his arms and whispered back, "You do not have to do anything you don't want to do."

She kissed him, "that is why I want to do this," she said gently, "you have proven time and time again you will not force your will on us, that is something I love about you and makes me want to possess a piece of you."

He chuckled slightly and kissed her, "then show me what you desire."

She took his hand and lay on the floor with him, gently stroking his chest, her fingers gently tracing the various scars he had on it. She stopped when she got to the scar over his heart, leaned in and kissed it.

It was as if he had been stabbed all over again, there was intense pain, but at the same time there was a feeling of longing.

Shar was surprised, when her lips touched his scar, she felt his entire body stiffen and his heart stop for a moment, and then suddenly there was a strong metallic taste in her mouth and blood on her lips. The wound opened at her touch, and she drank deeply of his life, before it closed back up and she felt a rush of energy poor into her body from all different directions. She sat up in surprise, she felt heat, and cold, electrifying shocks and the pressure of the earth. His blood dripped slightly from her mouth, and she felt the darkness of the shadows as they encased the two of them. As suddenly as the sensation had started, it stopped, and she found herself astride his body kissing him with a sense of urgency she had never felt before. "You must drink of my blood," she whispered as the kiss broke, "for we are as one."

Mortimer didn't question her, but simply sat up, and felt himself go inside her, as he licked gently at one of her scars. As she slowly unfolded her knees and brought her chest up to his face, he kissed her over her own heart and felt the skin peel back as she screamed, and her blood swelled out and into his mouth. He drank deeply and felt the powers around them grow even stronger, until he pulled his mouth away and the wound closed back up.

She dropped back down onto his lap, thrusting him back inside her, and smiled through the tears in her eyes. "That hurt like hell," she said as she pushed him back down to the floor and slid him deeper inside her. She knew something strange was going on, but now all she wanted was what he had given to all of the others. Shar smiled, something about the energy that ran through her drove her to new limits, but she felt everything was just out of reach, and then he shifted and rolled over on top of her.

He could feel her frustration, as he rolled on top of her and kissed her gently, then without warning, he bit her on the side of her neck, and listened to her gasp. He licked at the blood as it oozed from the wound, and then kissed her with bloody lips again.

She felt the sharp stabbing pain as he bit her, and once again felt as if she were flying, then as he kissed her with bloody lips, she reached out and felt as if she had landed amongst the stars. Her body lay there quivering with pleasure as her spirit came falling back into it, she had finally found a pleasure worth dying for.

Mortimer smiled at her, as she came back to her senses, every so often he would lick the blood from the wound on her neck, and revel in the coppery taste of her blood. "Are you alright?" he asked.

Shar returned his smile, "better than alright," she replied. "I feel amazing, so full of energy and yet at the same time so tired."

# Recovery

A musical laugh made both of them turn and look, the crimson witch stood there laughing happily, "Oh my, I can't believe you did that, nobody has had the audacity to complete such a spell in centuries." She smiled at Shar, "Congratulations my dear, you are the first non-magical human to drink a necromancer's blood and live, not to mention you gave him your blood as well. I suggest you control your temper until you find someone who can instruct you in the ways of magic, who knows what will happen if you lose your temper."

"What are you talking about?" Mortimer asked, suddenly very nervous.

The crimson witch smiled happily, "She has become a vessel for your power, and the power of all you. When she drank deeply of your blood, she filled that part of her that was empty, but she didn't just fill it with a piece of you, she filled it with all of the loose magic in the room. Didn't you realize you had created a gate with her at the center, and all of the magic that was still lying about the room got pulled through that gate and into her. Once trained, she will be able to use any form of magic, not as strong as any of the rest of you, but when combined together stronger than all of you."

"I think I understand," he replied, "the magic that was released when I was with each of the others, it kept swirling around where we made love, due to the enchantments on this room it couldn't dissipate as it normally would and instinctively none of the women let it overlap, thus creating a perfect summoning gate. Shar was the center of it, and when she drank my blood, it found an empty vessel and went to it. We could have easily put any object in the center and it would have been drawn to that instead and infused it with the magic."

"Correct," the crimson witch replied, "it is how the ancient magic weapons were given their power. It cost a lot to enchant a weapon though because finding someone with the control to pool their magic in five different places at one time was hard, and the alternative was finding a couple who were able to make love five times in a single day." She shook her head slowly, "from what I am seeing the ritual that frees my soul may become a very unique experience."

Mortimer shrugged, "I am finding it more and more difficult to proceed towards the ritual, but as I swore an oath, I must complete it, or die trying."

The crimson witch frowned, "I understand, and if you chose not to complete it I would not hold it against you, seeing how much you have sacrificed so far I find it hard to ask you to sacrifice anymore. I will rest now, I don't think you'll need me until you get home." She vanished with a sad smile on her face.

Mortimer frowned slightly, "I wonder if my grandfather felt my thoughts and that is why he hasn't been present nearly as much."

"I don't know," Shar said, and then groaned in pain as she felt her muscles tightening, her skin felt as if it were being stretched too tight upon her body, and she was suddenly itchy all over.

Mortimer watched her in shock, as she writhed in pain for a few minutes, her muscles became tighter, harder and larger. Her breasts swelled slightly and a tear developed over her heart. Quickly he rolled her onto her side and saw another tear start on her back, and he knew she was experiencing the pain of a sword being thrust through the heart.

Shar screamed in agony and arched her back until everyone heard it crack and pop repeatedly. Blood spurted from her chest and back at the same time, but didn't hit the floor, instead it spread out and enveloped the tear. Her heart stopped beating and then a few seconds later it started back up a slow and steady rhythm as the blood dried and a scab grew over the tears.

Mortimer held her steady as best he could as the others all rushed over to see if they could help.

Clarice tried to cast an ice cocoon, but for some reason the magic wouldn't work.

Scarlet tried to cast a hot fire on the wound to cauterize it, and again her body rejected the magic.

"Stop," Mortimer said, "it won't do any good, the shadow magic is preventing anything from touching her until the transformation is complete." He grimaced slightly, "It is up to her if she is going to survive this, there is nothing we can do to help her, beyond trying to make her as comfortable as possible."

"Then comfortable she shall be, "Zephyr suddenly replied, as she grabbed a loose blanket and headed for the door.

"I'm coming with you," Tara said as she too grabbed a blanket.

They returned quickly, Zephyr had a blanket full of feathers, and Tara a blanket full of sand. Mortimer didn't say anything, but watched as they quickly hung the blankets into a large hammock, and a pair of sailors came into the room carrying a large brazier full of coals.

Scarlet looked at the brazier and snapped her fingers, instantly flames burst forth from it and they moved it over next to the hammock.

The sailors were obviously very well trained, they neither looked at the women, nor made any comments as they left and returned with armloads of firewood, "Captain," once sailor said to Mortimer, "if it pleases you we would like to move her to the hammock."

Mortimor put his arms under Shar and said, "I can do that, can you please bring us a tub of water?"

"Fresh water or sea water?" the sailor asked as he moved out of the way.

"Sea water," Clarice and Lorelei said together.

Both sailors bowed to them and replied, "As the ladies wish."

Zephyr chuckled slightly, "My crew has seen me naked before, and they know that if I am addressing them without clothing, then they had better move fast."

Sure enough the two sailors returned shortly with a huge tub of sea water and placed it opposite the fire next to the hammock, "Does the captain require anything more or should we return to our normal duties."

"You may resume your normal duties," Mortimer replied, "I would appreciate it if our clothing could be rinsed and food brought to us here."

"Would it be alright if we have one of the lady passengers deliver the food and rinse your clothing?" one sailor asked.

Mortimer laughed, "I appreciate your concern for my lady's honor, yes that will be alright."

Zephyr laughed as the sailors gathered up the scattered clothing and left the room, "You know every sailor on this ship is going to be offering them rum to describe what they saw."

Mortimer laughed in response, "They can talk all they want, or keep it to themselves, I have a feeling most of them are terrified of all of us anyways."

"True," she replied, "those two have never talked before, I doubt they'll start now." She shook her head, "they grew up on the island and always dreamed of becoming knights, until they took the oath to serve me."

"Their dream might just come true," he replied with a wink.

Clarice looked at Shar and smiled, "She is sleeping now, I doubt she is in pain."

Mortimer shook his head slowly, "Her body may look asleep, but her soul is going through hell, at least she won't have to make a deal with death as she is covered under my contract."

A soft knock on the door and they all turned towards it, "come in," Scarlet called.

An older lady opened the door and entered the room with a basket full of dried meats, cheese, some dried fruit and a couple bottles of alcohol. "I was told to bring this to you," she said as she looked at Mortimer appraisingly. "I hope you're up to the challenge with all these ladies," she said with a wink at him.

Lorelei laughed, "he was more than up for the challenge," she said with a return wink.

"My word," the lady replied, "I should have brought some bandages for all those wounds, he must be one heck of a beast."

Tara laughed, "he is only the beast we desire him to be, otherwise he is quite sweet and caring."

Mortimer couldn't help but blush at this, "thank you for the food," he said to the lady.

She smiled, "no, thank you, I haven't seen a body like yours in ages. You all look to be in need of a bath. When I return with your clothing I hope you will be a bit cleaner." she said as she bowed to them and left.

Scarlet burst out laughing after she left, "Oh, she hit the nail on the head regarding the need for a bath. Clarice if you can summon us a pool of water. I would like to try and warm it a bit so we can get clean."

Clarice shrugged, and waved her hands in an intricate pattern, and a pool of water formed in front of her, "Don't heat it too much or it will try and evaporate."

Scarlet worked her magic, and soon the water was the perfect temperature.

Mortimer waved to Tara to go first, then when she was done, he pointed to Lorelei, after her it was Scarlet and then Clarice. Finally when they were all clean, he got into the water and with a sigh of contentment washed the blood and sweat from his body. It felt good to be clean and the two worked very well together at maintaining the water and its temperature just right.

The older lady returned shortly after they were done bathing, and had both their clothing and some bandages. She set the clothing down on a nearby table, and then proceeded to visually inspect each of them, "I believe I'll start with you young lady," she said to Lorelei. "It looks as if you were attacked by some wild beast."

Lorelei blushed, she knew the wounds would heal on their own, but also knew the lady would refuse to leave until she had bandaged them.

After she was done with Lorelei, she turned to Tara, "you're next honey," she said with a smile. "You are quite the petite one aren't you," she said as she tended to the bites and scratches.

The lady looked at Scarlet and Clarice and shrugged, "Which one of you two is next?"

Zephyr chuckled slightly, she knew it was hard to see the marks on her body due to the feathers.

Clarice pointed to Zephyr, "She should be next, trust me."

The lady shrugged and turned to inspect Zephyr closely, "My dear it looks as though someone thought you were a chicken," she poked and prodded Zephyr, occasionally plucking a few feathers and patching up her injuries.

She finished up with Zephyr, and turned to Clarice, "Come here child and let me take care of that bite."

Clarice frowned as she walked over to the lady, "It's not that bad, and will heal soon."

"Nonsense," the older lady replied, "any wound can get infected, and bites even more so than normal wounds. I swear there has to be a wild animal somewhere in this room." It didn't take her long to clean and bandage the bite, and then she turned to Scarlet. "My word child, were you the beast's chew toy?" she asked as she got a closer look at the wounds.

Scarlet laughed, "you could say that, but I also invited it and enjoyed it quite a bit," she answered.

"Then I suggest you cut back on the amount of fun you have until you are fully healed," the lady replied. "You may have scales, but that doesn't mean you can go around getting yourself all chewed up. It took her quite a while to clean and bandage all of the bites, but eventually she turned to mortimer and frowned.

"You look almost as bad as she did," she said to him.

Mortimer laughed, "I am sure I do, but my injuries are not important, I'd rather you checked Shar's injuries first, she is sleeping in the hammock."

The lady didn't say anything, but instead moved over to the hammock, "I haven't seen injuries like this since I worked as a nurse on the battlefield." She reviewed a few of the scars and smiled, "these bring back memories, I tended some of these wounds." She gently washed the fresh wounds, and double checked some of the older ones, "Someone did a good job at healing that cut in her side," she said with a smile. "The bites she endured will heal, but unlike you witches she will have a scar from them." She turned to Mortimer once more, "you need to be a little more gentle with your toys."

Mortimer snorted, "I try to be, but she insisted on being treated the same as the others."

She frowned at him and finished with Shar, as she turned to work on his wounds she said, "She is not a witch and you cannot treat her the same as you can treat them. You could accidentally kill her if you're not careful."

"She is stronger than you think, and I am careful with her, I hold back with all of them as much as I can," he replied. "You obviously know about magic, so you know the side effects of being a warlock, it is even worse for the necromancer." He looked her directly in the eyes, "you need not tend to my wounds, they will heal on their own, and serve as a reminder of the pain I caused to them."

The lady suddenly broke into a smile, "necromancer is it? You practice a lost art, I am impressed you didn't kill any of them. I will treat you as I never refuse to tend the wounded, besides I have a feeling if I didn't, these lovely ladies would be most upset with me." She grabbed his shoulders and forced him to sit down in front of her, "Apparently you received as well as you gave, and it's a good thing I am tending your wounds, you have a lot of magical debri in them." She picked at the bite on his neck with her fingernails and frowned, "My grandmother always told my brothers don't go playing with a witch in heat, didn't anyone ever explain that to you?"

Mortimer shook with suppressed laughter, "I didn't have a choice, we are all bound together by a blood bond."

"That explains most of the injuries," the lady replied with a sigh, "but it doesn't explain the sword wound on Shar."

"She took in some of my magic when we made love," he answered.

She cut him off with a slap, "you idiot, don't you know that if you share magic with a non-witch she will suffer the same fate as you? Don't they teach warlocks not to use their magic when in bed with a woman? The two strongest releases of magic are death and sex, you let your magic loose on her body while having sex and it amplified your power." She shook her head, "seriously don't they teach you kids anything these days?"

"My father is the only warlock I know besides myself," he replied, "I am the only necromancer in the world as far as I know, so I have had no teachers since I left my family."

The lady shook her head slowly, "Poor kid, you are using magic you know next to nothing about, no wonder these gals are so torn up. The pirate queen used to have an extensive library on magic, it is an ancient library, but it would serve you well to review the books in it on necromancy."

Zephyr suddenly spoke, "how do you know about the library?"

She laughed slightly, "I used to borrow books from it on occasion, it was no secret that it existed, but few pirates have a desire to read."

Zephyr laughed, "That is true, it is also true I brought the library on board this ship. We have been using its books to help us understand what has been going on with us."

Mortimer laughed slightly, as the lady picked at another bite wound, "The guard forbids witches from breaking their bonds, those that do are usually put to death, or learn to conceal their nature quite rapidly. They also have a very extensive library that they don't allow anyone to access."

The older lady laughed, "so they still don't allow men into the guard, and you're obviously not a witch hunter or these ladies would be dead." She looked at him closely and frowned, "that would mean you have to be part of the rose order, great warriors, but not necessarily great spellcasters."

Mortimer bowed his head slightly, "Mortimer DeRose at your service madame," he said, "direct descendent of the original count DeRose first to sacrifice himself to protect the guard from the witch hunters, in the hopes his son would be allowed to marry the woman he loved."

The lady laughed, "According to legend, on his death his son gained a great deal of power, and quickly became the most powerful of the warlocks."

He smiled at the lady, "actually, he became a necromancer, it was his fathers death that opened the path for him to make a contract with death itself. It is through his contract that I was able to summon death when I died and become a necromancer myself."

She shook her head, "So you have no teacher, since there hasn't been a necromancer around for quite a long time."

"Since my great grandfather gave up his life in order to save his wife's soul, after she sacrificed her life to try and save his life," he frowned, "The witch hunters are no more, I destroyed their power all together, next I will need to revive the old druid power to maintain balance, and after that it will be up to death itself to decide if my contract has been fulfilled."

The lady shook her head, "the druids are not all dead, they are simply in hiding, their magic is something that can be taught to a normal human, as it is the magic of life."

Scarlet laughed, "She would be a good match for that old druid in the woods."

"I agree," he replied, "so would that young sailor, the library should be returned to them as well, so that they can grow in numbers once more."

The older lady laughed softly, "you know I didn't like you when I saw the injuries these gals sustained, but now I am starting to appreciate why they are with you." She finished tending to his injuries and turned to leave, "I'll be back later, your clothing is on the table, you can get dressed when you feel like it."

They all watched her leave the room, and Mortimer chuckled, "she would definitely be a good start for rebuilding the druid race."

Tara shrugged, "I agree, now if you don't mind I am going to have that sailor bring us the rest of the books from the library." She grabbed her chemise and threw it on, it was a bit looser around the waist and dragged on the floor, but she simply pulled it up and tied her belt around her waist.

Mortimer picked up the book on necromancers, and started to read it, "at least I can start learning more about my nature."

The women all decided to get dressed, and took turns watching over Shar as she slept, at the same time sailors started bringing books to the room armloads at a time, while Scarlet and Zephyr sorted them by subject.

After several hours, Mortimer put a slip of paper between two pages and stood up, "that is a very interesting book, I have an idea now of how to wake Shar." He walked over to her, and gently kissed her. As he kissed her, he sent his magic into her lungs and gently pulled the air out of them.

Suddenly Shar gasped for breath and sat up, "What did you just do?" she asked in a slight panic, as she winced in pain.

He couldn't resist chuckling at the look on her face, "Easy I filled your lungs with the power of death and as such the power you took in earlier reacted and forced you awake." He smiled at her, "you were having too much fun playing in the realm of the dead."

She shook her head to clear it of the leftover images and smiled at him, "Damn I hurt, but why don't I have any wounds from that realm?"

Mortimer frowned, "The pain you feel is from the sword of shadow that pierced your heart, but because you are now filled with the power of death, you can no longer be harmed in death's domain."

Shar looked at the wound in her chest and frowned, "It looks exactly like yours."

"Yes," he replied, "when I shared my power with you, I shared the injury that gave me that power as well. If I had known, I never would have let my power enter you."

She smiled at him, "no, I am glad you did, I can deal with the pain, as it brings me closer to you."

"You understand, until you learn to control your power, you will feel the dying pain of every soul you take," he asked.

She nodded her head, "yes, but every soul I take will make me more powerful. Next question, why did my muscles grow suddenly?"

Scarlet put down the book she had been reading and smiled, "It is your true nature asserting itself, your ancestors were the barbarians that tamed the magical creatures and bred with them to become witches. As such your body has taken on a more barbarian form, increased muscle mass, possibly increased speed, and more than likely a much higher pain tolerance."

"Thank you, for explaining that," she replied, "that also explains why I have a serious craving for meat, I don't care if it's cooked, I just want meat."

Clarice laughed and threw a chunk of dried pork at her, "this will have to tie you over until we get to land in another week."

Tara looked up from where she was busy sewing, "I let out the seams on your clothing as much as possible, they may be a bit tight until we get some more cloth to make you new clothes." She indicated a pile of clothing set to one side, "Oh, I doubt your armor will fit anymore either." She went back to her work, as she worked on modifying all of their outfits so they would fit with their once more altered bodies.

Mortimer picked up a mirror and handed it to Shar, "I'm not sure how to tell you this, but white hair suits you."

She smiled at him and replied, "It suits you as well, but I liked it when your eyes were more blue and less gray."

He shrugged, "the cost of using death magic." He also realized it had been a while since he last dyed his hair, and privately wondered if he should do so before they got home.

"Leave it," Scarlet said, "it suits you very well, and honestly who cares if others believe it is a bad omen on the battlefield."

# Returning prisoners

For the next week, they spent all of their spare time studying the books in the library, some of them learned to read the old druid language, while the others learned more about their powers. They learned a vital piece of information during that week, the more they used their powers the more their bodies would change to that of their magical ancestors.

Shar discovered that she could call upon not only the shadows, but also any of the four elements, although they always had a shadowy presence to them.

Scarlet learned to create a blue healing fire, it sped up the healing process of anyone nearby, but drained her energy rapidly.

Tara discovered that she could entomb a person and force them to sleep as if dead so that their body could focus on healing, similar to Clarice's ice cocoon.

Lorelei learned how to utilize a combination of her voice and perfume to push the body to exert itself in ways she didn't realize, this left her with a strong sexual desire though and afterwards she had to rest, so did Mortimer after satisfying her desire.

Zephyr learned to control the air to the point she could actually force blood back into a wound and hold it shut while it was healing.

Clarice learned more about the abilities and limitations of her magic, she could control any liquid now, not just water and scared a group of sailors as she summoned a bottle of wine from the kitchen.

Mortimer learned that he could use his power over death to keep a person alive even after they sustained a mortal wound, although he did not get the opportunity to test this power out. He did test out using necrotic stitches to close wounds and allow them to heal faster.

All of them discovered by chance that their connection had grown stronger than they had originally thought possible, and now the blood bond worked both ways, and carried the sensation of pain from one to another. If one was hungry they all were suddenly hungry, if one was hurt they all felt the pain, and if one was aroused, they all became aroused. This happened a lot when Lorelei was trying new spells, it soon became obvious she didn't get her power from water, but actually got it from making love, which became a daily occurrence with her.

At first Scarlet got a little jealous of all the love Lorelei would be getting from Mortimer, until after the first morning when all of them felt the excitement of the love making, and she decided he could take turns with each of them.

Each day was the same routine, wake up, make love to a woman, eat breakfast, read for a bit, practice magic for a bit, make love with another wife, then eat lunch, discuss ideas about magic and possible new spells, try a few new spells and practice some more, then make love again, eat dinner and talk about what they had learned that day. Finally just before going to sleep, he would make love again, usually to Scarlet, as the others felt she should have more attention from Mortimer than the rest of them.

On occasion Zephyr and Tara would head up to the helm and check in on the ship's progress, but for the most part they left it to the first mate to handle the duties on the vessel.

On the day they were informed they were approaching land, Zephyr laughed and said, "You know I am thinking of giving the Golden Harpy to the first mate, what do you think love?"

Mortimer smiled at her as they had just had a wonderful mid air session of love making, "I was thinking the same thing, he has shown a great ability to handle her and I am certain he would use her to protect the village."

Scarlet laughed happily, "you forget, it will also be easier to transport a few people as opposed to an entire ship back to your home."

"True," he replied, "I am just worried as we have to have an exact mental image of where we wish the portal to end before we cast the spell, and with the amount of time we've been gone, anything could have changed."

"One thing should be consistent though," she replied, "the mural of the rose engraved on the floor at your fathers seat. I just can't see that changing, or being covered."

"Good point," he replied as he swung his feet down to the floor, "very well, we should get dressed and prepare to meet with the villagers. Clarice, did you send a message to the witch in the village?"

"Yes my love," she replied, "she will be at the end of the dock with the mayor of the village and probably half of the villagers as well."

They were soon dressed, and standing on the deck watching the land move closer to them. It was the first time since the battle that they carried their weapons, and Mortimer couldn't help but think Shar should be carrying a huge ax or club instead of a shortsword and dagger. Shar had grown quite a bit, and none of her armor fit her, even her clothing had been modified to being just a short skirt and a halter top. She was barefoot and her muscles twitched slightly to compensate for the movement of the ship.

Mortimer himself wore dragonskin trousers and a vest laced tight, and carried his sword on his hip as if it were a part of him.

Scarlet and Zephyr both wore dragon skin vocto, through the back of which small wings stuck out. Scarlet's were leathery while Zephyrs had feathers.

Tara wore a tight fitting dragon skin vest and trousers, and moved restlessly the closer they got to shore.

Clarice was resplendent in her dragon skin gown, and had her hair braided with pearls given to her by the sea.

Lorelei looked like the goddess of love, she wore a low cut dragon skin vest, it left little to the imagination, and a dragon skin skirt slit from ankle to hip.

All of the ladies except Shar had on slippers made from scraps of dragon skin and canvas, while Mortimer wore a pair of knee high black boots, folded down just below the knee, one of the crewmen had dubbed them captains boots.

The sailors seemed to think the group of them looked more like very successful privateers than a knight and his ladies, and often referred to them as the royal court.

They came into the harbor in early afternoon, and Lorelei kept glancing sidelong at Mortimer as they threw the mooring lines to the dock. "Patience," he replied to her glances, "I promise I will take care of you once we are alone."

The other ladies laughed, as they could all feel the desire Lorelei had for him, and they weren't sure if it was just her desire, or if it had something to do with the outfit.

Lorelei pressed up against him and purred, "you know with these outfits we could do it right now and nobody would know, just lower your pants and I'll do the rest."

At first Scarlet was shocked at this suggestion, but then she started to laugh, "She's right you know, just take her behind those crates and nobody will see a thing."

Mortimer chuckled softly, "They will be done pulling us in and tying the lines in a couple of minutes, we need to be the first ones off ship when they are done."

Lorelei pouted slightly, but understood why that was the case.

Sure enough, as Mortimer led the way down the gangplank, he saw many of the villagers held makeshift weapons. He waved to the witch and smiled, "Sorry for my appearance, but things got a little out of hand while we were retrieving your children."

The old witch laughed slightly as she noticed the women, "I can see that, it looks as though you had quite the adventure."

Mortimer noticed the crowd relaxing a little and laughed, "You could say that we discovered and destroyed the source of the pirates, but now we have a lot of people who need a home, and many of them are competent sailors."

Some of the villagers grumbled a bit at this, but they didn't charge the ship so that was a good sign. The mayor stepped forward, "We welcome home our children, and will do our best to make the newcomers feel welcome, can you be certain they won't revert to piracy?"

Lorelei stepped forward and smiled at the mayor, "trust me when I tell you, we only resorted to piracy due to the power of the bond placed on us by the pirate queen."

"Oh," the mayor said as he felt the influence of her magic, "what has happened to this pirate queen?"

Zephyr laughed as she leapt from the gangplank to stand next to Mortimer, "she found herself a king and gave him her throne, she too was held prisoner by this bond that required her to always expand the pirate fleet."

The mayor involuntarily took a step backwards and stared at Zephyr, "then where is this pirate king?"

Mortimer laughed, "have no fear, I was able to destroy the enchantment that was creating the bond, when I took the throne."

The witch stepped forward and put her hand on the mayor's shoulder, "this would explain the change in him and the others, the amount of magic he had to use in order to destroy such a spell would leave quite an obvious and permanent mark."

Some of the villagers pushed forward at this point, and stopped when Shar leapt off the ship and landed on the dock with a loud thud, "any who try to harm my lord will taste of my blade," she yelled.

Mortimer gently put a hand on her shoulder, "It's alright, they mean no harm."

She shrugged impressively, "I still stand by my words, if anyone wishes to hurt you they will have to go through me." She smiled at him, "I am not about to lose the best thing in my life."

The mayor rolled his shoulders back, and smiled at her, "I have heard the barbarians of the north are true to their word and if they put their trust in someone, then they are truly trustworthy." He waved a hand at the rumbles of the crowd, "Come let us see our children return, and let each person be judged for their actions from here on out."

Mortimer smiled and waved up to the ship, where a couple of sailors proceeded to help the young and elderly down the gangplank. He also saw many other passengers line the side of the ship and wave happily to their parents. "Take your time," he called out to the crew, "I don't want any injuries."

The crowd became quiet for a moment, and then grew louder as they greeted old friends and family members, several of the young men stood back and watched as the young women started to depart the ship.

After a while Mortimer looked up and saw the first mate standing at the top of the gangplank, "All are ashore captain," the first mate called down.

Mortimer waved for him to come down and join them, as he reached the end of the gangplank, he patted the first mate on the back and said, "Congratulations Captain, the ship is all yours, I just need that one piece of cargo brought off in the morning and you can do with her as you please."

The first mate stared at him in shock, and the mayor stepped up and said, "I hope you will be willing to keep her docked here to discourage any other pirates from raiding."

The newly promoted captain laughed, "I couldn't think of a better place to call home," he looked closely at the mayor and frowned, "you look very familiar."

The mayor laughed and said, "they've been raiding my village for who knows how long and he says I look familiar." He looked closely at the new captain and smiled, "you know you're about the age I was when the pirates took my son and daughter from me."

The village witch laughed and started to wave her hands in the air, a single disk of water appeared before them and in it they could see a young mayor. She looked at the reflection and then the new captain and started to laugh, "you should welcome your son home then mayor," she said as she showed him the image.

The mayor wrapped his arms around his son's neck and started to cry, too bad he didn't know where his daughter was.

"No," Scarlet said sternly to Mortimer, "we are not going looking for his daughter."

Zephyr laughed and looked a bit impish, "About that," she said looking at Lorelei who was surrounded by eager young men.

Lorelei turned as she felt the gaze upon her, "what aren't you telling us?" she asked.

"You were not born on the island," she replied, "you were stolen from this village as a baby and raised by us." Zephyr nodded her head towards the mayor's son, "he refused to let you go when we took him, and swore up and down he would protect you from us. It seems the sea runs deep within your family's veins."

Lorelei walked over to Zephyr, raised her hand as if she was going to strike her, and then gave her a hug, "I understand, the bond made us do many horrible things." She suddenly grabbed her in a tight hug, "thank you for telling me the truth, even if your mother hid it from me my entire life."

The mayor looked at her and said, "my wife is a beauty amongst beauties, but she never had scaly skin, fangs or claws." He carefully reached out and pulled her face close to his and smiled, "but I swear your eyes match hers perfectly."

"Where is your wife?" Mortimer asked the mayor.

"She is in the tavern, she wanted to be sure there was plenty of food and drink for the homecoming," he answered.

"Your wife is smart," Mortimer replied, "why don't you escort my wife to the tavern and we'll meet you there." He turned to the rest of his wives, "why don't the rest of you go with him, I will catch up."

Tara laughed, "That sounds good to me."

Scarlet and Clarice both shook their heads no, "Sorry," Scarlet said, as she took his arm. "I am not letting you out of my sight."

"I wish to talk to the witch," Clarice said as she moved away.

Zephyr shrugged and went with Lorelei, but Shar frowned and said, "it is my duty to protect you, I can't do that if I'm not with you."

"That's fine, we are all heading that way, I just thought it would be good for us to mingle a bit with the people," he replied.

Scarlet gave a low chuckle, "is there a reason you are putting off satisfying your wife?"

Mortimer smiled at her, "not really, I figured you would hang back with me, and I thought we might slip away for some private entertainment."

Shar laughed, "you know how upset Lorelei will be that she didn't get to jump your bones in that outfit?"

Scarlet laughed, "she can do that later, I get to be the first to have him, in this outfit, she can be second."

"Why not third?" Shar asked, "I'll gladly go second."

Clarice suddenly chimed up, "Sorry, but it goes in the order of marriage, I get to be second."

Mortimer frowned, this was not what he had in mind, but eventually he shrugged, "Very well, but we'll need some privacy."

A nearby old man chuckled, "Just slip behind those fishing nets over there, the kids do it all the time and if your ladies aren't too loud nobody will notice."

It turned out the old man was correct, there were several pillows and a cozy little nest hidden among the nets, and Scarlet wasted no time in pushing Mortimer to the ground and lowering her own trousers. She sat on his lap and felt him enter her, soon she was in the throes of passion as he grasped her breasts and gently nibbled at her neck.

When she was done, Scarlet winked at Clarice, "your turn honey."

Clarice was already breathing heavily, and leapt into his lap, as soon as he entered her, it felt as if he were making love to her mermaid body and she felt herself explode with pleasure.

Shar gave him a dark smile and said, "I believe it's Tara's turn next."

Mortimer laughed, "probably a good thing she isn't here."

"Really?" Tara asked as she bounded over the top of the nets and landed beside him. She didn't waste any time stripping down and landing in his lap, she gasped, "Oh, that actually hurt a little, let's try again." she rocked forward a bit and thrust herself down onto him even harder, "oh, I like that, no wonder Clarice always changes to a mermaid with you."

Tara had an endurance the others did not, and he realized she was keeping tight control of her body, but soon enough she groaned and collapsed backwards into his arms, "I'm undone," she said with a smile just before she kissed him.

"We should get to the tavern," he said suddenly, "I am sure the others are waiting."

As they entered the tavern, Zephyr tackled Mortimer and plastered him with a kiss, "I got us a room upstairs for a few hours," she winked at him, "one of my former sailors said we could use his."

She almost pulled him off his feet as she led him upstairs, such was her urgency. She was much more creative than the others, and she showed him how flexible she could be when she wanted to be. Finally she stopped with him inside her and kissed him passionately, "Don't be too hard on her," she said as she got dressed and opened the door for Shar.

Despite her size and muscle, Shar was very gentle, she simply kissed him as he got to his feet, and they made love standing up. He knew her body, and knew her self control, so when he felt her legs buckle, he simply went down with her onto the bed and kissed her sweetly. The room was filled with shadows at this point, and he called them back, it had been a couple days since he last caused her to lose control of her magic like that.

Shar smiled lazily, "It is much more enjoyable to make love with you, than to just feel it through another person."

He returned her smile, "but you have to admit it is strange feeling both your pleasure and your partners at the same time."

"Lorelei is very eager, are you sure you're ready for her?" she asked.

Mortimer laughed gently, "Her magic has a steep price, it is no wonder I have never heard of a witch that has her power."

"Only if you're a mortal," Shar replied, "I know you use your magic to augment your abilities, I have felt it many times."

Mortimer laughed, "I never kept that a secret from you women, I am surprised you bring it up."

"I only bring it up because she is in a sexual frenzy, and you may need every ounce of your power to make her happy," Shar replied as she stood and straightened her skirt.

Mortimer nodded thoughtfully, "alright," he said finally, "let her in before she destroys the inn in frustration."

He was amazed as Lorelei fairly flew through the door and into his arms. She flung her skirt to one side as she wrapped her legs around him and kissed him with a passion only she ever seemed to have.

It took quite a while to satisfy Lorelei's desire, but he knew it would, eventually after several different positions and quite a bit of biting and clawing, she was satisfied. Mortimer looked at her lying there and grinned, "is it my turn now?" he asked.

Lorelei melted like warm butter as he ran his hands up her thighs and to her breasts, she knew what he was going to do, and she welcomed it as he teasingly lowered his body between her legs and nibbled gently at her breasts. She arched her back in anticipation of the next round, and she heard groans from just outside the room.

He pulled on her nipples with his teeth, and he slowly penetrated her, he heard her moan and her eyes rolled up in the back of her head, as he suddenly thrust himself deep into her and his lips found hers. Gradually his lips moved from her mouth to her neck and then her shoulders, a single hard bite and she screamed in pleasure, her entire body in spasms of ecstasy, and yet he didn't stop, he kept going until she gasped for air as her body spasmed again, her fingernails dug deeply into his back and a trickle of blood ran down from her shoulder to her breast. Finally he was done, and he lay next to her slowly licking the fresh blood from her breast, up to her shoulder and drank once more from the wound.

She opened her eyes and smiled, "you can do that any time you want with me my love. I love the feeling of your teeth sinking into my flesh, devour me as you take me, and I shall recover and be ready for more."

Mortimer chuckled as he drew back from the bite mark on her shoulder, "I know, that is why I did it. You are a strange one, but I will give you any pain you wish if it will also bring you pleasure."

Lorelei returned his smile, "Then bite one more time and let me feel your teeth and claws pierce my flesh as your love has pierced my soul."

He hadn't heard her say that before, but did as she asked, he slid his arms under her, and dug his claws into her back at the same time he bit deeply at her breast as she arched her back. Her cry of pleasure drove him to bite deeper and he dug his claws in deeper, until finally she relaxed panting in his arms.

Mortimer frowned, he didn't like hurting her, but she was never satisfied if there wasn't some form of pain. He let his magic step in and stitch the wounds closed so they might heal properly, but at the same time he worried about her. "Happy now?" he asked.

She smiled at him, "yes, that one will definitely leave a mark." She didn't have the heart to tell him, he was all she desired, and she hated herself for causing him emotional pain by demanding he cause her pain.

Slowly they disentangled themselves from each other and got dressed, sure enough you could see the bite mark on her breast with the outfit she was wearing. "That should keep a few young men away," Mortimer said with a chuckle.

She shrugged, "I have no interest in other men or women." She paused for a moment, "well, excluding a few of the ones outside the door," she finished.

When they returned to the bar area of the tavern, the sailors all cheered, and one yelled, "at least it didn't take a week this time."

Mortimer laughed at the joke, and several villagers just stared at them questioningly, until another sailor close to Lorelei whistled and said, "you really were hungry weren't you?"

Lorelei blushed slightly, "he isn't the only one with an appetite you know," she replied with a grin that showed her fangs.

The mayor stepped in front of Mortimer and frowned, "I don't like the idea of you hurting my daughter," he said.

Lorelei stepped between them and smiled at her father, "I demanded he do this, so if you want to blame anyone for hurting me, blame me."

An older version of Lorelei stepped forward and frowned, "she will not be happy if she is not with a man who can physically handle her need for pain and pleasure, my grandmother told me that once when I was a child." She smiled, "she always said to stay away from magic or I would never be able to feel pleasure without a bit of pain. I never understood that, but now I think I do." She looked closely at Mortimer and her smile widened, "I can see the pain you keep to yourself child, some day you will have to share it with her in a way that she understands it."

Mortimer blushed slightly as Lorelei turned crimson with embarrassment. "I have already shown her enough pain to last a lifetime," he replied, "now I seek only to show her pleasure, however she desires it."

"Looks like they need to get a room," a nearby sailor laughed.

"Seriously I would think they would be tired of each other after spending an entire week locked in a room together," another sailor commented.

Mortimer laughed loudly and openly, "no, a week is not nearly long enough when I have devoted my life to them." He smiled at his wives and pulled them close to him.

The villagers seemed taken aback by his openness, but cheered along with the sailors as several people cried out, "well said."

The drinking and eating went long into the night, but nobody seemed to care, it was pretty obvious they were all just happy to see an end to the pirate raids without any more bloodshed on their part.

# Needless Battle

In the morning, Mortimer went to talk to the old witch, and get her advice on the fastest way home. He was tired of distractions at this point and just wanted to be able to rest without the constant feeling that he wasn't getting anything done.

She laughed and pointed generally westward, "you have about a month's ride in that direction, unless you can craft a portal," she replied. "If you can do that, then I suggest you use it, as I'm pretty sure you don't want to wade through the battlefield outside your home city."

Scarlet recognized the look on Mortimer's face and frowned, "If we go through the battlefield, we will also have to go through another session of expelling negative energy, I am not sure any of us are up to that."

Lorelei laughed, "I am," she said with a smile.

Shar shrugged, "I can handle myself on a battlefield, but I'd rather not spend another week trying to calm him down."

Clarice looked at her and smiled, "he wouldn't be the only one who needed to destress afterwards, you would be in the same place as him."

Zephyr frowned, "Let's try the portal spell, Scarlet you pick the location for the end of it, I don't think we can count on Mortimer not to land us in the middle of a battle."

"Very well," Scarlet answered, "You lead, as air magic is travel magic, and we'll add magic as it progresses."

Zephyr nodded her head in understanding and started to speak under her breath. The air started to twist and turn around them, then the ground jumped up to join it as water leapt from a nearby trough and swirled in the air, finally Scarlet raised her arms and a pillar of fire spun in amongst all the rest of it.

Gradually the rocks formed an arch with the fire circling along the inside of the arch. The water formed a shimmering surface through which you could see a statue of a kneeling angel, and the wind died down.

"Why would you choose to arrive in a cemetery?" the witch asked in amusement.

Scarlet smiled, "it is where I first met Mortimer and he saved my life." She turned to the others, "let's hurry. I'll go first, followed by Tara, after her it will be Mortimer, Clarice, Lorelei, Shar and finally Zephyr." With that she stepped through the portal.

It was a single step, and it felt as if the wind pushed you hard in the back, and then you were out of it.

Scarlet turned around and saw an archway before her, and through it the others came single file.

Tara leapt through and landed lightly on her feet, Mortimer a second behind her, his hair standing up as he felt the energy of the dead beneath his feet. Clarice and Lorelei both stepped through in quick succession and then Shar, with the egg and Zephyr came so close together it was as if Zephyr were riding Shar's back.

As the last of them exited the portal, it collapsed and the columns disappeared, "Come," Mortimer said, "we do not want to stay here too long."

Shar agreed, she could feel the power of the dead beneath her feet and she knew it could rapidly become addictive.

Mortimer led them rapidly through the cemetery, pausing only occasionally to talk with a spirit and let them know they were not there to feed. Once out of the cemetery, they all relaxed a bit, and their pace slowed down, "Do we go to the town gates or do we head for the order?" he asked in general.

"The gates they answered in unison," they could all feel the excitement which emanated from him, it was time to push back the enemies of the town and find out why they were there.

Mortimer led the way rapidly through the streets, those people not defending the city who saw them moved quickly out of their way. As they approached the gate, Mortimer laughed, he recognized many of the men and women on the walls and hailed several by name, "How large is the opposing force?" he asked.

"Not large," a nearby woman answered, "if we weren't worried about them slipping past us and killing civilians we would easily crush them on the field."

"Where'd the town get the money for so many mercenaries, and how many companies joined the attacker?" he asked as he drew his sword.

"We're doing this one for free," she answered with a smile, "too many of us owe our lives to you to let them destroy your home. As for the enemy, they have a couple of units from the west, and one from the north, those barbarians are the only ones we're truly worried about."

Shar smiled darkly, "Can you open the man gate to let me out?"

"Sure, they should be falling back any second now," the mercenary replied, "but are you sure you want to go alone?"

"She won't be alone" they all answered as one, as they drew weapons and headed for a small door with a heavy bar across it.

Sure enough, they heard the enemy fall back, and Mortimer snorted at the poor tactic, they lost more soldiers in the retreat than if they had stayed against the wall. "Now," he whispered to Shar, who simply grasped the bar with one hand and lifted it from it's brackets.

Mortimer stepped through the open door and kicked back a nearby soldier, followed quickly by Scarlet and Clarice. Tara slipped out with Lorelei and Zephyr, and Shar brought up the rear as soldiers closed the door behind them.

"Barbarians first," Shar said, "they will be the toughest opponents."

The enemy appeared to be surprised at this group of mostly women heading their way with no armor on, finally an enemy archer realized they might be enemies and fired an arrow at Mortimer, Zephyr waved her hand negligently and the arrow flipped in the air and returned to the soldier who fired it. He had a look of absolute shock on his face as the arrow embedded itself to the fletchings in his chest.

"You came here for me," Mortimer yelled at the troops in front of him, "well, here I am either attack me directly or turn and flee for your lives." He glared at all of the soldiers and several of them took a step backwards.

A group of large warriors stepped forward, "we came here to fight," the leader shouted. "We will not retreat unless we are defeated."

Shar laughed, "then consider yourselves defeated, "for you are nothing compared to us."

The leader of the barbarians looked at her and laughed, "Do you challenge us to combat? I cannot expect a decent fight unless it is fair, I will let you have the numbers, and will only send in four of my warriors, best them and I will accept your challenge to single combat."

Mortimer chuckled dryly, "I should have known, they want a good fight, not a slaughter."

Clarice shrugged and winked at Tara, "I believe they may find movement a bit difficult, don't you?"

Tara returned the laugh and spread her hands before her, suddenly a crack opened in the field, and large brown hands rose up to grasp the legs of the barbarians.

"You will accept my challenge now, or I will crush your entire force," Shar bellowed back at the leader.

The leader looked around at the rest of his troops and nodded his head, "Very well, challenge accepted, when shall we fight?"

"Now," Shar answered as she flipped her sword in the air like it was a dagger.

The barbarian leader charged at her with a roar, and Shar let the sword hang in the air as she leapt forward and ducked under his club. She didn't want to kill him, so she simply lashed out with her foot and kicked his own feet into each other.

The barbarian spun on the spot and stopped, "you are unarmed," he said slightly puzzled.

She pointed upwards and he saw the sword flipping high in the sky, and suddenly felt the pain of her fist landing on his jaw. He staggered back a step in complete surprise until a knee drove itself into his gut and doubled him up, she followed with the other knee directly into his nose and watched him fall backwards to the ground.

He grunted as he stood and smiled at her, "You are truly one of our people, why do you side with this man?" he asked as he started to circle her with his arms stretched out as if to try and catch her.

Shar smiled and pulled aside the strap of her halter top to reveal the scars from his biting her, "He is my husband by the law of bone and blood," she answered as she in turn circled the leader. "He is my husband in that I have drank of his power and joined our souls in the old ways," she continued as she stepped towards him. "He is my husband through honor and loyalty and thus I will kill any who seek to harm him," she said as she suddenly launched forward into the leader's grasp and pummeled him with several fast strikes to the face.

The barbarian leader eventually managed to catch her wrists, and hold her off to one side to avoid the bulk of her kicks that started coming in, "enough," he bellowed, "you have made your point. I ask that you at least let our shaman inspect you, if what you say is true then we will leave the field."

Shar stopped struggling and let the shaman approach, the leader looked over at Mortimer and laughed, "She has spirit, good luck to you little man."

Mortimer chuckled evilly, "that's nothing, she hasn't even gotten warmed up."

The shaman looked at Shar from a slight distance and whistled, "by the ancient magic, it is true, she is filled with his magic, along with the magic of several others. It would be impossible for our entire clan to take her down, the gods themselves would rain death upon us for all eternity."

The leader smiled darkly, "good luck little man, we will quit the field as agreed."

A soldier from the opposing force came forward and had words with the barbarians, but didn't look too happy with what the barbarians had to say as he returned to his ranks.

Meanwhile Mortimer had been watching the enemy and smiled slyly, "the two mercenary companies they hired appear to have lost the taste for battle with the barbarians leaving." He frowned slightly, "don't be surprised if they try to rush us."

Zephyr shrugged, "No arrows can get to us, so it will only be close combat."

Scarlet smiled, "that is fine, I enjoy a good barbeque."

Clarice laughed, "I prefer mine steamed or boiled."

Tara shrugged, "either way their bones will end up beneath my feet."

Lorelei purred slightly, "I can't wait to see the beautiful designs their blood shall make on my walls."

Shar looked at Mortimer and grinned, "Are you feeling as hungry as I am?"

The sound of bugles announced the charge, and Mortimer laughed as thousands of arrows flipped around and struck the people who fired them. He could feel his power growing, with each death he grew stronger and more dangerous.

Scarlet rolled her eyes, "I swore we said we were going to avoid this," she said as a wall of white hot fire launched out from her hands and bathed the enemy troops. Metal melted in the heat and flesh burst into flames, "I tried to make it so you don't suffer too long," she said as bits of molten metal collapsed amongst the ash.

Tara stomped her feet and the earth opened up and swallowed an entire unit of soldiers, "please don't make me do that again," she said as the next unit back stepped really fast.

Clarice waved her arm and shards of ice fell from the sky and pierced armor and flesh alike, killing horses and soldiers quickly, "cool off," she said to the next line of cavalry.

Lorelei stepped forward and they saw a wave of green gas come from her arms and encompass the troops before her, who dropped their weapons and started stripping out of their armor, "make love not war, or if war at least be better at it," she said as their flesh started to blister and melt. "They really are tasty," she said with a wink to Mortimer.

Shar rolled her eyes, "great, here we go again, you just had to let her get turned on didn't you," she said to Mortimer.

"I didn't know it was possible to turn her off," he replied. "You cover the back, I've got the front line."

Shar nodded her head in understanding and sprang to intercept a group of soldiers working their way around them and towards the town walls. As she charged, a large shadowy blade appeared in her hands, and she swung it with great force at the first soldiers she came upon. The blade cut through armor and flesh alike and she watched as people fell completely cut in two.

Mortimer didn't hesitate, he knew the person in charge would be at the back of the battlefield, and with a wave of his hand the nearby dead rose from the ground, "Do not let anyone leave this battlefield without my permission," he ordered the spirits, and watched as they charged the army in front of him. "You had the chance to leave," he said to the soldiers before him, "now that opportunity is lost and any who stand against me shall die."

His sword moved as if of its own volition, deflecting a blow here removing a head or other extremity there. He walked forward at a steady pace, stepping over dead bodies as necessary, tossing the wounded aside should they not move out of his way, soon he had a fairly clear path through the army as people moved rapidly out of his reach. In a brief time he came to a unit of mounted men in heavy armor, and he laughed, these would be the lords knights, sworn to protect him at all cost.

He waited patiently for them to charge at him, the first to reach him flew from the saddle as his sword cleaved the legs out from under his horse. A twist of the wrist and his blade swung back and removed the knight's head while he was still in mid air. The knights grew cautious and tried to encircle him, he simply slashed the air with his left arm and shadowy spikes sprung from the ground around him and impaled both rider and steed. "You bore me with your lack of tactics," he said as he once again moved forward.

A group of young nobles soon stood before him, courtly types with no real place on a battlefield, their flimsy swords meant more for show than actual battle pointed directly at him. Mortimer laughed, "the town's children could handle you lot," he said as he stepped towards them. He was mildly surprised when they launched themselves at him, their blades flashing in the sun. The look of surprise on their faces when their swords broke on contact with his made him laugh evilly, "you really should never have left your mother's arms," he said as with a single swing his blade whistled through the air and took their heads.

He looked at the next group before him and frowned, they were mercenaries, probably hired to protect the noble in charge of this farce. "You know that with every death on this battlefield I grow stronger, and hungrier. Why do you insist on feeding me?" He asked as several charged at him.

The first mercenary went down with a simple block and repost maneuver, the second however timed his attack perfectly and Mortimer felt a blow on his side. The strike did not hurt, it was as if something had absorbed the impact, but it irritated him that someone had struck him, so he punched the mercenary in the face with his left hand.

The mercenary stumbled back a step and laughed, "What are you," he asked, "that blow should have cut you in half."

"I am the hand of death until my contract expires," Mortimer answered as he switched his sword to his left hand and thrust rapidly through the man's heart. He chuckled as the man clutched at the cross guard of his sword, and simply let go as he turned back to the other four mercenaries that stood before him.

The next one charged, and he ducked under the sword, while his right arm swung out and grabbed her by the throat. With a twist of his body he pulled the mercenary backwards and flung her onto the ground. The force of the blow was so fierce his opponent's sword flew from her hand and clattered on the battlefield as the breath was knocked from her. As she gasped for breath on the ground, Mortimer stomped on the mercenary's stomach as she screamed in agony.

Mortimer knelt down, one foot on the mercenaries stomach and ripped off her helmet, "You are quite pretty," he said to the woman, "I think I will save you for later, my women will be quite hungry after this."

She looked him in the eyes and saw how black they were, and suddenly she stopped struggling, "Please," she begged, "do not kill me."

Mortimer laughed, "Oh, I do not wish to kill you, I claim you as my spoils, according to the mercenary code you are my prisoner and you shall behave as such." He didn't wait for her response, he simply stroked her cheek gently with a blood soaked hand. "Now go down that path towards the city gates and surrender yourself to my women." He looked at the three mercenaries who remained standing, "that goes for all of you."

Without a word, the three remaining mercenaries dropped their weapons and helped their companion to her feet. They weren't sure what they were walking into, but they knew their lives had just been spared.

Mortimer looked at the pavilion before him and laughed, inside on a single chair sat a young boy, at his side were two older gentlemen, all of them with a look of absolute terror on their faces. "You must be the ones in charge," he said as he stretched out his hand for his sword. They all heard a high pitched scream as it ripped itself out of the mercenary's chest and flew through the air into his hand.

The two older men rushed forward to attempt to stop him, "please, your lordship, take our lives but let our young lord go." they begged as they approached.

Mortimer smiled, his eyes still black as coal, as he flicked his sword sideways sending a spray of blood across both mens faces. "I do not kill children, not even children who have caused so much death."

One of the gentlemen flinched, "how can we be sure, you have slaughtered so many of our men," he replied.

Mortimer shrugged, "you can't, but you also know I could just as easily kill you and walk over your corpses to get to the boy. Why not stop the bloodshed and we can negotiate?"

The men turned to each other and nodded their heads, "very well," the one replied, "if we have your word it will be peaceful negotiations."

"You have my word," he replied as he sheathed his sword. "I never desired any killing, I was hoping to return home to peace, but apparently that was not to be."

The two men stepped aside and a trumpet blared calling for an end to the combat.

With a burst of wind, Zephyr was at Mortimer's side, "your wishes husband?" She blushed slightly when she saw his eyes, "besides that. What do you wish for us to do regarding the enemy?"

"Tend to their wounded," he replied, "and spread word to the others to cease hostilities and help the wounded." He grinned darkly, "tell the prisoners to help, and we will decide their fate depending on their behavior."

She chuckled, "That girl interests you, should I have her bathed and prepared for your pleasure?"

"No, they will all be bathed after this, and if she pleases my wives, we will find a position for her among the staff," he smiled at her, "I have no desire for any other woman than the ones I currently have."

Zephyr laughed and gave him a kiss, "I forgot how good you taste covered in blood," she whispered as she darted back to the others with the aid of the wind.

The two men looked bemused for a second, "I am going to have a busy afternoon it seems," he chuckled to himself and winked at the men.

The two men bowed slightly to him, "your name sir?" one asked.

"Mortimer DeRose, the hand of death," he replied as he followed them into the pavilion.

The older of the two led slightly, and as he approached the boy in the chair bowed deeply and said, "My lord, may I present to you, Sir Mortimer DeRose the hand of death and knight of the order of the rose."

The boy stiffened slightly, but showed no other reaction to this title, "Welcome Sir Mortimer, I did not know the killer of my father was of the order."

Mortimer bowed slightly, "I have killed many boys' fathers, when I worked as a mercenary."

"I am sure you did," the boy replied, "the problem is it was brought to my attention by my uncle that I must avenge his death at your hands if I am to ever take his title for my own."

"I take it your uncle is acting regent until you reach maturity," he replied.

"That is correct," the boy replied, "sadly after today I feel I may never inherit my fathers position."

Mortimer laughed softly to himself and sat down cross legged in front of the boy, "You'll have to pardon me, but it sounds more likely that your uncle has sent you here in the hopes you would be killed. If he had meant for your fathers death to be avenged, he would have sent a much more experienced general and would himself have come to watch the battle."

The boy nodded his head slowly, "my councilors have recently been saying the same thing, so I am beginning to believe you are correct."

"I am impressed with your bravery," he replied, "most boys would have fled by now, even most men. As it is, none may leave this battlefield until either I die, or I release the souls of the warriors I sent to prevent retreat." He sighed, "the question is are you willing to concede defeat and go home, or are we going to go back to killing all of your troops?"

A soldier approached the pavilion and bowed deeply, "my lord, a young woman wishes to speak with her husband, your will?"

The boy laughed, "Let her in, I do not wish anymore bloodshed for today."

Scarlet stepped into the tent and curtsied to the boy before she turned to Mortimer, "I am here to be sure you are alright, Zephyr mentioned she was worried about you."

Mortimer laughed as he looked at her, "I am fine, just having a chat with our young lord here."

She looked at the blackness in his eyes and gasped, "You've only gone this far once before, let us tend to you before you continue to negotiate." She waved a hand behind her and he saw his other wives just outside.

He couldn't resist smiling at her, "The difference is I am not wounded, now please go help tend to the wounded, show them mercy after the horrors of war."

Scarlet knelt down next to him, "I will leave Shar here just in case, she may not be as skilled as you, but she can at least hold you back until we arrive." With that and a kiss, she stepped out of the pavilion.

Shar stepped in, and Mortimer waved for her to sit next to him, "Come love there is no need to fear an attack, these men are not warriors."

She laughed, "only you would fear no attack when completely surrounded by enemy soldiers." She turned to the boy and bowed, "your lordship," she said as she sat down.

The boy laughed, "someday I will be powerful enough to command so many lovely ladies, but first I must decide what to do here."

Mortimer chuckled, "You have several choices, resume the attack and most likely die, retreat and hope your uncle doesn't find another way to get you killed, or be smart and hire a large enough mercenary force to overthrow your uncle. I am quite certain nobody has explained that there is no avenging a person who died on the battlefield, as they chose to be there in the first place."

The boy frowned, "you make it sound so simple, but it isn't. In order to take on the mantle of duke, I must first reach the age of maturity, until then I will always have a regent ruling in my stead, a regent who will be chosen by the council of dukes should my current regent die as he is the last relative I have."

"Does the regent have to be a noble?" Mortimer asked.

"They must have at least obtained the rank of knight in our courts," the boy answered.

"Do they have to be related by blood?" he asked.

One of the councilors stepped forward, "there are cases of the regent being an in law, why do you ask?"

Shar burst out laughing, "don't tell me you are going to arrange for this young man to marry an older woman and appoint her regent."

Mortimer laughed in response, "no, I am thinking of arranging a marriage to this young man with a girl his own age and appointing her father as regent, then all we have to do is kill the current regent."

"My uncle will not allow such a thing," the boy protested, "besides what if I don't like the girl you choose for me?"

"Why don't we declare a truce for the day," Mortimer replied, "this way the young lord can visit my home and meet a few of the daughters of the knights. Provided nothing untoward happens between his lordship and a knight's daughter, the betrothal can be canceled when the young lord becomes an adult."

"But what about my uncle?" the boy asked.

"If your uncle is presently at your keep, then I will send a messenger demanding his presence at once or he will forfeit his life for violation of the mercenary laws," Mortimer replied. "Your uncle seems to have forgotten that as regent he is required to be on the battlefield if any mercenaries are hired in the name of the lord." He winked at the councilors, "even without the arranged marriage he would have lost his position when my complaint reached the mercenary council and they took it to the surrounding rulers."

The boy laughed suddenly, "If I had been given military advisors instead of court councilors, they would have known this and would have prevented this entire mess."

"So, do we have a deal?" Mortimer asked the young lord.

"I will do my best to find a suitable wife within your order's walls," the boy said with a slight bow.

Mortimer smiled to himself, he knew the perfect young lady for this young lord, although his sister might be a bit upset with moving to a keep with her husband instead of living at home. "Then come, let us show unity and walk out together," he said as he stood and waved his left arm towards the lord.

Shar looked at him and asked, "what about the dead love?"

"Oops, can't forget them now can I," he drew his sword and placed it's point in the ground, a wave of shadows shot out from the point in all directions, soon a nearby corpse stood up and marched over to him.

"Your orders my lord," the corpse said in a hollow voice.

"Pass the word, people may come and go as they please once more, you have discharged your duty honorably and earned a place of rest in the afterlife," he said to the corpse.

The corpse bowed deeply, "it has been an honor to serve you my lord, we shall greet you as friends when you once again enter death's realm." with that the corpse collapsed and the shadows vanished from the ground.

Mortimer smiled and relaxed slightly, "That was a decent way to burn off the excess energy I had accumulated, I will have to teach you how to do that," he said to Shar.

Shar grunted, "I'd rather just jump your bones until it is all burned off," she replied and then blushed as she remembered the boy standing next to them.

Mortimer looked at the young boy and laughed, "you will understand someday," he said.

The boy laughed with him, "I am not yet old enough to be interested in girls, but I already understand the relationship between men and women. I'm just curious how you are so casual with them all, it's as if you can read their minds."

Shar burst out laughing, "he's already figured out your secret," she said with a wink.

Mortimer shook his head as they walked out into the light, "it has nothing to do with reading their minds, it has more to do with listening to their desires. You may learn it someday, but don't be upset if you get it wrong a few times, some people learn it quickly, and others never learn it."

# An old friend

He led the young lord and Shar through the battlefield to the town gate, "Open up," he bellowed, "the battle is over."

A female mercenary opened the gate and laughed, "Really Grim, you actually left some alive, I'm surprised." She ducked as a wash of flame flew towards her, "I see you still have that hot head with you," she said with a smirk.

"I see you are wearing my old armor," he replied. "We have declared a truce so that he might attend a meal at my family's house."

The woman rolled her eyes, "only you would invite the enemy over for lunch."

Mortimer shrugged, "what can I say I worked up an appetite?"

"I told you before I would be more than happy to fix that," she said with a smile as she ducked again, this time it was an ice shard that quivered in the wooden frame of the gate. "I swear, the people you bring home don't like me much."

Mortimer chuckled softly, "I suggest you apologize with a kiss, otherwise you might find your bed very uncomfortable." He raised his right hand and bellowed, "ladies, it is time to go see father."

The ground rumbled, rain fell nearby and a fireball burst in front of him as several of them appeared.

"Where's Zephyr and Lorelei?" he asked.

Lorelei sauntered towards him casually licking blood from her fingers, "sorry love, but my magic is not quite that flashy."

Zephyr laughed from the town wall above them, "I decided to wait up here until the others arrived, Scarlet seems a bit hot today." she said as she gently floated to the ground.

Lorelei looked at the mercenary and smiled, "who is this tasty looking morsel and can I have a bite?"

Mortimer shook his head as he put his hand on her shoulder and pulled her to him, "Scarlet first, this is an old friend," then he promptly bit her gently on the neck.

Lorelei melted like butter into his side, "do that again and we'll need a tent."

Scarlet couldn't help it, she burst out laughing at the two of them. "If I really meant you any harm, I would have hit you with that fire," she said to the mercenary. "It's good to see you are still alive."

The woman shook her head and laughed, "with you I never know what to expect, the last time we met you laid me out in front of my colleagues."

Scarlet grinned, "then I guess it's best to do as my husband suggests, and really give them something to talk about." She moved quickly and wrapped her arms around the mercenaries shoulders and gave her a kiss. She tasted salty, she thought as their lips met, she let the kiss get more passionate and when she felt the woman's mouth open slightly, slipped her tongue into her mouth. Her tongue explored the mercenaries mouth and partially down her throat, oh it was warm and inviting, and she could feel the poor woman melt into her embrace. "Oh my," she gasped as they ended the kiss, "Clarice you should apologize for that shard you threw at her."

"Very well," Clarice said as she took the woman from Scarlet's arms, "I'm sorry for throwing a spear at you, please accept my deepest apologies," she said as she too kissed the woman deeply and passionately.

This proved too much for the mercenary to handle, first the fiery hot tongue of Scarlet, followed by the icey coolness of Clarice, and she just melted into the woman holding her, she was suddenly very jealous of Mortimer. She heard a sensual voice behind her say, "my turn now." she turned her head to see the most amazing green eyes she had ever seen, and the scent of a field of flowers wafted over her.

Lorelei smiled sweetly at the mercenary and said, "I have nothing to apologize for, but you look so tasty, I just have to have a taste." She ripped the woman from Clarice's arms and kissed her with a passion the nearby mercenaries had never seen. She couldn't resist, her claws came out and dug into the chainmail as she kissed her victim, her tongue explored the woman's mouth and she sucked the air from her lungs, finally she released her, "she is tasty, but he tastes much better," she said as she turned to look at Mortimer.

Mortimer laughed and caught the mercenary in his arms, "I think you overdid it," he said to all three.

Scarlet smiled, "I hope she forgives me, I would hate to make her go through another apology."

Clarice laughed, "the only one here who owes her an apology is Mortimer, after all he set her up."

He shrugged, "Very well, I will apologize to her," he said and suddenly found her struggling to get free of his arms.

"Not yet," she gasped, "let me get my feet back under me before you even think of apologizing."

Scarlet grinned evilly, "if you make him wait too long, he will strip you down and consume your soul as he ravishes your body, after all you once called him the grim reaper."

The mercenary's head whipped up, "Red, why share him with me?"

"Because it scares the hell out of our prisoners," she answered.

The young lord gave a gentle cough, "I wonder if it wouldn't be better if we got to where we are going before things progress too far."

A nearby man in heavy plate armor laughed, "I am inclined to agree," he said as he removed his helmet. "Why don't I escort his lordship to my house while my son burns off his excess energy."

Scarlet recognized the face of Mortimer's father and dropped into a deep curtsy, "Your lordship," she said, still facing the ground. The others stared at her behavior, they had never seen her so submissive.

The knight laughed heartily and grasped her by the shoulders, "please call me father, you are my son's wife after all," he said as he pulled her into a hug.

The hug knocked the wind out of Scarlet for a moment, but she kept her composure and asked, "you know I am not his only wife?" she asked.

"How many," he asked softly.

"Six total," she answered, "but if we're not careful he might make it seven or eight before we make it to the house."

"I might have to move him to a bigger room," he laughed.

Scarlet waved to the others, and they came over for introductions.

Clarice blushed when he compared her to the legendary goddess of the sea.

Tara smiled and almost creased his armor when he commented on how petite she was.

Zephyr simply bowed her head and gave him a peck on the cheek when he remarked on how light she was.

Shar returned his welcoming hug with a hug of her own, lifting him off his feet slightly when he admired her strength.

Lorelei stepped forward and he was silent for a second before he called her the most venomous viper to walk on two legs. She stepped forward and bowed to him, "I dare not get too close, I am quite hungry and only your son can satisfy my hunger."

Mortimer's father laughed at this and wrapped her in a huge bear hug, "I have not seen a witch of sexual powers in a long time, it is good to see one again."

Lorelei almost cried, as she fought the urge to bite and try to control the man. As he put her back down, she gasped, her breasts swelling with every breath and her fangs slightly exposed. Suddenly Shar was there and she felt the calmness that came with her, "thank you," she gasped to Shar.

Mortimer's father bowed his head to Lorelei, "I shall have a room prepared for you when you arrive, I get the feeling you all will need it." He turned to Scarlet and smiled, "Thank you for keeping him alive, and even greater thanks for returning him to me." He bowed to all three of them and then turned and led the young lord through the town.

Scarlet turned to the others, "you have just been introduced to our husband's father, do any of you wish to flee?"

Lorelei raised her hand slightly, "I am terrified of being alone with that man, I don't want Mortimer to hate me if I lose control and that man makes my control slip."

Scarlet laughed, "he makes everyone lose control, even Mortimer," she waved over towards where he still held the poor mercenary woman close to his chest, his entire body shaking slightly. "I can't believe I'm going to say this, but Lorelei I need you to release your passion on Mortimer."

Lorelei smiled, "In public," she shrugged, "I can do that."

"Just don't let that mercenary go anywhere," she smiled at Lorelei, "she is going to be my test subject." She looked around at the few mercenaries standing nearby and grinned, "I see we have a few additional test subjects."

Instantly the area around them was devoid of people, "damn they move fast for wearing such heavy gear," Tara laughed.

"How are you doing?" Lorelei asked Shar suddenly.

"I feel much better," she replied, "you have this knack for draining the excess energy from the battle, it's almost as if you wash it away."

"That's good, now I had better go deal with Mortimer, before he crushes that poor woman to death," she replied as she licked her lips.

As she approached him, Lorelei could tell he wasn't out of control, he was just fighting his own battle, "he must have killed someone who had very strong feelings for that woman," she said to herself. She shrugged her shoulders and gently ran her fingers up his arm, he reacted instantly, the blackness of his eyes subsided and she saw a flicker of gray before they reverted to black. "How delicious," she said as she stroked the back of the woman's neck, "don't go anywhere honey, I will need you," she said as she gently pulled his arms from the lady and put them around her own neck.

Mortimer felt Lorelei touch him, he felt her guide his body, and then he felt her kiss him, she's offering herself to me, he thought as he accepted her offering and kissed her back. He didn't care they were both covered in blood, he didn't care if anyone was nearby, all he cared about was her and he knew instantly she was using her magic on him and he let her.

Lorelei guided him up against the wall, she loosened his pants, and she swung the front of her skirt out of the way, as she wrapped her legs around his waist and took him inside her. She had never tasted anything this sweet, she thought as she kissed him, he needed a gentle hand, and she wanted to be that hand. She rocked gently with his heartbeat, as she kept their lips locked together, soon she felt what she had been searching for and felt the power of death flow out of his body, as her own body quivered with pleasure and threatened to collapse.

Mortimer smiled at Lorelei as they finished, "that was most unexpected," he said as he kissed her again.

Lorelei returned his kiss and smiled, "I don't know what happened that time, I just wanted to taste you so badly, now go apologize to the woman so we can have some real fun."

He looked over to the lone mercenary and smiled, she looked terrified as she noticed she was surrounded by his wives and they all appeared to be smiling. Quickly he fixed his pants and blushing he said, "Sorry about that."

"A real apology," Lorelei said, "according to Scarlet this woman has desired you for a while, let her have a taste, but only a taste, if she follows you home then we can invite her to join the family."

The woman looked around again and laughed nervously, "Chainmail does not lend itself to romance," she said as she started to walk towards Mortimer.

Mortimer felt a presence and closed his eyes, he could see himself cutting the armor from her body in a single stroke, "Really Scarlet? Is that what you want?"

All of the women laughed, "it's what we all want," Lorelei answered as she licked her lips.

The mercenary stepped in close, "and what is it you all want?" she asked as she turned and looked Lorelei in the eye.

Mortimer chuckled evilly as he felt the shadows wash back in, "they want what I wanted in my youth," he answered as he drew his sword, deliberately sliding its edge along the side of her armor.

She looked down as she saw the cut in her armor and frowned, "are you going to kill me or what?" she asked. For some reason she was terrified, but at the same time she was curious.

He slid the blade up the length of her back, ever careful not to put too much pressure on it and watched as her armor slid forward and off her shoulders, "Let it fall," he said as he let go of his sword.

She couldn't resist, she relaxed her arms and watched the armor slide off, to the ground, thankful she still had a layer of leather and padding on, "what are you going to do to me?" she asked, "Are you going to give me what I asked for when you were a mercenary?"

Scarlet laughed, "oh you are so sweet, he is going to do much more than that."

Mortimer wrapped his arms around the mercenary and grasped the seam of her padding in both hands, with a jerk it tore from top to bottom and he ripped it from her body. "The more people die around me the stronger I become," he said to her as he wrapped his arms around her naked body. "You have a few more scars now than when you tried to seduce me in the past."

She blushed slightly, "I'm sorry, but the battlefield is rough on the body," she replied as she slid her hands into his vest and felt the scars on his own body. She let her hands slip to his waist and she frowned, "this one is new and very deep from the feel of it."

He laughed as he shrugged off his vest, "that one almost killed me and created a very messy situation." Slowly he leaned forward and kissed her, gently at first and then more deeply. As they separated from the kiss he smiled at her, "I'm sorry I turned you down in the past, but I had too many things on my mind back then. You should get dressed though, the townsfolk frown on nudity in public you know." He let her go and smiled as he surveyed her body, "you do taste good and look absolutely delicious, but I cannot be with you without others permission."

She looked around and Scarlet held out a cloak for her, "let me help you," she said as she wrapped it around the mercenary. "If you truly want to be with him, then come with us to his home, but know if you do you will need to discard your armor and don a dress."

The mercenary frowned slightly, "I would let you burn me to death if it meant I could be with him even once."

Lorelei laughed, "If you are with him once, then you will be bound to him forever, that is the price you pay to be with him," she said as she picked up Mortimer's vest and sword, "god this thing is heavy today."

Mortimer chuckled and simply opened his hand and the sword leapt into it so he could sheath it, "take me home before the shadows return," he said softly.

Scarlet instantly was at his side and guided him as if he was drunk, and she knew he was fighting the drunkenness of power. She winked at Lorelei who nodded to Clarice.

Clarice smiled as she wrapped an arm around the mercenary's shoulder and asked, "So what is your decision?"

She turned her head and smiled at Clarice, "I made the mistake of letting him walk away once, I am not about to do so again."

Clarice grinned at her, "Good, we better hurry to keep up with the others."

"He has changed a lot since I was on the battlefield with him," the mercenary said to herself, "he is far more confident than he was before and far more reckless."

Clarice couldn't help but laugh, "that would be Scarlet's influence on him," she paused for a moment before she continued, "I believe part of it is Lorelei's influence as well. Since she joined us he has been getting a bit friskier than we expected."

"I have seen him after many battles," the mercenary continued, "but he always would retire to a tent by himself for several days, before reappearing at the fire to listen to others brag." She laughed slightly, "it really upset some of the people that he wouldn't join in the bragging, especially when it came to their conquests of women."

"When he separated for those few days he was going through a cleansing ritual, in order to not get taken over by the power of death," Clarice replied, "it can be a very painful ritual, or at least it was until we discovered another way to release the energy. I have to ask you again, are you sure you want to be with him, no matter the pain?"

She looked Clarice directly in the eye, "Yes, although I am quite curious to know why you keep asking as if trying to dissuade me from making this decision."

"Because to join us, is a very painful experience," Clarice answered, "in case you haven't noticed most of us are no longer human." She frowned slightly, "even Shar went through a lot of transformation and continues to change the more she is around the power, soon none of us will be recognizable as humans."

She smiled at Clarice, "I had noticed the change in Scarlet, the rest of you I never met before, but I am not concerned about it. It is something I have wanted for a while, and never had the courage to chase after." She looked around her, "Don't tell me he lives here."

Clarice laughed, "Yes, he does, apparently a guard is waiting to escort us to his chambers." She pointed to the side where a single man in plate armor stood at attention, seeing her gesture towards him, he approached and bowed.

"Lady Clarice, mistress of the sea I presume," he said as he bowed.

"Yes, sir knight," Clarice replied.

The knight bowed again, "we were told to watch for your arrival with or without the Lady Rose."

"Where by chance did you hear that name?" the mercenary asked as she tensed up.

Sir Mortimer, knight of the order and king of the eastern sea pirates, most gracious lady," the knight responded politely.

Clarice laughed softly, "I take it you have a back entrance for us to use," she asked.

"Right this way ladies," the knight replied as he led them through the garden and to the stables. "There is one of the fey inside who will take you quickly to his lordship's chambers."

Rose frowned, "I haven't heard that name since before I ran away and became a mercenary, if my family knew I was here it would create a lot of trouble."

Clarice burst out laughing, "oh my you are innocent, he is going to love adding you to the family especially when his sister sends out the wedding invitations. You shall have to make certain your family gets an invitation."

Rose looked at her as if she was crazy and then almost leapt out of her skin when a silky voice spoke from behind her, "Ladies if you will please hold my hands, I will take you to your room in a moment."

The voice belonged to a petite little elf girl wearing a living dress of leaves and flowers, "I didn't mean to startle you, we'll be using a magic path to get to the chambers you will be staying in. My husband and children are already assisting the other ladies with their dresses for the night."

Rose blushed slightly as Clarice asked, "what of my husband?"

The elf smiled, "you mean Mortimer, oh he has been isolated temporarily, after he accidentally raised his mothers spirit upon entering the manor." She smiled sweetly at both of them, "now please we should hurry, we have a lot to do before dinner tonight."

They each took one of her hands and tried to relax as vines sprang up around them and encased them, gradually the vines opened up and they found themselves standing in a large room with a huge pool of water in the middle of it.

Scarlet walked in and waved to them, "You should both take a moment and get a quick bath, I have a dress picked out for you already Clarice, but I was not sure which would be best for our new friend."

"I will be there in a moment, and we can decide together," Clarice replied as she slipped into the pool and let her body revert to its natural form. Immediately she felt a presence in the water and started to gather her magic.

"The sprite won't hurt you," the elf said quickly, "she just wishes to inspect you for injuries and to get you properly cleaned up."

Clarice relaxed and looked at a nervous Rose standing at the edge of the water, "come on, I won't let you drown," she said with a smirk. "We can't properly present you to Mortimer until you are cleaned and properly dressed."

Cautiously Rose stepped into the tub and winced, it was hot, next thing she knew a wall of water came up behind her and dumped itself over her head, "I thought you said you wouldn't drown me," she spluttered.

"Oh, that wasn't me," Clarice replied, "that was the water sprites way of telling you to sit down and let her do her job." She giggled for a moment, "hey now, that tickles," she said as she playfully swatted the water.

The water rose up slightly and playful splashed her in return.

Rose decided it would be best to just relax and let them do as they pleased with her, she was quite certain they were planning something horrific, but she also knew they wouldn't do any permanent harm. Sure enough, she felt hands run over her body, and an angry hissing sound came from the water when it came across a scar. Then she felt someone pulling at her hair and she was dunked underwater completely, at first she panicked and then she realized there was a whirlpool of air covering her mouth and nose which allowed her to breath.

After several minutes, Rose resurfaced with her hair drawn out behind her like a red and yellow blanket, her skin sparkled in the light and she felt wonderful. "I don't remember my hair ever being this long," she said as she looked over at Clarice.

Clarice laughed, "That is the magic of the sprite, it can heal any wound without leaving a scar, and apparently it has decided our hair was damaged and needed to be repaired." Her own hair was gloriously long, and now reached down past her tail as she relaxed and leaned against the side of the tub. "I suppose I did promise Scarlet I would help her choose a dress for you, but it's going to take forever to dry off now."

Scarlet walked in and looked at the two of them, "you both look lovely, sprite can you please assist Clarice out of the pool so that I might dry her off?"

With a watery sigh, the water lifted Clarice up and set her gently on the floor outside the pool, before it receded back and started playing with Rose's hair.

"Thank you," Scarlet said with a smile and a flick of her wrist, "you may do as you please with her, but remember she is a gift for Mortimer." A small flame appeared in Scarlet's hand and she ran it rapidly over Clarice's body, drying her out so she could more readily return to human form. "Come deer, we will show you the dresses while the children do your hair." she said to Clarice.

Clarice stood and followed her out of that room and into a huge room with a massive bed in the center with clothing hanging from all of the walls around the room, "your mannerism is different here, why?"

Scarlet laughed, "I don't know, I noticed the same thing the last time I was in the manor, somehow it changes the way you think and feel, as if all of the bad thoughts get washed away or something."

"And where is Mortimer?" She asked.

"He is having a conversation with his mother and father," Scarlet answered, "now I found the perfect white, blue and green dress for you, but I have no idea what would be good for our friend in there."

Clarice chuckled, "you mean Rose? I would think something in the way of leather and steel would be good."

Scarlet laughed, "Rose is it, well that narrows things down a bit." She pushed Clarice into a nearby seat, "let's get your hair done up before we get your dress on you."

Immediately a dozen little elf children ran over with brushes and ribbons and went to work on her hair, Clarice couldn't remember ever having it this long. She noticed all of the others wore dresses that accentuated their ancestry and smiled, Tara was resplendent in a brown dress with an overlayer of green leaves. Shar wore a close fitting fur and leather dress that accentuated her muscles. Zephyr looked amazing in a feathery dress of blues, white and yellow. Lorelei looked as if a snake had slithered up her body and melted to it, her dress was a green skin tight scaly looking material with a collar of what looked to be actual snakes teeth. Scarlet's dress was a mixture of reds sewn together to appear as if she was walking through flames, the top of it was a crimson colored bodice made of scales, which really accentuated her figure nicely. For Clarice they brought out a white, green and blue dress sewn to appear as if whoever wore it was walking through the waves, attached to it was a bodice of blue/white scales.

Soon enough, Rose came into the room with the rest of them, and frowned, she had never seen a room full of such beautiful women. "I get the feeling I don't belong here," she mumbled to the elf girl who pulled her in by the hand.

The elf girl laughed musically and dragged her over in front of a mirror, "just stand here for a minute, and let the mirror show you what the others think you should wear."

Rose stared at the mirror and laughed as a dress appeared in it, she shook her head, "I am not a fragile flower," she said with a frown. The image was replaced with a green and black dress, and a black leather bodice with beautiful blood red roses embroidered into it. She couldn't help but smile, "that's pretty, but I doubt it would look good on one such as I."

Instantly she felt a pair of clawed hands grab her by the shoulders and throw her across the room onto the bed, Scarlet stood above her a fury in her eyes as she stared down at her and said, "that is the dress you will be wearing tonight and you will look amazing in it."

Rose cowered back from Scarlet, she knew this woman could kill her in a heartbeat, but was even more afraid of the look in her eyes, "yes ma'am," she replied with a gulp.

Scarlet took a deep breath and visibly calmed herself, "sorry," she said. "Can I tell you a secret?" she asked.

"If you want to," Rose answered, still nervous about her anger.

"Do you know the real reason I hit you the first time we met?" she asked.

"I figured it was to show how tough you were," Rose answered, growing even more nervous.

Scarlet laughed, "Honey, to do that I could have just set the bar on fire." She smiled at her, "it was because I was jealous of you," she said.

"Jealous of me?" she asked, "but why?"

Scarlet turned slightly red, "because of how pretty you were, even wearing that armor, and because you had spent all that time fighting alongside Mortimer. The fact that he never slept with you after all of your offers, shows how much he respected you as a warrior." She smiled at Rose, "during my travels with him, I have learned a lot about him, and I know I cannot compete with you or him on a battlefield without magic. It made me realize just how special you had to be, and as such when I saw you on the battlefield today I marked you so that I could make certain you stayed safe." She sat down next to Rose on the bed and put an arm around Rose's shoulders, "I was the one who decided to test you, I was the one who decided we should open our arms to you, and apparently in doing so I have created a complication for the ritual."

Rose stared at Scarlet, half in fear and half in awe, "but why?"

Lorelei laughed happily, "because you look so tasty, and you will please Mortimer when we are gone."

"What do you mean gone?" Rose asked.

Shar laughed, "it is no secret we could all die during this ceremony, and if that is the case we want you to be here to take care of Mortimer the way we would have."

Rose took a deep breath and steadied herself, "I am not sure I could please him nearly as much as you ladies do."

Scarlet laughed, "don't doubt yourself until you've tried. Now let's get you into that dress and get your hair prepped."

Rose nodded her head in agreement and stood up on shaky legs, these women were crazy if they thought she could replace them all if something happened to them.

Soon enough a knock came to the door and when they opened it a young guard stood outside, "Pardon me ladies, but your presence is requested in the altar room," he said with a bow.

"Lead the way," Scarlet said as she waved for the others to follow her.

The guard escorted them down the hall and through a doorway into a steep stairway, "Please watch your step," he said as he lit a nearby lantern and picked it up.

The stairway wound downward quite steeply for a long way, Tara frowned slightly at one point and said, "we are at least a hundred feet below the manor."

"Correct, m'lady," the guard said as he led them further down the stairs. "The altar room is down further and was built upon the bones of your ancestors."

# Ritual

Eventually they came to a large thick door with a single metal plate in the center of the door. The guard set down the lantern and drew a sharp knife from his belt, "I bring the saviors of a lost soul and crave admittance," he said as he cut open the palm of his hand and placed it upon the metal plate.

The door swung open easily at his touch and a voice replied, "then enter and be welcome."

The guard stepped to one side and waved the women through, after the last of them entered the chamber, the guard touched the steel plate once more, turned and walked back up the stairs.

They watched as the door closed behind them and multi-colored flames arose along the walls. "Welcome," a beautiful young woman standing in the middle of the room said, "please stand in a circle so that I may properly see you."

As they formed a circle around the woman, Scarlet asked, "where is Mortimer?"

The lady smiled sadly, "he will not be joining us just yet. Now please let me get a good look at you." She glided smoothly around the inside of the circle and smiled, "you have grown a lot since I last saw you," she said as she stopped in front of Scarlet. "We have a slight problem with the ritual," she said as she glided back to the center of the circle.

"As you know you all share a blood bond with my son," she looked at Rose, "well, except you honey, you have been spared that so far." She looked around at them all again, "the problem is the necromancer's bond you made which can only be broken by death itself."

She looked around again, "the other problem is through that bond you have already filled the chosen vessel." She frowned slightly, "the blood bond is necessary for the ritual, the necromancer's bond is an obstacle and the filled chalice is another obstacle." She smiled slightly, "normally we would just proceed with the ritual and due to the necromancer's bond you would all die, including my son, but the crimson witch has forbidden us from making this demand of you." She chuckled slightly, "apparently you have all really impressed her or she really enjoys watching your lives, I'm not sure which."

The ghostly woman paced around in the circle for a bit before she continued, "So we are here to decide on our course of action, you can all sacrifice yourselves and my son to free the witch, or you can continue to live the way you are living now, continuing to grow more powerful and him constantly struggling with the corruption of death magic." She smiled slightly, "the original ritual you would have sacrificed yourselves and been reborn in a single body with all of your powers and minds converged into one. Now, we are not sure if that will work, the crimson witch believes though that we can use the hand maiden as a vessel to save my son's life and contain all of your powers. I will let you ladies discuss it, while I check on my son." The ghostly figure vanished instantly, and they were left alone in the room.

Shar laughed loudly, "I for one will give my life if they believe they can save Mortimer with it."

Lorelei shrugged, "I do not have a life without him, and told him when he ripped the bonds from my flesh that he could do with my life as he pleased, so I leave it up to him."

Rose frowned, "I feel out of place as I am not bonded and so my feelings have no bearing on your decisions."

Clarice and Scarlet looked at each other and laughed, "we swore to free the witch from the blade and as such we shall give our lives to do so."

Zephyr shrugged, "my life was forfeit when he defeated me, it is simply my time to pay the price for my crimes."

Tara shook her head, "it is against my own desires, but like the rest of you I will give my life if it will save him."

The ghostly figure returned and asked, "has a decision been reached?"

"Yes," Scarlet answered, "we are willing to sacrifice ourselves for Mortimer, but what is Rose's part?"

The ghost laughed and it sounded as if a small river were flowing between the branches of a nearby tree, "she must decide if she desires to be bound to my son and the rest of you forever, and if she is willing to commit an atrocity according to most people in order to have that bond." She turned directly to Rose, "I must tell you, if you do this you will never be alone, for their souls will be tied to yours and while you will gain their magical abilities, you will also feel their feelings and have their desires."

"What is this atrocity you speak of?" Rose asked, she wondered if her goddess would approve.

"You must first decide if you are willing to be magically bound to my son," the ghost replied.

Rose snorted with derision, "I wouldn't be here if I didn't desire such." She didn't mention the bond she shared with him already.

The ghost smiled, "I am glad to hear that, now to answer your question, you will need to drink of their blood after they die, and then you must share said blood with my son via a kiss."

Scarlet laughed, "A different sort of necromancer's bond."

"Not quite," the ghost replied, "the drinking of the blood is part of the ritual to use the blood bond to release the spirit. The sharing of the blood through a kiss is the necromancer's bond to bring my son back to life."

"Why is it you never say Mortimer's name?" Rose asked.

The ghost smiled at her, "because to say the name of the dead is to summon their attention to you, and as a necromancer he has all of the powers of the dead."

Scarlet laughed, "and you don't want him to be aware of this conversation."

"Correct," she answered, "he would not be happy about us having this conversation. If you are all ready to proceed with the ritual, please come with me," she said as she turned and floated gracefully towards a nearby wall.

The others followed her and were surprised to find the wall was permeable, it felt as if they were pushing through water for a few minutes and then suddenly they were in another room with a table and several chairs arranged around it. Along the far wall more chairs were lined up as if waiting to be used and on the table there was a single bone goblet. In front of each chair there was a bone funnel. Mortimer stood scowling in the far corner, all of the crimson blades and his sword sat on a table before him.

"If I thought it would do any good," he said softly as they approached, "I would forbid you all from participating, but you bound me to this fate when you used your own souls to heal me."

"I would do it again in a heartbeat knowing what I know now," Scarlet said with a smile.

Lorelei cried slightly, "my only regret is not being able to bear your children my lord."

Mortimer's scowl deepened into a frown, "if you insist on doing this, pick your blade, I am forbidden from interfering in any way other than words. After you have chosen your blade, please find the seat that corresponds to your magic and take it." He turned to Rose and spoke, "I am sorry to have put you in this situation, please feel free to back out at any time, it will not change the ritual, it will simply prevent me from coming back to life."

Rose walked up to him and slapped him, "do you think so little of me that I wouldn't bring you back from the dead a thousand times if necessary? I swear to the goddess, after I bring you back I will demand each of your wives possess me and have their way with you, until you beg them for forgiveness." She then turned and looked at the ghost, "where do you want me to be?"

The ghost laughed musically once more, "my child you have a fire to rival that of a dragon, the patience of the water, the decisiveness of the wind and the stubbornness of the earth, you will make a fine vessel. You will be seated in the red leather throne next to Mortimer." She looked at Mortimer and frowned, "you my most insolent of children will sit in the throne next to her and accept the fate you have woven for yourself."

Mortimer couldn't help it, he smiled at his mother, "as you wish, but one question is it possible for my wives to possess Rose after this ritual?"

"Child," she burst out laughing, "have no fear, your wives will still be with you after this and I won't say more on the matter."

The women all chose different blades, and Shar picked up Mortimer's own sword, then they found their seats and sat down.

The ghost smiled, "an old friend is going to walk you through the ceremony, please do not be afraid, he will not harm you."

A booming voice came from behind them, "it is good to see you are continuing with your quest no matter the consequences. You simply need to tell the spirit in the blade you hold that you are releasing it, and then you must cut a major vein and let yourself bleed out into the funnels. Your blood will then run into the chalice and once full I shall take the chalice to the vessel and she shall drink it." He grinned at Rose, "you must drink all of the blood in the chalice and before you wipe the blood from your lips you must promise the one you love to love them forever and then kiss them with the blood still on your lips." He looked at all of them, "any questions."

"Just one," Clarice said with a smile, 'can I give you another gift?"

Death walked over and leaned down close to her, "I am still feeling the impact of your last gift, what else would you give to me?"

She smiled at him, "I would give you everything I am and the best night of your life if you will be sure to protect my husband."

He couldn't help but laugh, "I appreciate your concern and I do not require such a bargain, you belong with your husband and not with me."

Clarice reached up and pulled Death close to give him a kiss on his boney cheek again, "I alway knew you were not a bad person."

Death shook his head and turned a little red, "once again you are the first person to ever truly treat me as another person, and that is why I am going to make certain you and your husband are reunited."

He turned to the women and slowly said, "you may begin the ritual, remember to do it in unison as the necromantic bond could prevent the entire ritual from finishing."

All six of them lifted their blades and rested the tips between their breasts, and as one they cried out, "I release you from your prison," as they plunged the blades into their hearts and watched as the blood flowed out of them and into the chalice.

Mortimer screamed in agony, it felt as if a thousand blades had pierced his heart at the same time. He looked down and saw his own blood flowing from the scar on his chest, then he looked over at Rose and smiled, "at least I saved you from dying." His chin dropped to his chest and he sat there lifeless.

Rose almost leapt from her seat, as she watched the women's bodies start to dissolve, until a pair of ghosts stood behind the women holding hands. The ghosts did not look happy, but instead kept looking towards the chalice with a worried look on their faces.

Death grinned at the two ghosts, "it is good to see you will be entering my dominion finally. Would you do me the honor and present to her the chalice, it is your choice, if she does not drink from it they will remain in my domain, but if she does, you know what will happen."

The red ghost glared at death, "do you promise they will not be used the way we were?"

"That is something for the world of man to decide," Death answered, "but I do promise I will do everything in my power to prevent such a cruel fate."

The shadowy ghost squeezed the red ghost, "we cannot choose their path for them, they did this knowing what could happen, the best we can do is try to honor them by completing the ritual." He frowned slightly, "once again we have failed the mermaid's family."

The red ghost slowly walked forward and picked up the chalice, "as it did in my lifetime, this chalice holds more than its size would indicate."

The shadowy ghost stepped forward and helped her as she brought it before Rose, "the choice is yours, but know that if you drink this it will be a painful transformation."

Rose laughed, "pain of the flesh is nothing compared to the pain of the soul," she said as she took the chalice and began to drink from it. At first it was fiery hot and burned as it went down, it tasted of sulfur and something she could not identify, then as she kept drinking it turned cool and tasted of salt as if she drank deeply of the sea. It progressed rapidly and thickened slightly as it took on a mossy flavor and she smelled the freshly dug up earth. As she continued it got really thin and it was as if she was drinking the air immediately after a lightning strike. Suddenly it was sweet and mildly intoxicating, she felt as if she would burst if she didn't get to her love soon. Finally it tasted of ash and shadows, she felt as if she were drinking death itself. As she finished she wanted to wipe the blood from her face, but stopped herself and turned towards Mortimer.

She looked at him and tilted his head back, very gently she kissed him on the lips, and she felt this urge she had never felt before and drove her tongue into his mouth, searching for she knew not what. She kissed him deeply, passionately and with all of her heart and soul, "please come back to me," she whispered as she broke from him, "I swear I will never leave you again and I will always be by your side."

Rose didn't care about the dress she was wearing, she didn't care about the ritual, all she cared about was getting him back, as she threw herself from her seat and landed in his lap. She had nothing to clean his wound with, so she bent over and licked at the blood covering his chest, she reveled in the taste of it and the feeling of his flesh beneath her tongue. She felt a slight beat from his heart and renewed her efforts to get the blood cleaned off of him so she could see to the wound.

Gradually the heartbeat got stronger, and she looked up to see his eyes showed signs of life, immediately she pulled him close to her and kissed him deeply, "I am so glad it worked," she said, just before she screamed. The world was darkness and pain, she felt her bones stretch and snap, her joints popped, her skin burst open. One second she was falling through the air, the next she was buried in the earth, then she was cold and wet, followed rapidly by heartbreak of a love that was lost and finally she felt the agony of hundreds of weapons as they pierced her flesh and crushed her bones.

Then the pain was gone and she was in Mortimer's arms as he stared into her face a worried look in his eyes, "are you alright?" he asked.

Rose panting slightly from the memory of the pain and nodded her head, "I can't really describe it, but it was extremely painful."

"Is the chalice completely empty?" Mortimer's mother asked from beside them.

"Yes," Rose answered as she double checked it, "there isn't even a mark from the blood."

"Good, then it cannot be used to control you," she replied. "Now come children, there is much to do to prepare for your wedding."

Mortimer chuckled dryly, "can we just have a simple ceremony? I can't wait to have my wife to myself."

His mother shook her head, "honey, you know your sister has been looking forward to this day for a long time, and you've already made it complicated enough without trying to weasel your way out of it."

He bowed his head, "very well mother, we'll just retire to my chambers to get ready."

She shook her head, "you may return to your chambers to get ready, she will come with me to my chambers to get ready."

Rose looked at her questioningly, "what happened to the quiet homecoming?"

The ghost shook her head, "sorry dear, but we had to alter things a bit due to the battle this morning, but don't you worry we will have everything arranged and ready by nightfall. Besides, I believe you had best have a look in the mirror before you decide to show yourself to the public."

Puzzled, Rose followed the ghost through another wall and up a long flight of stairs until they came to a doorway.

"Through this doorway you will find a hallway, the third door on your right will put you in the guest room we have assigned for your use," she smiled slightly, "my daughter will be there shortly to help you adjust."

Rose followed her directions and was amazed at the room they had given her, it was painted in such a manner that depending on where you looked you felt as if you were in a different element. She spent a good five minutes turning around in a circle, first in a volcano, then in the air, then underwater and finally underground. There was a heart shaped doorway in one corner, she walked through it and found herself in a room that just screamed romance, the only thing in the center of the room was a large heart shaped bed covered in rose petals of various colors and the entire room smelled of roses. Off to one side was a small doorway which led into a small room filled with dresses and nightgowns, which led into a room with a wash basin built into the floor.

# Wedding

She knelt next to the wash basin and looked at her reflection in the water and almost screamed, her face was covered in blood, the once beautiful dress she was wearing was covered in blood as well, and had scorch marks and tears all over it. Her eyes stared back at her, their color kept shifting and she suddenly had a thought in her head, telling her to relax and let them sort it out.

"Scarlet?" she asked.

"Yes, I am here," her own voice answered back, "give us a few more minutes to figure out how this works."

"I'm going to take a bath," she said out loud and promptly let herself fall into the wash basin. She was not surprised when wet hands caught her and started to undress her as she lay face down in the water. She was surprised when she realized she was face down in the water and could breath. Gradually she rolled over and stared at the ceiling.

"I see you have decided to take a bath," a woman's voice said suddenly from the doorway. "That's good, it will help you to relax a bit."

Rose laughed wildly, "relax? Who can relax? I have no idea what I have become, or who I am anymore."

The woman chuckled, "that is to be expected. I may have some answers for you if you would like to hear them."

"Sure," she replied, curious to see what the woman had to say.

"Concentrate on any of the women whose blood you drank," the woman replied, "then look at your reflection."

She concentrated on Clarice, since she had been the one she'd spent the most time with, then she raised her hand and a small sheet of water came up with it and showed her, her reflection. A pair of ice blue eyes stared back at her, her hair was white and when she looked down she discovered she had Clarice's curves and her fish tail, "but how?" she asked and her voice sounded just like Clarice's had.

The woman laughed, "oh, you are a natural. You have their essence within you, and when you concentrate you can take on their powers, their attributes, or if you want you can even let them take control." The woman stepped forward and Rose almost fainted, she looked like a female version of Mortimer, "Do you mind if I join you in the bath?"

"I don't mind," she replied as she watched the young woman drop her robe and step lithely into the water. "You're gorgeous," she said without thinking about it.

"Thank you," the woman replied, "I was going to say the same about you. Why don't you concentrate on yourself?"

Rose thought about it for a moment, and concentrated, "I am not sure if I can do it, I'm not even sure of who I am."

"Tell me," the woman continued, "were you happy when you were a mercenary?"

"Only when Mortimer was around," she answered.

"Were you happy as a princess?" she asked.

"No," she said bluntly and it felt as if something melted away from her.

"Would you be happy as a farmer?" she asked with a strange look on her face.

"If it was with mortimer then yes," Rose answered with a smile. "I would be happy to be anything as long as he was with me."

The woman laughed, "then I know who you are, you are my brother's wife. You just have to figure out what kind of wife you want to be."

Rose thought of all the times she had sat next to Mortimer in the hospital tent tending his wounds as he laughed about how he had gotten them, she couldn't help but smile, and suddenly she felt another shift in her body. She raised her arm and the water came up with it, but this time the face that looked back at her was her own, her body was her own although her breasts looked larger than before, and her hips still muscular looked as if they broadened a little and she found herself to be a bit more flexible than she had been since being a child.

"Now, focus on this image of yourself and tie it to your name," the woman said, "then whenever you want you can switch between all of the bodies of his wives." She smiled evilly, "if you want you can even let them take over your body when you're not in a mood for his attention and they are."

"How do you know all this?" she asked as she felt someone brushing out and cleaning her hair.

"I read my great grandmother's journal," she answered with a smile. "We have contacted your family and the guard has agreed to provide a passage for them to witness the wedding. The question is who is going to be in charge of the body during the ceremony?"

Rose laughed, "I am, the others are still deciding on how this works."

"Good, it sounds as if they have already come to terms with their situation. Come, we should get you dressed for the ceremony," she said as she stood up and stepped out of the water.

Rose laughed at Lorelei's thought and accidentally spoke, "if I was a man I'd want to spend the night with you."

The woman laughed, "that can be arranged if my brother and husband agree, maybe when they go on a hunting trip together."

Rose stared in shock for a moment, "is this normal in your family?"

"Yes," she answered, "my sister died before bearing a child for her husband, and as she was dying she asked that I provide him with a child. My husband agreed and thus my son is his child and my daughters are my husband's children. Everyone was happy with the arrangement, and both family lines can continue to expand."

"Would you bear your sister's husband another child?" Rose asked.

"No, I fulfilled my duty to my sister and he does not seek my attention," she answered.

"You are a strange family," Rose said as she too stepped out of the water.

"Well, my little chimera, you have chosen a good body," Mortimer's sister said as she looked approvingly down the length of Rose's body, "my brother will be pleased."

Rose blushed slightly and walked into the room full of dresses, "what should I wear?" she asked out loud.

"This," Mortimer's sister answered as she pulled a colorful dress from amongst all of the others. It goes well with your alignment of the elements, and the white base is suitable considering your lack of a marriage bond to date."

"I see you are not concerned about my virtue," Rose said with a wry grin.

"Why should we be?" she replied, "it's none of our business, it is between you and your future husband."

Rose suddenly turned pale, "oh, I just realized he knows of my past, how can he take me seriously knowing I am not pure?"

"You forget who you're talking about, he is as far from pure as any man can get," she replied to Rose, "besides he is not one to judge others on their past mistakes, only on the decisions they make in the future."

Rose burst out laughing, "and what will he say when I tell him seeing him wounded turned me on?"

Mortimer's sister burst out laughing as well, "he will probably laugh, considering he has already told me about all the time you spent in the hospital tent tending his wounds. You have to remember, he was a mercenary too and understands the feeling of lust when one survives a life or death battle."

Rose smiled at the thought and then shook herself back to reality, "if I don't get my mind out of the gutter, I am going to need another bath."

"A bath won't clean a dirty mind," Mortimer's sister replied, "come let's get this dress on you and then I can do your hair."

Rose was amazed at how quickly she was able to slip into the dress, and also at how tight the bodice fit, "does it have to be so tight?" she asked when she was done being laced in.

"No, but it does make you look absolutely delicious, as one of his wives would say," the woman replied.

It seemed to take forever to get her hair done, Mortimer's sister would brush it out, then braid it, then change her mind, and finally ended up with just brushing it out and weaving some roses into her hair to form a sort of crown. When she was done, she said, "Perfect timing, I can hear the music in the hall announcing the arrival of our guests."

Rose followed her out of the room and listened to all of her instructions as they went down the hall; this sounded like a very complicated ceremony, she thought. Finally she was handed off to Mortimer with a final piece of advice, "if all else fails just follow Mortimer's lead."

Mortimer took her hand and smiled at her, "You didn't have to change for me you know," he whispered to her.

Rose blushed slightly, "yes, I did, because I couldn't see you with anything less than the perfect woman."

"You are more than the perfect woman, you are my perfect woman," he said to her with a wink. "Come, let us greet our guests and get this over with."

"Agreed," she replied, "I'm not sure if it's me that wants to strip you out of that suit so badly or someone else."

"Let her out for a moment and we can ask her," he replied.

She thought about it for a moment and then laughed, "no, she says that would be a bad idea as we would be late for our own wedding. They all say you look absolutely delicious and can't wait until we can devour you at our leisure."

Mortimer laughed, "you definitely fit in well with them my love," he said as he gave her a quick kiss.

Rose felt her body temperature rise slightly and smiled, oh yes she was going to enjoy tonight.

The greeting of the guests went by quite rapidly, with a mixture of jealousy and relief from many of the women in the great hall. The ceremony itself involved a lot of ritual chants and prayers, and then a small sharp knife was brought out.

Suddenly the priest doing the ceremony said in a deep booming voice, "may no human or god separate these two, for they are bound in death as they are in life and I look forward to their long and happy life." He pricked both of their fingers and stirred them into a crystal wine goblet.

Rose thought it odd that nobody seemed to notice how the priest's face had suddenly turned into a skull when he spoke those words, or how the whine in the goblet changed colors several times before it settled back to a deep dark red.

"Drink and be one," the skull said as they drank from the goblet.

After that everything went by in a blur, dinner, dancing, a toast from Mortimer's father, more dancing, cake and finally the last dance, where she was surprised to see the ghostly figures from the blades dancing alongside them. "Thank you my children," the red ghost said in passing, "I am sorry to have caused you so much pain."

Rose smiled at the ghost, "without it we would not have found so much pleasure, thank you." She watched as the ghosts faded from view, finally able to rest.

"You are far more gracious than I would have ever imagined," Mortimer said with a smile, "most people would have resented them for what you had to go through."

She laughed gently, "I would have walked through the pits of hell to be here by your side, and to some extent I did. I can see and feel all of the horrors they went through, and yet I also feel their love for you. My only question is why did it have to be that way?"

"You ask a very good question, and I don't have an answer to it," he replied, but someday we will find out."

"When do we get to escape this dance floor and retire to our own room?" she asked with a grin.

Mortimer laughed softly, "we can go anytime you want my love, but I believe your parents would be upset if we left before they got a chance to talk to you."

"Very well, let's go talk with them," she replied with a sigh.

They walked over to where her parents sat at a small table, and Mortimer pulled out a chair for her to sit down, before he took a seat himself.

"I'm surprised you came," Rose said right away, "I know I have always been a disappointment to you."

Her father snorted, "I wouldn't call you a disappointment, a problem child with wild ideas maybe, but never a disappointment. What ever gave you the idea we could be disappointed in you?"

She blushed slightly, "maybe it was the fact that you always wanted a son to take your place, or maybe it was the fact I broke the nose of every man you tried to arrange a marriage to, or it could be that I escaped the castle and became a mercenary."

Her father laughed, "just because I wanted a son does not mean I was disappointed with a daughter. I will admit I was a bit taken aback the first couple of times you fought with potential suitors, but I got a laugh out of it when you punched that pompous prince in the snout and told him to go marry a beggar if he wanted someone to worship him." He took a deep breath and frowned, "when you ran away I panicked, and then when my scouts found you I knew there was no way for me to force you to come home, especially when they said you had spent a week in the healers tent tending to a young man who had almost died." He smiled at her slightly, "I was kind of hoping you would send me a letter and invite me to meet the young man whom you cared so deeply about."

Rose smiled slightly, "well to be honest I wasn't planning on it. Clarice was the one who insisted on inviting you to the wedding."

"Clarice?" her mother asked, "who is she and when do we get to meet her?"

"She is his second wife," Rose answered with a smile, "if you would like you can meet her and the rest of his wives right now."

Mortimer chuckled slightly as her parent's choked on their wine, "are you sure you want to introduce them?' he asked Rose.

"Yes," she replied with a purr to her voice, "besides Scarlet really wants to meet my parents."

"How many wives does he have?" her father asked.

"Rose is the seventh," Mortimer answered.

"Oh, did they attend the wedding?" he asked.

Rose laughed, "Oh yes, they most certainly did, after all they were part of the ceremony."

Rose's parents looked a bit confused by this comment, and Mortimer finally said, "you had better introduce them, it's the only way your parents will understand."

Rose gave him an evil grin, and suddenly he was sitting next to Scarlet, "hello love," she said to him as she turned to Rose's parents and smiled. "As you can imagine, your daughter will never be alone."

In the blink of an eye, Scarlet was replaced with Clarice, "This is going to prove to be quite entertaining," she said with a smirk. "Oh, don't worry, we wouldn't think of taking over your daughter's body without her permission," she said.

Clarice was replaced with Tara, who simply looked at Mortimer and smiled, "I love you," she said as she vanished and was replaced by Zephyr.

Zephyr laughed happily, as she reached over and kissed Mortimer, "don't worry, they'll come to accept us all just as you did."

She was replaced by Shar, who blushed slightly, "you will have to understand there was a lot at stake and your daughter chose to house us in order to save our husband."

Shar quickly changed out for Lorelei, and Mortimer tensed up a little as she said, "your daughter has the most delectable body, I can't wait for tonight." She turned to Mortimer and smiled graciously, "oh don't worry, Rose forbid me from using any magic right now." She then turned and kissed him passionately, "I can't wait to sink my teeth into you once again my love."

Rose returned, and everyone visibly relaxed a bit, "as you can tell, I am very happy with them and they are very happy with me."

"They look a bit scary," her mother said, "especially the first and last ones, what are they?"

"Witches," she answered, "Scarlet has draconic ancestry, Clarice is half mermaid, Tara is part subterranean elf, Zephyr is part harpy, Shar is a direct descendant of barbarians, and Lorelei is related to the water serpents of old. Each of them specializes in a type of magic, and through them I have access to all of their magic."

"That last one acted as if she were a type of temptress," her mother said with a frown.

Rose laughed, "oh, that would be an understatement, she could probably teach you a few things about making love."

The color drained from both her parents' faces, as they looked at each other, "I'm not sure if I'm comfortable with this marriage," her father whispered to her mother."

Mortimer laughed loudly, "it's not like there is much of a choice, as the priest said, no one shall undo what he has done today."

"Yes well," her father started, "maybe it would be best if you came and lived with us, after all I don't want my daughter consorting with witches and dead people."

Mortimer was about to say something, when his father spoke up from behind him, "they will be living here until they decide where they wish to live. I do not order this, I simply offer my home to my son and new daughter, they are adults and can make their own decisions. As for your comment about the dead, I don't think you realize that wherever they live the dead will visit them and I am quite certain the witches guard will send out people to check on them regularly as well, so if you don't want to continuously have witches and ghost show up at your castle it might be best to let them stay here."

"I do believe our conversation has reached its conclusion," Mortimer said to Rose, "shall we retire to our bed chambers?"

Rose smiled at him and replied, "certainly my love, I hope the bed doesn't make too much noise."

Mortimer's father laughed, "I highly doubt you will be nearly as noisy as some of our previous tenants, but rest assured the walls of your room are thick enough to muffle even a dragon's roar of pleasure."

"How can you be so cavalier about this?" Rose's father asked in shock.

Mortimer's father bowed to Rose, "my daughter, would you be so kind as to tell Lorelei to go ahead and have some fun, the important guests have left and these two need to unwind a bit."

Rose smiled and waved her hand towards the table, "sure thing father."

Mortimer caught a whiff of roses and lavender, as Rose grabbed him by the hand and kissed him. "We shall retire for the night, good evening everyone," he said as he fairly dragged Rose out of the great hall.

They heard the doors to the great hall lock behind them as they left and Rose laughed evilly, "your father has a devious sense of humor."

"Yes," he replied, "it's going to be a wild party in there, father hasn't lain with a woman since mother died and the delegation from the witches guard was still in the room when he locked it."

"Oops," she replied, "when he told Lorelei to have a little fun, she cast a very strong aphrodisiac spell upon the room, unless they had some very powerful protection, they will be going at it all night with anyone who is in the room."

Mortimer laughed, "Father, your parents, a dozen guards, and an equal number of witches, I wonder what father is playing at."

"I did make certain your sister wasn't in the room," she replied.

Mortimer laughed, "my sister doesn't need a spell to get wild ideas into her head, it's a family curse to always be lusty."

"That's a blessing, not a curse," she said under her breath. "You realize, this is something I have wanted for a long time, and it keeps getting put off, how do I know it won't be put off again?"

Mortimer laughed as he turned and swept her off his feet, "I promise you it won't get put off again, I'll rip your clothes from your body if need be."

"I'd like to see you try," she replied as he kicked in a thick wooden door.

# Dead again

He kicked the door closed once they were through it and took three steps before he kicked open another thick wooden door, "Father promised we wouldn't be heard," he said as he kicked that door closed as well, "he meant it, the walls in this room are over five feet thick of solid stone." He carried her to the center of the room and threw her down onto an extremely soft bed.

She landed in the bed and smiled, "this is not quite what I expected."

Mortimer chuckled as he climbed on top of her, "care to see how fast I can get you out of that dress?" he asked with a grin.

"If you really want me, you should make it quick," she replied as she tried to decide the fastest way to get him out of his clothing.

Mortimer grinned at her, and slid his hand down her back, his sharp claws came out and severed the laces holding her bodice tight, then simply grabbed the shoulder straps and yanked her entire outfit off in a single move.

"Oh," she replied, "that's not fair." She put her arms around his neck and pulled him in for a kiss, as she kissed him she felt her own nails extend and become clawlike. She raked them down his back and felt the fabric of his shirt tear in ribbons, with a sirk she ran her claws down his waist and thighs and watched as his pants just fell apart.

He smiled at her, and stood up to allow his clothing to fall to the floor, "now where to begin" he asked, as he grabbed her legs and pulled her to him. He couldn't resist, as he felt her thighs with his hands, he slowly slid his hands up to her hips, and gently he kissed her thighs before gradually biting them, lightly at first, and then harder as he felt her pulse quicken. He gradually moved up to her stomach, as she arched her back in pleasure, her claws tearing ribbons of cloth out of the bedcovers.

She wasn't sure she could take much more of his delays, she was burning with desire, and he had already sent her to the heavens once, but the feel of his lips and teeth slowly making their way up her stomach was driving her crazy. She felt his claws dig into her breasts, followed by his tongue gently licking them, and she screamed in pleasure once more as he bit gently at her nipples. "You're killing me," she gasped as he worked his way up to her neck and mouth.

He found it difficult to take his time, but he continued to explore her entire body, until finally his lips reached hers and he let himself slide into her body. As he held her lips to his, he felt her claws dig into his back and smiled, she now felt the passion he had felt in all of his relationships, and he gently rolled to the side pulling her on top of him.

"You're a beast," she said as she pulled away from his lips, sat up and let her claws rake gently over his chest. She saw the large scar on his chest and frowned, as she remembered the blood pouring out of it, very gently she stroked the scar, "this is my fault," she said as she thrust herself down onto him suddenly. She let herself fall into the passion and felt him respond to her passion, as she bit and clawed at his chest and shoulders, until finally she collapsed sobbing for air on his chest. "Do with me what you will," she whispered, "I don't deserve to be happy after almost getting you killed." She heard the voices in the back of her head screaming at her not to blame herself, but she didn't care.

"Anything?" he asked, an evil sort of hiss in his voice.

"Anything," she agreed.

He moved with great deliberation, as he sat up on the bed with her still in his lap. Suddenly he leaned forward and stood up, his arms holding her tightly against him as he lurched across the room and slammed her back into the wall.

The impact surprised her and forced her head to bounce off his left hand.

He pressed her against the wall, holding her there with his body as he grabbed her wrists and pulled them above her head, "you cannot blame yourself for my decision, and it is a decision I do not regret one bit," he said as he stared into her eyes. He watched her cry for a moment until she finally took a moment to catch her breath and return his stare, then he simply bent his neck down and kissed her. "What am I going to do with you?" he asked as he pulled back from the kiss.

"Anything you want," she answered, as she realized how uncomfortable the wall was. She shifted her body slightly and saw the look in his eyes, it was a look of excitement mixed with fear.

"Am I hurting you?" he asked softly.

Rose couldn't resist, she smiled at him, "no," she answered, "but I wish you would hurt me the way I have hurt you?"

He stared at her for a long time, until she once again squirmed against his body, slowly he took a step back, "I can't do that to you," he replied as he turned and walked back to the bed to sit down.

She stood there in shock, her hands still over her head and her back against the wall, "why not," she finally asked, "isn't that the reason you finally agreed to bed me?"

Mortimer shook his head, "no, it's not," he replied. "The number of times you took care of my shattered body, the number of times you patched me back together, the number of times you asked me to join you in your tent and I declined, that is the reason I decided I wanted you." he smiled at her, "for all your anger and rage, when it came down to it you had no place on the battlefield, you were a kind hearted person, why do you think I always asked you to watch my back, it was so I could watch yours, I knew you wouldn't be able to kill someone to protect yourself, it's not in your nature, you always pulled that blow back a second too soon and that's what got you in trouble on the battlefield, but it made you into a great friend, and I wanted to have a great friend as my partner in life."

Rose was shocked, he didn't harbor any ill will towards her for all the injuries he had received by stepping in front of her on the battlefield, suddenly she realized he didn't care what body she wore, he truly wanted to be with her, the failed mercenary. She felt her body shift and old aches and pains came back, she knew her scars were visible and for some reason she didn't care. Slowly she walked over and sat next to him, "I'm sorry," she said to him, "I still see the blood dripping off the blade of the sword as it came out of your back and you standing there gripping his hand with your own and swinging your sword around to remove his head, and all I can think is that it is my fault because I wasn't fast enough or strong enough. Can you forgive me and we can try to consummate this marriage thing again?"

He smiled at her, "I never blamed you for my choices, I forgive you for blaming yourself, but if we are going to do this, this is the body I want when I am with you."

She couldn't help herself, in her excitement she threw herself on him and kissed him passionately. She felt his body react and this time she took it slow and steadily built up the pace as she reveled in the feeling of his hands caressing her back and his lips wandering from her mouth to her neck, down to her breasts and then slowly back up to her mouth. This was better than earlier, this felt pure.

They didn't get much sleep that night, but they also didn't leave their room for several days until a cautious knock at the door announced a visitor, just before someone came into the room. "Just making certain you two are still alive," she said as she opened the door.

Rose laughed as she looked over at Mortimer, he returned her look and glanced towards where they lay, comfortably in each other arms, a small pool of blood surrounded them.

Mortimer looked around and laughed, "was it all a dream?" he asked.

"Yes and no," she answered, "you really did try and save my life, but at least I was able to be with you until the end."

"What about the others?" he asked.

"They were all me, all parts of my soul, all designed to be perfect for you, and yet you cast them all aside to choose me," she answered.

They heard a musical laugh from behind them, and turned to see a beautiful woman with alabaster skin and black hair floating before them. "That was a wonderful ceremony you had, we have never had such a ceremony in the realm of the dead." She smiled sweetly at them and held out her hand, "Come with me children, I will not hurt you, I am simply here to guide you to the afterlife."

They hesitated a moment and the woman laughed musically again, "the goddess of death has never lied, I have no need to. I am curious though about that potion, the kiss of death, I have never kissed you, so how do you know what the kiss of death feels like?"

Mortimer looked at Rose who winked at him and stepped forward, she looped one arm around death's neck, drew her in and kissed her, "yes, it tasted like that," she said as she pulled away from death's surprised face. "You kiss her and tell me, if I'm correct."

He stepped forward and was slightly bemused at how the angel of death moved back slightly before she braced herself as if about to be attacked. Very gently, he reached up and stroked her cheek with his fingertips, "I have always wondered what death would be like, I never imagined it would be so beautiful," he said as he twisted his fingers into her hair and pulled her in for a kiss. Her mouth was as cold as the grave, but full of flavor, she tasted of blood, sweat, ash and had a strong flavor of clove. "You are correct, that has got to be the most wonderful flavor in the world," he said as he let death pull away, "but I prefer the way you taste," he said as he turned to Rose.

Rose smiled sweetly at him, "as a handmaiden of death, I am sworn to the goddess death, it is up to her if I may continue to be with you."

Death laughed, "after that, I kind of want him for myself, no one has dared touch me like that in the past, you may stay with him, you have earned it."

"I will do whatever you desire if it means I can be with Rose," Mortimer answered.

"As the goddess wishes," Rose replied with a smile, for she knew the goddess of death had no need of servants, in the afterlife

"Then come with me children, we have spent too much time here and I would show you to your new home," the goddess said with a smile. "I am so glad I sent you back with a new body to guide him to me."

"What of the unborn child?" Mortimer asked.

"Your sister carries it now," the goddess replied, "she is quite the competent witch to transfer an unborn child from the womb of the dying to the womb of the living."

Made in the USA
Columbia, SC
15 November 2022